Giles Fletcher

The Complete Poems of Giles Fletcher

Giles Fletcher

The Complete Poems of Giles Fletcher

ISBN/EAN: 9783337406929

Printed in Europe, USA, Canada, Australia, Japan

Cover: Foto ©Andreas Hilbeck / pixelio.de

More available books at **www.hansebooks.com**

Early English Poets.

GILES FLETCHER, B.D.

Early English Poets.

THE
COMPLETE POEMS

OF

GILES FLETCHER, B.D.

EDITED,

WITH

Memorial=Introduction and Notes,

BY THE

REV. ALEXANDER B. GROSART.

London:
CHATTO AND WINDUS, PICCADILLY.
1876.

Preface.

I INCLUDED the Poems of the FLETCHERS very early in my Fuller Worthies' Library; and within a few months of their private issue, the entire impressions were distributed among my fellow-students and lovers of our elder poetic literature. The number of copies (106 8vo, and 156 12mo) was so limited that I have had since to disappoint many applicants from far and near. It gives me accordingly no little pleasure to respond to the wish of the Publishers that I should furnish certain of the Fuller Worthies' Library to the general public. Giles will pave the way for Phineas Fletcher; and the Fletchers, with Sir John Davies and Sir Philip Sydney, which are to be almost contemporaneously published, afford access to a wider circle to some of those literary treasures that *for the first time* it has been my privilege to collect and edit critically and worthily.

Throughout I have re-collated every line and word with the Author's own texts—not without advantage in various ways, in that my earlier Worthies were printed at a provincial press, and with un-instructed and merely mechanical workmen, so much so that even a second and third revise-proof failed to secure attention to my corrections.

I add to this new edition of Giles Fletcher a bright little poem from the Tanner MSS., first printed by me as an appendix to his Father's Poems ("Licia," &c.) in the Fuller Worthies' Miscellanies. I have also been enabled to add to the facts and criticisms of the Memorial-Introduction. As a Maker of real and unique genius, Giles Fletcher is only in these later days winning his deserved renown. By his great poem he has never ceased to hold across the centuries the "fit audience tho' few;" and to-day he is a living *motif* and impulse in the line of "Sursum :"

> "Onward and upward, whatever the way ;
> Gloomy or glad, through darkness and day :
> Vow'd to the end, be it distant or soon,
> Under the banner of Christ to march on ;
> Strong in His armour to war against ill ;
>   With a will, with a will,
>   Onward and upward."[1]

ALEXANDER B. GROSART.

FROM MY STUDY,
St George's, Blackburn, Lancashire.

---

[1] Hymns by F. T. Palgrave, 1870 (Macmillan), 3d ed.

To

FRANCIS TURNER PALGRAVE, ESQ.,

late Scholar of Balliol and Fellow of Exeter College, Oxford ;

a

" Sweet Singer "

and a

Penetrative and judicially-deliberate Critic ;

𝕴 𝕯𝖊𝖉𝖎𝖈𝖆𝖙𝖊

This first complete and worthy edition of an old Poet :—

Very faithfully and admiringly,

ALEXANDER B. GROSART.

Contents.

MEMORIAL-INTRODUCTION.

I. *BIOGRAPHICAL.*

PHINEAS, and not GILES FLETCHER as usually supposed—was the first-born of his Family; and hence such new facts and details as I have had the good fortune to discover (and recover) concerning the FLETCHERS, find most fitting place in the Memoir of him prefixed to our collection of his 'Poems.'[1]

The father of our Poets was GILES FLETCHER, LL.D., brother of RICHARD FLETCHER, who died Bishop of London. He was a man who did valorous and varied service to his Country: his visit to THEODORE IVANOWICH, 'czar' of Russia, and his book about it, being the most notable. Dr GILES FLETCHER was son of good RICHARD FLETCHER, the first REFORMATION 'pastor' of CRANBROOK in Kent, and in his somewhat stormy and wandering life, he is found flitting to and fro between the paternal Vicarage and London. PHINEAS was born—as elsewhere we prove—in CRAN-

---

[1] In the Fuller Worthies' Library, 4 vols. 1869. Sooner or later to be published uniform with this.

A

BROOK ; but Giles was born in London by the testimony of THOMAS FULLER in his 'Worthies.'[1] His informant was the Rev. JOHN RAMSEY of 'Rougham in Norfolk' who married the widow of our Poet.[2] It is to be regretted that his birth-date was not given by FULLER. CHALMERS'[3] conjecture of 1588 seems improbable, as in the present volume will be found his 'Canto' upon the death of Elizabeth, originally published in 1603, that is, in such case, when he was in his 14th or 15th year. I do not forget that at the same age, if not younger, Milton put forth "the shooting of the infant oak which in later times was to overshadow the forest" —as Dr SYMMONS with unwonted vivacity describes his translations from the Psalms. But while these Psalms owe perhaps their choicest epithets and most vivid touches to Sylvester ('du-Bartas') the 'Canto' is strictly original and altogether too prodigious a production for

[1] Vol. II. 82 (edt. 1811 by Nichols).

[2] Fuller and after him his editors, and even Willmott, misspell this excellent man's name 'Rainsey.' It is RAMSEY, as appears by a volume of his 'Sermons,' of ripe learning and rare quaintness and memorableness of thinking and style—which is in my library, viz : 'Præterita or a Summary of several Sermons : the greater part preached many years past in several places, and upon sundry occasions. By JOHN RAMSEY, Minister of East Rudham in the County of Norfolk,' 1650 (4°). The 'Registers' of his Church and Parish are all gone till within a century of the present time ; and hence no memorial of him remains there. I have not met with another copy of his 'Præterita.' In his Epistle Dedicatory to Duport, he describes it as a 'second mite into the Churches Treasury : the common gazophylacium of the Press.'

[3] Biog. Dict. *sub nomine.*

a mere youth. The reader can turn to the 'Canto' and judge for himself.

Our first new fact—and a valuable one—we are able to add here viz: that his mother's name was JOAN SHEAFE of CRANBROOK, Kent, daughter of one of the wealthy clothiers of the place. The 'Register' shews that the marriage of this 'fair lady' with GILES FLETCHER Senr., took place on 16th January, 1580 (o.s.) that is 1581.[1]

It is to be noted that Anthony a-Wood gives a place of honour to the son of Thomas Sheafe of Cranbrook, viz: Dr Thomas Sheafe, who lies in the Chapel of St George's, Windsor. In all probability this dignitary was brother of Joan, mother of our two poets.[2]

FULLER further states that at an early age he was sent to 'Westminster' School, and that he was elected from it to Trinity College, Cambridge. On this WILLMOTT—than whom few have been more painstaking, as none had keener insight, or finer poetic sympathies, or a more unerring taste—remarks:—

[1] I must heartily acknowledge the ungrudging labour of Mr WILLIAM TARBUTT of CRANBROOK, in aiding my Fletcher-researches. Painstaking, persevering and intelligent, without pretence, Mr TARBUTT is an enthusiast in all that honours his native town. We trust he will one day expand his occasional Lectures, and give us a 'History' of it. Mr TARBUTT's investigations have yielded me important contributions to the Memoir of PHINEAS FLETCHER and the Family generally.

[2] Athenæ Oxon: by Bliss, *sub nomine:* his censure of another related SHEAFE for leaving his money to 'laymen' and not the Church, is mere abuse, and utterly unwarranted.

"This is the relation of Fuller; but I am unable to reconcile it with the declaration of GILES FLETCHER himself. In the dedication of 'Christ's Victorie' to Dr NEVILLE, he speaks, with all the ardour of a young and noble heart, of the kindness he had experienced from that excellent man. He mentions his having reached down 'as it were out of heaven, a benefit of that nature and price, than which he could wish none (only heaven itself excepted) either more fruitful and contenting for the time that is now present, or more comfortable and encouraging for the time that is already past, or more hopeful and promising for the time that is yet to come.' And further on, he expressly states that he was placed in Trinity College by Dr Neville's 'only favour, most freely, without either any means from others, or any desert in himself.' This praise could not have been consistent with truth, if Fletcher had obtained his election from Westminster School; and a careful examination of the Register-Book enables me to add that he was not upon the Foundation."[1]

This is decisive; and yet no one will bear hard on dear FULLER, with such a mass of material to assort. I can testify, after following him in many recondite and special lines of inquiry, that his general accuracy is not less amazing than his immense industry.

[1] Lives of the English Sacred Poets: by Robert Aris Willmott. 2nd edition, 2 vols. 12mo, 1839 : Vol I. p. 64. This is preferable here to the first edition, as it corrects previous errors, and is fuller : but the first edition is preferable in other respects, as will appear.

The patronage of Dr NEVILLE must have been well-timed; for through the paternal responsibilities incurred as executor of his Bishop-brother, the Family were enduring at the period, painful hardships as an extant Letter—elsewhere to be used—gives pathetic evidence.[1] It is probable that the Fletchers of Liversedge, Yorkshire, held places of trust in the service of the lordly house of the Nevilles there.[2]

That the 'Canto' of young Master GILES found so prominent a place in so prominent a volume as 'Sorrowe's Joy:' wherein the 'wisest Fool' (King JAMES) was welcomed by nearly all the University 'singers,' including PHINEAS FLETCHER—would seem to argue premature recognition. And yet very slender are the records of him even in his own College—renowned Trinity. Cooper's ATHENÆ CANTABRIGIENSES strangely fails us altogether, though already covering the years of GILES' attendance.[3] Wood's ATHENÆ designates him 'batchelour of divinity of Trinity College,' and adds with rare feeling for him " equally beloved of the muses and graces."[4] Does the mention of the 'Graces' point to his personal beauty? If so—it recalls the 'comeliness'

---

[1] See our Memoir of Phineas as before : and Bond's ' Preface' to Dr Fletcher's book on Russia, pp. cxxv-vi.

[2] See Memorial-Introduction to Poems of Giles Fletcher, LL.D., in Misc. of F. W. L., as before, pp. 8-10.

[3] Vol. I., 1500-85 : Vol. II., 1586-1609. Are we never to get Vol. III.?

[4] Fasti (by Bliss) I. 190, 191.

and noble presence of his uncle (Bishop FLETCHER) that
so 'took' Elizabeth.

We are enabled to add to his TRINITY dates.   In the
Scholars' Admission Book is the following entry in his
own handwriting, under 'April 12th, 1605.'

'Ægidius Fletcherus, Discipulus juratus.'

His name also occurs among the B.A. scholars in the
Senior Bursar's Book for 1606.   He is there shewn to
have received two quarterly payments of 3s. 4d.   The
book for 1605 is missing, as is that for 1607 ; but in
1608 his name appears as a B.A. scholar, and he receives
four quarterly payments of 3s. 4d.   In 1614–5, in the
Senior Bursar's Book, are these two entries :   *Item*,
Paid to Mr Fletcher for a quarter's allowance, at 3s. 4d.
the wecke from St. Ladie day to Midsomer for Mr Gar-
diner—xliijs. iiijd. : 1615.   *Item*, Spent in carring [*sic*]
of letters gratulatory to the King and Prince to Gren-
wiche by my selfe [1] and Mr Fletcher, man and horse, 5
days, vl. xviijs. : 1617.   Finally, in the Conclusion Book
is this : January 24th. : Mr Fletcher and Mr Kin-
aston added to Catechise to those already appointed.

---

[1] This Bursar ('myselfe') was a Thomas Fortho.   With reference
to the last entry it may be well to explain that Fellows who wished
to qualify themselves for College preachers had to expound the
Catechism a certain number of times in Chapel.   Under the old
statutes the College Preachers had certain privileges with regard
to livings which they were allowed to hold with their Fellow-
ship.

Such is all of 'Register'-memorial left; slight but all new facts.[1]

There can be no doubt that from 1603 of the 'Canto,' to 1617, he was laying up those stores of various learning and of scholastic Divinity, for which he was afterwards so remarkable.

In 1610, he published the poem—'Christ's Victorie'—on which his Fame will rest immovably 'while there is any praise.'[2] A second edition was not issued until 1632. It is sufficiently clear that no more than the immortal 'Folio' of 1623, 'Paradise Lost,' or 'Silex Scintillans,' was this consummate poem 'popular;' while from his brother's Lines it is evident that 'malicious tongues' depreciated it; and that otherwise he was not sufficiently estimated. We must here read the loving fraternal 'Lines.' "Upon my brother Mr G. F. his book entituled 'Christ's Victorie and Triumph.'

Fond lads, that spend so fast your posting time,
(Too posting time, that spends your time as fast)
To chant light toyes, or frame some wantom rhyme,
Where idle boyes may glut their lustfull taste;
Or else with praise to clothe some fleshly slime
With virgin roses and fair lilies chaste;
  While itching blouds and youthfull eares adore it;
But wiser men, and once yourselves, will most abhorre it.

But thou (most neare, most deare) in this of thine
Hast prov'd the Muses not to Venus bound;
Such as thy matter, such thy Muse, divine;

---

[1] I am deeply indebted to Mr W. ALDIS WRIGHT, M.A., of Trinity College, for discovering these entries for me.

[2] Southey's British Poets: Chaucer to Jonson, p. 807.

Or thou such grace with Mercie's self hast found,
That she herself deignes in thy leaves to shine ;
Or stoll'n from heav'n, thou brought'st this verse to ground,
    Which frights the nummèd soul with fearfull thunder,
And soon with honeyed dews thawes it 'twixt joy and wonder.

Then do not thou malicious tongues esteem ;
(The glasse, through which an envious eye doth gaze,
Can eas'ly make a mole-hill mountain seem)
His praise dispraises, his dispraises praise ;
Enough, if best men best thy labours deem,
And to the highest pitch thy merit raise ;
    While all the Muses to thy song decree
Victorious Triumph, triumphant Victorie." [1]

That 'Christ's Victorie' had one supreme 'student' in
JOHN MILTON every one discerns ; and the 'one' is
compensating renown.   Surely and permanently, if
slowly, the majority came round to the 'one ;' and now
whoever knows aught of English Literature, knows 'by
heart' the 'thoughts that breathe and words that burn'
of this truly divine and imperishable Poem.   If GILES
had lived to see his brother's 'Sicelides' (1631) ; and
perchance he did see it in the Manuscript—he would
doubtless have found cheer in these lines of the 'Epi-
logue' in answer to the question 'What euer feast could
every guest content ?' viz :

" In this thought, this thought the Author eas'd
Who once made all, all rules—all neuer pleas'd ;
FAINE WOULD WE PLEASE THE BEST, IF NOT THE MANY
AND SOONER WILL THE BEST BE PLEASED THEN ANY ;
OUR REST WE SET IN PLEASING OF THE BEST,
So wish we you what you may give us : Rest."

[1] 'Poeticall Miscellanies,' pp. 101, 102 (1633).

Fuller has neglected to inform us in what year our 'sweet Singer' received ordination; but while in residence at Cambridge he was much sought after as a 'preacher.' His pulpit was sacred 'St. Mary's' from which have come perhaps the grandest Sermons ever spoken by mortal tongues, and to the most large-brained auditories found anywhere, not excepting 'Paule's Crosse.'[1] A peculiarity of his 'prayers,' was that they usually consisted of one entire allegory 'not driven, but led on, most proper in all particulars.'[2] It is scarcely a loss that 'prayers' of this type have not been preserved, and yet one would have liked to see a specimen, as one rejoices that in sequestered places one may still see Gardens of the antique sort, wherein the God-made sylvage is transformed by art into all manner of Dutch fantastiques of beds and knots, 'without a leaf astray,' as 'Our Village' describes.

In '1612' Fletcher edited and published at Cambridge the 'Remains' of a remarkable 'Oxford' man— NATHANIEL POWNOLL. The 'Epistle Dedicatory' is addressed to John King, Bishop of London.;[3] and is a bit of terse, thoughtful English. Willmot laments that he had not been able to obtain the book as "it would certainly tend to illustrate the poet's history." Between the first edition of his 'Lives' (1834) and the second

---

[1] Cf. my Memoir of Dr Richard Sibbes, Vol. I. pp. lii., liii.: and Masson's 'Milton.'

[2] Fuller, as before.

[3] See my Memoir of Bishop King prefixed to reprint of his 'Jonah' [4to.] in Nichol's Puritan Commentaries.

(1839) he seems to have despaired of ever seeing it, and drops out all mention of it.[1] I am very pleased to be able to produce it from SELDEN's copy of POWNOLL, preserved in the 'Bodleian.'[2] Here it is :—

'To the Reverend Father in God John L[ord] Bishop of London.

Right woorthie and reuerend Father in God :

Blame not your ancient Obseruer, if nowe, after he hath recouered in a manner, at Cambridge, that life which he lost at his departure from Oxford, he rises aniew, as it wear out of his ashes, to do his humble seruice to his Lordship ; and, indeede, to whome can any fruit that comes from him, bee with more right pre-

---

[1] Cf. the former, p. 34 : In a foot-note here, WILMOTT is perplexed with a contradiction between WATT's 'Bibliotheca Brittannica' and the antiquary COLE, because the former describes Pownoll's volume as printed at 'Canterbury :' but the explanation is that there was a mistake of Watt's editors (for his work was posthumous) in reading Cant[abrigiæ] : = Cambridge, as Canterbury.

[2] The following is the full title-page 'The Young Divines Apologie for his continuance in the Universitie with Certain Meditations, written by Nathaniel Pownoll, late student of Christ-Church in Oxford. Printed by Cantrell Legge, Printer to the Vniversitie of Cambridge ; and are to be sold in Paul's Church-yard by Matthew Lownes at the signe of the Bishop's head,' 1612, [12mo.] Another edition of the 'Young Divine's Apology' was published at Oxford in 1658 'printed for T. Robinson' and to this are added (1) His Meditation upon the calling of the Ministrie at his first institution unto it. (2) A Meditation upon the first of the seauen penitentiall Psalmes of David. (3) His daily Sacrifice.

sented then to him, in whose garden, and onder whose
shadow it griew? Into whose hand should this small
book, though wanting his owne Epistle, be deliuered,
but onto that, to which it hath before given so many
Epistles? whear can it looke for protection with more
hope than whear it hath formerly, with all fauour founde
it?

If your Lordship thearfore will be pleased to be the
defender of this Apologie, and to breath as I may truly
say, the breath of life againe into his sequent Meditations, that so beeing annimated aniew with those on-
speakable sighs, and alike feruent zeale of spirit, wher-
with they wear first, as in fierie chariots, carried up into
heau'n; I doubt not but they will seeme, beeing so
quickned, to any that shall reade them (especially if, as
Job wished in a case not much onlike, his soule wear in
his soules stead) no cold, or dull, or dead letters; and
in so doing, you shall not onely follow him into his
graue, but call him out of it with this so speciall a benefit, binding with the dead in one knot of thankfulnesse
all his friends that yet liue, and cannot but ioy to see
your Lordship's fauour out-liue the person on whom it

These last three are contained in one volume at the end of the
'Apologie' 1612. I notice that in the Will of our Giles' Uncle—
Bishop RICHARD FLETCHER—he bequeaths, among other things
the following: 'Item,' I geue vnto my sister Pownoll twenty
poundes. (Dyce's Beaumont & Fletcher, Vol. I. lxxxviii.) Was
this the mother of our Pownoll? If so then we have a key to our
poet's interest in editing and publishing his 'Remaines:' in such
case he was his cousin.

is bestowed: of whome my selfe, being the leaste, shal
euer thinke I am most bound to be.

Your L. to command in all good scruice

G. FLETCHER.'

To this falls to be added an equally good ' Epistle '
to ' the Reader ' which follows :—

' The Authour of this small discourse, or rather (giue
mee leaue so to call him) the Swan that, before his
death, sung this diuine song, is now thear, whear he
neither needs the praise, nor fears the envy of any :
whose life, as it deserued so it was covetous of no mans
commendation ; himselfe being as farre from pride as
his desert was neere it, yet because it was his griefe,
that hee should die before he was fit to doe God the
seruice hee desired ; and his friends desire, that beeing
so fit as hee was for his service, hee might (if it had
been possible) neuer have died at all; thearfore his
booke was bould to thrust itselfe into that world which
the Author of it had lately left, thereby to satisfye both
his Makers desire, in doing the church of God some
seruice ; and his friends griefe, in not suffering him altogether to lie dead.

And truely what better seruice can it doe, then to
persuade with reason, since Authoritie forces not, our
young Neophytes to abide awhile in the schooles of the
Prophets, at Bethel, before they presume to enter the
Temple at Hierusalem ; and if reason can doe little
with them, because happily they want it, yet let his ex-

ample (an argument that prevails much with the common people, of whome such prophets are the tayle) make them at least see, and confesse, though they know not how to amend, their fault. Ten yeares had hee liued in the Uniuersitie, eight languages had hee learnt, and taught his tongue so many seueral waies by which to expresse a good heart ; watching often, daily exercising, alway studying, in a word, making an end of himselfe in an ouer-feruent desire to benefit others ; and yet, after hee had, as it wear out of himself, sweat out all this oyle for his lampe, after hee had with the sunne ran so many heauenly races, and when the sunne was laied abed by his labours, after hee had burnt out so many candles to giue his minde light (hauing alwaies S. Paul's querie in his minde τις προς ταυτα ικανος) hee neuer durst adventure to doe that, after all these studies done, and ended, which our young novices, doeing nothing, coumpt nothing to doe : but still thought himselfe as unfit, as hee kniew all men weare unworthy of so high an honour, as to be the Angells of God.

I could wish that he had left behinde him, if not all his learning, yet some of his modesty to be diuided among these empty sounding vessels, that want both ; but since in him so great examples of piety, knowledge, industrie, and unaffected modesty are all fallen so deeply asleep, as I am afraid we shall hardly find in any of his age the like, (which I speak not to deny iust praise to the liuing; but who will not afford a fiew flowers to strowe the cophine of the dead ?) thear was

no way to awaken them, and in them him, but by layeing them up, not with him in his graue, but in these immortal monuments of the presse, the liuing Tombes
proper to dead learning, wherein these flowers may liue,
though their roote be withered, and though the trunk be
dead, the branches flowrish.

Let rich men therefore in the guilded sepulchres and
proud monuments of their death, beg for the memory of
their liues: the righteous shall be had in euerlasting
remembrance, without any such proud beggary; nor
shall he euer be beholding to a dead stone for the
matter; and good reason, Righteousness being a shadow
of that divine substance, which hath in it no shadow of
change much less of corruption : only I could wish their
liues wear as long as their memories ; that so this crooked
age might haue as great store, as it hath need of them.

G. F.'

Prefixed to the 'Bodleian' copy of Pownoll is this
Latin M.S. Epitaphum.

> ' Flos juvenum, decus Oxonii, spes summa parentum
>   Te tegit ante diem (matre parante) lapis.—
> Hoc satis est cineri : reliqua immortalia coelo
>   Condit amorque hominum, condit amorque Dei.'

When our Fletcher left Cambridge is not known;
but as we have seen he was appointed to 'catechise' in
1617, and thus must have remained at the University
until then at least.

That he was a Divinely-'called' not merely Bishop-
ordained 'minister of the Gospel' is certain. For in

the invocation of his great Poem he adoringly acknow-
ledges *the* one mighty change within, the gentle yet
awful dower that alone warrants a man to accept the
august office. As PHINEAS has like definite and deep
words concerning the same central thing—as fully
appears in his Memoir—it would almost seem as though
the two brothers were moved, inclined, and enabled to
give themselves to their Lord at the same time. With
hush of awe, not without white tears, one reads the
goldenly precious self-revelation, modest but frank, frank
because confiding. They must find place here :

> . . . . . . "The obsequies of Him that could not die
> And death of life, ende of eternitie,
> How worthily He died, that died vnworthily ; . . . . . .
> Is the first flame wherewith my whiter Muse
> Doth burne in heauenly love, such love to tell.
> O Thou that didst this holy fire infuse,
> And taught'st this brest, *but late the graue of hell,*
> *Wherein a blind, and dead heart liu'd,* to swell
> With better thoughts, send downe those lights that lend
> Knowledge, how to begin, and how to end
> The loue, that neuer was, nor euer can be pend."[1]

Thus baptized with Fire 'from the Altar' he became a
servant-Shepherd under the Owner-shepherd.

FULLER says "He was at last (by exchange of his
living) settled in Suffolk." On this WILMOTT observes
"It seems improbable that he would have relinquished
any other preferment for a situation which is supposed
to have hastened the period of his death;" and he
continues "[He] did not live long to reap the advan-

[1] Part I. s. 1, 3. . . . . . .

tage of his preferment; the unhealthiness of the situation combined with the ignorance of his parishioners, to
depress his spirits and exhaust his constitution; a lonely
village in the maritime part of Suffolk, more than two
hundred years ago, had few consolations to offer to
one accustomed to the refined manners and elegant
occupations of an University. We are told by Fuller
in the quaint manner for which he is remarkable, that
Fletcher's 'clownish and low-parted parishioners (having
nothing but their shoes high about them) valued not
their pastor according to his worth, which disposed him
to melancholy and hastened his dissolution.'"[1]

We are reminded of HERRICK's like experience among
his 'clownish' Devonshire parishioners. Unfortunately
the 'Registers' of ALDERTON—the 'living' of Fletcher
—only go back to 1674; so that there are no accessible
records to get at Facts and dates.

[1] As before, p. 67: "He may have been" suggests Willmott
here, "presented to the living by Sir Robert Naunton, whose
family were the patrons of the Church and had their residence in
the parish. Naunton was Public Orator during several years of
Fletcher's residence at Cambridge, and being himself a member of
Trinity was, probably, well acquainted with his poetry and genius."
On this, in a little Paper which appeared in the Ipswich Journal,
(March 12th, 1853) a local Writer adds "If Scipio departed from
Rome to fix his residence in some remote locality, it was but
natural that he should sigh for the companionship of his beloved
Lælius." It is discreditable in no common degree to Suffolk that
an appeal by the (then) Rector for funds in order to place a marble
tablet in the wall of the 'old Rectory' in memory of Fletcher,
remains (1875) un-responded to and the pious project unperformed.
O Shame where is thy blush?

While 'Rector' I do not doubt he discharged faithfully the functions of his office ; and his prose in the form of ' Epistles ' and ' Prefaces ' already given, and those which precede his Poem, should alone warrant us in conclud ing that he had preaching-power.　But besides it is our rare happiness to have before us a copy—one of three known to exist, and only three—of a prose treatise by our Worthy, that gives us in all likelihood the substance. of a series of sermons.　As this book has escaped the knowledge of all our Fletcher's previous Biographers, I shall give first of all the title-page, next the ' Epistle De-dicatory,' and thereafter extracts illustrative of its thought and style.

There is first the title-page

The
REWARD
of the Faithfull.
Math. 5. 6.
They shall be satisfied.

THE LABOVR OF
the Faithfull.
Genes. 20. 12.
Then Isaac sowed in that Land.

THE GROVNDS
of our Faith.
Acts 10. 43.
To him giue all the Prophets witnesse.

At London printed by B. A. for
Beniamin Fisher, and are to
be sold at the signe of the *Tal-*
bot in Pater-noster row
1623.[1]

---

[1] I owed my use of this precious volume originally to my accomplished friend George W. Napier, Esq., of Alderley Edge, near

The ' Epistle ' refers to 'favours' conferred by BACON. It is saddening that we cannot know more of their nature. Was it the ' presentation ' to Alderton? and the graciousness of it ?   It would almost seem so, for in Bacon's *Liber Regis* (ed. 1786, p. 782), under the head of Alderton I find this :—"Sir James Bacon pro duabus vicibus, olim Patr." Thus it is not improbable that the living was in the gift of the Bacons, and that *the* Bacon may have presented him to it.

The ' Epistle' is as follows :

' To the right Honorable and Religious, Sir Roger Townshend, Knight Baronet;[1] all grace and peace.
Honourable Sir,

Benefits, they say, are alwayes best giuen when they are most concealed, but thanks when they are made most knowne.   Giue my priuate estate leaue therefore

Manchester.   It is daintily covered with satin and silver wire-work in flowers—which kind of binding is usually ascribed to the ladies of Little Gidding.   Since, I received the gift of a perfect copy (Mr Napier's lacking the title-page), and recently the British Museum has added a third to its treasures.

[1] Sir John Townshend, Bart, M.P., married Anne, eldest daughter and co-heir of Sir Nathanael Bacon, K.B., half-brother of *the* Bacon.   The eldest son of this marriage was the Roger of this Dedication, created a Baronet in 1617.   From him descend the present Marquis Townshend, Viscount Sydney, Baron Bayning, &c. (See ' Notes and Queries ' 4th Series, May 23rd, 1868, p. 499). Phineas also dedicates his ' Locustae ' to Sir Roger, and his English ' Locusts ' to Lady Townshend.   See our edition of Phineas Fletcher, *in loco.*   John Yates dedicates his ' Saints' Sufferings and Sinners' Sorrowes ' (1631) to Sir Roger Townsend, &c.   G.

to borrow the Art of the Printer, which is the publike
Tongue of the learned, to expresse my selfe (though
with no other learning then what your kinde respects
haue taught mee) most gratefull vnto you : who indeed
am bound, though principally, yet not onely to your
Honoured selfe, but *totj Gentj tuæ*, to the worthy Lady
your mother, the religious Knight, Sir Nathaniel, your
second Father, & without thought, not beyond my desire, to your most noble & learned Vncle, the Right
Honorable Francis Lord Verulam, Viscount Saint Al-
bones, my free and very Honourable Benefactor, whose
gift, as it was worthy his bestowing, so was it speedily
sent, and not tediously sued for; Honourably giuen,
not bought with shame, to one whom he neuer knew or
saw, but onely heard kindly slaundered with a good re-
port of others, and opinion conceiued by himselfe of
sufficiencie and worth. For by your Fauours I confesse, my estate is something, but the sence of my
pouertrie much more increased. For if we may beleeue
Nero's wise Maister and Martyr ; ' There is none so
poore, as he who cannot requite a benefit :' [1] but I am
glad your Estates will be alwayes beyond any retaliating [2]
kindnesses of mine who could not, indeed, without
doing you much iniury, wish my selfe able to make you
amends.

[1] Seneca. G.
[2] An example of a now disused sense of this word, such as illus-
trates and confirms Trench's remarks on it in his well-known
' Study of Words.' G.

As therefore Aristippus came to Dionysius, so doe I to you ʾΕτί τῷ μεταδώσειν ὧν ἔχω καὶ μεταλήψεσθαι ὧν μὴ ἔχω Hauing received what I wanted, to returne what I had.[1] Though in trueth this small present may bee better sayed to bee giuen by you to others, then by my self to you, who thought it worthy of more mens reading then your owne, which I pray God it may be. Surely if there be any worth in it, it is in the dignitie of the matter, and the fitnesse of it, for our nature and times. The matters are the Grounds, Exercise and Reward of the faithfull, Heauenly Light, Bodily labour, Spirituall rest. The first of which brings with it light for our Soules; the second, Health for our bodies, and the third for them both eternal Blessednesse. But in our times there are three vertues are so great strangers, in which there are so many euill heartes of vnbeliefe, all standing ready to depart from the liuing God, that wee had need to offer a holy violence to our nature, and to fall out with our times, that fall so fast away from God, or else it is to be feared least the tide and streame of them both carry vs not into the riuers of Paradise, there to bee landed vpon the mountaines of our saluation, but into the riuers of Brimstone, whether all are wafted that depart from God : as himselfe telleth vs ; ‘ Depart from mee yee cursed into euerlasting fire.’

And so much the more need had wee, that liue in this last Age of the world, to looke to the infirmitie of our

---

[1] Diogenes Laertius, *Vita Aristippi* ii. 77. G.

natures and diseases of the time : because natural infirmities are alwayes greatest Tyrants in our Age, and it is
no otherwise in this old world, then in old persons : If
we were borne weake sighted, it is a venture but in age
a great dimnesse, if not a totall blindnesse doe not be-
fall vs. If a lame hand by nature hath disabled the
actions of our youth; the hand which in youth could
doe little, will doe nothing in our age ; if we have tra-
duced a personal inclination from our parents to any
vice, it is a grace if that inclination grow not to an
affection in our youth, and in our age to a habite. So
fast grow the ill weedes of Nature when Nature it selfe
decayes in vs.

Now wee cannot bee ignorant that in the very Spring
of nature, these three strong infirmities were seeded in
vs. The first vpon the effacing of God's Image, a
dimme eye-sight or darknesse in our soule : the second
a lame hand or idlenesse in the body, which grew when
Mortalitie first broke in vpon vs, and left our nature
consumed of that first-borne strength it then flowrished
with : bringing in vpon our labour an accursed sweat,
vpon our sweat, wearinesse, and consequently faynting,
and languishing the whole body with vnrest, and disease :
The third vpon the losse of our heavenly inheritance, an
inclination and affection of the whole man to such a
happinesse, as wee cannot build for our selues, out of the
beautie and delights of this world : which Salomon happily alluded vnto Eccles. 3. 11. where speaking of
Humane happinesse, to reioyce, and doe good, that is,

to eate and to drinke, and to enioy the good of all our
Labour, verse, 3, (Which questionlesse is therefore lawfull, because it is there sayd to bee the gift of God) hee
telleth vs; that, ' God hath made every thing beautifull
in his season, and hath set הָעֹלָם *cœlum*, the worlde, as
it is translated, or the desire of perpetuitie in their
heartes, so that no man can finde out the worke that
God maketh from the beginning to the end.' Whereas
it seemes to me, Salomon allowing vs this Humane felicitie, as good in it selfe, yet secretly accuseth it (by
reason of the immoderate affection, and desire of perpetuitie wee cast after it) for blinding the eye of our
consideration so farre, as thereby wee cannot find out
the worke that God maketh from the beginning to the
end, which doub[t]lesse [1] can be no other then his worke
of our Redemption, purposed from all eternitie in Christ
our Lord who therefore as himself is called πρωτότοκος
πάσης κτίσεως, the first-borne of all creatures, so his day
is cald *Nouissimus Dierum*, the last of all dayes, he
onely being (as himselfe witnesseth) A and Ω and the
First [2] and the Last, the beginning of all things and the
ende of all things Colos. i., [3] 15; and in this worke onely
consists the knowledge of our perfit happines wherein is
both perpetuitie and sufficiency, which work of God's,
most men therefore cannot finde out, because they ac-
quiet their desires with this humane felicitie, and lie
downe vnder Issachars blessing, which indeed, is but a

[1] Misprinted ' doublesse.'   [2] Misprinted ' Frst.'
[3] Misprinted ' 11.'

cursory and viatorie happinesse, seruing vs onely for the time and by the way.

These then are the three great diseases of our soules, bodies, and persons : Blindnesse of Spirit, Idlenesse of Body, Loue and rest in the world ; which the beginning of the world, made by corruption, naturall ; and the Age of the world, by the second nature, and of custome, hath made delightfull to vs. And truely, if our owne experience did not teach vs how most men in our daies pleased themselues in these infirmities, and with what delight wee are ignorant, idle, and enamored of the world : yet the Oracles of God would plainely euidence it vnto vs, wherein wee shall finde it prophecied of this last tempest of the world, that it should bee full of seducing Spirits to infidelitie, of idle busie-bodyes, of louers of pleasures more then louers of God. To cure which three great diseases[1] of our natures, and our times I haue sent abroade by your perswasion (and therefore haue burdened you with the Patronage of it) this short Præscript, which I pray God may worke by the power of his Spirit, soundnesse in vs. To the riches of whose grace, I most entirely commend you, and rest Your Worships in all hearty affection and Christian seruice.

GILES FLETCHER.

I now proceed to select such portions of the work itself as have arrested my attention in reading it.[2] Taken

---

[1] Misprinted 'diseased.'

[2] The texts are St. Matthew v., 6, 'They shall be satisfied,' pp. 1-127 ; Genesis xxvi., 12, pp. 127-302 ; Acts x., 43, pp. 303-419.

as a whole it is scarcely worthy of a reprint; but our
gleanings will, it is believed, interest. The 'verse'
bits will be found in their own place among the poems.
I submit our extracts *seriatim* from the commencement
to the close.[1]

(1) "So much almes, and often fasting & due pay-
ment of tithes, what goodnesse haue they, if the almes
must bee trumpeted abroad, and the fast must set a
sowre face vpon the matter, and the tithes must bee
boasted of, and layed as it were in Gods dish, when he
comes to pray before him in the Temple, as though God
who giues him all, were beholding to him, for restoring
him the tenth part of his owne?" (p. 9.)   Again :—

(2) " Now it is a speech of our Sauiour which it may
bee euery man remembers, but few men marke, when
after fourty dayes fast in the wildernesse, he was tempted
to satisfie his hunger by making bread of stones, he
answered, That man liu'd not by bread onely, but by
euery Word that proceeded out of the mouth of God.
Which speech though a prophane Ignorant will perhaps
derisively [2] scoffe at, as thinking it impossible to liue by
words, yet such words as proceed out of the mouth of
God haue more vitall sweetnesse, and nourishable sap
in them, than all his corne, and oyle, and wine haue.
Was not the whole world made by the word of God ?

---

[1] It is remarkable that this prose treatise of our Poet should not
hitherto have been known after Phineas's well-known verses given
onward.

[2] Misprinted ' derisonly.'

Was not the soule of euery reasonable creature made by the same word, and so imbreathed into the body of the first father of our humane nature? and is now still infused into euery one of our bodies, when they are perfectly instrumented, and made fit for the soule to dwell in?" (pp. 19–21.)   Again :—

(3) "If a man digging in a field, find a mine, we cal this fortune : but a mine must bee first there by nature, before any can finde it there by fortune.   And therefore fortune that comes alwayes after nature, cannot bee the cause of nature." (p. 24.)   Again :—

(4) "What nature in earth obsueres the different motions of the heavenly bodies, and admires the methodicall wisedom of God in them, and thinkes vpon his couenant of mercy, when he sees the token of it shining in the waterie cloud (sweetly abusing the same waters to bee a token of his mercy, which before were the instrument of his iust revenge.") (p. 30, 31.) Again :—

(5) "Whose eye lookes beyond the bright hilles of time, and there beholds eternity, or sees a spirituall world beyond this body, esteeming that farre discoasted region, his native country,[1] but onely man? (p. 31.) Again :—

(6) So with the body.   But we cannot drinke too much of our spirituall rocke, nor eate too much of our heauenly Manna, after which we haue feasted our hearts with, we shall find noe more hunger, or thirst; feele noe

---

[1] Misprinted 'countey.'

more iniuries of age, or time ; feare noe more spoiles of
mortality, or death.   Neither is the soule nourished by
this diuine food, as the body is, by wasting that whereby
it selfe is preserued, and consuming that to maintaine it
selfe, whereby it selfe is kept from corruption : but as
the sight of al eyes is preserued and perfected by
the light of the Sunne, whose beames can neuer be
exhaust, so our spiritual life is nourished by the partici-
pation of the life of Christ which is indeed πηγάζων
ζωὴ, *annona cœli,* the flower of heauen, neuer engrost by
possessing, nor lost by vsing, nor wasted by nourishing,
nor spent by enioying but hath that heauenly, and
vnconsumable nature in it (being to nourish immortall
soules) that it preserues al without decaying itselfe, it
diuides it selfe to all without losse or diminution of it
selfe ; it is imparted to all and replenished, and not
impayred by any of those soules that banquet vpon it."
(pp. 37–40.)   Again :—

(7) "Like the twilight of an euening, or the first
breake of day in which the shadows of earth, and the
light of heauen are confused." (p. 42.)   Again :—

(8) "Makes vs of one spirit and one soule, as it
were, with the Diuine being; not by the vnion of
essence and information, but by inhabitance and par-
ticipation." (p. 61.)   Again :—

(9) "But when the morning of glory shall arise,
wherein our soules shall awaken from the heauy eye-lid
of our flesh, and the veyle of our body shall first be
remoued, and after being depur'd from his drosse, be

refined into a bright and spirituall body, wee shall then
see God as he is." (pp. 73, 74.)   Again :—

(10) " So that looke as you see the very bright image
of the Sunne so reflected vpon the water somtimes,
that the dull Element seemes to haue caught downe the
very glorious body it selfe, to paint her watry face with,
and lookes more like a part of heauen, then like it selfe ;
who in the absence of the Sunne, is all sabled with
blacknesse and darknesse, and sad obscurity ; but vpon
the first beames of the heauenly body, is glazed with a
most noble & illustrious brightnesse ; so is it with our
whole man.   For when God shall thus imprint and
strike himselfe into our darke being, O how beautifull
shall the feet of Gods saints bee?   Esay 52. 7.   What
a Diadem of stars shall crowne their glorious heads?
Reuelat. 12.   How shall their amiable bodies shine in
Sun-like Majesty?   Mat. 13. 4." (pp. 77, 78.)   Again :—

(11) " This carried the heart of olde Simeon into such
a holy extasie of religious delight, that earth could hold
him no longer, but he must needs, as it were, breake
prison, and leape out of his olde body into heauen.   O
what a desire of departure to it, doth a true sight of this
saluation kindle !   ' Lord,' saies he, ' now lettest,' &c.
As if he should say, Lord, now the child is borne, let
the olde man die, now thy son is come, let thy seruant
depart, now I haue seene thy saluation, O let mee goe
to enioy it.   Now I haue beheld the humanity of thy
sonne, what is worth the looking vpon, but the diuinity
of such a person, who is able to make my young Lord

heere euen proud of his Humilitie. For so great a ioy
of spirit can neuer be thrust vp into so small a Vessell,
as an olde shrunke-vp body of earth is. Since therefore
I haue testified of thy Christ, since I haue made an end
of my dying note, and sung thee my Christmasse song ;
since I haue seene thee, O thou holy one of Israell,
whom no flesh can see & liue, what haue I to do to liue,
O Lord? What should I weare this olde garment of
flesh any more? Thou hast left thy fatnesse off, O
thou faire Oliue Tree and the oyle of it hath made mee
haue a cheerefull countenance : thou hast forsaken thy
sweetnesse, O thou beautifull Vine, and thy fruit hath
warm'd thine olde Seruant at the very hart. Now therfore being thou hast powred thy new wine into this old
vessell, O giue the old bottle leaue to breake, O let
me depart in peace ; for I haue enough, I haue seen,
mine eyes haue seene thy saluation." (pp. 111–114.)
Again :—

(12) " Exod. 20. 9 . . . which is not to be vnder-
stood as a Permission, but as a Precept : as though God
gaue vs onely leaue, & not charge to labour. For hee
sayes not, six daies thou Maist labour, but six daies
thou Shalt labour." (p. 131.)   Again :—

(13) "Are not al things imbrightned with vse, and
rustied with lying still? Let but the little Bee become
our mistresse. Is shee not alwaies out of her artificiall
Nature, either building her waxen Cabinet, or flying
abroad into the flowry Meadowes or sucking honey
from the sweete plants, or loading her weake thighes

with waxe to build with, or stinging away the theeuish
Droan that would fain hiue it selfe among her labours,
and liue vpon her sweete sweat? *Ignauum, fucos, pecus
a præsepibus arcent.*[1] And shal this little creature, this
Naturall goode hous wife thus set her selfe to her businesse, and shall we droane away our time in idlenesse,
and which alwaies followes it, vicious liuing?" (pp. 138,
139.)   Again:—

(14) It is indeede a naturall Truth, *Omne Corpus
naturale quiescit in loco proprio.* Euery naturall body
is quiescent in his owne proper place : and yet wee see
though all gladly rest in their owne regions, and inuade
not the confines of their neighbour Elements, yet they are
alwayes mouing and coasting about in their owne orbes
and circuits, thereby teaching vs to labour euery man in
the circle of his owne calling, and not to busie-body
out abroad with other newe workes. The Aire breakes
not into the quarters of heauen and yet, wee see, it is
alwayes fann'd from place to place, and neuer sleepes
idly in his owne regions: the reason is, because otherwise it would soone putrifie it selfe and poyson vs all
with the stinking breath of it, did not the diuine prouidence of God driue it about the World with his
Windes, that so it might both preserue it selfe and serue
to preserue us, which otherwise it could never doe.
. . . . . . So that in a word, euery thing moues for
man, & should man only himselfe be idle and stand
still." (pp. 143–146.)   More fully:—

[1] Virgil. *Georg.* IV. 168. G.

(15) "A faithfull Minister is a great labourer. I
would not willingly make comparisons betweene him
and the husbandman, and say his labour is beyond
theirs; but this I may safely say, that God himselfe
compares him not onely to a husbandman, but to shew
the greatnesse of his labour, to euery calling indeed that
is most sweated with industrie and toyle. I know all
men thinke their owne callings most laborious, but
whether thinke you it easier to plow vpon hard ground,
or vpon hard stones? whether to commit your seed to
those furrowes that will return you fruitfull thankes; or
those that for your labor will spoyle your seed, & requite
you with reproch and slander? whether to such ground
as is good, and naturally opens her bosome to drinke
in the dewes of heauen that fall upon her, and gladly
recciues the Sunne beames shed from God to warm and
make fruitfull the seede credited to her wombe, or such
ground as neuer thirsts after the watering of Apollos,
though as Moses speakes (Deut. 32. 2.) his words drop
as the raine, and his speech distill as the dew; neuer
can indure the light of heauen to shine vpon it, but lies
alwayes in darkenesse and in the shadowes of death?
yet such ground (stones I should haue sayd) did the
diuine courage of Stephen meet with in Ierusalem (Act.
7. 59), such S. Paul wrought on at Lystra (Act. 14. 19.),
such Moses and Aaron and Iosua toyled vpon in the
wildernes (Num. 14. 10.) such the prophets (Matt. 21,
25.) such the Prince of the prophets found in his owne
inheritance, though he had before (as we see in Esay 5.

2.) pickt all the stones himselfe out of it (John 8, 59). What one difficultie or danger is the roughest calling assaulted with, that his is not. Does the plowmans labour know no end, but is it as the Poet speakes of it:

> Labor actus in orbem,
> Quique in se sua per vestigia voluitur?[1]

So is his. Does the Shepheard, the sun-burnt and frosted shepheard, watch ouer his flockes by night, strengthen the diseased, set apart the sound, binde vp the bruised, seek out the lost, rescue those that are preyed vpon? So does he. Marches the soldier before the face of death? liues hee among the pikes of a thousand dangers? walks he throgh his owne wounds and blood? So does he: but as the ground this spirituall plowman tils is harder, so the wolves & Lyons this Shepheard watches against are fiercer, and the Armies he graples with of another temper then such as are made like himselfe of flesh and blood; being Powers and Principalities, spirituall wickednesses, & worldly gouernors, one of whom could in a nights space strike dead the liues of a hundred fourescore and fiue thousand souldiers at once, all armed and embattayld together Isay 37. 36. Let all the Princes of valour that euer liued bring into the field their most tried and signall warriour, whose face and brest stand thickest with the

---

[1] More accurately " Redit agricolis labor actus in orbem, Atque in se sua per vestigia volvitur annus."—Virgil *Georg. ii.,* 401, 402. **G.**

honourable scarres [1] of braue aduentures; if I doe not
single out to encounter him one souldier that beares in
his body the markes of the Lord Iesus, who shall haue
broken through an Iliad of more dangers and perils, then
he, let Gath and Ascalon triumph ouer Sion once againe,
& let it be said that a second and more noble Saul is
falne vpon his high places, then euer yet fell before.
For wee shall finde him all the world ouer in labours
more abundant, in iourneys more often, in more perils
in the city, in the wilderness, in the sea, more often in
watchings, and fastings, in hunger and thirst, in cold &
nakednesse, in prison more frequent, and ofter in wearinesse and death 2 Cor. 11. 23. &c.   Let not him therefore that sowes the earth with his labor, slander the
spirituall tilth of our soules with lazie thoughts.   Alas!
in the time of peace contempt is the greatest haruest we
reape and in the tempests of persecution, our blood is
the first seed is sowne in the Church." (pp. 155—162).
Again :—

(16) " Isaac (1) a religious person sowes.   (2) sowes
in a time of famin and dearth.   (3) ground of strangers.
(4) reward."   Again :—

(17) " What would one of our small heires say, should
I now turne Farmour.   I thanke God I haue beene
brought vp after another fashion, and haue ground
enough of mine owne to liue upon by other mens
labours.   Well I make no question but Isaac was as

---

[1] The original has ' honourable starres,' but ' markes' onward,
shews it to be a misprint for ' scarres' as above.   G.

well brought vp as such idle, out of calling gentlemen, and yet he plowes, and sowes, not only another mans ground, but the ground of straungers, where hee could expect nothing but hard dealing, which indeed hee found." (pp. 171, 172.)   Again :—

(18) "God . . . . His are no Court-promises prodigally made, and purposely forgotten. (p. 177.) Again :—

(19) " All these mischiefes happen not to rich men, but to men that will bee rich, not to men that haue money but to men that loue money and set their heart vpon it.   ' If riches increase,' &c., saies Dauid.   A man may haue riches, but riches must not haue the man." (p. 183.)—

(20) " It may be thou art godly and poore.   Tis well : but canst thou tell whether, if thou wert not poore, thou wouldst be godly?   Sure God knows vs better then wee ourselues doe, and therefore can best fit the estate to the person." (pp. 211, 212.)   Again :—

(21) " Rest therefore thy selfe content with that estate God hath set thee in, that is best for thee, if thou beest a childe of God, and it is not God's order to giue thee his blessings to hurt thee with." (p. 212.)   Again :—

(22) " A covetous man is the poorest man aliue.   For must not he needs be poore, whom God himselfe doth not satisfie ? " (p. 218.)   Again :—

(23) " But indeed to say true.—A couetous man that rauines and snatches at other mens goods is no more properly in God's sight a rich man, then we would call

him that had stollen a great summe of mony from another man, rich. We shall doe him no wrong if we call
him a rich theefe. For yee know wee neuer reckon the
goods of theeues their owne goods, because as soon as
they are taken notice of, their goods are all seiz'd vpon
to the King's vse : And so many times as soone as God
sends out his pale Pursuiant to attach this couetous
wretch, the goods presently are disposed of, all [as] God
will have them : sometimes it may be to his honest
heire, or perhaps to the destruction of such as inherit
with his sinne his substance, as the rich Epulœs Brothers :
but many times to the building of Hospitals or the
erecting of Grammar Schooles, or putting out of Pren-
tises or redeeming of Prisoners or founding of Colledges
or releeuing of maimed Soldiers, or making of good
waies, such as himselfe never walkt in (or which now is
a rare point of pietie) in doing some good to the Church
of God, by restoring to the right vse, vsurped and impro-
priate tithes, or buying them from the dead hands they
lie in, and laying them vpon God's Altar, that feedes not
vnder the Gospel any mortmaines, such as were the
hands of the Romane Clergie : but such as are more
free, and active in the seruice of the Prince, and Commonwealth, then any in the whole bodie politique of
double their abilitie, and strength." (pp. 220—223.)—

(24) "God's love is the beginning, and thy glory is
the last end, the loue of God will bring thee to : but
there be many meanes betweene the beginning and the
ende, his loue and thy glory. First, God's loue elects

thee to be iustified, and to worke thy iustification he cals thee, and that thou maiest be called, he infuses into thy heart faith in Christ, and that thou mightst beleeue, he causes thee to heare the word, that thou mightst heare, his Prophets must preach it to thee, before they can preach, they must be sent : So that in briefe, The Minister is sent to preach, he preaches that thou maist heare, thou hearest, that thou mightst be called, thou art called to beleeue in Christ, thou beleeuest that thou maiest be iustified, being iustified, thou art sure of thy Crowne of Glorie, and this glory the loue of God by all these meanes sets as it were vpon thy head. Betweene therfore our glory which is the end, & God's loue which is the beginning and cause of it, many interiacent meanes, you see, are cast betweene." (pp. 239—241.) Again :—

(25) "If the Sunne be risen, wee shall finde him sooner by his beames vpon the tops of the Mountaines, then in the Orient of Heauen it selfe ; and so the Loue of God is sooner discouered to rise in thy heart by the beames of Grace it there shows abroad, then by the flame of it self that shines in his owne breast in heauen. If then grace imbrighten thy heart, thou maist from Grace assure thy selfe of God's loue, and thine own glorie : but if thou findest in thy selfe an impenitent and incorrigible heart, thou mayst then iustly worke vpon thy selfe a sence of thy misery : I dare not say thou art sure of God's wrath, but I must say, except thou repent, and God change thy heart, thou art yet in a fearefull and

lost estate ; say not therefore thus.—God hath cast me
out from his fauour, therefore my heart is obdurate, impenitent, incorrigible.   For this is to argue from that
thou knowest not, whether God fauors thee or no : but
thus rather, My heart is obdurate, impenitent, incorrigible, therefore if I so continue, God will surely cast mee
out from his fauour and presence.   And this thou maist
securely doe, because thine owne conscience is both a
witnesse and a iudge of thy life, whether it be impenitent or not." (pp. 251—3.)   Again :—

(26) " Nor was it a miracle to see rich mens daughters (vnacquainted with new tires, and most fashionable
dresses) busie themselues in laborious (and not curious
needle) work, but it was ordinary in that old world to
meete the young and beautifull Rachel tending her
father's sheepe, and watering the flocke, and Rebecca
with a pitcher vpon her shoulder, drawing water both
for her owne vse, and to water the Camels of Abraham's
servant, an office that our nice virgins, who dresse vp
themselues like so many gay silke-worms would thinke
scorne of." (pp. 262—3.)   Again :—

(27) " Thus were the opinions of the old world, but
it is a world to see now the prodigious change of Nature,
when not onelie most men count Husbandrie a base and
sordid businesse, vnfit to soyle their hands with : but
some, who thinkes his breast tempered of finer clay then
ours of the vulgar sort, call such as haue spent their
times in the studies of Diuinity, no better then *rixosum
disputatorum genus quorum vix in coquendis oleribus con-
silium admittit.*" (pp. 274-275.)   Again :—

(28) "Others bestow their time in Legall, and Callings vsefull to the Common-wealth, but as they abuse them, neyther honest, nor iustifiable before God. Such are our Tap-houses, and Gaming Innes : I meane not harbouring and viatory Innes, which questionless, in fit places, and where Iustice is neere at hand, if rightly vsed, are not onely lawfull and profitable, but necessarie and honest : for to lodge weary Trauellers as Rahab did the Spies of Israel, or to let the poore labouring man to have iust allowance of bread and drinke for his money can be accounted no other then necessary relief : but for our Tipling Innes in small and vntract Hamlets, without which our Country-Diuels of drunkennesse, Blasphemy, Gaming, Lying, and Queaning, could amongst vs finde no harbor (though perhaps in places of more resort they haue credit enough to be entertained in fairer lodgings) they are eyther the Diuel's vncleane Warehouses for his spiritual wickednesses to trade in; or in our plaine world hee hath no traffique at all." (pp. 291-93).

(29) " It was Eliah's speech from God to Ahab : ' Hast thou slaine, and also taken possession ;' and it may well be his Churche's to either of theirs. Hast thou taken possession, and wilt thou slay also ? not the body once, but for euer the soules, of innocent men. Let no man quarrell with me, as Ahab did with Eliah. ' Hast thou found me O mine Enemie ? ' If he doe, I must borrow Saint Paule's answer 'Am I thine enemy, because I tell thee the Truth ? ' No (I speake not out of rash, but charitable zeale) thou art thine owne Enimie, thou art God's

Enimie, thou art the enimie of his Church. For if thou
didst loue him, thou wouldst feede his flock, feede his
Sheepe, feede his Lambs. If thou diddest loue his
Church, thou wouldest shew thy loue by thy obedience
to it. Who enioynes euery one eleuen moneths residence vpon his cure, and graunts him but one month's
absence, whereas it is a venture, but without long search
you may finde one that absents himselfe eleuuen
moneths, and is resident but once a yeare, and that is
perhaps at haruest, or peraduenture at Easter, when his
owne, and not so much the Church's profit calles him to
his benefit, not his Benefice. He would being resident
preach euery Sunday, as shee commaunds him in her
45. Cannon. Hee would labour to conuince Heretiques
(which now in his absence growes vppon her) or see
them at least censured as shee bids him in her 65. and
66. Canons. He would keepe the sound in safety,
and visit the sicke, as shee directs him in her 67.
Canon. Thus he would do, and not laugh at them that
did thus, and would haue him doe so, as men more precise, than wise, of more heate than discretion. I am
not so intemperate as to rage against all Non-residency,
which in case of insufficiencie of one Liuing, or publique,
and necessarie imployment, either in Vniversities or
Court, must needs be allowable : but either our Church
it selfe is precise, that bids him doe thus : or he that
does the contrary without any ouerballancing reason,
prooues himselfe a Bastard, and none of hir Children.
A double wound it is our Church receiues from these

men. For as themselues haue not the grace to correct their owne sinne, so they haue commonly in their roomes certaine vnder-curats, so grossely ignorant. as not to know theirs. They that know nothing themselues, are set by these to teach others, of whom we cannot say *dies dici*, but *nox nocti indicat scientiam*. One night teaches another, a blinde Prophet a blinde People." (pp. 397-402.)   Again :—

(30) " Those Ecclesiastical home-Droanes of our owne, which hiue themselues vnder the shadow of our Church (the wicked thiefe money, that siluer dropsie, that now raigns in vnconsionable Patrons, making way for them), and so beare indeed either no witnesse to Christ at all, or but very slight, and rash witnesse" (p. 397).

He is very severe on non-residence at page 399 *seqq :* as earlier (page 371) he had passionately exclaimed (28) " O that there were not in Christ's militant Church, as there were in Othoe's military Campe, so many men, so few Soldiers, so many professors, so few Christians."

That he could wield the lash effectively has already appeared : but here is an out-burst on contemporary literature somewhat unexpected :

(31) " Among the crowde of this ranke (idlers) wee may thrust in our idle pamphleteers and loose poets, no better than the priests of Venus, with the rabble of stage-players, balleters and circumferaneous fidlers and brokers : all which if they were cleane taken out of the world there would bee little misse of them." Further:—

(32) " I do not deny but that God is able to perfect his power in these mens weaknesse : [The under-curates

left by non-residents] For it is not impossible for our spirituall Sampson (as hee ouercame his enemies, and was refreshed with a iawe of the seely beast) so to make the waters of Life spring between the teeth of these simple creatures : but these unsent Runners might do well to content themselues with one Cure, and not to be too busie in trudging between many, as some of them are." (p. 404.)

(33) "Neyther doe I denie but that such trading Preachers may find work enough for their mouths by making other mens labours runne through them. But this is to get their Liuing by the sweat of other men, and to wipe it off to their owne browes" (p. 405.)

He then gets sorrowfully vulgar, abusive, and illogical, and apologetical, thus :—

(34) "Pardon mee (right deerly beloued in our Lord and Sauiour) if when Thorns and Thistles grow vpon God's Altar, as the Prophet Hosea speakes, I am forced to vse a little fire of Zeale to consume them." (p. 413.)

Besides these fuller specimens I have marked a number of brief ones containing unusual words and turns of expression : *e.g.*

(1) The name of the wicked ' rots '—" And therefore our Sauiour in the Storie of Lazarus, and Dives, keepes the poore man's name aliue to the worlde's end, but industriously leaues the rich man's name at vncertaintie, with ' There was a certaine rich man.' " (p. 207.)

(2) " Purpled in glory by the bloud royall of our deere Lord " (p. 239.)

(3) "Those two mayne iettes . . . . Selfe-sufficiency and Perpetuitie." (p. 121.)

(4) "Scioyn'd one from another." (p. 122.)

(5) "Apting the bodies of men " (p. 269.)

(6) " Our nakednesse was then our glory, it is now our shame : it was a curse to till the earth then, it is now a blessing to haue earth to till : so that wee haue learnt to turne by the corruption of our nature, our apparell that should couer our shame, to proclaime our pride : and our Lands that should feede vs by our labour, to the food of our luxurie " (pp. 277, 278.)

(7) "They had need to be embalm'd as well before, as after their deaths." (p. 298.)

(8) " Lessoned our reason by sence " (p. 304.)

(9) " The noon-Sunne." (p. 307.)

(10) " The Christian impaths himselfe." (p. 321.)

(11) "Defalke as much from God's word." (p. 323.)

(12) " Some of these again spanging out of the Canon of the New Testament, all the Reuelation of S John. (p. 325.)

(13) " Others farsing *into* the Canonicall writings, Apocriphall and vnknowne Authors." (p. 325.)

(14) " The strict keeping of decorum, in figuring them [the four Evangelists] like beasts ['the four Beasts'] such as the Lamb himselfe is." (p. 331.)

(15) " The bulletting of a whole commonwealth." (p. 394.)

(16) " An irrepugnable truth." (p. 30.)

(17) " Were they not eftsoons reymbark't and stock't
againe into the Tree of Life." (p. 43.)

(18) " The first fulnesse or saturity." (p. 50.)

(19) " Indeflowrishing and vnattainted health." (p. 51.)

(20) " Measured them out by God, to vessel it up in."
(p. 53 and again p. 91.)

(21) " This is a retruse, and hidden, but in truth a
very diuine motion " (p. 69.)

(22) " The similitude it hath with it, in the act of in-
tellection." (p. 70.)

(23) "Inspired, and I may so speake, Spirited with
the Holy Ghost." (p. 76.)

(24) " Euigilant soules." (p. 85.)

(25) " Imbondaged." (p. 107.)

I know not that I leave anything worth-while in this
VOLUME : but surely we have in these words from it,
'APPLES of GOLD' in a 'BASKET of SILVER.' Biogra-
phically, our longer extracts numbered 15. and 17. are
most interesting : and there are other personal touches
that make the recovery of the ' Reward of the Faithfull'
no common treasure-trove toward our all too scant
knowledge of this Worthy.

That he was human is clear enough : infirm of temper
and perchance over-vehement and over-Churchly, and in
relation to the lowly men who outside of the Church of
England sought to 'speak' for the One Saviour and of
the One 'Salvation' mournfully without the large charity
of the illustrious JEREMY TAYLOR in his ' Liberty of

Prophesying'—which may be called the 'Magna Charta' of ' Ecclesiastical History,' so potent is it still.

FULLER leaves the death-date of our Poet imperfect thus 162.. but ANTHONY A-WOOD supplies it, viz., 1623.[1] " I beheld," says the former, " the life of this learned poet, like those half-verses in Virgil's Æneid, broken off in the middle, seeing he might have doubled his days according to the ordinary course of nature." [2] That 1623 was our Worthy's death-year is confirmed inferentially by PHINEAS'S over-looked verses headed " Upon my brother's book called, The grounds, labour and reward of faith," than which nothing can more meetly close the 'memorial' part of our Introduction :

> " This lamp fill'd up, and fir'd by that blest Spirit
> Spent his last oyl in this pure, heav'nly flame ;
> Laying the grounds, walls, roof of faith: this frame
> *With life he ends ;* and now doth there inherit
> What here he built, crown'd with his laurel merit:
>   Whose palms and triumphs once he loudly rang,
>   There now enjoyes what here he sweetly sang.
> This is his monument, on which he drew
> His spirit's image, that can never die ;
> But breathes in these live words, and speaks to th' eye:
> In these his winding-sheets he dead doth shew
> To buried souls the way to live anew,
>   And in his grave more powerfully now preacheth:
>   Who will not learn, when that a dead man teacheth ? " [3]

No stone,—and so no 'golden lie' of epitaph—or any other outward memorial whatever, marks GILES

---

[1] As before, *s. n.*   [2] As before: ' Worthies ' *s. n.*
[3] Poeticall Miscellanies, pp. 101, 102 (1663).

FLETCHER's last resting-place.   He left a Widow—as
we have already seen—who transferred herself to another and neighbouring Rectory.   Who she was, and
whether she bore a family to her first husband, has not
been 'written,' only it is recorded that Letters of Ad-
ministration were issued 12th November 1623, in the
Prerogative Court of Canterbury " on the estate of Giles
Fletcher of Alderton, county Suffolk, S. T. B. " to his
relict Anne; so that here we have the double-fact of *his*
death in 1623, and *her* Christian name ' Anne.'

And so the little life-story is told of one, concerning
whom loveable old LIVESEY's eulogium of CHETHAM,
holds, " They who excell[ed] him in grace, came short
of him in learning : and they who excell'd him in learning came short of him in grace." [1]   Remembering then
his noble Poem

> " Now his faith, his works, his ways,
>   Nights of watching, toilsome days,
>   Borne for Christ, 'tis meet we praise."

---

[1] ' Greatest Loss,' page 9.

ORDINARILY one might feel called on to apologize for coming between the Reader and his book with 'critical' remarks; but while to the necessarily select circle into which the Poetry of the Fletchers and their associates is likely to come, the works themselves should suffice—each being left to search out what of rare and vivid, beautiful and memorable, is to be found therein,—it nevertheless is my hope that some little service and help may be rendered to them—as to others—if from many-yeared loving and reverent familiarity with these fine old Singers, I illustrate successively their characteristics, estimate, or give materials for estimate, of their distinctive worth, and trace their influence, contemporary and later; and so guide, perchance, to a higher recognition than is common of their place in the lustrous roll of the Poets of England. With reference to all the Fletchers extant criticism has been based on the merest 'shreds and patches'—'purple patches' I allow—of extracts, and second-and-third-hand traditionary common-places of quotation; *e.g.* we have—and they are typical—on the one hand Henry Headly (in his "Select Specimens") telling us that "Christ's Victorie" is a "rich and picturesque poem unenlivened by IMPER-SONATION"—the antithesis of the fact in so far as 'impersonation' is concerned, as will appear; and more recently even such-an-one as S. C. Hall (in his " Book of Gems ") lavishing (apparently) well-weighed epithets in laudation of 'Elegies' that have no existence, and confirming his own verdict on Phineas Fletcher's ' Piscatory Eclogues' with learning from Coleridge *on another altogether* in a way that self-convicts him of never having read them, inasmuch as though their title be ' Piscatory' they have nothing whatever to do with ' angling,' save in their slight framework.   His condemnation of classical names and allusions brought together at random from scattered stanzas manifests amazing if also amusing ignorance, alike of them and the Poem.   It may be as well to find a place for this egregious criticism, as thus :—" Of Christ's Victory we may speak in terms of the highest praise.   The Poet has exhibited a fertility of invention and a rich store of fancy, worthy of the sublime subject.   The style is lofty and energetic, the descriptions natural and graphic, and the construction of the verse graceful and harmonious.   But unhappily he has introduced among his sacred themes—the birth, temptation, passion, resurrection and ascension of the Saviour—so many characters from and allusions to profane history, as often to jar upon the sense and to render the poet justly liable to the charges of bad taste and inconsistency.   Giles Fletcher indeed had no power in selecting his thoughts, or his reputation might have equalled his genius.   He refers to the Graces, Mount Olympus, the Trojan boy, the Titans, ' wild Pentheus,' 'staring Orestes,' Orpheus, Deucalion, Bacchus, Pan, Adonis, Arcady, Mount Ida, and the honey of Hybla— references that bear us away from the solemn grandeur of his great theme." On this empty twaddle three things may be said (*a*) Surely it is about time that objections to illustrations drawn from Greek Mythology being used by Christian writers, were decently buried and forgotten? For it is clear that our Fletchers and Milton did not regard these myths as merely heathen fables but as adumbrations of great truths to be revealed at the advent of Christianity. Of this there is striking exemplification in Giles Fletcher's "Christ's Triumph over Death" (st. 7, 8.)

> " Who doth not see drown'd in Deucalion's name
> (When earth his men, and sea had lost his shore)
> Old Noah? and in Nisus' lock, the fame
> Of Sampson yet alive ; and long before
> In Phaëthon's, mine own fall I deplore :
> *But he that conquer'd hell, to fetch againe*
> *His virgin widowe, by a serpent slaine,*
> *Another Orpheus was then dreaming poets feigne:*" *&c. &c.*

(*b*) That any man who could place between quotation-marks 'wild Pentheus' and 'staring Orestes' and 'Ida' and pronounce against the supremely grand text which contains them, proclaims his own utter incapacity and provides an admirable addition to the " Curiosities of Criticism " if a second D'Israeli ever arise to prepare such a volume : (*c*) That ' Lycidas ' and ' Comus ' might be similarly travestied by shovelling together their classical names and allusions.[1]

Our Memoirs show that Phineas, and not Giles as usually supposed—was the elder of the two brothers ; but as the quaint Puritan Preachers were wont quaintly to play on the ancient story of Esau and Jacob, the younger gat the blessing from the first-born ; or in plainer prose, published his chief poem long before his brother's appeared—albeit without one touch of ' *supplanting*' ; for never was there more winsome friendship than theirs.   (It is evident indeed by " Christ's Triumph after Death " (st. 49, 50) that Giles must have read the " Purple Island " in manuscript.   Probably " Christ's Victorie " and the " Purple Island " were written at the same time and mutually communicated :

> " But let the Kentish lad, that lately taught
> The oaten reed the trumpet's silver sound."

(Cf. P. I. II. st. 2)

> " Who now shall teach to change my oaten quill
> For trumpet 'larms.")

Turning then to " Christ's Victorie and Triumph in Heaven and Earth, over and after Death," it is due to the Poet to keep in mind its date, viz. 1610.   Preceding thus, even in publication and much longer in composition, by upwards of half-a-century ' Paradise Lost ' and ' Paradise Regained,' it has the distinction of having

[1] The Book of Gems : The Poets and Artists of Great Britain. By S. C. Hall.   3 vols. 8vo, 1848.

been the first 'sacred' poem of any considerable length, that has left its mark on English Literature. I am very well aware that prior to 1610, Antiquarianism has dug up so-called religious verse; but comparison therewith were an outrage. You may cull from some of them a radiant metaphor, a melodious couplet, a finely-touched epithet, a pregnant thought; but you have no other single poem before 'Christ's Victorie' whose whole warp and woof, substance and adornment, are 'sacred:' so that in the outset, as the pioneer of England's religious poetry in epic or semi-epic form, Giles Fletcher demands grateful praise. We can only surmise wistfully the deduction that might have been called for from this, had we the lost treasure of Spenser's 'Ecclesiastes,' 'Canticum Canticorum,' 'Hours of our Lord,' and the 'Sacrifice of a Sinner.' WITHER and QUARLES, HERBERT and CRASHAW and VAUGHAN, followed not preceded him. SOUTHWELL'S 'St Peter's Complaint' is much too short to be named with 'Christ's Victorie' even if it were not in his lesser pieces that the saintly Jesuit wrought most cunningly. NICHOLAS BRETON indeed was earlier and contemporary, and he verily has sung sweetly and divinely. Cognate with this honour of firstness—if the word be allowable—among the 'sacred' Singers of our Country, is the simple, idiomatic, capital English, of 'Christ's Victorie.' Hitherto your perfunctory editors and compilers have with stupid and uncritical supererogation modernized the orthography of the great Poem. Never was the irreverent process less called for; never

D

so like to rough-handed brushing off the exquisite
powder from a moth's wing or the fine meal from an
auricula.   Our text—as in every case—is from the
Poet's own, and the most hasty perusal will satisfy, that
the great body of the wording is pure un-archaic English, easily intelligible, terse, compact, musical.   With all
one's allegiance to SPENSER, it is trying to feel, much
more to think, one's way through the tropically thorny
luxuriance of his language.   And yet Master GILES
FLETCHER was a 'growing lad' when 'dear Colin' was
laid softly in Westminster.   Comparing 'Christ's Victorie' with earlier and later Poems, I think it deserves
no common praise for the naturalness, spontaneousness,
inevitableness, of its English.   The stanza is a modifi-
cation of what is called the Spenserian, and it is
astonishing how little of the contortion of the Sybil
there is with the flood-tide of her inspiration, how much
of the naked strength and disdainful greenness of the
old English oak, without its nodosities.   The perfection
of the thought is equalled by the perfection of its utterance.   There is the grand simplicity about it of our
English Bible of 1611.   And hence a familiar, sweetly
'common' sound in its every line almost.   I open a
chance page : and how vital, how modernlike are these
stanzas that first meet my eye !   He is describing 'the
faire Idea' of God as 'Mercie.'

> ' If any aske why roses please the sight?
> Because their leaues vpon Thy cheekes doe bowre:
> If any aske why lillies are so white?
> Because their blossoms in Thy hand doe flowre:

Or why sweet plants so gratefull odours shoure?
 It is because Thy breath so like they be:
 Or why the Orient sunne so bright we see?
What reason can we giue, but from Thine eies, and Thee?

Ros'd all in liuely crimsin ar Thy cheeks,
Whear beawties indeflourishing abide,
And, as to passe his fellowe cither seekes,
Seemes both doe blush at one another's pride;
And on Thine eyelids, waiting Thee beside.
 Ten thousand Graces sit, and when they mooue
 To Earth their amourous belgards from aboue,
They flie from Heau'n, and on their wings conuey Thy loue.

All of discolour'd plumes their wings ar made,
And with so wondrous art the quills ar wrought,
That whensoere they cut the ayrie glade,
The winde into their hollow pipes is caught:
As seemes the spheres with them they down haue brought:
 Like to the seauen-fold reede of Arcadie,
 Which Pan of Syrinx made, when she did flie
To Ladon sands, and at his sighs sung merily.

As melting hony, dropping from the combe,
So'still the words, that spring between Thy lipps:
Thy lippes, whear smiling Sweetnesse keepes her home,
And heau'nly Eloquence pure manna sipps:
He that his pen but in that fountaine dipps,
 How nimbly will the golden phrases flie,
 And shed forth streames of choycest rhetoric,
Welling celestiall torrents out of pöesie!

Like as the thirstie land in Summer's heat,
Calls to the cloudes, and gapes at euerie showre,
As though her hungry clifts all heau'n would eat,
Which if high God into her bosom powre,

Though much refresht, yet more she could deuoure ;
So hang the greedie ears of angels sweete,
And euery breath a thousand Cupids meete,
Some flying in, some out, and all about her feet.'[1]

Again of CHRIST :

' IIe is a path, if any be misled,
He is a robe, if any naked bee ;
If any chaunce to hunger, IIe is bread,
If any be a bondman, IIe is free,
If any be but weake, howe strong is IIee !
To dead men life IIe is, to sicke men health,
To blinde men sight, and to the needie wealth,
A pleasure without losse, a treasure without stealth.'[2]

Subsequent appropriations have vulgarized and made
(now) trite the illustrations here : but this only the more
calls for our appreciation of their *original.*   By the way,
the dainty fancies of the ' portraicture ' of ' Mercie '
have always reminded me of THOMAS CAREW'S 'Song '
(1642)
' Aske me no more where Ioue bestowes
When Iune is past, the fading rose:
For in your beautie's orient deep
These flowers, as in their causes, sleepe '[3]

The light-hearted ' Sewer in Ordinary to his Majesty '
had a deeper and more serious vein : and I think it
were not difficult to produce other reminiscences of our

---

[1] Christ's Victorie in IIeaven, st. 45—49.
[2] *Ibid.* st. 77.
[3] Poems by Thomas Carew, Esquire . . . . . 2d. edn. 1642,
p. 180.

Poet unconsciously taken—as the flavour of musk or rose-attar is by mere contact.

Another noticeable thing about 'Christ's Victorie' as in the mightier 'Paradise Lost' is the atmosphere of personal devoutness which surrounds it. While contemporaries were invoking after the Pagan fashion, the 'Muses' and other shadowy Patronesses, and seeking at most the refreshment of Helicon not 'Siloa's brook,' GILES FLETCHER with adoring faith, and glowing gratitude for what 'the grace of God' had done for him, turns to the Giver of every good and perfect gift and looks to Him for inspiration and 'fit words.' A Critic, already named, has remarked hereon : " Milton's invocation to the Holy Spirit in Paradise Lost is considered by Dunster 'supremely beautiful :' it does not surpass the solemn and enraptured piety of Fletcher."[1] Another has made the same comparison and doubted whether MILTON "equals this splendid and massive invocation."[2] We may read this earlier Introduction and 'Invocation,' which it will be remembered we saw to be of profound biographic value :

> ' The birth of Him that no beginning knewe,
> Yet giues beginning to all that are borne ;
> And how the Infinite farre greater grewe
> By growing lesse, and how the rising Morne

---

[1] Willmott's 'Lives' as before : 1st. edn. page 42: 'Paradise Regained' is by oversight referred to for Paradise Lost.

[2] Review of Willmott in Frazer's Magazine, October 1839, Vol. xx. p. 401.

That shot from heau'n did[1] backe to heau'n retourne:
The obsequies of Him that could not die,
And death of life, ende of eternitie:
How worthily He died, that died vnworthily ;—

How God and Man did both embrace each other,
Met in one person, Heau'n and Earth did kiss ;
And how a Virgin did become a Mother,
And bare that Sonne, Who the world's Father is,
And Maker of His mother ; and how Bliss
   Descended from the bosome of the High,
   To cloath Himself in naked miserie,
Sayling at length to Heau'n, in Earth, triumphantly,[2]

---

[1] CHALMERS and SOUTHEY misprint here ' and ' for ' did ' :
and so throw the fine opening stanza into (grammatical) confusion.

[2] In this place of ' Christ's Victorie,' I refer to Palmer's ' Christian Paradoxes.' Besides Fletcher himself, I have met with kindred
' Paradoxes ' elsewhere, indeed abundantly. I note here the gentle
SOUTHWELL in his "Nativity of Christ" published along with
"St. Peter's Complaint" in 1634, and so long subsequent to our
Poet:
  ' Behold the father is His daughter's sonne,
   The bird that built the nest is hatchd therein,
   The old of yeres an hower hath not outrunne,
   Eternall life to live doth nowe beginn,
  The Worde is dumm, the Mirth of heaven doth weepe,
  Mighte feeble is, and Force doth fayntely creepe.'
           (Poems by me : p. 128.)
So too CRASHAW, later still, in his ' Steps to the Temple ' (1646):
  ' Wellcome all wonders in one sight !
   Eternity shutt in a span !
   Sommer in Winter ! Day in Night !
   Heauen in Earth ! and God in man !
   Great little One, Whose all-embracing birth
   Lifts Earth to Heauen, stoopes Heauen to earth.'
  (' Hymn of the Nativity :' Works by me : Vol. I. pp. 73-4.)
Cf. also his ' Sospetto d'Herode,' stanzas 21—24.

Is the first flame, wherewith my whiter Muse
Doth burne in heauenly loue, such loue to tell:
O THOU THAT DIDST THIS HOLY FIRE INFUSE,
AND TAUGHT'ST THIS BREST—BUT LATE THE GRAUE OF HELL,
WHEREIN A BLIND AND DEAD HEART LIU'D—TO SWELL
   WITH BETTER THOUGHTS, SEND DOWNE THOSE LIGHTS THAT
   LEND
   KNOWLEDGE, HOW TO BEGIN, AND HOW TO END
THE LOUE, THAT NEUER WAS, NOR EUER CAN BE PEN'D.' [1]

I grant, if it be pressed, that there is in the outset
somewhat of the 'conceits' of a later age (curiously
enough): but the informing 'ideas' are grand and as
stated they found subsequently larger utterance in the
'Christian Paradoxes' of HERBERT PALMER, that were
deep and wise enough to usurp unchallenged for two
centuries, the great name of BACON. The 'conceits'
in them are in kind with the 'clothing-adornments'
male and female, of the Period: fantastic ruff, but of
the 'finest linen,' oddly-shapen head-dress, bosom-dress,
foot-dress: but gleaming with jewels of the first water:
stiff, cumbrous, awkward altogether, yet the vesture of
foremost, steep-browed men and 'ladies fair.'

The intensity of the Poet's own Love and Faith, Hope
and Graciousness lies over his Poem—like a bar of sunlight—as one has seen such shattering itself in dazzling
glory against a heath-purpled mountain-side. In unexpected turns, in equally unexpected places, you are
reminded that you have no mere Singer working artisti-
cally but a 'Saint'—in the Bible not Mediæval meaning

---

[1] Christ's Victorie in Heaven, st. 1-3.

—pouring out the glad Worship of his whole nature—a nature rich of faculty in itself and enriched with celestial riches.   This inworking into the very 'stuff' of his Poem, of his own personality, imparts a tender humanness to it : and came of that brave self-estimate or in another sense fine naturalness, which belongs to the greatest of our great names among those who have insight,—SHAKESPEARE, and touchingly BACON, MILTON, SIR THOMAS BROWNE.   Approve or condemn, accept or reject, it is something to feel as you read that a man's own warm blood not the mere ink of his pen, flows and thrills through his book.   I apprehend that everything immortal in Literature has had this basis of reality and personalness.   Thus I explain the abidingness of your lilt of a Song when the ambitious outside-fashioned great Poem has passed into forgetfulness.   WILLIAM COWPER and ERASMUS DARWIN were contemporaries : but how has the lowlier russet outlasted the glittering Bal-masque costume, a genuine human heart beneath the one, a piece of mechanism, like a skeleton-clock, within the other : the one pure, true, beating, the other movement without life, energy without appliance.   The bearing of this on our Poet—and in his favour—needs not to be pointed out.

Passing now to the subject and plan of 'Christ's Victorie' the former must be admitted to have been well and definitely chosen : and the latter if it have disadvantages has also rare advantages to one of the cast of genius of GILES FLETCHER.

With respect to his subject, as we have seen, it sprung very much out of the Poet's heart-wish to ‘ magnify’ his Saviour, to exalt His ‘ triumph ’ and to command allegiance by commending Him as the potent but gentle, gentle but potent Conqueror. With respect again, to the Plan of the poem, while the more carefully and vigilantly comparison is made, it will be found that the Personifications of ‘ Christ's Victorie ’ hold their own against those of ‘The Fairie Queen ’ it must be conceded that the ground-idea of a succession of such Personifications is to be traced to SACKVILLE in his ‘ Induction ’ to the Mirrour for Magistrates, and to SPENSER. SACKVILLE, LORD BUCKHURST, would be none the less dear to FLETCHER, that ‘uncle RICHARD ’—afterwards Bishop—had obtained from him his first Living—as seen in the Memoir of Phineas—and both the brothers take every opportunity of paying homage to SPENSER— as will appear more fully in our examination of PHINEAS'S Poetry. In the ‘ Epistle ’ to ‘ the Reader ’ of our GILES, it will be remembered he thus speaks “ our—I know no name more glorious than his own—Mr. Edmund Spencer.”

Thus ‘ led ’ of his master to elect Personification as the medium whereby he would give ‘ form and pressure ’ to his thick-coming conceptions, very magnificent is the Gallery of ‘portraitures ’ into which he introduces us, some having the sharp-defined lines and ‘breathing’ expression of Sculpture, and some the glow, the radiance, the life, of the ancient Masters of portrait-painting, and

not a few having those accessories of landscape back-
ground and clouded or luminous sky, for which they are
scarcely less remarkable.

It was not at all difficult to so opulent a mind as our
Poet's to discern the fitness of such a subject as ' Christ's
Victorie' for such a treatment as self-evidently, he designed from the commencement. Looking at the first
part which sings of the ' Victorie ' in Heaven, there
were at once all the attributes of ALMIGHTY GOD to
hinder the ' salvation' of fallen and guilty Man, and
these in apparent conflict.   And so there rose up before
the creative imagination of the Singer his splendid ' Personifications ' of JUSTICE and MERCY, and in association
with them and in the same large, grand mould, REPENT-
ANCE and FAITH, and subsidiary to each, attendants
admitting of equally striking Personification.   Looking
at the second part or the ' Victorie ' of Christ on Earth,
there was The Temptation—afterwards selected by MIL-
TON for ' Paradise Regained'—with its three-fold ' lures '
to DESPAIR, PRESUMPTION, and VAIN-GLORY, with their
varying elements and contrivances : than which it is
scarcely possible to conceive more apt materials for his
purpose of Personification, or more affluent in circumstance or more suggestive in agencies, inviting thereto.
Given the ' temptation' to DESPAIR, how real does it
make the whole, to have Christ face-to-face with a Being
in his ' cave ' of dolour and darkness : given the
' temptation' to PRESUMPTION, how most actual is it to
have her taking the Lord to her ' pavilion ' of phantom
and insecure attainment: and given the ' temptation' to

VAIN-GLORY, how life-like to find her in the gorgeous 'Garden,' and in that Garden, LUXURY and AMBITION, LUST and AVARICE. Looking at the third part, or the 'Victorie' of Christ over Death and the fourth part, or his 'Victorie' after Death, the Personifications in them have the same character of inevitableness. Throughout—much more than in Spenser and equal to the 'Induction'—the Personifications are substantive not shadowy, intensely even awfully real Beings, wherewith you are haunted as by the 'characters'—shall I say?—in JOHN BUNYAN's immortal Allegory. The Personifications of COLLINS and GRAY are bloodless, bodiless, beside the outstanding creations of GILES FLETCHER. The later Poets describe, the earlier makes appear, the former give you a felicitous epithet, the latter acts, that make the blackness or brightness of the personality fall across his page and your spirit. It may be treason to traditional criticism to say so : nevertheless I must say that the Personifications of the 'Ode to the Passions' and the 'Progress of Poetry' grow thin and ghostly beside the great Personalties of SPENSER and SACKVILLE and the FLETCHERS. There is a *dilettantism* about COLLINS and GRAY's imaginative Poetry that to me is decisive of the question of 'genius' as distinguished from talent and artistic skill. The 'Ode' to the memory of THOMSON and the 'Elegy,' belong to a different region altogether.

Returning upon this matter of the Personifications of 'Christ's Victorie :' which,—as the chosen medium whereby he would reveal his poetic genius and whereon he lavished his most cunning workmanship,—is *the* distinguishing characteristic of the Poem, I would now present a few examples. For power such as MICHAEL ANGELO alone among men has shewn in his 'wizard sphere,' JUSTICE stands out preeminent, as for loveliness does MERCY : and these two may suffice. Mercy is introduced as 'pleading' with God the Father for Man : but JUSTICE stands forth, and her interposition is grandly conceived. I italicize some lines for after-reference.

' But IUSTICE had no sooner MERCY scene
 Smoothing the wrinkles of her Father's browe,
 But vp she starts, and throwes her selfe betweene :
  As when a vapour, from a moory slough,
  Meeting with fresh Eoüs, that but now
    Open'd the world, which all in darknesse lay,
    Doth heau'n's bright face of his rayes disaray,
  And sads the smiling Orient of the springing day.

 She was a Virgin of austere regard ;
 Not as the world esteemes her, deafe and blind ;
  But as the eagle, that hath oft compar'd
  Her eye with Heau'n's : so, and more brightly shin'd
  Her lamping sight ; for she the same could winde
    Into the solid heart, and with her eares
    The silence of the thought loude speaking heares,
  And in one hand a paire of euen scoals [scales] *she weares.*

 No riot of affection reuell kept
 Within her brest, but a still apathy
 Possessèd all her soule, which softly slept
 Securely, without tempest ; no sad crie
 Awakes her pittie, but wrong'd pouertie,
    Sending her eyes to heau'n swimming in teares,
    With hideous clamours euer struck her eares,
  Whetting the blazing sword, that in her hand she beares.

The wingèd lightning is her Mercury,
And round about her mightie thunders sound :
Impatient of himselfe lies pining by
Pale Sicknes with his kercher'd head vpwound,
And thousand noysome plagues attend her round ;
    And if her clowdie browe but once growe foule,
    The flints doe melt, and rocks to water rowle,
And ayrie mountaines shake, and frighted shadowes howle.

Famine, and bloodles Care, and bloodie Warre,
Want, and the want of knowledge how to vse
Abundance, Age, and *Feare, that runnes afarre*
Before his fellow Greefe, that aye pursues
His wingèd steps ; for who would not refuse
    Greefe's companie, a dull and rawebon'd spright,
    That lankes the cheekes, and pales the freshest sight,
Vnbosoming the cheereful brest of all delight.

Before this cursed throng, goes Ignorance,
That needes will leade the waye he cannot see :
And, after all, *Death, doeth his flag aduance,*
And, in the midst, Strife still would roaguing be,
Whose ragged flesh and cloaths did well agree :
    And round about amazèd Horror flies,
    And ouer all, Shame veiles his guiltie eyes,
And vnderneath Hell's hungrie throat still yawning lies.

Vpon two stonie tables, spread before her,
She lean'd her bosome, more then stonie hard ;
There slept th' vnpartiall Iudge, and strict restorer
Of wrong or right, with paine or with reward ;
There hung the skore of all our debts, the card
    Whear good, and bad, and life, and death were painted :
    Was neuer heart of mortall so vntainted,
But when that scroule was read, with thousand terrors fainted.

Witnes the thunder that mount Sinai heard,
When all the hill with firie clouds did flame,
And wandring Israel with the sight afeard,
Blinded with seeing, durst not touch the same,
But like a wood of shaking leaues became.
  On this dead Justice, she, the Liuing Lawe
  Bowing herselfe with a majestique awe,
All heau'n, to heare her speech, did into silence drawe.' [1]

Then follows the address of JUSTICE—somewhat un-
equal but frequently sublime and impressive—and its
effect is thus magnificently given :

' She ended, and the heau'nly Hierarchies,
  Burning in zeale, thickly imbranded weare ;
  Like to an armie that allarum cries,
  And euery one shakes his ydraded speare,
  And the Almightie's Selfe, as He would teare
    The Earth and her firme basis quite in sunder,
    Flam'd all in iust reuenge and mightie thunder ;
  Heau'n stole it selfe from Earth by clouds that moisterd vnder.' [2]

' The awful grandeur of the celestial indignation '
observes WILLMOTT, ' seems to lift itself up in the
majesty of these lines. The sudden preparation of the
heavenly warriors, the clangor of arms and the uprising

---

[1] Christ's Victorie in Heaven, st. 9-16. SOUTHWELL later,
puts the whole into a couplet in his delightful little poem, ' At
home in Heaven '—though mis-directed from Christ to Mary's
' beauty :'

    " It made the rigour of His justice yelde,
    And crownèd Mercy, Empresse of the feilde."

Works by me, p. 88. Turnbull misreads ' vigour.'

[2] Christ's Victorie in Heaven, st. 40.

of the Deity himself, are splendid images, which are known to the reader of Paradise Lost not to have escaped the notice of MILTON. The pause at the beginning of the stanza is a note of solemn preparation.'[1]

Surely this long—not too long—and sustained passage from a poem dating in publication 1610, and in composition probably ten years if not more prior, were sufficient to vindicate for GILES FLETCHER a far superior recognition to that which he has met. The gifted Biographer of the 'Sacred Poets' it will be noticed, recals that MILTON had 'read' 'Christ's Victorie.' There can be no question that both the FLETCHERS added to the splendid 'spoils' from all books, of the great Poet. This indebtedness to the 'Purple Island' and 'Locustæ' and 'Apollyonists' and other lesser obligations, I shew in my Study of PHINEAS FLETCHER'S Poetry. But meanwhile glancing back upon the delineation of JUSTICE interposing between the Almighty and MERCY, the fine image of the Eagle is transferred to the 'Areopagitica:' the 'Scales' of one hand reappears in 'Paradise Lost' and the hush and stillness of the entire Universe waiting in awe for the opening of Justice's lips is reproduced in 'Paradise Regained,' when at the conclusion of the address of the Eternal Father to the angel Gabriel

> . . . . . . 'all heaven
> Admiring stood a space, then into hymns
> Burst forth' [B. I. v. 170]

---

[1] Lives as before, Vol. I. p. 74.

The happy phrase 'blinded with seeing' is one of many similar, over which MILTON lingered admiringly. 'Dark with excess of bright' cannot be said to surpass it. The whetted 'blazing sword,' the marshalling of the 'Shadows,' the Figure of 'Fear' on his swift far race, the whirling, centrifugal 'Horror,' the 'wood of shaking leaves' as in the outset the 'vapours from the moory slough,' will arrest the most stone-eyed reader.

From out the tumult and terror of celestial wrath, when JUSTICE had spoken, Mercy steps 'like Morning brought by Night' or as in Frazer 'like a rainbow in the storm.'

> 'As when the cheerfull sunne, clamping wide,
>   Glads all the world with his vprising raye,
>   And wooes the widow'd Earth afresh to pride,
>   And paints her bosome with the flowrie Maye,
>   His silent sister steales him quite away,
>   Wrap't in a sable clowde, from mortall eyes ;
>   The hastie starres at noone begin to rise,
>   And headlong to his early roost the sparrowe flies.
>
> But soone as he againe dishadowed is,
>   Restoring the blind world his blemish't sight,—
>   *As though another day wear newely ris,*
>   The cooz'ned birds busily take their flight,
>   And wonder at the shortnesse of the night :
>   So Mercie once again her selfe displayes,
>   Out from her sister's cloud, and OPEN LAYES
>   THOSE SUNSHINE LOOKES, WHOSE BEAMES WOULD DIM
>   A THOUSAND DAYES.'[1]

Then dazzled by the vision of his own creation, the Poet exclaims,

[1] Christ's Victorie in Heaven, st. 41, 42.

'How may a worme, that crawles along the dust,
Clamber the azure mountaines, thrown so high,
And fetch from thence thy faire Idea just,
That in those sunny courts doth hidden lie,
Cloath'd with such light, as blinds the angels' eye;
   How may weake mortall euer hope to file
   His vnsmooth tongue, and his deprostrate stile?
O raise Thou from his corse Thy now entomb'd exile!"[1]

Earlier in these remarks we have introduced the 'portrait' of Mercy that follows this. I add here the richworked delineation of her 'kind offices to man.'

" If any wander, Thou doest call him backe;
If any be not forward, Thou incit'st him;
Thou doest expect, if any should grow slacke;
If any seeme but willing, Thou inuit'st him;
Or if he doe offend Thee, Thou acquit'st him;
   Thou find'st the lost, and follow'st him that flies,
   Healing the sicke, and quick'ning him that dies:
Thou art the lame man's friendly staffe, the blind man's eyes.

So faire Thou art that all would Thee behold;
But none can Thee behold, Thou art so faire:
Pardon, O pardon then Thy vassal bold,
That with poore shadowes striues Thee to compare,
And match the things, which he knowes matchlesse are,
   O thou vive mirrhour of celestiall grace,
   How can fraile colours pourtraict out Thy face,
Or paint in flesh Thy beawtie in such semblance base?"[2]

Mercy now pleads with God the Father, with the noble passion sprung of compassion, and presents the 'Holy

---

[1] Christ's Victorie in Heaven, st. 41-43.   [2] *Ibid.* st. 51, 52.

E

Child.' Very matterfull and melodious is this 'intercession,' with its great cry:

> " Oh let not Iustice' yron sceptre breake
> A heart alreadie broke ; that lowe doth creep,
> And with prone humblesse her feets' dust doth sweep :
>   Must all goe by desert ? is nothing free ?
>   Ah ! if but those that onely woorthy be,
> None should Thee euer see, none should Thee euer see." [1]

The result is to daring thus told :

> " With that the mightie thunder dropt away
> From God's vnwarie arme, now milder growne,
> And melted into teares : as if to pray
> For pardon, and for pittie, it had knowne,
> That should haue been for sacred vengeance throwne :
>   Thereto the armies angelique devo'wd
>   Their former rage, and all to Mercie bow'd ;
> Their broken weapons at her feet they gladly strow'd." [2]

Then turning her look toward the Earth, where—as one of our Poet's finest lines puts it—to guide the Shepherds to the manger-cradle

> ' A Star comes dauncing up the Orient '

in words that might have been interwoven in his cousin's ' Faithful Shepherdess,' or ' Comus ' itself, the infant JESUS is thus welcomed by MERCY:

> ' Bring, bring, ye Graces, all your silver flaskets,
>   Painted with euery choicest flowre that growes,
>   That I may soone vnflow'r your fragrant baskets,
>   To strowe the fields with odours whear He goes,
>   Let what so e're He treads on be a rose.

---

[1] Christ's Victorie in Heaven, st. 75.   [2] *Ibid.* st. 84.

So downe shee let her eyelids fall, to shine
Vpon the rivers of bright Palestine,
Whose woods drop honie, and her rivers skip with wine.'[1]

Place beside this, Crashaw's later 'welcome' in his
' Hymn of Nativity :'

——' when young April's husband-showrs
Shall blesse the fruitful Maja's bed,
We'l bring the first-born of her flowrs,
     To kisse Thy feet, and crown Thy head.
To Thee, dread Lamb ! Whose loue must keep
The shepheards more then they the sheep.

To Thee, meek Majesty ! soft King
Of simple Graces and sweet Loues !
Each of vs his lamb will bring,
     Each his pair of sylver doues !
Till burnt at last in fire of Thy fair eyes,
Ourselues become our own best sacrifice.'[2]

Reverting to the striking account of Mercy's ' preva-
lence' with GOD (the Father,) it is very clear from text
and context alike, especially the parallels of ' the Earth '
and ' the Air ' and ' the Sea ' and ' the third Heaven ' in
their relation to Mercy,—that THOMAS FULLER drew his
inspiration thence in his vivid ' intercession ' of ' The
Lamb' with ' The Father' in David's behalf.   These two
stanzas out of many will prove this :

" Strait from His throne the Prince of Peace arose
And with embraces did His Father binde,
Imprisoning His armes, He did so close
(As loving iyve on an oak did winde

---

[1] Christ's Victorie in Heaven, st. 85.
[2] Works by me, vol. i. pp. 75-6.

> And with her curling flexures it betraile)
> IIis Father glad to finde IIis force to fayle
> Strugel'd as one not willing to prevaile :
>
> Thus then began the Spotlesse Lamb to speake
> One word of Whom would rend the sturdy rocke,
> Make hammer-scorning adamant to breake,
> And vnto sense perswade the senselesse stocke,
>   Yea God IIimselfe that knowes not to repent
>   Is made by IIis petitions penitent,
>   IIis Justice made with Mercy to relent." [1]

Besides these figures of larger mould that we have thus far looked at, there are companion lesser ones, grouped around them as the 'Twelve' stand around THORWALDSEN's 'Christ.' These will be 'sought out' by every reader who has one particle of poetic sympathy. MICHAEL ANGELO's chisel never smote the marble into a more sternly-grand 'creation' than one of these, namely 'Judas' in his weird remorse, with its spectral back-ground and haunting voices. I can only spare space for a small portion of this supreme portraiture :

> " As when wild Pentheus, growne madde with fear,
> Whole troupes of hellish haggs about him spies ;
> Two bloodie sunnes stalking the duskie sphear,
> And twofold Thebes runs rowling in his eyes ;
> Or through the scene staring Orestes flies,

---

[1] Our edition of Fuller's Poems, p. 56. On our Poet's Personi-fication of Justice and Mercy, Dr. GEORGE MACDONALD in his Antiphon has made certain Theological-critical remarks, which I feel constrained to traverse. See Note at the close of these remarks.

With eyes flung back vpon his mother's ghost,
  That, with infernall serpents all embost,
And torches quencht in blood, doth her stern sonne accost :

Such horrid Gorgons, and misformèd formes
Of damnèd fiends, flew dauncing in his heart,
That, now, vnable to endure their stormes,
' Flie, flie ' he cries, ' thyselfe, what ere thou art,
Hell, hell, already burnes in eu'ry part.'
  So downe into his torturer's armes he fell,
  That readie stood his funeralls to yell,
And in a clowd of night to waft him quick to Hell.

Yet oft he snatch't, and started as he hung :
So when the senses halfe enslumb'red lie,
The headlong bodie, ready to be flung
By the deluding phansie, from some high
And craggie rock, recovers greedily,
  And clasps the yeelding pillow, halfe asleep
  And, as from heav'n it tombled to the deepe,
Feeles a cold sweat through euery trembling member creepe.

Thear let him hang, embowellèd in blood,
Thear neuer any gentle shepheard feed
His blessed flocks, nor euer heav'nly flood
Fall on the cursed ground, nor holesome seed,
That may the least delight or pleasure breed :
  Let neuer Spring visit his habitation,
  But nettles, kixe, and all the weedie nation,
With empty elders growe : and signes of desolation !

Thear let the Dragon keep his habitance,
And stinking karcasses be throwne avaunt ;
Faunes, Sylvans, and deformèd Satyrs daunce,
Wild-cats, wolues, toads, and skreech-owles direly chaunt ;
Thear euer let some restles spirit haunt

With hollow sound, and clashing cheynes, to scarr
The passenger, and eyes like to the starr
That sparkles in the crest of angrie Mars afarr."[1]

The scholarly critic already quoted, has remarked
here, ' Euripides might have written these stanzas in the
season of his solemn inspiration.   In the 'staring Orestes'
we seem to behold the wretched mourner burst from the
enfolding arms of the weeping Electra, and fleeing in
horror from the furies surrounding his couch '—[2]   The
English Poet by no means suffers from comparison with
the classical original :

> OP.   Ὦ μητερ, ἱκετευω σε μηπισει εμοι
> Τας αιματωπους καὶ δρακοντωδεις κορας
> Αυται γαρ αυται πλησιον Θρωσκουσι μου
> Ὦ φοιβ' αποκτενουσι ᾧ αἰ κυνωπιδες
> Γοργωπες, ενερων ἱεριαι δειναι θεαι.
>
> [Orestes ll. 250-255.]

In sweet contrast with this dark Figure is the ' Joseph
of Arimathea' by the Cross—pathetic as any 'Saint' of
FRANCIA :

> . . . . "Long he stood, in his faint arms vphoulding
> The fairest spoile heau'n euer forfeited,
> With such a silent passion griefe vnfoulding
> *That, had the sheete but on himselfe beene spread,*
> *He for the corse might haue been buriēd* ' . . . .[3]

How soft as the dropping of Innocence's white tears,

---

[1] Christ's Triumph over Death, st. 47-51.
[2] WILLMOTT, Lives, as before, vol. i. p. 84.
[3] Christ's Triumph over Death, st. 54.

the 'lament' of the Mourners! How suggestive these thick-coming questions!

" Are theas the eyes that made all others blind ?
　Ah ! why ar they themselues now blemishèd ?
　Is this the face, in which all beawtie shin'd !
　What blast hath thus His flowers debellishèd ?
　Ar these the feete that on the watry head
　　Of the vnfaithfull ocean passage found ?
　　Why goe they now so lowely vnder ground ?
Wash't with our woorthlesse tears, and their owne precious wound ?

One hem but of the garments that He wore
Could medicine whole countries of their paine ;
One touch of this pale hand could life restore ;
One word out of these cold lips reuiue the slaine :
Well, the blinde man, Thy Godhead might maintaine :
　What, though the sullen Pharises repin'd ?
　He that should both compare, at length would finde
The blinde man onely sawe, the seers all wear blinde." [1]

Then ' the end :'

　. . . . . " Here burie we
　This heau'enly earth ; here let it softly sleepe,
　The fairest Sheapheard of the fairest sheep :
　So all the bodie kist, and homeward went to weepe." [2]

We have seen that the subject of the second part or canto of ' Christ's Victorie' is ' The Temptation :' and that interpreting the three ' snares' as ' tempting' the Saviour successively to Despair, Presumption and Vainglory, the Poet brings each before us as a Personality, and with circumstance and surrounding suited to them.

---

[1] Christ's Triumph over Death, st. 59, 60.　　[2] *Ibid.* st. 64.

From this portion of the Poem I will only select two typical specimens, viz. : the descriptions of the Cave of Despair and of the 'enchanted Garden.' Accompanying the Saviour is the disguised 'Tempter,' who leads Him to 'Desperation' who is 'character'd by his place :'

> " Ere long they came neere to a balefull bowre,
>   Much like the mouth of that infernall caue,
>   That gaping stood, all commers to deuoure.
> " Darke, dolefull, dreary,—like a dreary graue,
>   That still for carrion carkasses doth craue :"
>   The ground no hearbs but venomous, did beare,
>   Nor ragged trees did leaue, but euery whear
>   Dead bones and skulls wear cast, and bodies hanged wear.
>
> Vpon the roofe, the bird of sorrowe sat
>   Elonging ioyfull day with her sad note,
>   *And through the shady aire, the fluttring bat*
>   *Did waue her leather sayles, and blindely flote :*
>   While with her wings the fatall skreech-owle smote
>   Th' vnblessed house ; thear, on a craggy stone,
>   Celeno hung, and made his direfull mone,
>   And all about the murdered ghosts did shreek and grone.
>
> *Like clowdie moonshine, in some shadowie groue,*
>   Such was the light in which Despaire did dwell ;
>   But he himselfe with night for darknesse stroue.
>   His black uncombèd locks dishevell'd fell
>   About his face ; through which, *as brands of Hell,*
>   *Sunk in his skull, his staring eyes did glowe,*
>   *That made him deadly looke :* their glimpse did showe
>   Like cockatrice's eyes, that sparks of poyson throwe.
>
> His cloaths wear ragged clouts, with thornes pind fast ;
>   And, as he musing lay, to stonie fright
>   A thousand wild Chimeras would him cast :

As when a fearefull dreame, in mid'st of night,
Skips to the braine, and phansies to the sight
   Some wingèd furie, strait the hasty foot,
   Eger to flie, cannot plucke vp his root,
The voyce dies in the tongue, and mouth gapes without boot.

Now he would dreame that he from heauen fell,
And then would snatch the ayre, afraid to fall ;
And now he thought he sinking was to Hell,
And then would grasp the earth ; and now his stall
Him seemèd Hell, and then he out woulde crawle;
   And euer, as he crept, would squint aside,
   Lest him, perhaps, some furie had espide,
And then, alas ! he would in chaines for euer bide.

Therefore he softly shrunke, and stole away,
Ne euer durst to drawe his breath for feare,
Till to the doore he came, and thear he lay
Panting for breath, as though he dying were ;
And still he thought he felt their craples teare
   Him by the heels backe to his ougly denne ;
   Or faine he would haue leap't abroad, but then
The Heau'n, as Hell he fear'd, that punish guilty men." [1]

HEADLEY—who has been, as a critic, ignorantly over-praised—having quoted the above, has the audacity to say of it, ' the most material features of this description, are taken from SPENSER's ' Fairy Queen ' lib. i., canto 9, stanzas, 33, 36 ' and adds ' This is a curious instance of plagiarism, and seems to show us how little ceremony the poets of that day laboured under in pilfering from each other.' The criticism is a more ' curious instance ' of pert presuming on the ignorance of general readers :

[1] Christ's Victorie on Earth, st. 23-28.

and I do not marvel that even the gentle WILLMOTT in his 'Lives' is roused to retort 'if GILES FLETCHER had been living, he would probably have thought the critics of this day laboured under very little ceremony in accusing the " poets of that day " of thefts, without sufficiently examining their extent."[1]

Any one on turning to the two stanzas alleged from SPENSER will see that from the former, two lines are taken *verbatim*, viz :

> ' Darke, dolefull, dreary, like a greedy grave,
> That still for carrion carkasses doth crave '

and therefore intentionally, as a quotation from his 'dear Master' and only by oversight of the Printer probably, forgotten to be marked as such—as similarly, lines from Spenser's ' Ruines of Time ' in ' The Purple Island ' are inadvertently unmarked. And what of the 'material features remain ' to be designated ' plagiarism ? ' Only the ' ragged clouts ' and the ' thorns ' that fastened them ! Who but a man with nose for ' plagiarism' as eager-nostrilled as that of your ' orthodox' hunter after ' heresy,' will deem these of any moment ? It is to be remembered also that SPENSER owes a great deal more than trifles like these to Sackville and Ariosto and *Amadis de Gaul*: also that our Singer was dead before a second edition of his Poem was published, and so such petty oversights might readily be left uncorrected.

I take this opportunity of observing, that whoever

----

[1] As before.

comparcs thoughtfully and penetratively the after-concep-
tions and delineations of GILES FLETCHER will readily
distinguish the 'influence' of the Master on his reverent
scholar from any vulgar charge of 'plagiarism' and
discern those ineffable touches of light and shadow that
reveal an original mind working on existent materials,
precisely as each new, genuine Poet, looks on the same
old ever-new world of Nature, and transfigures it with
his own mystic insight, through his own open-lidded eyes.
I say more on this in relation to PHINEAS FLETCHER
and 'The Purple Island.'

Following the Cave of Despair is the 'Garden of
Delight' created in the cold white altitude of the
mountains. One very remarkable line felicitously in-
dicates the supernatural suddenness and loveliness of
the scene

    ' As if the snow had melted into flow'rs '

and then succeeds such rich classical allusions and
'large utterance,' as might have come from the golden
mouth of MILTON. These four stanzas for brilliance,
quaint beauty, daintiness of colour and richness of
imagination, will not easily be matched :

    " All suddenly the hill his snowe deuours,
      In liew whereof a goodly garden grew,
      As if the snow had melted into flow'rs,
      Which their sweet breath in subtill vapours threw,
      That all about perfumèd spirits flew :
        For what so euer might aggrate the sense,
        In all the world, or please the appetence,
      Heer it was powrèd out in lavish affluence.

Not louely Ida might with this compare,
Though many streames his banks besiluered ;
Though Xanthus with his golden sands he bare,
Nor Hibla, though his thyme depasturèd
As fast againe with honie blossomèd ;
    Ne Rhodope, ne Tempe's flow'ry playne :
    Adonis' garden was to this but vayne,
Though Plato on his beds a flood of praise did rayne.

For in all these, some one thing most did grow,
But in this one, grew all things else beside ;
For sweet Varietie herselfe did throw
To euery banke : here all the ground she dide
In lillie white ; there pinks eblazèd wide ;
    And damask't all the earth ; and here shee shed
    Blew violets, and there came roses red ;
And euery sight the yeelding sense, as captiue led.

THE GARDEN LIKE A LADIE FAIRE WAS CUT,
THAT LAY AS IF SHEE SLUMBER'D IN DELIGHT,
AND TO THE OPEN SKIES HER EYES DID SHUT :
THE AZURE FIELDS OF HEAU'N WEAR 'SEMBLED RIGHT
IN A LARGE ROUND, SET WITH THE FLOW'RS OF LIGHT :
    THE FLOWR'S-DE-LUCE, AND THE ROUND SPARKS OF DEAW,
    THAT HUNG VPON THE AZURE LEAUES, DID SHEW
LIKE TWINKLING STARRS, THAT SPARKLE IN TH' EAU'NING
    BLEW." [1]

The weird eye of Edgar Allan Poe of America, melted
before the loveliness of the last stanza : and he placed
it as a motto to his own brilliant Essay, ‘The Landscape
Garden.’ [2]

‘Paradise Regained’ reflects the vision of Vain-delight

---

[1] Christ's Victorie on Earth, st. 39-42.
[2] Works, Vol. IV. p. 336 (edn. New York, 4 Vols. 1856)

conjured up by the 'wicked spirits' for the Temptation. The 'Wooing Song'—a commonplace of quotation as an example of our Poet—preceded ROBERT HERRICK's delicious 'Gather the rosebuds' song.

I differ *toto cœlo* from WILLMOTT in his criticism on the delineation of 'the Person' of Christ Himself in this Canto. He is most unfortunate in condemning FLETCHER for 'want of judgment' herein, on the ground that such (so-called) 'fantastical colouring' in a 'sacred poem' is displeasing, for as he himself stultifyingly admits, the 'portrait' is principally drawn from the 'Canticles'—which, in our ignorance, we have been wont to regard as a 'sacred poem.' Moreover as the margin-references shew, traits are fetched from Genesis and Isaiah and the Psalms, and elsewhere. There are exquisite things in the delineation :

> " His haire was blacke, and in small curls did twine,
> *As though it wear the shadowe of some light,*
> *And vnderneath, His face, as day did shine,*
> But sure the day shinèd not halfe so bright,
> *Nor the sunne's shadowe made so darke a night.*
>   Vnder His louely locks, her head to shroude,
>   Did make Humilitie her selfe growe proude,
> *Hither, to light their lamps, did all the Graces croude.*"
>
> [*Ibid.* st. 8]

The comparison of the 'raven' locks and the beaming Face of Jesus, to 'the shadowe of some light' and 'the shining Day' seem to me surpassingly beautiful : and I think that every reader will agree that in the last line, which is to be linked on to the prior naming of

Christ 'the Sun,' we have the prototype of one of MIL-
TON's choice gems in ' Paradise Lost' [VII. 364, 365]

> ' Hither as to their Fountain other Starrs
> Repairing, in their golden Urns draw Light.'

Very musically begins c. 3rd.

> "So downe the siluer streames of Eridan,
>   On either side bank't with a lilly wall,
>   Whiter then both, rides the triumphant swan,
>   And sings his dirge, and prophesies his fall,
>   Diuing into his watrie funerall :
>   But Eridan to Cedron must submit
>   His flowry shore ; nor can he ennie it,
>   If when Apollo sings, his swans doe silent sit.
>
> That heau'nly voice I more delight to heare,
>   Then gentle ayres to breath, or swelling waues
>   Against the sounding rocks their bosomes teare,
>   Or whistling reeds, that rutty Iordan laues,
>   And with their verdure his white head embraues,
>   To chide the windes, or hiuing bees, that flie
>   About the laughing bloosms of sallowie,
>   Rocking asleepe the idle groomes that lazie lie." [1]

---

[1] With reference to these stanzas (1st and 2nd) I gladly avail
myself of the notes on the places by Dr Macdonald in Antiphon.
On Eridan and the swan, he annotates "The Eridan is the Po—
As regards classical allusions in connexion with sacred things, I
would remind my reader of the great reverence our ancestors had
for the classics, from the influence they had in reviving the literature
of the country.—I need hardly remind him of the commonly-re-
ceived fancy that the swan does sing once—just as his death draws
nigh. Does this come from the legend of Cycnus changed into
a swan while lamenting the death of his friend Phæton? or was
that legend founded on the yet older fancy? The glorious bird

I must here content myself with these vivid opening
lines of the third Part of our Poem, as it has already
furnished illustrative passages. I pass to the conclusion
—'Christ's Trivmph after Death.' If our quotations
thus far, have mainly shewn the POWER of our Poet to
conceive, and that calm, steady-gazing eye to look and
describe,—such as belonged to Rubens when unblench-
ingly, as the tradition runs, he slowly painted his
'Crucifixion' from a criminal slowly crucified before
him—abundant evidence remains behind that while the
rugged and terrible, the stern and awful, were perhaps
most congenial to him, he could change to the gentle
from the fearful, from the appalling to the winsome, with
swift versatility and wide sweep. It is as though one
walked in a fair Garden a-gathering flowers to read the
last 'Triumph.' How consummately lovely are these
—taken almost with 'prick of pin,' as the old Puritans

looks as if he ought to sing." On last line of stanza 1st "If when
Apollo sings, his swans do silent sit," he says "The poet refers
to the singing of the hymn before our Lord went to the garden by
the brook Cedron." On stanza 2nd, 1-3, he remarks "The construction is obscure just from the insertion of the *to* before *breath*,
where it ought not to be after the verb *hear*. The poet does not
mean that he delights to hear that voice more than to breathe
gentle airs, but more than to hear gentle airs (to) breathe. *To hear*,
understood, governs all the infinitives that follow : among the rest,
the winds (*to*) chide." On 'rutty' st. 2nd, line 4th, there is this :
"*Rut* is used for the sound of the tide in Cheshire. (See *Halli-
well's Dictionary*.) Does *rutty* mean *roaring?* or does it describe
the deep, rugged shores of the Jordan?" (p. 153). *O si sic omnia !*
—On *rutty* cf. our note *in loco.*

were wont to say and do in selecting their sermon-texts.
The commencement has the flush of colour, and the
melody of notes, rather than simple words :

"BVT now the second morning, from her bowre
  Began to glister in her beames ; and nowe
  The roses of the Day began to flowre
  In th' easterne garden ; for heau'ns smiling browe
  Halfe insolent for ioy begunne to showe :
      The early sunne came liuely dauncing out,
      And the bragge lambs ranne wantoning about,
  That heau'n and earth might seeme in tryumph both to shout.

Th' engladded Spring, forgettfull now to weepe,
  Began t' eblazon from her leauie bed ;
  The waking swallowe broke her halfe-yeare's sleepe,
  And euerie bush lay deepely purpurèd
  With violets ; the wood's late-wintry head
      Wide flaming primroses set all on fire,
      And his bald trees put on their greene attire,
  Among whose infant leaues the ioyeous birds conspire." [1]

Not less rich are these :

" Ye primroses and purple violets,
  Tell me, why blaze ye from your leauie bed,
  And wooe mens hands to rent you from your sets,
  As though you would somewhear be carrièd,
  With fresh perfumes and velvets garnishèd ?
      But ah ! I neede not aske, t'is surely so,
      You all would to your Sauiour's triumphs goe :
  There would ye all waite and humble homage doe.

---

[1] St. 1, 2.

Thear should the Earth herselfe with garlands newe
And louely flowrs embellishèd, adore :
Such roses neuer in her garland grewe,
Such lillies neuer in her brest she wore,
Like beautie neuer yet did shine before :
　　Thear should the sunne another sunne behold,
　　From whence himselfe borrowes his locks of gold,
That kindle heau'n, and earth, with beauties manifold." [1]

Rising from Earth to the Sky, take this lustrous ' picture :'

" So fairest Phosphor, the bright morning starre,
　But neewely washt in the greene element,
　Before the drouzie Night is halfe aware,
　Shooting his flaming locks with deaw besprent.
　Springs liuely vp into the Orient,
　　And the bright droue, flece't all in gold, he chaces
　　To drinke, that on the Olympique mountain grazes,
　The while the minor planets forfeit all their faces." [2]

JEREMY TAYLOR has not more orient ' eloquence' or more majestic march of comparison of the excelling glory of Heaven, than this :

" Gaze but vpon the house whear man embowrs ;
　With flowrs and rushes pauèd is his way,
　Whear all the creatures ar his seruiturs ;
　The windes do sweepe his chambers euery day ;
　And cloudes doe wash his rooms ; the seeling gay,
　　Starrèd aloft, the guilded knobs embraue :
　　If such a house God to another gaue,
　How shine those glittering courts, He for Himselfe will haue ?

---

[1] Christ's Triumph after Death, st. 7, 8.　　　[2] *Ibid.* st. 12.

F

And if a sullen cloud, as sad as night,
In which the sunne may seeme embodied,
Depur'd of all his drosse, we see so white
Burning in melted gold his wat'rie head,
Or round with yuorie edges siluerèd,
  What lustre super-excellent will He
  Lighten on those that shall His sunneshine see,
In that all-glorious court in which all glories be?

If but one sunne with his diffusive fires,
Can paint the starres, and the whole world with light ;
And ioy, and life into each heart inspires,
And eu'ry saint shall shine in heau'n, as bright
As doth the sunne in his transcendent might,
  (As faith may well beleeue what Truth once sayes)
  What shall so many sunnes' united rayes,
But dazle all the eyes that nowe in heau'n we praise?" [1]

Then in Heaven itself you have a radiant, exultant
'vision' of the redeemed Multitudes. Dr J. M. NEALE
pronounces the 'string of pearls' of his selected stanzas
from this final 'Triumph' to be 'unsurpassed in the
whole range of English sacred Poetry.' I can only
give one peerless stanza :

" No sorrowe nowe hangs clowding on their browe,
  No bloodles maladie empales their face,
  No age *drops on their hayrs his siluer snowe,*
  No nakednesse their bodies doeth embase,
  No pouertie themselues and theirs disgrace,
    No feare of death the ioy of life deuours,
    No vnchast sleepe their precious time deflowrs,
  No losse, no griefe, no change, wait on their wingèd hours." [2]

---

1 Christ's Triumph after Death, st. 27-29.   2 *Ibid.* st. 35.

As illustrating the fine mysticism and profounder
'thought' of our Poet—and there is a mass of pure
thought underneath all—I cannot withhold his 'Beatificall Idea,' stately as MILTON and anticipating HENRY
MORE and JOHN NORRIS in verse, and EVERARD and
PETER STERRY in prose.

" About the holy citie rowles a flood '
Of moulten chrystall, like a sea of glasse ;
On which weake streame a strong foundation stood :
Of liuing diamounds the building was,
That all things else, besides itself, did passe :
   Her streetes, instead of stones, the starres did paue,
   And little pearles, for dust, it seem'd to haue ;
On which soft-streaming manna, like pure snowe, did wave.

In midst of this citie cœlestiall,
Whear the Eternall Temple should haue rose,
Light'ned the Idea Beatificall :
End, and beginning of each thing that growes ;
Whose selfe no end, nor yet beginning knowes ;
   That hath no eyes to see, nor ears to heare ;
   Yet sees, and heares, and is all-eye, all-eare ;
That nowhear is contain'd, and yet is euery whear :

Changer of all things, yet immutable ;
Before and after all, the first and last ;
That, moouing all, is yet immoueable :
Great without quantitie ; in Whose forecast
Things past are present, things to come are past ;
   Swift without motion ; to Whose open eye
   The hearts of wicked men vnbrested lie ;
At once absent and present to them, farre and nigh.

It is no flaming lustre, made of light ;
No sweet concent, or well-tim'd harmonie :
Ambrosia, for to feast the appetite,
Or flowrie odour, mixt with spicerie ;

No soft embrace, or pleasure bodily ;
   And yet it is a kinde of inwarde feast,
   A harmony, that sounds within the brest,
An odour, light, embrace, in which the soule doth rest.

A heav'nly feast no hunger can consume ;
A light vnseen yet shines in euery place ;
A sound, no time can steale ; a sweet perfume
No winds can scatter ; an intire embrace
That no satiety can ere vnlace :
   Ingrac't into so high a fauour, thear
   The saints, with their beawpeers whole worlds outwear ;
And things vnseene doe see, and things vnheard doe hear."[1]

Throughout, as distinguished from these fuller passages, the most cursory reader will ever and anon come on vivid epithet, or arresting metaphor, or quaint fancy, or suggestive allusion, or felicitously-vowelled lines—ringing out from the centre of a stately stanza, like the softened sound of distant vesper-bells. But it were endless to point these out. Let them be 'searched' for. Even in his youthful 'Canto' on Elizabeth you have this unforgetable description :

     ————' So let the hissing snake
     Sliding with shrinking silence never take
     Th' unwary foot.'

Finally, I would briefly call attention to the influence of our FLETCHER—as of his brother—on MILTON. With genius so supreme as SHAKESPEARE'S and MILTON'S, any charge of plagiarism were simply monstrous,

————————————
[1] Christ's Triumph after Death, st. 38-42.

and even ludicrous. For their's is the magnificent
appropriation that conqueror-like, being superior to all,
places all under contribution, and that, to enrich themselves only that they may enrich their kingdom—all
taken too with no more consciousness of despoiling
than in taking from God, as with eye ' in a fine frenzy
rolling' they glance 'from heaven to earth' and fetch
thence tribute to their creations. I disavow therefore,
any idea of paltry reading-after our immortal Poet in
order to convict him of plagiarism, and equally would I
avoid confounding of coincidence therewith. But it
cannot fail to interest the thoughtful if I can shew, that
to ' Christ's Victorie' MILTON turned over and over as
to a classic : a fact sufficient to give renown to any
Poem.

Our previous references incidentally and our foot-notes
in their places, have already put the vigilant reader on
the alert : but I propose to adduce a few specific examples. Take these :

In Paradise Lost, Book V. line 44, we read of Eve

> —————' *Heaven wakes with all his eyes*
> Whom to behold but thee, Nature's desire ?'

The Commentators brought together by the indefatigable
if cumbrous TODD, have found the source of this in
SPENSER'S Fairy Queen—iii. XI. 45 :

> ——————' With how many eyes
> High Heaven beholds.'

but how much nearer is this in ' Christ's Victorie,' part i. st. 78 ?

> ———' *Heaven awaken'd all his eyes*
> To see another sunne *at midnight rise'*

and it must be remembered that this long preceded CRASHAW : remembered that MARINO and CRASHAW alike, were anticipated by the Fletchers in some of their grandest and most often-quoted conceptions. Again : in Paradise Lost, Book viii. lines 577–578, we have

> ' A broad and ample road, *whose dust is gold,*
> *And pavement stars.'*

and elsewhere 'star-paved' (P. L., iv. 976.)

Many years before ' Parthenia Sacra' (1633) and Gius-tiniano (1620) and Holyday (1618) and Drummond of Hawthornden (1616) and Sylvester's du-Bartas (1621) and all the usual authorities and parallels was our Poet's description of the ' Holy City :'

> ' Her streetes, instead of stones, *the starres did paue*
> And little pearles, for dust it seemed to haue.'
>
> [c. iv. 38.]

The representation of The Tempter under the guise of an 'aged man' or hermit, is found in nearly all the Mediæval ' Preachers' and in early Art : but whosoever compares MILTON's description in ' Paradise Regained' with our Fletcher's, will readily see that ' Christ's Vic-torie' and not rude ' prints' was before the great Poet : so that he is found in his old age returning to his youth-ful favorite. That this particular conception of the

Tempter of our Fletcher, had deeply impressed Milton, seems additionally confirmed by the reappearance of one choice word in this scene, in ' Lycidas ' *e.g.*

> ' Next Camus, reverend sire, went *footing slow* '

which is the echo of

> ....' an aged sire, farre off He saw
> Come *slowly-footing.*' (c. II. 15)

Similarly, the student will read Fletcher's and Milton's account of the effect of our Lord's presence on the wild-beasts.[1] Even more unmistakeable is the original of the famous objurgation of the ' herd of the people' by the Poet-Republican—here most anti-Democratic—read in the light of our Poet's vehement rebuke of the change-ful multitude.[2] Not less unmistakeable is the ' Circe' of Comus placed beside the ' Circe' transformation in Fletcher's ' Bower of Vaine Delight.'[3]

One magnificent conception, perhaps the very grandest in all ' Paradise Regained' is that of the 'globe' of angels descending at the close of The Temptation to ' minister' to the Saviour : [B. IV. lines 581–582.]

> ' So Satan fell : and straight *a fiery globe*
> *Of angels* on full sail of wing flew nigh.'

---

[1] See P. R., Book i. lines 310–314, and C. V., Part ii. 4, 5.
[2] See P. R., Book iii. lines 46–56, and C. V., Part iii. st. 31. Cf. also earlier, Sackville, Lord Buckhurst's ' Induction ' and Legend of Henry Stafford, Duke of Buckingham, pp. 147 *seqq.* (Works by R. W. S-West, 1859.)
[3] See Comus, 50-53 and C. V., part ii. stanza 49.

Once more ' Christ's Victorie' anticipates this :

> ....' Out thear flies
> *A globe of wingèd angels,* swift as thought '   (c. IV. 13.)

' Paradise Lost ' (B. II. line 512) had before employed it :

> ....' Him round
> A globe of fiery Seraphim enclos'd '

Virgil's ' globus ' (Aeneid X. 373) to which with pedantry rather than genuine scholarship, Bishop NEWTON refers, is as a child's marble to the ' globe ' itself; and equally so to Fletcher's splendid image.   It also arrested Dr. JOSEPH BEAUMONT : for in his ' Psyche or Love's Mystery ' (1648-1702) you have this, in the story of the Annunciation :

> " As we for joy at these strange tidings started,
>   Behold, *a sudden globe of pliant Light*
>   Into a stranger apparition parted,
>   And with new merveils entertain'd our sight :
>   For at a diamond Table fair and wide
>   A numerous quire of Angels we descry'd."
>
> [c. VII. st. 217.][1]

---

[1] I ought to have noticed in its place *ante* (p. 86) the parallel passages containing Milton's and our Fletcher's conception of Satan as a ' monk,' or ' aged Sire.'   See Paradise Regained, b. i. lines 314-320 and Christ's Victorie, part ii. st. 15-18.   It may be noted here that in the " English Metrical Homilies from Manuscripts of the 14th century " edited with rare painstaking by the cultured Librarian of the University of Edinburgh (John Small, M.A.). Satan appears not in the guise of a Monk, but as ' tempting ' the Monks in the guise of a Physician.   See Mr. Small's Introduction, pp. viii.-x.   (I vol. 4to, 1862.)

Another of the *memorabilia* of MILTON is the Lady's pure and nobly disdainful speech in ' Comus,' and especially its close, wherein one seems to catch the shiver and crash of the idle pageant-vessels of Sin :

> ' The brute Earth will lend her nerves, and shake
> Till all thy magick structures, rear'd so high
> Were shatter'd into heaps o'er thy false head'
>
> (lines 797–799)

' Christ's Victorie' brings before us the 'Sorceresse' endeavouring to ensnare our Lord in precisely the same manner as Comus does the Lady. The effect of her Song was, that

> ....' He her charms dispersèd into winde
> And her of insolence admonishèd
> *And all her optique glasses shatterèd*' (c. II. 60.)

In their places in ' Christ's Victorie' I have noted various Miltonic words there-from. How grand is this of the ' dead Christ '

> " One touch of this PALE HAND could life restore "

(c. III. 60] These are some others :

> ....' the thicken'd sky
> Like as a dark cieling stood.'
>
> [Paradise Lost : B. XI. 742-3]

FLETCHER had long previously written of the sky similarly ' the seeling (= ceiling) gay, starrèd aloft : ' [c. IV. st. 27]—translating the Latin *cœlum* no doubt. MILTON in his ' Hymn on the Nativity ' grandly sings

'the oracles are dumb' as in 'Paradise Regained,'
later, 'henceforth oracles are ceas't.' (B. I. l. 456.)
CRASHAW has it :

> ' He saw the falling idols all confess
> A coming Deity'

(Works in F. W. L.)

Fletcher before either, had written

> 'The Angells caroll'd lowd their songs of peace
> *The cursed oracles were strucken dumb.'*

(c. I. st. 82)

Milton clothes Jordan's banks with 'whispering *reeds*'
(P. R., B I. l. 26): Fletcher has 'whistling *reeds*' there
also (c. III. st. 2).   Milton in 'Comus' exhibits the
polluted crew in '*swill'd* insolence' (line 178): Fletcher
in like manner had exhibited his vile herd :

> ....'Others within their arbours *swilling* sat,
> With laughing Bacchus'

(c. II. st. 51)

Milton in that marvellous piece of 'dulcet music' the
Song to 'Sabrina fair' places Ligea sitting on 'diamond
rocks' (p. 881): but Fletcher anterior to Peacham's
'Period of Mourning'(1613) as to Habington's 'Castara'
(1635) had his 'maine rocks of diamound' (I. st. 61.)

It were easy to multiply examples : but I will only add
that the 'preface' to *Sampson Agonistes* reveals in its
authorities cited, recent reading of our Fletcher's
'Epistle' to the Reader in vindication of sacred
Poetry: while one line in Phineas Fletcher's Verses

to his brother, prefixed to 'Christ's Victorie' shews, that even they were not overlooked by MILTON. He in 'Paradise Regained,' in the celebrated passage already referred to in condemning the 'democracy' says

'Of whom to be disprais'd were no small praise'
(B. III. l. 56)

PHINEAS FLETCHER similarly in his filial tribute had before comforted his brother as against the fault-finding of some 'adversary,'

'His praise dispraises, his dispraises praise'

QUARLES, HERRICK and FULLER, GRAY and COLLINS, and others easily recognized, equally studied and turned to account our Fletchers.[1]

Altogether I pronounce GILES FLETCHER to be a true 'Maker' in the full, creative sense, and a 'Singer' inevitable as a bird, and 'Christ's Victorie' in its four-fold wholeness, a complete Poem and as a work of art,

---

[1] The first named—Quarles—has inadvertently omitted to place within quotation-marks, two lines taken almost bodily from 'Christ's Victorie' in his 'Emblems'—the first edition of which was not published until 1635 or twenty five years subsequent to our Giles Fletcher's Poem. The lines are these.
  "Ah ! if but only those that active be
  None should Thy glory see, none should Thy glory see."
So in "Christ's Victorie" (I. st. 75)
  "Ah ! if but those that onely worthy be
  None should Thee euer see, none should Thee euer see."
A friend suggests that surely our Poet intended to say
  'None should Thee euer seek, none should Thee euer see."

a 'perfect chrysolite'. Some of the facets—to pursue the second figure—may perchance be unskillfully cut, and the light broken in consequence : but the consummate jewel is there 'shooting its sparks at Phœbus.' It is original and definite in its conception. Its conception is noble. Its execution fulfills (= fills full) its conception. Throughout, it is marked by compression : compressed, purged thought, compressed learning, compressed imagination. Everywhere you have the sense of power in reserve, resources undrawn on. With few exceptions, he is sustained in his loftiest flights. He has rarely 'conceits'—those phantasms of 'conceptions'—as a whole he is melodious in rhythm and rhyme, if exceptional dissonance do not permit us to say of him what WILLIAM CARTWRIGHT said of BEN JONSON :

> "Nor would'st thou venture it unto the ear,
>   Until the file would not make smooth but wear."[1]

We have amply evidenced his magnificent faculty of impersonation. Would that Dorè had his cunning genius turned to ' Christ's Victorie !' What I very earnestly desire for our Poet is brooding study. It only requires that he be KNOWN, to win for him that larger estimate and study he deserves. ' Christ's Victorie ' can never die save with the language : but our generation would profit by familiarity with it. It will live on and be unhurt : neglecters of it lose.[2]

---

[1] Poems 1651, page 313.
[2] I place here the appreciative words of a scholar ripe and good

For it is of the asbestos 'stuff' that is imperishable and shall abide the 'Touchstone' of all generations—no fear of William Allingham's catastrophe :

> " A man there came, whence none could tell,
>   Bearing a TOUCHSTONE in his hand ;
>   And tested all things in the land
> By its unerring spell.
>
> Quick birth of transmutation smote,
>   The fair to foul, the foul to fair ;
>   Purple nor ermine did he spare,
> Nor scorn the dusty coat.
>
> Of heir-loom jewels, prized so much,
>   Were many changed to chips and clods,
>   And even statues of the gods
> Crumbled beneath its touch."

ALEXANDER B. GROSART.

---

and a critic of fine taste (Hugh James Rose, B.D.) and the verdict of a standard authority, the 'Encyclopedia Britannica.' First, Rose in his Biographical Dictionary : *s.n.* " Christ's Victory is a poem of singular beauty." Next the ' Encyclopedia ' (probably the cultured MACVEY NAPIER (?) : " Christ's Victory is a kind of narrative of the Redemption of man, reminding us to some extent of MILTON's Epic, and bearing in *form* at least, a still more striking resemblance to that of SPENSER. The animation of the narrative, the liveliness of the fancy and the deep pathos that pervades the whole work, contribute to make it in its totality one of the most beautiful religious poems in any language, and as Southey remarks, ' will preserve the author's name while there is any praise.' It has been complained that it abounds too much in allegory : and though the charge may be partly true, the interest of the poem is admirably maintained to the last."

NOTE.

Page 68.—Dr. George Macdonald's 'Antiphon' on Justice and Mercy as personifed in 'Christ's Victorie.'

I give the passage referred to *in extenso:* "To understand the first, [extract] it is necessary to explain, that while Christ is on earth a dispute between Justice and Mercy, such as is often represented by the theologians, takes place in heaven. We must allow the unsuitable fiction, attributing distraction to the divine Unity, for the sake of the words in which Mercy overthrows the arguments of Justice. For the Poet unintentionally nullifies the symbolism of the Theologian, representing Justice as defeated. He forgets that the grandest exercise of justice is mercy. The confusion comes from the fancy that justice means *vengeance upon sin,* and not *the doing what is right.* Justice can be at no strife with mercy, for not to do what is just would be most unmerciful." (p. 151) ("England's Antiphon. By George Macdonald, LL.D. (Macmillan) 1869 cr. 8vo.)

For the genius and fine nature and nurture of Dr George Macdonald, I have admiration and love that words were empty to express the depth of: but none the less, rather all the more—because of his wide and potent influence—must I be rude enough to reject all this, absolutely, as being at once mistaken in its application to the poetry under review, and fundamentally untrue in its teaching on the *thing.* I submit these counter remarks :

(*a*) The 'divine Unity' is left untouched by our Poet. 'Distraction' is the reverse of the matter-of-fact. Justice and Mercy are personified in accord with the ground-plan of the Poet—as shewn in our Essay *ante*—and the Personifications demand that we shall regard them as outside of the 'divine Unity,' that unity being guarded by the 'pleading' of Justice and Mercy as two Personalities addressing themselves to God (the Father). Unless you

deny that there are entities which we name Justice and Mercy,
you can't refuse their impersonation, you can't insist (rightfully) on
impersonation being an 'unsuitable fiction,' you can't 'confuse'
impersonation with the 'divine Unity.' These particular Personifications are as much outside of the 'divine Unity' as, for example,
are the Passions in Collins' Ode, outside of any one individuality.
Or looking in another direction, you can personify the Five Senses
without interfering with the human Unity.

Besides all this, there is a ground-work laid for such Personifications in the Holy Scriptures, *e.g.* Psalm lxxxv. 10, 11 : "Mercy
and Truth are met together, Righteousness and Truth have kissed
each other. Truth shall spring out of the Earth : and Righteousness shall look down from heaven."

(*b*) Conceding—and it must be conceded—that Personification
or Impersonation is legitimate, then if they were to be in character
and keeping, it was equally demanded that Justice and Mercy
should appear in opposition, even strife. I speak of Justice and
Mercy *per se*, not as in the 'divine Unity' where opposition were
impossible. I look at the two Personifications in their *apparent*
attitude toward man as fallen, and guilty in his Fall. So regarding
Justice and Mercy, who that has adequately pondered the problem
in debate, of man's guilt and the Plan of Redemption for that
guilt, will gainsay *apparent* conflict, as between Justice and
Mercy. Well! This *appearance* is sufficient ground for poetic
treatment, and it seems to me uncritical to pronounce it an 'unsuitable fiction'—as much so as to 'confuse' the Personifications
in their separate utterances with their existence as attributes in the
'divine Unity.' This 'confusion' by Dr Macdonald is the more
remarkable, in that while objecting to Fletcher's Personifications
he himself singles out Justice and Mercy and pronounces against
possible 'opposition' between *them*.

(*c*) It is the very antithesis of the matter-of-fact once more, to say
that Mercy "*overthrows* the arguments of Justice," and that "the
Poet unintentionally nullifies the symbolism of the theologian (by)
representing Justice as *defeated.*" 'Overthrows' and 'defeated' are
the worst possible words here. For how is it that Mercy achieves
her 'pleading?' Not by the 'overthrow' of the arguments of Justice

—for she admits their solidity—not by the 'defeat' of Justice—
for Justice acquiesces—but through turning to and presenting Him,
Who in His divinely-human and humanly-divine Person sustains the
full demands of Justice—and so,—but only *so*—warrants the exercise
of mercy : or to adhere to the Impersonation, affirmative response to
the appeal of Mercy to God (the Father).   It is transcendently
necessary to remember—what Dr. Macdonald forgets—that it is not
mercy as mercy *per se:* but Mercy pointing to a given WORK (of
atonement) that wins from GOD (the Father) man's pardon and
Salvation.

  (*d*) With reference to the words "*unintentionally nullifies* the
symbolism of the theologian " they seem to me even more profoundly
and pervadingly mistaken and pernicious, seeing that the burden of
the poem as it bears in its four-fold title and in its entire working out,
is the Victory of CHRIST not of Mercy *per se*, and His Victory not
over Justice, but as the Poet himself puts it over ' Satan ' and ' Death.'
As he quaintly describes in the ' Argument ' of the ' Victorie in
Heaven,' Mercy (through Faith) " translates the principal fault vnto
the Deuil " and Christ stands forth " as sufficient to satisfie as man
was impotent."   This *the* idea and ' intention ' of our Singer does
not 'nullify' but vindicate the ' symbolism of the theologian ' but
most emphatically—with all respectfulness I must be permitted to
say—'nullifies' the hasty ' criticism ' of the Commentator.   It is
something monstrous (and the word is not too strong) to represent
Mercy through Christ as a ' *defeat* ' of Justice—as other than SU-
PREMELY JUST.   Or regard it from another stand-point—the very
love of righteousness on the part of God must move Him to do
what will produce righteousness in His creatures, and so (in a sense)
the very work of Righteousness will be peace.   So that as Mercy
finds One to satisfy the *rightful* demands of Justice, to withhold
mercy were most unjust.

  (*e*) Given the Facts of man's guilt as before Justice, it is sorrowfully amazing to read that " the grandest exercise of justice is mercy."
Nay verily : ' the grandest exercise of Justice ' is TO BE JUST, and to
be just is often to be merciless.   To be merciful to the guilty *per se*
involves injustice.   Then behind such sentimentalism as this, the
questions are started as one reads it, if mercy be " *the grandest exercise*

of Justice" whence the terrible, close-grinding wheels of Providence —every wheel 'full of eyes' and so looking down on the track and cognisant of all there, even to the 'little children' lying across it? whence the nameless sorrow and suffering everywhere? whence the palpable retribution on wrong-doing even here? GOD is not the weak, soft Being that this 'grandest exercise' assumes. As another Poet hath it "A God all mercy were a God un-just."

(f) Justice does mean in relation to a specific thing, as in the poetry before us, "*vengeance upon sin:*" but maugre the taunt at the 'Theologians' again, that is no contradiction to "*the doing of what is right.*" To punish the guilty (or sin) is to take 'vengeance:' and who will say it is not 'doing right?' On the other hand 'for Christ's sake' to exercise mercy toward every one accepting The Substitute, is equally 'doing right.'

(g) Granted that "not to do what is just would be most un-merciful." But it is a *petitio principii :* for where guilt is—*apart* from the Redemption of Christ—Justice as 'just' can shew no mercy—as toward the guilty *per se*, is absolutely and tremendously merciless. In Jesus Christ 'God manifested in the flesh' the awful mystery of sin (as the Bible and the God of the Bible are true) is counter-worked, and in and from Him, Mercy is gloriously available to ALL—thank God to ALL,—but let the provided and offered Salvation be rejected or neglected there can only be the execution of the penalty on the individual transgressor: and that is '*to do right.*'

WILLIAM SHAKESPEARE instructs us all on the double problem :

> " Why all the souls that were, were forfeit once ;
> ....Alas ! alas !
> And He that might the vantage best have took,
> Found out the remedy. How would you be,
> If He, which is the top of judgment, should
> But *judge you as you are?* Oh ! think of that ;
> And mercy then will breathe within your lips,
> Like man new made."
>
> ('Measure for Measure' ii. 2.)

G

SOUTHWELL in his 'St Peter's remorse' has also these fine and deep words:

> ...." sith so vile a worm
>   Hath wrought His greatest spite,
> Of highest treasons, well Thou may'st
>   In rigour him indite.
> But Mercy may relent
>   And temper Justice' rod,
> For Mercy doth as much belong
>   As Justice to a God."

Works, as before, in F. W. L.)

and conversely, Justice as much as Mercy.

(*h*) Returning upon the words "a *dispute* between Justice and Mercy, such as is often represented by the *Theologians*" as well might Dr Macdonald overweigh the true Poet by the crudities of abounding Versifiers, as class with 'Theologians' those who make such representations. I will grant that Dr Macdonald may have received provocation from some 'popular' Preacher. I myself have listened to sermons in which Justice and Mercy debated (as in a College Club) and the Father was perplexed (so-to-say) till the Son stepped in and offered to suffer, and the Spirit added 'I will anoint Him' &c. But (1) such Preachers are no 'Theologians' and (2) in these debates it was not Mercy that triumphed in argument but always Justice. Mercy always found One to meet the claims of Justice: and so while the representation might be inaccurate, truth under-lay it. Further: I will concede that if you have regard to Justice and Mercy *theologically* and not as in Fletcher poetically, a two-fold evil result attends any separation of Justice and Mercy as divine attributes *i.e.* If (mentally) we give a sort of supremacy to either justice or mercy, we are like to miss somewhat of the glory of the One eternal God. (*a*) A man who sees righteousness filling the Universe *may* come to imagine that God the *just* needs reconciling to God the *merciful :* and so you have him crying out as a Hymn makes the sinner do :

> " Where shall the chief of sinners fly
>   Eternal Justice from Thine eye !"

the question being, How to escape from God *the just.* On the other hand (*b*) When mercy seems the ruling attribute you get all sorts of sentimentalism, and Christian 'virtue '—in its deep, robust Pauline meaning—loses its grandeur and force.

But save for DR MACDONALD'S anxiety to get a hit at the ' Theologians,' it was a mistake, and a wrong—and to those who hold him in deepest love, a sorrow,—to drag such matters into a criticism of a purely ' poetical' representation—albeit as we have seen, regarded theologically, Fletcher's Personifications and the substance and event of their ' pleading' alike, rest on the firmest basis of Theology-proper.

I give two additional examples of the theologic-poetic conception of Justice and Mercy in agreement with Fletcher. First, DR JOSEPH BEAUMONT in his " Psyche "—a poem that bears the deep impress of both our Fletchers. The great ' Sacrifice' of Calvary has been ' offered' and accepted :

> ...." Justice NOW had nothing more to say ;
> The blood which down the Cross its torrents threw
> All her objections had wash'd away ;
> And every page of her black Volume grew
>   Full as serene and fair as is the skies
>   Pure face when rescu'd from the clouds disguise.
>
> Dismissing therefore all her horrid train,
> Her satisfied self she strait withdrew :
> When Jesus looking up to Heav'n again,
> Perceiv'd the veil, which shadow'd had till now
>   His Father's Face, remov'd.   O blessed sight !
>   O cheerful Morning after heavy Night !"
>
> [C. XIV. 203, 204.]

Again trenchantly :

> ...." Hell at length will prick on mortall wit
> Against this Passion's MERIT to dispute,
> And all their syllogizing batteries set,
> In order their Redemption to confute.
>   Thus to their Reason must their Faith give way ;
>   Though God be satisfy'd yet will not they.

No ; they'll account IIis Mercy injur'd by
Allowing Justice to be fully pay'd.
Ah learnèd fool ! is Mercy's majesty
Not here triumphant, when the load is lay'd.
    On God's own Son, to bear what else would crack
    Proud though you be, for evermore your back."

                                [C. XIV. 221, 222.]

The other is SAMUEL SPEED in his " Prison-Pietie " (1677).

"ON JUSTICE AND MERCY.

Justice doth call for vengeance on my sins,
    And threatens death as guerdon for the same ;
Mercy to plead for pardon then begins,
    With saying, Christ hath under-gone the shame.
Justice shews me an angry God offended,
    And Mercy shews a Saviour crucifi'd :
Justice says, I that sinn'd must be condemnèd :
    Mercy replies, Christ for my sins hath di'd.
Grim Justice threats with a revengeful rod :
Meek Mercy shews me an appeasèd God.
    Lord ! though my sins make me for Justice fit
    Through Christ let Mercy triumph over it."

                                [pp. 151, 152.]

IIowever regarded therefore, our Poet is true and his Critic profoundly un-true : for as St Paul long since grandly argued out
" All have sinned, and come short of the glory of God : being justified freely by IIis grace, through the redemption that is in Christ
Jesus : Whom God hath set forth to be a propitiation through
faith in His blood, to declare His righteousness for the remission
of sins that are past, through the forbearance of God ; to declare,
I say, at this time His righteousness : that IIe might be just, *and*
the justifier of him which believeth in Jesus " (Rom. iii. 23-26).
I rejoice that Dr Macdonald's mistakes as a very poorly-furnished
Theologian in this instance, has not dimmed his vision as a Poet,
or abated his high praise of our Singer. Nor am I forgetful or
ungrateful for much genial and keen exposition of our old Worthies,
albeit some of his judgments, as on Cowley, are as perverse as they
are superficial.—G.

CHRIST'S
VICTORIE AND TRIUMPH.

NOTE.

THE original title-page, as well as those of the second and third editions, will be found annexed : also collation of each edition. The changes from the first (1610) are wholly modernization of the spelling. Our text is that of 1610; to the orthography of which, throughout, we adhere strictly—save that the usual mark of apostrophe of the possessive case is inserted e.g. Rome's not Romes, and that the capitals and italics are occasionally diminished and occasionally encreased—the former in the Divine names—nouns and pronouns—and in Impersonations. The punctuation is also accommodated to modern usage : the original consists mainly of a profusion of commas. As the Poet was dead before the second edition appeared, the text of 1610 is the only one that bears his authority. Exemplifications of the faulty character of re-prints hitherto, will be found in the foot-notes, where the most flagrant mis-prints, etc., etc., of three of the best are given viz. (1) RICHARDSON's : " Christ's Victory and Triumph in Heaven and Earth, over and after Death, in Four Parts. By Giles Fletcher. With an Original Biographical Sketch of the Author, &c. Also some Choice Pieces from the Poetical Writings of the Rev. George Herbert, Late Orator of the University of Cambridge.   London : Published by T. Richardson, 98, High Holborn, and B. Clark.   1824.   cr. 8vo. pp. xiv. and pp. 130." This is a somewhat ambitious but a very poor edition.   There is nothing 'original' in the 'Biographical Sketch' except that while adding nothing to former scanty materials it contrives to multiply 'blunders.'   The orthography is modernized throughout and the sense repeatedly mistaken.   Probably the Publisher—who was also the Printer—was his own Editor.   I designate it by Richardson : but he is not to be confounded with DR. RICHARDSON, to whom we have frequent occasion to refer in our notes (2) SOUTHEY's : in his 'British Poets: Chaucer to Jonson.'   (1831, 8vo.)   He disclaims responsibility for the proof-sheets : but he must be held responsible for the selection of his texts.   (3) CATTERMOLE's : in his "Sacred Poetry of the 17th Century."   (1836, 2 vols. 12mo.) both modernized and carelessly read.   I have not deemed it worth-while to add the like mis-prints and corruptions of the general collections of what are called 'The Poets' by Dr. Anderson and by Chalmers. That of 1783 (8vo) along with 'The Purple Island' is beneath criticism.   Throughout I have added foot-notes as required—passing over trite classical allusions and names.   I have very heartily to acknowledge the scholarly aid of my friend W. ALDIS WRIGHT, Esq.,

M.A., of Trinity College, Cambridge, in verifying and
correcting such allusions and quotations as I found
any difficulty with. He has rendered me careful and
ungrudging help in all my labours on these Poets. I
have also to thank my excellent correspondent GEORGE
H. WHITE, Esq., Glenthorne, Torquay, for various most
painstaking and suggestive communications on this and
other of my Worthies.

G.

(*a*) 1st edition :

CHRISTS

VICTORIE, AND TRI-

umph in Heauen, and Earth,

over, and after death.

A te principium, tibi desinet, accipe iussis
Carmina cæpta tuis, atque hanc sine tempora circum
Inter victrices hederam tibi serpere lauros.

[Wood-cut fleur-de-lis : motto ' Domino confido.']

CAMBRIDGE
Printed by C. LEGGE. 1610. [small 4to.]

Collation : Title-page—Epistle Dedicatory pp. 3—Nethersole's
'Verses' 1 page—to the Reader pp. 5—Phin. Fletcher's and
Nethersole's 'Verses' pp. 4—[unpaged]—Poem pp. 83 and Latin
'Lines' 1 page. Opposite blank reverse of page 45 is a separate
title-page 'Christ's Trivmph ouer and after Death. Vincenti
dabitur. Printed by C. Legge, 1610. After page 79 by an
oversight mispages 81 and so runs—

(*b*)   2nd edition :

CHRISTS

VICTORIE AND

TRIUMPH IN HEAVEN

AND EARTH, OVER

AND AFTER DEATH.

A te principium, tibi desinet : accipe jussis
Carmina cœpta tuis, atq. hanc sine tempora circum
Inter victrices hederam tibi serpere lauros.

The second Edition.

[Wood-cut.   Hinc . Lvcem . et . Pocvla . Sacra . Alma Mater.]

CAMBRIDGE :
Printed for Francis Green.   1632.   [Small 4to.]

Collation : Title-page—Epistle Dedicatory pp. 3—Nethersole's
' Verses ' 1 page—to the Reader pp. 4—Phin. Fletcher's and
Nethersole's ' Verses ' pp. 4—[unpaged]—Poem pp. 83 and Latin
' Lines ' on page 84.   Opposite page 42 is the separate title as
supra 'Christ's Triumph ouer and after Death.   Vincenti dabitur.
Printed by the Printers to the Universitie of Cambridge.   Ann.
Dom.   1632.'

(*c*) 3rd edition.

CHRISTS

VICTORY

AND

TRIVMPH.

In *Heaven* and *Earth*, over and after

Death.

$$\text{Wherein is} \atop \text{lively figured} \Bigg\} \text{His} \begin{cases} Birth. \\ Circumcision. \\ Baptism. \\ Temptation. \\ Passion. \\ Resurrection. \\ Ascention. \end{cases}$$

In foure divine Poems.

———

Cambridge :

Printed by *Roger Daniel*, for *Richard Royston.*   1640.

[Small 4to.]

Collation: same as 2nd edition: and seven engravings as
described in our Appendix to the Poem.   The above separate
title not in 3rd edition.   G.

To the Right Worshipvll, and Reverend Mr. Doctour
Nevile, Deane of Canterbvrie, and the Master of Trinitie
Colledge in Cambridge.[1]

Right worthie, and reverend Syr :

As I haue alwaies thought the place wherein I liue,
after heauen, principally to be desired, both because I
most want and it most abounds with wisdome, which is
fled by some with as much delight, as it is obtained by
others, and ought to be followed by all : so I cannot but
next unto God, for euer acknowledge myselfe most bound
vnto the hand of God, (I meane yourselfe) that reacht
downe, as it were out of heauen, vnto me, a benefit of
that nature, and price, then which, I could wish none,
(onely heauen itselfe excepted) either more fruitfull, and
contenting for the time that is now present, or more
comfortable, and encouraging for the time that is alreadie
past, or more hopefull, and promising for the time that is
yet to come.

For as in all mens iudgements (that haue any iudge-
ment) Europe is worthily deem'd the Queene of the

---

[1] For notice of Dean NEVILLE see TODD's 'Account of the
Deans of Canterbury.' He died May 2, 1615. G.

world, that Garland both of Learning, and pure Religion beeing now become her crowne, and blossoming vpon her head, that hath long since laine withered in Greece and Palestine ; so my opinion of this Island hath alwaies beene, that it is the very face, and beautie of all Europe, in which both true Religion is faithfully professed without superstition, and (if on earth) true Learning sweetly flourishes without ostentation : and what are the two eyes of this Land, but the two Vniversities; which cannot but prosper in the time of such a Prince, that is a Prince of Learning as well as of People :[1] and truly I should forget myselfe, if I should not call Cambridge the right eye : and I thinke (King Henrie the 8. beeing the vniter, Edward the 3. the Founder, and your selfe the Repairer of this Colledge, wherein I liue) none will blame me, if I esteeme the same, since your polishing of it, the fairest sight in Cambridge : in which beeing placed by your onely fauour, most freely, without either any meanes from other, or any desert in my selfe, beeing not able to doe more, I could doe no lesse, then acknowledge that debt, which I shall neuer be able to pay, and with old Silenus, in the Poet (vpon whome the boyes—*injiciunt ipsis ex vincula sertis*[2] making his garland, his fetters) finding my selfe bound vnto you by so many benefits, that were giuen by your selfe for ornaments, but are to me as so many golden cheines, to hold me fast in a kind of desired bondage, seeke (as he doth) my freedome with

---

[1] James I. G.   [2] Virgil Ecl. VI. 19. G.

a song, the matter whereof is as worthie the sweetest
Singer, as my selfe, the miserable Singer, vnworthie so
diuine a subiect : but the same fauour, that before re-
warded no desert, knowes now as well how to pardon all
faults : then which indulgence, when I regard my selfe, I
can wish no more ; when I remember you, I can hope
no lesse.

So commending these few broken lines vnto your's, and
your selfe into the hands of the best Physitian, IESVS
CHRIST, with Whome, the most ill affected man in the
midst of his sicknes, is in good health, and without
Whome, the most lustie bodie, in his greatest iollitie, is
but a languishing karcase, I humbly take my leaue, ending with the same wish, that your deuoted Obseruer, and
my approoued Friend doth, in his verses presently
sequent, that your passage to heauen may be slow to vs,
that shall want you here, but to your selfe, that cannot
want vs there, most secure and certeyne.

Your Worship's, in all dutie, and seruice

G. FLETCHER.

THOMAS NEVYLE.
MOST HEAVENLY.

As when the Captaine of the heauenly host,
Or else that glorious armie doth appeare
In waters drown'd, with surging billowes tost,
We know they are not, where we see they are ;
 We see them in the deepe, we see them mooue,
 We know they fixèd are in heauen aboue :

So did the Sunne of righteousnesse come downe
Clowded in flesh, and seem'd be in the deepe :
So doe the many waters seem to drowne
The starres his Saints, and they on earth to keepe,
 And yet this Sunne from heauen neuer fell,
 And yet these earthly starres in heauen dwell.

What if their soules be into prison cast
In earthly bodies? yet they long for heauen ;
What if this worldly Sea they haue not past?
Yet faine they would be brought into their hauen.
 They are not here, and yet we here them see,
 For euery man is there, where he would be.

Long may you wish, and yet long wish in vaine,
Hence to depart, and yet that wish obtaine.
Long may you here in heauen on earth remaine,
And yet a heauen in heauen hereafter gaine.
 Go you to heauen, but yet O make no hast,
 Go slowly slowly, but yet go at last.
  But when the Nightingale so neere doth sit,
  Silence the Titmouse better may befit.

        F. NETHERSOLE.

THEAR are but fewe of many that can rightly iudge of Poetry; and yet thear ar many of those few, that carry so left-handed an opinion of it, as some of them thinke it halfe sacrilege for prophane Poetrie to deale with divine and heauenly matters, as though David wear to be sentenced by them, for vttering his graue matter vpon the harpe : others something more violent in their censure, but sure lesse reasonable (as though Poetrie corrupted all good witts, when, indeed, bad witts corrupt Poetrie) banish it with Plato out of all well-ordered Commonwealths. Both theas I will strive rather to satisfie, then refute.

And of the first I would gladlie knowe, whither they suppose it fitter, that the sacred songs in the Scripture of those heroicall Saincts, Moses, Deborah, Ieremie, Mary, Simeon, Dauid, Salomon (the wisest Scholeman, and wittiest Poet) should bee eiected from the canon, for wante of grauitie, or rather this erroure eraced out of their mindes, for wante of truth. But, it maye bee, they will giue the Spirit of God leaue to breath through what pipe it please, & will confesse, because they must needs, that all the song dittied by him, must needs bee, as

H

their Fountaine is, most holy: but their common clamour is, who may compare with God? true; & yet as none may compare without presumption, so all may imitat, and not without commendation: which made Nazianzen, on[e] of the Starrs of the Greeke Church, that now shines as bright in heauen, as he did then on earth, write so manie diuine Poems of the Genealogie, Miracles, Parables, Passion of Christ, called by him his χριστὸς πάσχων:[1] which when Basil, the Prince of the Fathers, and his Chamber fellowe, had seene, his opinion of them was, that he could haue deuised nothing either more fruitfull to others: because it kindly woed them to Religion, or more honourable to himselfe οὐδὲν γὰρ μακαριώτερον ἐστι τοῦ τὴν ἀγγέλων χορείαν ἐν γῇ μιμεῖσθαι, because by imitating the singing Angels in heau'n, himselfe became, though before his time, an earthly Angel.[2] What should I speake of Iuvencus, Prosper, and the wise Prudentius? the last of which, liuing in Hierom's time, twelue hundred yeares agoe, brought foorth in his declining age, so many, & so religious poems, straitly charging his soule, not to let passe so much as one either night or daye without some diuine song, *Hymnis continuet dies, Nec nox ulla vacet, quin Dominum canat.*[3]   And as sedulous Prudentius, so prudent Sedulius was famous in this poeticall diuinity,

---

[1] The Cento called *Christus Patiens* is printed in his Works, Vol. II. 253 (Paris 1636).   G.

[2] Epist. ad Gregorium Theolog. 1.   G.

[3] Prudentius, Cathemerinon liber, præf. 37, 38.   G.

the coetan[1] of Bernard, who sung the historie of Christ
with as much deuotion in himself, as admiration to
others; all which wear followed by the choicest witts of
Christendome; Nonnius translating all Sainct Iohn's
Ghostpel into Greek verse, Sanazar, the late-liuing
Image, and happy imitator of Virgil, bestowing ten
yeares vpon a song, onely to celebrat that one day when
Christ was borne vnto vs on earth, & we (a happic
change) vnto God in heau'n : thrice-honoured Bartas, &
our (I know no other name more glorious then his own)
Mr. Edmund Spencer (two blessed Soules) not thinking
ten years inough, layeing out their whole liues vpon this
one studie : Nay I may iustly say, that the Princely
Father of our Countrey (though in my conscience, God
hath made him of all the learned Princes that euer wear
the most religious, and of all the religious Princes, the
most learned, that so, by the one, hee might oppose him
against the Pope, the peste of all Religion and by the
other, against Bellarmine the abuser of all good Learning)
is yet so far enamour'd with this celestiall Muse, that it
shall neuer repent mee—*calamo triuisse labellum*, when-
soeuer I shall remember *Hæc eadem ut sciret quid non
faciebat Amyntas?*[2] To name no more in such plenty,
whear I may finde how to beginne, sooner then to end,
Saincte Paule, by the Example of Christ, that wente
singing to mounte Oliuet, with his Disciples, after
His last sup[p]er, exciteth the Christians to solace them-

---

[1] Contemporary. G. [2] Virgil, Ecl. II. 34, 35. G.

selues with hymnes, and Psalmes, and spirituall songs; and thearefore by their leav's, be it an error for Poets to be Divines, I had rather err with the Scripture, then be rectifi'd by them: I had rather adore the stepps of Nazianzen, Prudentius, Sedulius, then followe their steps, to bee misguided: I had rather be the deuoute Admirer of Nonnius, Bartas, my sacred Soueraign, and others, the miracles of our latter age, then the false sectarie[s] of these, that haue nothing at all to follow, but their own naked opinions: To conclude, I had rather with my Lord, and His most divine Apostle sing (though I sing sorilie) the loue of heauen and earthe, then praise God (as they doe) with the woorthie guift of silence, and sitting still, or think I dispraisd Him with this poetical discourse. It seems they haue either not read, or clean forgot, that it is the dutie of the Muses (if wee maye beeleeue Pindare, and Hesiod) to set allwaies vnder the throne of Iupiter, *eius et laudes et beneficia* ὑμνειοὐσας which made a very worthy German writer conclude it *Certò statuimus, proprium atque peculiare poetarum munus esse, Christi gloriam illustrare,* beeing good reason that the heauenly infusion of such Poetry should ende in His glorie, that had beginning from His goodnes, *fit orator, nascitur Poeta.*

For the secound sorte thearfore, that eliminat Poets out of their citie gates; as though they wear nowe grown so bad, as they could neither growe woorse, nor better, though it be somewhat hard for those to bee the onely men should want cities, that wear the onely causers

of the building of them and somewhat inhumane to
thrust them into the woods, to liue among the beasts,
who wear the first that call'd men out of the woods,
from their beastly, and wilde life, yet since they will
needes shoulder them out for the onely firebrands to
inflame lust (the fault of earthly men, not heauenly
Poetrie) I would gladly learne, what kind of professions
theas men would bee intreated to entertaine, that so
deride and disaffect Poesie: would they admit of Philosophers, that after they haue burnt out the whole candle
of their life in the circular studie of Sciences, crie out at
length, *Se nihil prorsus scire?* or should Musitians be
welcome to them, that *Dant sine mente sonum*—bring
delight with them indeede, could they as well expresse
with their instruments a voice, as they can a sound? or
would they most approve of Soldiers that defend the life
of their countrymen either by the death of themselues,
or their enemies? If Philosophers please them, who is
it, that knowes not, that all the lights of Example, to
cleare their precepts, are borrowed by Philosophers from
Poets; that without Homer's examples, Aristotle would
be as blind as Homer: If they retaine Musitians, who
euer doubted, but that Poets infused the verie soule into
the inarticulate sounds of musique; that without Pindar
& Horace the Lyriques had beene silenced for euer: If
they must needes entertaine Soldiers, who can but confesse, that Poets restore againe that life to soldiers, which
they before lost for the safetie of their country; that
without Virgil, Æneas had neuer beene so much as heard

of. How then can they for shame deny commonwealths
to them, who wear the first Authors of them ; how can
they denie the blinde Philosopher, that teaches them,
his light; the emptie Musitian that delights them, his
soule ; the dying Soldier, that defends their life, immortalitie, after his owne death; let Philosophie, let
Ethiques, let all the Arts bestowe vpon vs this guift,
that we be not thought dead men, whilest we remaine
among the liuing : it is onely Poetrie that can make vs
be thought liuing men, when we lie among the dead, and
therefore I think it vnequall to thrust them out of our
cities, that call vs out of our graues, to thinke so hardly
of them, that make vs to be so well thought of, to deny
them to liue a while among vs, that make vs liue for
euer among our Posteritie.

So beeing nowe weary in perswading those that hate,
I commend my selfe to those that love such Poets, as
Plato speakes of, that sing divine and heroical matters,
οὐ γὰρ οὗτοι εἰσίν, οἱ ταῦτα λέγοντες, ἀλλ ὁ Θεὸς, αὐτός ἐστιν
ὁ λέγων,[1] recommending theas my idle howers, not idly
spent, to good schollers, and good Christians, that haue
ouercome their ignorance with reason, and their reason,
with religion.

----

[1] Plato *Ion.* p. 181. D :   G.

PRELIMINARY VERSES.

FOND ladds that spend so fast your poasting time,
(Too poasting time, that spends your time as fast)
To chaunt light toyes, or frame some wanton rime,
Where idle boyes may glut their lustful tast ;
Or else with praise to cloath some fleshly slime
With virgins roses and faire lillies chast ;
 While itching bloods and youthfull cares adore it ;
But wiser men, and once yourselues, will most abhorre it.

But thou (most neere, most deare) in this of thine
Ha'st proov'd the Muses not to Venus bound ;
Such as thy matter, such thy Muse, divine ;
Or thou such grace with Merci's selfe hast found,
That she herself deign's in thy leaues to shine ;
Or stol'n from heav'n, thou broughts[t] this verse to ground,
 Which frights the nummèd soule with fearefull thunder,
And soone with honied dewes melts it 'twixt ioy and wonder.

Then doe not thou malitious tongues esteeme ;
The glasse, through which an envious eye doth gaze,
Can easily make a mole-hill mountaines seeme :
His praise dispraises, his dispraises, praise ;
Enough, if best men best thy labours deem,
And to the highest pitch thy merit raise ;
 While all the Muses to thy song decree
Victorious Triumph, Triumphant Victorie.
PHIN. FLETCHER, Regal.

In 1632 edition there is added here a couplet :

Defuncto fratri,
Think (if thou cans't) how mounted on his spheare
In heaven now he sings : thus sung he here.
                                PHIN. FLETCHER. Regal.

QVID ô, quid Veneres, Cupidinesque,
Turturesque, iocosque, passeresque,
Lascivi canitis greges, poëtæ?
Etiam languidulos amantum ocellos,
Et mox turguidulas sinu papillas,
Iam risus [1] teneros, lachrymulasque,[2]
Mox suspiria, morsiunculasque,
Mille basia ; mille, mille nugas ?
Et vultus pueri, puellululæve
(Heu fusci pueri, puellulæque)
Pingitis nivibus, rosunculisque,
(Mentitis nivibus, rosunculisque)
Quæ vel primo hyemis rigore torpent,
Vel Phœbi intuitu statim relanguent.
Heu stulti nimiùm greges poetæ !
Vt, quas sic nimis, ah nimis stupetis,
(Nives candidulæ & rosæ pudentes)
Sic vobis pereunt statim labores :
Et solem fugiunt severiorem,
Vel solem gelida rigent senectâ :
     At tu qui clypeo, haud inane nomen
       (Minervæ clypeo Iovisque) sumens
Victrices resonas Dei Triumphos,
Triumphos lachrymis, metuque plenos,
Plenos lætitiæ, et spei triumphos,
Dum rem carmine, Pieroque dignam
Aggrederis, tibi res decora rebus

---

[1] 'Fletus' 1632 edn.   G.   [2] 'Cachinnulosque' *ib.*   G.

Præbet carmina, Pieroque digna.
Quin ille ipse tuos legens triumphos,
Plenos militia, labore plenos;
Tuo propitius parat labori
Plenos lætitiæ et spei triumphos.

PHIN. FLETCHER, Regal.

Π' Μαριὰμ
Μὴ μιαρά.

BEATISSIMA virginum Maria,
Sed materque simul beata, per quam
Qui semper fuit ille cœpit esse:
Quæ Vitæ dederisque inire vitam:
Et Luci dederis videre lucem:
Quæ fastidia, morsiunculásque
Passa es quas grauidæ solent, nec unquam
(Audebas propior viro venire)
Dum clusus [1] penetralibus latebat
Matricis tunicâ undique involutus,
Quem se posse negant tenere cœli.
Quæ non virgineas premi papillas
Passa, virgineas tamen dedisti
Lactandas puero tuo papillas.
Eia, dic age, dic beata virgo,
Cur piam abstineas manum timesque
Sancta tangere, Sanctuariumque
Insolens fugias? an inquinari
Contactu metuis tuo sacrata?
Contactu metuit suo sacrata
Pollui pia, cernis en ferentem,
Lenimenta Dei furentis, illa
Fœdatas sibi ferre quæ iubebat.
Sis felix noua virgo-mater opto,
Quæ mollire Deum paras amicum.

---

[1] 'Clausus' *ib.* G.

Quin hîc dona licet licet relinquas,
Agnellumque repone, turturemque,
Audax ingrediare inanis ædes
Dei, tange Deo sacrata, tange
Quæ non concubitu coinquinata,
Agnellum peperitque, Turturemque,
Exclusit, facili Deo litabit
Agno cum Deus insit, et columbæ.

Nor can I so much say as much I ought,
Nor yet so little can I say as nought,
In praise of this thy worke, so heauenly pend,
That sure the sacred Dove a quill did lend
From her high-soaring wing : certes I know
No other plumes, that makes man seeme so low
In his owne eyes, who to all others sight
Is mounted to the highest pitch of height :
Where if thou seeme to any of small price,
The fault is not in thee, but in his eyes :
But what doe I thy flood of wit restreine
Within the narrow bankes of my poore veyne?
More I could say, and would, but that to praise
Thy verses, is to keepe them from their praise.
For them who reades, and doth them not aduance,
Of envie doth it, or of ignorance.

                                    F. NETHERSOLE.[1]

---

[1] NETHERSOLE was 'Public Orator' of the University (of Cambridge), in which office he was succeeded by GEORGE HERBERT, who, like GILES FLETCHER, was a *protégé* of Dean Nevile. Lowndes calls him Sir Francis as author of a forgotten Latin tractate (See *s. n.*) Nethersole fell under the scorpion lash of JOHN GOODWIN, who had been assailed by him very grossly and unrighteously. G.

CHRIST'S
VICTORIE AND TRIUMPH.

THE ARGUMENT.[1]

The Argument propounded in generall: Our redemption by Christ : st. 1, 2.—
The Author's inuocation for the better handling of it : st. 3, 4.—The Argument
[in particular]: Man's redemption expounded from the cause—Mercie dwell-
ing in heauen, and pleading for man now guiltie, with Justice described by her
qualities: st. 5—11. Her retinue : st. 12—14.—Her subiect : st. 15, 16.—Her
accusation of man's sinne : st. 17. And (I.) of Adam's first sinne : st. 18, 19.
—Then of his posteritie's, in all kinde of Idolatrie : st. 20—24. How hopelesse
any patronage of it : st. 25—27.—All the creatures hauing disleagued themsclues
with him for his extreame vngratefulnes: 28—34,—So that beeng destitute of
all hope or any remedie, he can look for nothing but a fearful sentence : st. 35—
39.—The effect of Iustice, her speech: the inflammation of the heauenly Powers
appeased by Mercie, who is described by her cherfulnes to defend man : st.
40—42.—Our inabilitie to describe her : st. 43, 44.—Her beautie resembled by
the creatures, which are all fraile shadows of her essentiall perfection : st.
45, 46.—Her attendants: st. 46, 47.—Her persuasiue power : st. 48—50.—Her
kind offices to man : st. 51, 52.—Her garments, wrought by her owne hands,
wherewith shee cloaths herselfe, composd of all the creatures : st. 53.—The
Earth : st. 54.—Sea ; st. 55, 56.—Ayre : st. 57, 58.—The celestiall bodies : st.
59, 60.—The third heauen : st. 61, 62.—Her obiects : st. 63.—Repentance : st.
64—66.—Faith : st. 67—69.—Her deprecative spech for Man ; in which she
translates the principal fault vnto the Deuill ; and, repeating Iustice her
aggrauation of man's sinne, mittigates it. (1) By a contrarie inference : (2) By
interessing[1] her selfe in the cause, and Christ : st. 70—75.—that is, as sufficient
to satisfie, as Man was impotent : st. 76, 77. Whom shee celebrates from
the time of His natiuitie : st. 78. From the effects of it in Himselfe : st. 79,
80.—Egypt : st. 81.—The angels [and] men : st. 82, 83.—The effect of
Mercie's speech : st. 84.—A transition to Christ's second victorie : st. 85.

---

[1] In the author's own edition and in those of 1632 and 1640,
'The Argument' is dispersed over the margins opposite the several
stanzas. It has been thought better to bring it together at the
commencement of each Part. G.

[2] Richardson, Southey, and Cattermole, misprint 'intercessing'
=interceding ; Fletcher himself as *supra*. G.

Christ's Victorie in Heaven.

1.

THE birth of Him that no beginning knewe,
    Yet giues beginning to all that are borne ;
And how the Infinite farre greater grewe,
By growing lesse, and how the rising Morne,
That shot from heau'n, did [1] backe to heau'n retourne ;
   The obsequies of Him that could not die,
   And death of life, ende of eternitie,
How worthily He died, that died unworthily ;—

2.

How God and Man did both embrace each other,
Met in one person, Heau'n and Earth did kiss ;
And how a Virgin did become a Mother,
And bare that Sonne, Who the world's Father is,
And Maker of His mother ; and how Bliss
   Descended from the bosome of the High,
   To cloath Himselfe in naked miserie,
Sayling at length to Heau'n, in Earth, triumphantly— [2]

[1] Southey and Chalmers misprint here 'and' for 'did.' C.
[2] I may be allowed to refer to my " Lord Bacon not the Author

3.

Is the first flame, wherewith my whiter Muse
Doth burne in heauenly loue, such loue to tell.
O Thou that didst this holy fire infuse,
And taught'st this brest—but late the graue of
    hell,
Wherein a blind and dead heart liu'd—to swell
    With better thoughts, send downe those lights that
        lend
    Knowledge, how to begin, and how to end
The loue, that neuer was, nor euer can be pend.[1]

4.

Ye Sacred Writings, in whose antique leaues
The memories of Heau'n entreasur'd lie,
Say, what might be the cause that Mercie heaues
The dust of sinne aboue th' industrious skie,
And lets it not to dust and ashes flie?
    Could Iustice be of sinne so ouer-wooed,
    Or so great ill be cause of so great good,
That bloody man to saue, man's Sauiour shed His
    blood?

of 'The Christian Paradoxes,' being a re-print of Memorials of
Godliness and Christianity, by Herbert Palmer, B.D. With Introduction, Memoir and Notes." 8vo, 1865. Probably Palmer
had the 'Paradoxes' suggested by Fletcher. G.
    [1] 'Penned'=written or described : but cf. stanza 17, line 7
=confined. G.

5.

Or did the lips of Mercie droppe soft speech
For traytrous man, when at th' Eternall's throne
Incensèd Nemesis [1] did Heau'n beseech
With thundring voice, that Iustice might be showne
Against the rebells, that from God were flowne?
   O say, say how could Mercie plead for those
   That, scarcely made, against their Maker rose?
Will any slay his friend that he may spare his
    foes?

6.

There is a place beyond that flaming hill,
From whence the starres their thin apparance shed;
A place, beyond all place, where neuer ill,
Nor impure thought, was euer harbourèd,
But sainctly heroes are for euer s'ed [2]
   To keepe an euerlasting Sabbaoth's rest,
   Still wishing that, of what th' ar still possest,
Enioying but one ioy,—but one of all ioyes best.

7

Here, when the ruine of that beauteous frame,
Whose golden building shin'd with euerie starre
Of excellence, deform'd with age became,
Mercy, remembring peace in midst of warre,
Lift vp the musique of her voice, to barre

[1] = Personification of Conscience.   Cf. Hesiod, Theog.
223. G.
   [2] Southey 'su'd:' Cattermole 'said:' Query = savèd? G.

Eternall Fate, least it should quite erace
That from the world, which was the first world's
    grace,
And all againe into their nothing—Chaos—chase.

8.

For what had all this All, which man in one
Did not vnite? the earth, aire, water, fire,
Life, sense, and spirit, nay, the powreful throne
Of the diuinest Essence, did retire,
And His owne image into clay inspire :
    So that this Creature well might called be
    Of the great world the small epitomie,
Of the dead world, the liue and quicke [1] anatomie.

9.

But Iustice had no sooner Mercy seene
Smoothing the wrinkles of her Father's browe,
But vp she starts, and throwes her selfe betweene :
As when a vapour, from a moory slough,
Meeting with fresh Eoüs,[2] that but now
    Open'd the world, which all in darknesse lay,
    Doth heau'n's bright face of his rayes disaray,
And sads the smiling Orient of the springing day.

---

[1] Living, alive, as Shakespere, (Hamlet v. 1.) "'Tis for the
dead, not for the quick." Cf. Numbers xvi. 30. G.

[2] Eos : in Latin, Aurora, the goddess of the Morning who brings
up the light of Day from the East. Cf. Hesiod. Theog. 371
&c. G.

10.

She was a Virgin of austere regard ;
Not as the world esteemes her, deafe and blind ;
But as the eagle, that hath oft compar'd
Her eye with Heau'n's, so, and more brightly shin'd
Her lamping sight ; for she the same could winde
    Into the solid heart, and with her cares
    The silence of the thought loude speaking heares,
And in one hand a paire of euen scoals [1] she weares.

11.

No riot of affection reuell kept
Within her brest, but a still apathy
Possess'd all her soule, which softly slept
Securely, without tempest ; no sad crie
Awakes her pittie, but wrong'd pouertie,
    Sending her eyes to heau'n swimming in teares,
    With hideous clamours euer struck her eares,
Whetting the blazing sword, that in her hand she beares.

12.

The winged lightning is her Mercury,
And round about her mightie thunders sound :
Impatient of himselfe lies pining by

[1] Scales. G.

I

Pale Sicknes with his kercher'd [1] head vpwound,
And thousand noysome plagues attend her round;
　　But if her clowdie browe but once grow foule,
　　The flints doe melt, and rocks to water rowle,
And ayrie mountaines shake, and frighted shadowes
　　howle.

13.

Famine, and bloodles Care, and bloodie Warre,
Want, and the want of knowledge how to vse
Abundance; Age, and Feare that runnes afarre
Before his fellowe Greefe, that aye pursues
His wingèd steps; for who would not refuse
　　Greefe's companie, a dull and rawebon'd spright,
　　That lankes the cheekes, and pales the freshest sight,
Vnbosoming the cheereful brest of all delight.

14.

Before this cursed throng, goes Ignorance,
That needes will leade the way he cannot see:
And, after all, Death doeth his flag aduance,
And, in the midst, Strife still would roaguing [2] be,
Whose ragged flesh and cloaths did well agree:
　　And round about amazèd Horror flies,
　　And ouer all, Shame veiles his guiltie eyes,
And vnderneath, Hell's hungrie throat still yawning lies.

---

[1] Milton has 'Chercheft' in Il Pensoroso, l. 125 'But Cherchef't
in a comely Cloud' G.　　　　　　　　　[2] Raging.　G.

15.

Vpon two stonie tables, spread before her,
She lean'd her bosome, more then stonie hard;
There slept th' vnpartiall Iudge, and strict restorer
Of wrong or right, with paine or with reward;
There hung the skore of all our debts, the card
   Whear good, and bad, and life, and death were
     painted:
Was neuer heart of mortall so vntainted,
But when that scroule was read, with thousand terrors
   fainted.

16.

Witnes the thunder that mount Sinai heard,
When all the hill with firie clouds did flame,
And wandring Israel, with the sight afeard,
Blinded with seeing, durst not touch the same,
But like a wood of shaking leaues became.
   On this dead [1] Justice, she, the Liuing Lawe
   Bowing herselfe with a majestique awe,
All heau'n, to heare her speech, did into silence drawe.

---

[1] 'Dead:' Cf. st. 15. ll. 1, 2. On this 'dead Justice,' that is
the tables of the Written Law, the Living Law "bowed herself,"
leaning her elbows as it were on the Tables as she proceeded to
speak. The emendation, which formerly I too hastily accepted, of
'dread' destroys the antithesis between the *dead* letter or decalogue
and personified Justice. G.

17.

' Dread Lord of spirits, well Thou did'st deuise
To fling the world's rude dunghill, and the drosse
Of the ould Chaos, farthest from the skies,
And thine Owne seate, that heare [1] the childe of losse
Of all the lower heau'n, the curse and crosse,
  That wretch, beast, caytiue monster—Man,—might
   spend,
  (Proude of the mire in which his soule is pend)
Clodded in lumps of clay, his wearie life to end.

18.

' His bodie dust : whear grewe such cause of pride ?
His soule Thy image : what could be enuie ?
Himselfe most happie : if he so would bide,
Now grow'n most wretched, who can remedie ?
He slewe himselfe, himselfe the enemie,
  That his owne soule would her owne murder wreake :
  If I were silent, Heau'n and Earth would speake
And, if all fayl'd, these stones would into clamours
   breake.

19.

' How many darts made furrowes in his side,
When she, that out of his owne side was made

---

[1] Richardson has 'hear,' Cattermole misprints 'there.' G.

Gaue feathers to their flight?[1] whear was the pride
Of their newe knowledge? whither did it fade,
When, running from Thy voice into the shade,
   He fled Thy sight, himselfe of sight bereau'd;
   And for his shield a leauie armour weau'd,
With which, vain man, he thought God's eies to haue
     deceau'd?[2]

20.

'And well he might delude those eyes, that see,
And iudge by colours : for who euer sawe
A man of leaues, a reasonable tree?[3]
But those that from this stocke their life did drawe,
Soone made their father godly, and by lawe
   Proclaimèd trees almightie : gods of wood,
   Of stocks, and stones with crownes of laurell stood
Templed, and fed by fathers with their children's blood.

21.

'The sparkling fanes, that burne in beaten gould,
And, like the starres of heau'n in mid'st of night

---

[1] Cf. Æschylus, Myrmidones, frag. Bp.'Butler in his note on this fragment, quotes Waller's sonnet commencing ' That Eagle's fate, &c. Byron applies it pathetically to Kirke White. See a learned discussion of the whole question, by Gataker, Advers. Misc. Posth. cap. xii. G.

[2] The close of this stanza has suffered from the Editors. Southey misprints (line 6th) ' light ' for 'night,' and (line 7th) ' heavy ' for ' leauie '=leafy, and Cattermole drops (line 8th) ' vain man.' G.

[3] = Adam so concealed in, and as it were blended with, the tree as to deceive human though not divine vision. G.

Blacke Egypt, as her mirrhours doth behould,
Are but the denns whear idoll-snakes delight
Againe to couer Satan from their sight :
  Yet these are all their gods, to whome they vie
  The crocodile, the cock, the rat, the flie :
Fit gods, indeede, for such men to be serued by.

22.

' The fire, the winde, the sea, the sunne, and moone,
The flitting [1] aire, and the swift-wingèd how'rs,
And all the watchmen, that so nimbly runne,
And centinel about the wallèd towers
Of the world's citie, in their heau'nly bowr's ;
  And, least their pleasant gods should want delight,
  Neptune spues out the lady Aphrodite,
And but in Heauen proude Iuno's peacocks skorne to
      lite.

23.

' The senselesse Earth, the serpent, dog, and catte,
And woorse then all these, Man, and woorst of men,
Vsurping Ioue, and swilling [2] Bacchus fat,
And drunke with the vine's purple blood ; and then
The fiend himselfe they coniure from his denne,

------

  [1] Moving, changing. Cf. "Christ's Triumph after Death," st.
6. 1. 7. G.
  [2] Richardson and Cattermole misread 'swelling.' G.

Because he onely yet remain'd to be
Woorse then the worst of men : they flie from thee,
And weare his altar-stones out with their pliant knee.

24.

' All that he speakes (and all he speakes are lies)
Are oracles ; 'tis he (that wounded all)
Cures all their wounds, he (that put out their eyes)
That giues them light, he (that death first did call
Into the world) that with his orizall [1]
   Inspirits Earth : he Heau'ns al-seeing eye,
   He Earth's great prophet, he, whom rest doth flie,
That on salt billowes doth, as pillowes, sleeping lie.

25.

' But let him in his cabin restles rest,
The dungeon of darke flames, and freezing fire,
Iustice in Heau'n against man makes request
To God, and of his angels doth require
Sinne's punishment : if what I did desire,
   Or who, or against whome, or why, or whear,
   Of, or before whom ignorant I wear,
Then should my speech their sands of sins to mountaines
     rear.

[1] Query ' rising' as of the sun ? But I have not met with the
word elsewhere. G.

26.

' Were not the heau'ns pure, in whose courts I sue ;
The Iudge, to whom I sue, iust to requite him ;
The cause for sinne, the punishment most due ;
Iustice her selfe the plaintiffe to endite him ;
The angells holy, before whom I cite him ;
 He against whom, wicked, vniust, impure ;
 Then might he sinnefull liue, and die secure,
Or triall might escape, or triall might endure.

27

' The Iudge might partiall be, and ouer-pray'd ;
The place appeal'd from, in whose courts he sues ;
The fault excus'd, or punishment delay'd,
The parties self-accus'd that did accuse ;
Angels for pardon might their praiers vse :
 But now no starre can shine, no hope be got.
 Most wretched creature, if he knewe his lot,
And yet more wretched farre, because he knowes it not.

28

' What should I tell how barren Earth is growne,
All for to sterue her children : didst not thou
Water with heau'nly showers her wombe vnsowne,
And drop downe cloudes[1] of flow'rs? didst not thou
  bowe

---

[1] Southey misprints ' clods.'   G.

Thine easie eare vnto the plowman's vowe?
  Long might he looke, and looke, and long in
    vaine
  Might load his haruest in an emptie wayne,
And beat the woods, to finde the poor okes' hungrie
    graine.

29.

' The swelling Sea seethes in his angrie waues,
And smites the Earth, that dares the traytors nourish ;
Yet oft his thunder ther light corke outbraues,
Mowing the mountaines, on whose temples flourish
Whole woods of garlands ; and their pride to cherish,
    Plowe through the scae's greene fields, and nets
      display
  To catch the flying winds, and steale away,
Coozning the greedie Sea, prisning their nimble
    prey.

30.

' How often haue I seene the wauing pine,
Tost on a watrie mountaine, knocke his head
At Heau'ns too patient gates, and with salt brine
Queench the moone's burning hornes, and safely fled
From Heau'ns reuenge, her passengers all dead
    With stiffe astonishment tumble to Hell?
  , How oft the Sea all Earth would ouerswell,
Did not thy sandie girdle binde the mightie well?

31.

' Would not the aire be fill'd with steames [1] of death,
To poyson the quicke [2] riuers of their blood,
Did not thy windes, fan with their panting breath,
The flitting region? would not the hastie flood
Emptie it selfe into the Sea's wide wood,
 Did'st not thou leade it wand'ring from his way,
 To giue men drinke, and make his waters strey,
To fresh the flowrie meadowes, through whose fields
  they play?

32.

' Who makes the sources of the siluer fountaines
From the flint's mouth, and rocky valleis slide,
Thickning the ayrie bowells of the mountaines?
Who hath the wilde-heards of the forest tide
In their cold denns, making them hungrie bide
 Till man to rest be laid? can beastly he,
 That should haue most sense, onely senseles be,
And all things else, beside himselfe, so awefull see?

33.

' Wear he not wilder then the saluage beast,
Prowder then haughty hills, harder then rocks,
Colder then fountaines, from their springs releast,
Lighter then aire, blinder then senseles stocks,

---

[1] Richardson, Southey, and Cattermole misprint ' streams.' G.
[2] ' Living,' ' alive,' as before. G.

More changing then the riuers curling locks :
   If reason would not, sense would soone reprooue
      him,
   And vnto shame, if not to sorrow, mooue him,
To see cold floods, wild beasts, dul stocks, hard stones
      out-loue him.

34.

' Vnder the weight of sinne the Earth did fall,
And swallowed Dathan ; [1] and the raging winde,
And stormie sea, and gaping whale, did call
For Ionas ; [2] and the aire did bullets finde,
And shot from Heau'n a stony showre, to grinde
   The fiue proud kings, that for their idols fought ; [3]
   The sunne it selfe stood still to fight it out,[4]
And fire from heau'n flew downe, when sin to heau'n
      did shout.[5]

35.

Should any to himselfe for safety flie ?
The way to saue himselfe, if any were,
Wear to flie from himselfe : should he relie
Vpon the promise of his wife ? but there,
What can he see, but that he most may feare,

---

[1] Numbers c. XVI.   [2] Jonah I. I seqq. II. I–10, &c. G.
[3] Joshua X. II. G.   [4] Joshua X. 12 seqq. G.
[5] Genesis XVIII. 20, and XIX. 24.

A syren, sweete to death : vpon his friends ?
Who that he needs, or that he hath not, lends ;
Or wanting aide himselfe, ayde to another sends ?

36.

'His   strength ? but   dust :   his   pleasure ? cause   of
          paine :
His hope ? false courtier : youth or beawtie ? brittle :
Intreatie ? fond :[1] repentance ? late, and vaine :
Iust recompence ? the world wear all too little :
Thy loue ? he hath no title to a tittle :
    Hell's force ? in vaine her furies Hell shall gather :
    His seruants, kinsmen, or his children rather ?
His child, if good, shall iudge ; if bad, shall curse his
          father.

37.

'His life ? that brings him to his end, and leaues
          him :
His end ? that leaues him to beginne his woe :
His goods ? what good in that, that so deceaues him ?
His gods of wood ? their feete, alas, are slowe
To goe to helpe, that must be help't to goe :
    Honour, great woorth ? ah, little woorth they be
    Vnto their owners : wit ? that makes him see
He wanted wit, that thought he had it, wanting Thee.

[1] Foolish. G.

38.

' The Sea to drinke him quicke ? [1] that casts his dead :
Angells to spare? they punish : night to hide ?
The world shall burne in light; the Heau'ns to
        spread
Their wings to saue him ? Heaun it selfe shall
        slide,
And rowle away like melting starres, that glide
  Along their oylie threads : his minde pursues
    him :
  His house to shrowde, or hills to fall and bruse
    him ?
As sergeants both attache, and witnesses accuse him.

39.

' What need I vrge, what they must needs confesse,
Sentence on them, condemn'd by their owne
        lust ?
I craue no more, and Thou canst giue no lesse,
Then death to dead men, iustice to vniust ;
Shame to most shamefull, and most shameles
        dust :
  But if Thy mercie needs will spare her friends,
  Let Mercie there begin where Iustice endes.
'Tis cruel Mercie, that the wrong from right defends.'

---

[1] ' Living,' ' alive,' as before. G.

40.

She ended, and the heau'nly Hierarchies,
Burning in zeale, thickly imbranded[1] weare;
Like to an armie that allarum cries,
And euery one shakes his ydraded[2] speare,
And the Almightie's Selfe, as He would teare
  The Earth and her firme basis quite in sunder,
  Flam'd all in in iust reuenge and mightie thunder;
Hea'un stole it selfe from Earth by clouds that moisterd[3]
  vnder.

41.

As when the cheerfull sunne, clamping[4] wide,
Glads all the world with his vprising raye,
And wooes the widow'd Earth afresh to pride,
And paints[5] her bosome with the flowrie Maye,
His silent sister steales him quite away,

---

[1] CATTERMOLE explains this as 'mustered in arms;' but this is a mere adaptation to the context. RICHARDSON in his great Dictionary says 'Perhaps armed with brands,' and then quotes from Fletcher, as above. 'Brand,' which means a 'torch' is also used for a 'sword,' because in motion it glitters like a burning torch or fire-brand. Skinner. G.

[2] Ydraded *i.e.* dreaded : Richardson and Cattermole substitute 'terrific.' G.

[3] Moistured, refreshed = dropt moisture or tears of rain. Southey and Cattermole misprint 'moisten'd.' G.

[4] Enlightening like a lamp : Cf Spenser, Fairie Queen III. c. 3, s. 1 : and first Sonnet. Dr Richardson as before, quotes above. G.

[5] Misprinted 'paint :' but in 1632 ed. corrected to 'paints' as *supra.* G.

Wrap't in a sable clowde from mortall eyes;
The hastie starres at noone begin to rise,
And headlong to his early roost the sparrowe flies.

42.

But soone as he againe dishadowed is,
Restoring the blind world his blemish't sight,
As though another day wear newely ris,[1]
The cooz'ned birds busily take their flight,
And wonder at the shortnesse of the night;
   So Mercie once againe her selfe displayes,
   Out from her sister's cloud, and open layes
Those sunshine lookes, whose beams would dim a
   thousand dayes.

43.

How may a worme, that crawles along the dust,
Clamber the azure mountaines, thrown so high,
And fetch from thence thy faire Idea iust,
That in those sunny courts doth hidden lie,
Cloath'd with such light, as blinds the angels' eye;
   How may weake mortall euer hope to file
   His vnsmooth tongue, and his deprostrate stile?
O raise Thou from his corse Thy now entomb'd exile!

---

[1] Richardson, Southey and Cattermole, again sadly mar this line, by mis-reading from the previous one 'world' for 'day' and 'his' for 'ris' G.

44.

One touch would rouze me from my sluggish hearse,
One word would call me to my wishèd home,
One looke would polish my afflicted verse,
One thought would steale my soule from her thicke
  lome,
And force it wandring vp to Heau'n to come,
  Thear to importune, and to beg apace
  One happy fauour of Thy sacred grace,
To see—what though it loose her eyes?—to see Thy
  face.

45.

If any aske why roses please the sight?
Because their leaues vpon Thy cheekes doe bowre :
If any aske why lillies are so white?
Because their blossoms in Thy hand doe flowre :
Or why sweet plants so gratefull odours shoure?
  It is because Thy[1] breath so like they be :
  Or why the Orient sunne so bright we see?
What reason can we giue, but from Thine eies, and
  Thee?

46.

Ros'd all in liuely crimsin ar Thy cheeks,
Whear beawties indeflourishing abide,
And, as to passe his fellowe either seekes,
Seemes both doe[2] blush at one another's pride ;

Southey misprints 'their' G.   [2] Here also misprints 'to.' G.

And on Thine eyelids, waiting Thee beside,
   Ten thousand Graces sit, and when they mooue
   To Earth their amourous belgards [1] from aboue,
They flie from Heau'n, and on their wings conuey Thy
    loue.

47.

All of discolour'd plumes their wings ar made,
And with so wondrous art the quills ar wrought,
That whensoere they cut the ayrie glade,
The winde into their hollowe pipes is caught:
As seemes the spheres with them they down haue
    brought:
   Like to the seauen-fold reede of Arcadie,
   Which Pan of Syrinx made, when she did flie
To Ladon sands, and at his sighs sung merily. [2]

48.

As melting hony, dropping from the combe,
So 'still the words, that spring between Thy lipps:
Thy lippes, whear smiling Swetnesse keepes her home,
And heau'nly Eloquence pure manna sipps:
He that his pen but in that fountaine dipps,
   How nimbly will the golden phrases flie,
   And shed forth streames of choycest rhetoric,
Welling celestiall torrents out of poësie!

---

[1] *Belles regardes* 'beautiful looks:' Richardson, as before, quotes
Fletcher as above: Cf Spenser F. Q. III. c. 9.

[2] Cf. Ovid. Met. i. 691 &c.: Virgil, Eclog. ii. 31. G.

K

49.

Like as the thirstie land in Summer's heat,
Calls to the cloudes, and gapes at euerie showre,
As though her hungry clifts all heau'n would eat,
Which if high God into her bosome powre,
Though much refresht, yet more she could deuoure ;
   So hang the greedie ears of angels sweete,
   And euery breath a thousand Cupids meete,
Some flying in, some out, and all about her fleet.

50.

Vpon her breast Delight doth softly sleepe,
And of Eternal Ioy is brought abed :
Those snowie mountelets, through which doe creepe
The milkie riuers, that ar inly bred
In siluer cisternes, and themselues do shed
   To wearie trauailers, in heat of day
   To quench their fierie thrist, and to allay
With dropping nectar floods, the furie of their way.

51.

If any wander, Thou doest call him backe ;
If any be not forward, Thou incit'st him ;
Thou doest expect, if any should growe slacke ;
If any seeme but willing, thou inuit'st him ;
Or if he doe offend Thee, Thou acquit'st him ;

Thou find'st the lost, and follow'st him that flies,
Healing the sicke, and quickning him that dies :
Thou art the lame man's friendly staffe, the blind man's
    eyes.

52.

So faire Thou art, that all would Thee behold ;
But none can Thee behold, Thou art so faire ;
Pardon, O pardon then Thy vassal bold,
That with poore shadowes striues Thee to compare,
And match the things, which he knowes matchlesse are :
    O Thou vive [1] mirrhour of celestiall grace,
    How can fraile colours pourtraict out Thy face,
Or paint in flesh Thy beawtie in such semblance base ?

53.

Her vpper garment was a silken lawne,
With needle-worke richly embroidered,
Which she her selfe with her owne hand had drawne,
And all the world therein had pourtrayèd,
With threads so fresh and liuely colourèd,
    That seem'd the world She newe-created thear,
    And the mistaken eye would rashly swear
The silken trees did growe, and the beasts liuing wear.

---

[1] Richardson and Cattermole translate 'vive' into 'living' and
drop the 'O.'
Drummond of Hawthornden has the word and rhyme, *c.g.*
        'O well-spring of this all,
          Thy father's image vive,
        Word, that from neught did call
        What is, doth reason, live.' G.

54.

Low at her feet the Earth was cast alone,
(As though to kisse Her foot it did aspire,
And gaue it selfe for her to tread vpon,)
With so vnlike and different attire,
That euery one that sawe it, did admire [1]
  What it might be, was of so various hewe ;
  For to it selfe it oft so diuerse grewe,
That still it seem'd the same, and still it seem'd a newe.

55.

And here and there, few men she scatterèd,
(That in their thought the world esteeme but small
And themselues great,) but she with one fine thread
So short, and small, and slender, woue them all,
That like a sort of busie ants, that crawle
  About some molehill, so they wanderèd ;
  And round about the wauing Sea [2] was shed :
But, for the siluer sands, small pearls were sprinklèd.

56.

So curiously the vnderworke did creepe,
And curling circlets so well shadowed lay,
That afar off the waters seem'd to sleepe ;
But those that neare the margin pearle did play,
Hoarcely enwauèd wear with hastie sway,

---

[1] Wonder. G.   [2] = The sea in waves. G.

As though they meant to rocke the gentle eare
And hush the former that enslumbred wear :
And here a dangerous rocke the flying ships did fear.

57.

High in the ayrie element there hung
Another clowdy Sea, that did disdaine
(As though his purer waues from heauen sprung)
To crawle on Earth, as doth the sluggish maine :
But it the Earth would water with his raine,
   That eb'd and flow'd, as winde and season would,
   And oft the Sun would cleaue the limber[1] mould
To alabaster rockes, that in the liquid rowl'd.

58.

Beneath those sunny banks, a darker cloud,
Dropping with thicker deaw, did melt apace,
And bent it selfe into a hollowe shroude,
On which, if Mercy did but cast her face,
A thousand colours did the bowe enchace,
   That wonder was to see the silke distain'd
   With the resplendance from her beawtie gain'd,
And Iris paint her locks with beames, so liuely feign'd.

59.

About her head a cyprus[2] heau'n she wore,
Spread like a veile, vpheld with siluer wire,

---

1 Yielding. Cf. Milton P.L. 'wav'd their limber fans.' VII.
476. G.

2 'Cyprus' is our modern word 'crape,' French 'crespecrape.'

In which the starres so burn't in golden ore,
As seem'd, the azure web was all on fire:
But hastily, to quench the sparkling ire,
  A flood of milke came rowling vp the shore,
  That on his curded waue swift Argus bore,[1]
And the immortall swan, that did her life deplore.

60.

Yet strange it was, so many starres to see
Without a sunne, to give their tapers light:
Yet strange it was not, that it so should be;
For, where the sunne centers himselfe by right,
Her face, and locks did flame, that at the sight
  The heauenly veile, that else should nimbly mooue,
  Forgot his flight, and all incens'd with loue
With wonder, and amazement, did her beautie prooue.

61.

Ouer her hung a canopie of state,
Not of rich tissew, nor of spangled gold,
But of a substance, though not animate,
Yet of a heaun'nly and spirituall mould,
That onely eyes of spirits might behold;

Therefore the text is = a canopy of crape. Cf. Milton, Il
Pensoroso,
       'Sable stole of Cipres lawn
       Over thy decent shoulders draw'n.' G.
  [1] Southey repeats the misprint of ' wore ' here, from 1632 edn.
G.

Such light as from maine[1] rocks of diamound,
Shooting their sparks at Phebus, would rebound,
And little angels, holding hands, daunc't all around.

62.

Seemèd those little sprights, through nimbless bold,
The stately canopy bore on their wings
But them it selfe, as pendants, did vphold;
Besides the crownes of many famous kings :
Among the rest, thear Dauid euer sings,
    And now, with yeares growne young, renewes his
      layes
    Vnto his golden harpe, and ditties playes,
Psalming aloud in well-tun'd songs his Maker's prayse.

63.

Thou Self-Idea of all ioyes to come,
Whose loue is such, would make the rudest speake,
Whose loue is such, would make the wisest dumbe,
O, when wilt Thou Thy too-long silence breake
And ouercome the strong to saue the weake !
    If Thou no weapons hast, Thine eyes will wound
    Th' Almightie's selfe, that now sticke on the ground,
As though some blessed obiect thear did them empound.

64.

Ah ! miserable abiect[2] of disgrace,
What happines is in thy miserie ?

---

[1] Sea-rocks. G.   [2] Southey misprints 'object.' G.

I both must pittie and enuie thy case ;
For she that is the glorie of the skie,
Leaues heauen blind, to fix on thee her eye.
    Yet her (though Mercie's selfe esteems not small)
    The world despis'd ; they her Repentance call,
And she her selfe despises, and the world, and all.

65.

Deepely, alas ! empassionèd she stood,
To see a flaming brand, tost vp from hell,
Boyling her heart in her owne lustfull blood,
That oft for torment she would loudely yell ;
Nowe she would sighing sit, and nowe she fell
    Crouching vpon the ground, in sackcloath trust :[1]
    Early and late she prayed, and fast she must,
And all her haire hung full of ashes, and of dust.

66.

Of all most hated, hated most of all
Of her owne selfe she was ; disconsolat
(As though her flesh did but infunerall
Her buried ghost) she in an arbour[2] sat
Of thornie brier, weeping her cursed state ;
    And her before, a hastie river fled,
    Which her blind eyes with faithfull penance fed,
And all about, the grasse with tears hung downe his
        head.

[1] Trussed, *i.e.* dressed or girded. G.
[2] Southey has 'harbour.' G.

67.

Her eyes, though blind abroad, at home kept fast;
Inwards they turn'd, and look't into her head:
At which shee often started, as aghast
To see so fearfull spectacles of dread;
And with one hand, her breast she martyrèd,
    Wounding her heart, the same to mortifie;
    The other a faire damsel held her by,
Which if but once let go, shee sunke immediatly.

68.

But Faith was quicke and nimble as the heau'n,
As if of loue and life shee all had been,
And though of present sight her sense were reauen,
Yet shee could see the things could not be seen:
Beyond the starres, as nothing wear between,
    She fixt her sight, disdeigning things belowe:
    Into the Sea she could a mountaine throwe,
And make the sun to stande, and waters backewards
        flowe.

69.

Such when as Mercie her beheld from high,
In a darke valley, drown'd with her owne tears,
One of her Graces she sent hastily,
Smiling Eirene,[1] that a garland wears
Of guilded oliue, on her fairer hears,[2]

[1] Peace. G.   [2] Hairs. G.

To crowne the fainting soule's true sacrifice ;
  Whom when as sad Repentance comming spies,
The holy Desperado wip't her swollen eyes.

70.

But Mercie felt a kinde remorse to runne
Through her soft vaines, and therefore, hying fast
To giue an end to silence, thus begunne :—
' Aye-honour'd Father, if no ioy Thou hast
But to reward desert, reward at last
    The deuil's voice, spoke with a serpent's tongue,—
    Fit to hisse out the words so deadly stung,—
And let him die, death's bitter charmes so sweetley sung.

71.

' He was the father of that hopeles season,
That, to serue other gods, forgot their owne :
The reason was, Thou wast aboue their reason :
They would haue any [1] gods, rather then none,
A beastly serpent, or a senselesse stone :
    And these, as Iustice hates, so I deplore ;
    But the vp-plowèd heart, all rent and tore,
Though wounded by it selfe, I gladly would restore.

72.

' He was but dust ; why fear'd he not to fall ?
And, beeing fall'n, how can he hope to liue ?

---

[1] Southey misprints ' other.'   G.

Cannot the hand destroy him, that made all?
Could He not take away, aswell as giue?
Should man depraue, and should not God depriue?
  Was it not all the world's deceiuing spirit,
    (That, bladder'd vp with pride of his owne merit,
Fell in his rise) that him of Heau'n did disinherit?

73.

'He was but dust: how could he stand before Him?
And being fall'n, why should he feare to die?
Cannot the hand that made him first, restore him?
Deprau'd of sinne, should he depriuèd lie
Of grace? can He not hide[1] infirmitie
  That gaue him strength? vnworthy the forsaking,
    He is, who euer weighs, without mistaking,
Or Maker of the man, or manner of his making.

74.

'Who shall Thy temple incense any more?
Or at Thy altar crowne the sacrifice?
Or strewe with idle flow'rs the hallow'd flore?
Or what should Prayer deck with hearbs and spice
Her vialls, breathing orisons of price?
  If all must paie that which all cannot paie?
    O first begin with mee, and Mercie slaie,
And Thy thrice honour'd Sonne, that now beneath doth
      strey.

---

[1] Southey misprints 'find.' G.

75.

' But if or He or I, may liue, and speake,
And Heau'n can ioye to see a sinner weepe ;
Oh let not Iustice' yron sceptre breake
A heart alreadie broke ; that lowe doth creep,
And with prone humblesse her feets' dust doth sweep.
 Must all goe by desert ? is nothing free ?
 Ah ! if but those that onely woorthy be,
None should Thee euer see, none should Thee euer see.

76.

' What hath man done, that man shall not vndoe,
Since God to him is growne so neer a kin ?
Did his foe slay him ?   He shall slay his foe :
Hath he lost all ?   He all againe shall win :
Is Sinne his master ?   He shall master Sinne :
 Too hardy soule, with Sinne the field to trie :
 The onely way to conquer, was to flie ;
But thus long Death hath liu'd, and now Death's selfe
  shall die.

77.

' He is a path, if any be misled,
He is a robe, if any naked bee ;
If any chaunce to hunger, He is bread,
If any be a bondman, He is free,
If any be but weake, howe strong is Hee !
 To dead men life He is, to sicke men health,
 To blinde men sight, and to the needie wealth ;
A pleasure without losse, a treasure without stealth.

78..

'Who can forget—neuer to be forgot—
The time, that all the world in slumber lies,
When, like the starres, the singing angels shot
To Earth, and Heau'n awakèd all his eyes,
To see another sunne at midnight rise
    On Earth? Was neuer sight of pareil[1] fame;
    For God before, man like Himselfe, did frame,
But God Himselfe now like a mortall man became.

79.

'A Child He was, and had not learn't to speake,
That with His word the world before did make;
His mother's armes Him bore, He was so weake,
That with one hand the vaults of Heau'n could shake;
See how small roome my infant Lord doth take,
    Whom all the world is not enough to hold!
    Who of His yeares, or of His age hath told?
Neuer such age so young, neuer a child so old.

80.

'And yet but newely He was infanted,
And yet alreadie He was sought to die;
Yet scarcely borne, already banishèd
Not able yet to goe, and forc't to flie:
But scarcely fled away, when, by and by,

---

[1] 'Equal.' G.

The tyran's[1] sword with blood is all defil'd,
And Rachel, for her sonnes, with furie wild,
Cries, 'O thou cruell king, and, O my sweetest child!'

81.

'Egypt His nource became, whear Nilus springs,
Who, streit to entertaine the rising sunne,
The hasty haruest in his bosome brings;
But now for drieth[2] the fields wear all vndone,
And now with waters all is ouerrunne:
　　So fast the Cynthian mountaines powr'd their snowe,
　　When once they felt the sunne so neere them glowe,
That Nilus Egypt lost, and to a sea did growe.

82.

'The angells caroll'd lowd their song of peace;
The cursed oracles wear strucken dumb;[3]
To see their Sheapheard, the poor sheapheards press;
To see their King, the kingly Sophies[4] come;
And them to guide vnto his Master's home,

---

[1] The contemporary and later spelling of 'tyrant's.'　G.
[2] Drought.　G.
[3] Cf: Milton's Ode 'on the Morning of Christ's Natiuity'
stanza 19:
　　　　　　'The Oracles are dum,
　　　　　　No voice or hideous humm
　　　　　　Runs through the arched roof.'............G.
[4] Wise men.　Cf: Milton, P.L., X. 435 'Bactrian Sophi'　G.

A starre comes dauncing vp the Orient,
That springs for ioye over the strawy tent,
Whear gold, to make their prince a crowne, they all
    present.

83.

' Young Iohn, glad child ! before he could be borne,
Leapt in the woombe, his ioy to prophecie : [1]
Old Anna, though with age all spent and worne,
Proclaimes her Sauiour to posteritie : [2]
And Simeon fast his dying notes doeth plie.[3]
    Oh, how the blessed soules about Him trace !
    It is the Sire [4] of Heau'n thou dost embrace :
Sing, Simeon, sing—sing, Simeon, sing apace ! '

84.

With that the mightie thunder dropt away
From God's vnwarie [5] arme, now milder growne,

---

[1] St. Luke I. 41.   G.   [2] St. Luke II. 36.   G.
[3] St. Luke II. 29.   G.   [4] Southey misprints 'fire.'   G.
[5] Cf. 'The Purple Island' canto VI. stanza 19, lines 3, 4, where
this special bit is finely praised, and where 'unwares' shews that
Phineas Fletcher understood it as = ' unwary.'

> "And charm'd the nimble lightning in Thy hand,
>   That all *unwares* it dropt in melting tears."

This is bold, perhaps over-bold, but the whole conception of the
contest between Justice and Mercy is carried out with startling
audacity.   See st. 40 and read it in the light of st. 84.   The idea
if not the word itself means—appeased rather than (literally)
unwatchful or unexpecting.   G.

And melted into teares: as if to pray
For pardon, and for pittie, it had knowne,
That should haue been for sacred vengeance throwne:
   Thereto the armies angelique devo'wd
   Their former rage, and all to Mercie bow'd;
Their broken weapons at her feet they gladly strow'd.

85.

'Bring, bring, ye Graces, all your silver flaskets,
Painted with euery choicest flowre that growes,
That I may soone vnflow'r your fragrant baskets,
To strowe the fields with odours whear He goes,
Let what so e're He treads on be a rose.'
   So downe shee let her eyelids fall, to shine
   Vpon the rivers of bright Palestine,
Whose woods drop honie, and her rivers skip with
      wine.

CHRIST'S
VICTORIE AND TRIUMPH
ON EARTH.

L

THE ARGUMENT.

Christ brought into the place of combat, the wildernes, among the wilde beasts : Mark I., 13 : st. 1.—Described by His proper attribute, the Mercie of God : st. 2, 3—Whom the creatures cannot but adore : st. 4, 5,—by His unitie with the Godhead : st. 6.—His proper place : st. 7.—The beautie of His body, Cant. v., 11 ; Psal. XLV., 2 ; Gen. XLIX., 13 ; Cant. v., 10 ; and Isa. LIII., 2 : st. 8—15.—By preparing Himself to the combate with His adversarie that seem'd what he was not : st. 14, 15.—Some devout Essene : st. 16—19.—closely tempting him to despaire of God's prouidence, and prouide for Himself ; st. 20,—But was what he seemed not, Satan, and would faine haue lead Him, 1—To Desperation, characterd by his place, countenance, apparell, horrible apparitions, &c. : st. 21—30.—2—To Presumption : character'd by her place, attendants, &c. : st. 31—36.—and by her temptation st. 37.—3—To Vainglorie : poetically described from the place where her court stood ; a garden : st. 38—49,—from her court and courtiers : st. 51.— (1.) Pleasure in Drinking : st. 50, 51 ; in Luxury ; st. 52 ; (2.) Avarice : st. 53— 55 ; (3.) Ambitious honour : st. 56 ; from her throne, [and] from her temptation : st. 57—59.—The effect of this victorie in Satan : st. 60 ; the angels : st. 61 ; the creatures : st. 62.

1.

THEAR, all alone, she spi'd, alas the while !
  In shadie darknes, a poore Desolate,
That now had measur'd many a wearie mile,
Through a wast desert, whither heau'nly Fate
And His owne will, Him brought ; He praying sate,
    And Him to prey, as He to pray began,[1]
    The citizens of the wilde forrest ran,
And all with open throat would swallowe whole the man.

2.

Soone did the Ladie to her Graces crie,
And on their wings her selfe did nimbly strowe,
After her coach a thousand Loues did flie ;
So downe into the wilderness they throwe ;
Whear she, and all her trayne that with her flowe
    Thorough the ayrie waue, with sayles so gay,
    Sinking into His brest that wearie lay,
Made shipwracke of themselues, and vanish't quite away.

---

[1] Cf. Fuller :
    ' On her that pray'd so long, doth prey at last,'
        ' DAVID'S HEAVIE PUNISHMENT : st. 14.' G.

3.

Seemèd that Man had them devourèd all,
Whome to deuoure the beasts had made pretence;
But Him their saluage thirst did nought appall,
Though weapons none He had for His defence :
What armes for Innocence, but innocence ?
   For when they saw their Lord's bright cognizance
   Shine in His face, soone did they disadvaunce
And some vnto Him kneele, and some about Him
   daunce.

4.

Downe fell the lordly lion's angrie mood,
And he himselfe fell downe in congies[1] lowe ;
Bidding Him welcome to his wastfull wood ;
Sometime he kist the grasse whear He did goe,
And, as to wash His feete he well did knowe,
   With fauning tongue he lickt away the dust ;
   And euery one would neerest to Him thrust,
And euery one, with new, forgot his former lust.

5.

Vnmindfull of himselfe, to minde his Lord,
The lamb stood gazing by the tyger's side,
As though betweene them they had made accord ;
And on the lion's back the goate did ride,
Forgetfull of the roughnes of the hide :

---

[1] Bows = salutations.   G.

If He stood still, their eyes upon Him bayted,
If walkt, they all in order on Him wayted,
And when He slept, they as His watch themselues con-
ceited.

6.

Wonder doeth call me vp to see—O no,
I cannot see, and therefore sinke in woonder :
The Man that shines as bright as God,—not so,
For God He is Himselfe, that close lies vnder
That Man,—so close, that no time can dissunder
That band ; yet not so close, but from Him breake
Such beames, as mortall eyes are all too weake
Such sight to see,—or it, if they should see, to speake.

7.

Vpon a grassie hillock He was laid,
With woodie primroses befreckelèd ;
Ouer His head the wanton shadowes plaid
Of a wilde oliue, that her bowghs so spread,
As with her leavs she seem'd to crowne His head,
And her greene armes to embrace the Prince of
Peace ;
The sunne so neere, needs must the Winter cease,
The sunne so neere, another Spring seem'd to increase.

8.

His haire was blacke, and in small curls did twine,
As though it wear the shadowe of some light ;

And vnderneath, His face, as day did shine—
But sure the day shinèd not halfe so bright,
Nor the sunne's shadowe made so darke a night.
    Vnder His louely locks, her head to shroude,
    Did make [1] Humilitie her selfe growe proude :—
Hither, to light their lamps, did all the Graces croude.

9.

One of ten thousand soules I am, and more,
That of His eyes, and their sweete wounds com-
        plaine :
Sweete are the wounds of Loue, neuer so sore—
Ah ! might He often slaie me so againe !
He neuer liues that thus is neuer slaine.
    What boots it watch ? those eyes for all my art,
    Mine owne eyes looking on, haue stole my heart :
In them Loue bends his bowe, and dips his burning
        dart.

10.

As when the sunne, caught in an aduerse clowde,
Flies crosse the world, and thear a-new begets
The watry picture of his beautie proude :
Throwes all abroad his sparkling spangelets, [2]
And the whole world in dire amazement sets,

---

[1] Cattermole reads 'meek.' G.
[2] Spangles = rays of sunlight broken into drops, *i.e.* diminutive
of 'spangles.' G.

To see two dayes abroad at once ; and all
Doubt whether nowe he rise, or nowe will [1] fall :
So flam'd the Godly flesh, proude of his heau'nly thrall.

11.

His cheekes as snowie apples, sop't in wine, [2]
Had their red roses quencht with lillies white,
And like to garden strawberries did shine,
Wash't in a bowle of milk, or rose-buds bright
Vnbosoming their brests against the light :
  Here loue-sick soules did eat, thear dranke, and made
  Sweete-smelling posies, that could neuer fade,—
But worldly eyes Him thought more like some liuing
  shade.

12.

For Laughter neuer look't upon His browe,
Though in His face all smilling ioyes did bide :
No silken banners did about Him flowe—
Fooles make their fetters ensignes of their pride :
He was the best cloath'd when naked was His side.[3]

---

[1] Richardson and Cattermole misprint 'he.' G.

[2] This seems a curious figure ; but a friend informs me that many years ago when he was young, there was a species of apple called "sops o' wine "—a dark red skin, but the flesh when peeled of most exquisite white and red as if dipped in bright red wine. It is probable that our Poet knew of this apple. G.

[3] Cf. Fuller

  ' Who most was nak't when cloathèd in his weeds '

' David's Heavie Punishment' III. 6. See also the first of his before unpublished Epigrams. G.

A Lambe He was, and wollen fleece He bore,[1]
Woue with one thread : His feete low sandalls wore ;
But barèd were his legges,—so went the times of yore.

13.

As two white marble pillars that vphold
God's holy place, whear He in glorie sets,
And rise with goodly grace and courage bold,
To beare his temple on their ample ietts,[2]
Vein'd euery whear with azure riuulets :
    Whom all the people on some holy morne,
    With boughs and flowrie garlands doe [3] adorne—
Of such, though fairer farre, this temple was vpborne.

14.

Twice had Diana bent her golden bowe,
And shot from hea'un her siluer shafts, to rouse
The sluggish saluages, that den belowe,
And all the day in lazie couvert drouze,
Since Him the silent wildernesse did house :
    The heau'n His roofe and arbour harbour was,
    The ground His bed, and His moist pillowe, grasse ;
But fruit thear none did growe, nor riuers none did
    passe.

---

[1] Richardson and Cattermole misprint 'wore.' G.
[2] 'Projections :' it occurs thus in Sir John Davies. G.
[3] Southey misprints 'to.' G.

15.

At length an aged Syre farre off He sawe
Come slowely footing ; euerie step he guest
One of his feete he from the graue did drawe ;
Three legges he had—the wooden was the best ;[1]
And all the waie he went, he euer blest
   With benedicities, and prayers' store ;
   But the bad ground was blessèd ne'r the more ;
And all his head with snowe of age was waxen hore.

16.

A good old hermit he might seeme to be,
That for deuotion had the world forsaken,
And now was trauailing some Saint to see,
Since to his beads he had himselfe betaken,
Whear all his former sinnes he might awaken,
   And them might wash away with dropping brine,
   And almes, and fasts, and churche's discipline ;
And dead, might rest his bones vnder the holy shrine.

17.

But when he neerer came, he lowted lowe
With prone obeysance, and with curt'sie kinde,
That at his feete his head he seemd to throwe ;—
What needs him now another Saint to finde ?

---

[1] ' You are now come to go on three legs :'   Livesey's ' Greatest
Loss,' as before. G.

Affections are the sailes, and faith the wind,
   That to this Saint a thousand soules conueigh
   Each hour: O happy pilgrims thither strey!
What caren they for beasts, or for the wearie way?

18.

Soone the old palmer his deuotions sung,
Like pleasing anthems, modulèd in time;
For well that aged Syre could tip his tongue
With golden foyle of eloquence, and lime,
And licke his rugged speech with phrases prime.
   'Ay me, quoth he, how many yeares haue beene,
   Since these old eyes the sunne of heau'n have
      scene!
Certes the Sonne of Heau'n they now behold, I weene.

19.

'Ah, mote my humble cell so blessed be,
As Heau'n to welcome in his lowely roofe,
And be the Temple for Thy Deitie!
Loe how my cottage worships Thee aloofe,
That vnder ground hath hid his head, in proofe
   It doth adore Thee with the seeling lowe—
   Here honie, milke, and chesnuts wild doe growe;
The boughs a bed of leaues vpon Thee shall bestowe.

20.

'But oh! he said, and therewith sigh't full deepe,—
The heau'ns, alas! too enuious are growne,

Because our fields Thy presence from them keepe ;
For stones doe growe where corne was lately sowne :
(So stooping downe, he gather'd vp a stone :)
    But Thou with corne canst make this stone to care.
    What needen [1] we the angrie heau'ns to fear?
Let them enuie vs still, so we enioy Thee here.'

21.

Thus on they wandred : but those holy weeds
A monstrous serpent, and no man, did couer :
So vnder greenest hearbs the adder feeds :
And round about that stinking corps did houer
The dismall Prince of gloomie night, and ouer
    His euer-damnèd head the Shadowes err'd [2]
    Of thousand pecant ghosts, vnseene, vnheard,
And all the Tyrant feares, and all the Tyrant fear'd.

22.

He was the Sonne of blackest Acheron,
Whear many frozen soules doe chattring lie,
And rul'd the burning waues of Phlegethon,
Whear many more in flaming sulphur frie,
At once compel'd to liue, and forc't to die ;
    Whear nothing can be heard for the loud crie
    Of ' Oh ! ' and ' Ah ! ' and ' Out alas ! that I
Or once againe might liue, or once at length might
    die ! '

---

[1] Richardson and Cattermole misread ' What need we their....'
G.   [2] Wandered = hovered. G.

23.

Ere long they came neere to a balefull bowre,
Much like the mouth of that infernall caue,
That gaping stood, all commers to deuoure.
"Darke, dolefull, dreary,—like a dreary graue,
That still for carrion carkasses doth craue :"[1]
    The ground no hearbs but venomous, did beare,
    Nor ragged trees did leaue, but euery whear
Dead bones and skulls wear cast, and bodies hangèd
    wear.

24.

Vpon the roofe, the bird of sorrowe sat
Elonging[2] ioyfull day with her sad note,
And through the shady aire, the fluttring bat
Did waue her leather sayles, and blindely flote ;
While with her wings the fatall shreech-owle smote
    Th' vnblessèd house ; thear, on a craggy stone,
    Celeno[3] hung, and made his direfull mone,
And all about the murdered ghosts did shreek, and
    grone.

25.

Like clowdie moonshine, in some shadowie groue
Such was the light in which Despaire did dwell ;

---

[1] Spenser : F. Q., B. i. c. 9. st. 33 : ' dreary '=greedy? G.
[2] Lengthening : Dr Richardson, as before, quotes Fletcher
above. G.
[3] Celæno : one of the harpies. Cf. Æneid. iii. 211. G.

But he himselfe with night for darknesse stroue.
His black uncombèd locks dishevell'd fell
About his face ; through which, as brands of Hell,
  Sunk in his skull, his staring eyes did glowe,
    That made him deadly looke : their glimpse did
    showe
Like cockatrice's eyes, that sparks of poyson throwe.

26.

His cloaths wear ragged clouts, with thornes pind
    fast ;
And, as he musing lay, to stonie fright
A thousand wild Chimeras would him cast :
As when a fearfull dreame, in mid'st of night,
Skips to the braine, and phansies to the sight
  Some wingèd furie, strait the hasty foot,
    Eger [1] to flie, cannot plucke vp his root,
The voyce dies in the tongue, and mouth gapes without
    boot [2]

27.

Now he would dreame that he from heauen fell,
And then would snatch the ayre, afraid to fall ;
And now he thought he sinking was to hell,
And then would grasp the earth ; and now his stall
Him seemèd Hell, and then he out would crawle ;

---

[1] Eager. G.   [2] To no purpose = dumb. G.

And euer, as he crept, would squint aside,
Lest him, perhaps, some furie had espide,
And then, alas ! he should in chaines for euer bide.

28.

Therefore he softly shrunke, and stole away,
Ne euer durst to drawe his breath for feare,
Till to the doore he came, and thear he lay
Panting for breath, as though he dying were ;
And still he thought he felt their craples teare[1]
   Him by the heels backe to his ougly denne ;
   Out faine he would haue leap't abroad, but then
The Heau'n, as Hell he fear'd, that punish guilty men.

29.

Within the gloomie hole of this pale wight
The serpent woo'd Him with his charmes to inne ;
Thear He might baite the day, and rest the night :
But vnder that same baite a fearful grin[2]
Was readie to intangle Him in sinne,
   But He vpon ambrosia daily fed,
   That grew in Eden, thus He answerèd :
So both away wear caught, and to the Temple fled.

---

[1] 'Claws:' Spenser F. Q., v. S. 40. G.

[2] = Gin or trap, as in the English Bible of 1611 in Job XVIII, 9 :
Psalms, CXL., 5: CXLI., 9 Consult Mr W. Aldis Wright's inesti-
mable 'Bible Word-Book' under 'gin.' No one who values genuine
help toward better Bible-knowledge will go without this Word-
Book.' It is truly *multum in parvo.* G.

30.

Well knewe our Sauiour this the serpent was,
And the Old Serpent knewe our Sauiour well;
Neuer did any this in falshood passe,
Neuer did any Him in truth excell:
With Him we fly to Heau'n, from Heau'n we fell
   With him: but nowe they both together met
   Vpon the sacred pinnacles, that threat,
With their aspiring tops, Astræa's starrie seat.

31.

Here did Presvmption her pauillion spread,
Ouer the Temple, the bright starres among;
(Ah! that her foot should trample on the head
Of that most reuerend place!) and a lewd throng
Of wanton boyes sung her a pleasant song
   Of loue, long life, of mercie, and of grace;
   And euery one her deerely did embrace,
And she herselfe enamour'd was of her owne face.

32.

A painted face, belied with vermeyl store,
Which light Euëlpis[1] euery day did trimme,
That in one hand a guilded anchor wore;

---

[1] 'Good Hope' personified: I have not found it elsewhere. Cf. 'The Purple Island,' c. IX. st. 32, where she is personified as Elpinus. G.

Not fixed on the rocke, but on the brimme
Of the wide aire, she let it loosely swimme :
 Her other hand a sprinkle [1] carried,
 And euer, when her Ladie wauerèd,
Court holy-water all vpon her sprinkelèd.

33.

Poor foole ! she thought herselfe in wondrous price
With God, as if in Paradise she wear ;
But, wear she not in a foole's paradise,
She might haue seene more reason to despere :
But Him she, like some ghastly fiend, did feare ;
 And therefore, as that wretch hew'd out his cell
 Vnder the bowels, in the heart of Hell,
So she aboue the moon, amid the starres would dwell.

34.

Her tent with sunny cloudes was seel'd aloft,
And so exceeding shone with a false light,
That heau'n it selfe to her it seemèd oft ;
Heau'n without cloudes to her deluded sight,
But cloudes withouten heau'n it was aright ;
 And as her house was built, so did her braine
 Build castles in the aire, with idle paine,
But heart she neuer had in all her body vaine.

 [1] A vessel having a 'rose' for scattering water finely, as used in a garden : here perhaps the thing used in Roman Catholic churches for 'sprinkling' holy water. G.

35.

Like as a ship in which no ballance [1] lies,
Without a pilot, on the sleeping waues,
Fairely along with winde and water flies,
And painted masts with silken sayles embraues,[2]
That Neptune' selfe the bragging vessel saues,
    To laugh a while at her so proud aray;
    Her wauing streamers loosely shee lets play,
And flagging colours shine as bright as smiling day:

36.

But all so soone as heau'n his browes doth bend,
She veils her banners, and pulls in her beames,
The emptie barke the raging billows send
Vp to the Olympique waues, and Argus seemes
Againe to ride vpon our lower streames:
    Right so Presvmption did her selfe behaue,
    Tossèd about with euery stormie waue,
And in white lawne shee went, most like an angel braue.

37.

Gently our Sauiour shee began to shrive,[3]
Whether He wear the Sonne of God, or no;
For any other she disdeign'd to wive:
And if He wear, shee bid Him fearles throw
Himselfe to ground; and thearwithall did show

---

[1] Qu: ballast? G.   [2] Beautifies. G.
[3] To examine as a confessor. G.

M

A flight of little angels, that did wait,
Vpon their glittering wings, to latch [1] Him strait,
And longèd on their backs to feele His glorious weight.

38.

But when she saw her speech preuailèd nought,
Her selfe she tombled headlong to the flore :
But Him the angels on their feathers caught,
And to an ayrie mountaine nimbly bore,
Whose snowie shoulders, like some chaulkie shore,
    Restles Olympus seem'd to rest vpon,
    With all his swimming globes : so both are gone,
The Dragon with the Lamb—Ah, vnmeet paragon !

39.

All suddenly the hill his snowe deuours,
In liew whereof a goodly garden grew,
As if the snow had melted into flow'rs,
Which their sweet breath in subtill vapours threw,
That all about perfumèd spirits flew :
    For what so euer might aggrate the sense,
    In all the world, or please the appetence,
Heer it was powrèd out in lavish affluence.

40.

Not louely Ida might with this compare,
Though many streames his banks besiluerèd ;

----

[1] Catch: Dr Richardson, as before, quotes Fletcher above. Richardson and Cattermole misread 'launch.' G.

Though Xanthus with his golden sands he bare,
Nor Hibla,[1] though his thyme depasturèd
As faste againe with honie blossomèd ;
   Ne Rhodope, ne Tempe's flow'ry playne :
   Adonis' garden was to this but vayne,
Though Plato on his beds a flood of praise did rayne.

41.

For in all these, some one thing most did grow,
But in this one, grew all things else beside ;
For sweet Varietie herselfe did throw
To euery banke : here all the ground she dide
In lillie white ; there pinks emblazèd wide ;
   And damask't all the earth ; and here shee shed
   Blew violets, and there came roses red ;
And euery sight the yeelding sense, as captiue led.

42.

The garden like a ladie faire was cut,
That lay as if shee slumber'd in delight,
And to the open skies her eyes did shut ;
The azure fields of heau'n wear 'sembled right
In a large round, set with the flow'rs of light,
   The flowr's-de-luce,[2] and the round sparks of deaw,
   That hung vpon the azure leaues, did shew,
Like twinkling starrs, that sparkle in th' eau'ning blew.

[1] Hybla.
[2] Query—Ben Jonson's ' Plant and Flower of Light '= Lily. G.

43.

Vpon a hillie banke her head shee cast,
On which the bowre of Vaine-delight was built;
White and red roses for her face were plac't,
And for her tresses marigolds wear spilt :
Them broadly shee displaid, like flaming guilt,
   Till in the ocean the glad day wear drown'd;
   Then vp againe her yellow locks she wound,
And with greene filletts in their prettie calls[1] them
    bound.

44.

What should I here depeint her lillie hand,
Her veines of violets, her ermine brest,
Which thear in orient colours liuing stand ;
Or how her gowne with silken leaues is drest ;
Or how her watchmen, arm'd with boughie crest,
   A wall of prim[2] hid in his bushes bears,[3]
   Shaking at euery winde their leauie spears,
While she supinely sleeps, ne to be wakèd fears !

45.

Ouer the hedge depends the graping[4] elme,
Whose greener head empurpulèd in wine,

---

[1] Caul=small caps. Cf. Aldis Wright, as before. G.
[2] Privet. G.
[3] The construction is—Or how a wall of prim . . . bears (*i.e.*
a verb)—her watchmen armed, &c. G.
[4] =Grape-supporting. G.

Seemèd to wonder at his bloodie helme,
And halfe suspect the bunches of the vine;
Least they, perhaps, his wit should vndermine.
  For well he knewe such fruit he neuer bore:
  But her weake arms embracèd him the more,
And with her ruby grapes laught at her paramour.

46.

Vnder the shadowe of these drunken elmes
A fountaine rose, where Pangloretta vses
(When her some flood of fancie ouerwhelms,
And one of all her fauorites she chuses)
To bath herselfe, whom she in lust abuses,
  And from his wanton body sucks his soule,
  Which, drown'd in pleasure in that shaly [1] bowle
And swimming in delight, doth amarously rowle! [2]

47.

The font of siluer was, and so his showrs
In siluer fell, onely the guilded bowles
(Like to a fornace, that the min'rall powres)
Seem'd to haue moul't it in their shining holes;
And on the water, like to burning coles,
  On liquid siluer, leaues of roses lay:
  But when Panglorie here did list to play,
Rose-water then it ranne, and milke it rain'd they say

---

[1] Shallow. G.
[2] Nearly all this stanza is omitted by Cattermole. G.

48.

The roofe thicke cloudes did paint, from which three
    boyes
Three gaping mermaides with their cawrs[1] did feed,
Whose brests let fall the streame, with sleepie noise,
To lions mouths, from whence it leapt with speede,
And in the rosie lauer seem'd to bleed.
    The naked boyes unto the water's fall,
    Their stonie nightingales had taught to call,
When Zephyr breath'd into their watry interall.

49.

And all about, embayèd in softe sleepe,
A heard of charmèd beasts aground were spread,
Which the faire witch in goulden chaines did keepe,
And them in willing bondage fetterèd ;
Once men they liu'd, but now the men were dead,
    And turn'd to beasts ; so fablèd Homer old,
    That Circe with her potion, charm'd in gold,
Vs'd manly soules in beastly bodies to immould.

50.

Through this false Eden, to his leman's bowre,
(Whome thousand soules devoutly idolize)
Our first destroyer led our Sauiour :
Thear in the lower roome, in solemne wise,
They daunc't around, and powr'd their sacrifice

---

[1] Ewers = vases.   G.

To plumpe Lyæus,[1] and among the rest,
  The iolly priest, in yuie garlands drest,
Chaunted wilde orgialls, in honour of the feast.

51.

Others within their arbours swilling sat,
(For all the roome about was arbourèd)
With laughing Bacchus, that was growne so fat,
That stand he could not, but was carrièd,
And euery euening freshly waterèd,
  To quench his fierie cheeks, and all about
  Small cocks broke through the wall, and sallied out
Flagons of wine, to set on fire that spueing rout.

52.

This their inhumèd soules esteem'd their wealths,
To crowne the bouzing kan from day to night,
And sicke to drinke themselues, with drinking healths;
Some vomitting, all drunken with delight.
Hence to a loft, carv'd all in yvorie white,
  They came, whear whiter ladies naked went,
  Melted in pleasure and soft languishment,
And sunke in beds of roses, amourous glaunces sent.[2]

53.

Flie, flie, Thou holy Child, that wanton roome!
And thou, my chaster Muse, those harlots shun,

---

[1] Bacchus. G.

[2] Cattermole drops out st. 51 & 52 without indicating the omission. G.

And with Him to a higher storie come,
Whear mounts of gold, and flouds of siluer run,
The while the owners, with their wealth vndone,
   Starve in their store, and in their plenty pine,
   Tumbling themselues vpon their heaps of mine,[1]
Glutting their famish't soules with the deceitful shine.

54.

Ah! who was he such pretious perills found?
How strongly Nature did her treasures hide,
And threw vpon them[2] mountains of thicke ground,
To darke their orie lustre! but queint Pride
Hath taught her sonnes to wound their mother's side,
   And gage[3] the depth, to search for flaring shells,
   In whose bright bosome spumie[4] Bacchus swells,
That neither heau'n nor earth henceforth in safetie dwells.

55.

O sacred hunger of the greedie eye,
Whose neede hath end, but no end covetise,
Emptie in fulnes, rich in pouertie,
That hauing all things, nothing can suffice,
How thou befanciest the men most wise!

---

[1] = Heaps from the mine. G.
[2] Richardson and Cattermole misread 'him.' G.
[3] Gauge. G.
[4] Foamy: Dr Richardson, as before, quotes Fletcher above. Cf. Milton P.L., VI. 479 'fierie spume.' G.

The poore man would be rich, the rich man great,
The great man king, the king, in God's owne seat
Enthron'd, with mortal arme dares flames and thunder
    threat.

56.

Therefore aboue the rest Ambition sat;
His court with glitterant pearle was all enwall'd,
And round about the wall in Chaires of State,
And most majestique splendor, were enstall'd
A hundred kings, whose temples wear impal'd
   In goulden diadems, set here and thear
   With diamounds, and gemmèd euerywhear,
And of their golden virges [1] none disceptred wear.

57.

High over all Panglorie's blazing throne,
In her bright turret, all of christal wrought,
Like Phœbus' lampe, in midst of heauen, shone;
Whose starry top with pride infernall fraught,
Selfe-arching columns to vphold wear taught:
   In which her image still reflected was
   By the smooth christall, that, most like her glasse,
In beauty and in frailtie, did all others passe.

58.

A siluer wande the sorceresse did sway,
And, for a crowne of gold, her haire she wore;

---

[1] Rods : Dr Richardson here also quotes Fletcher. G.

Onely a garland of rose-buds did play
About her locks; and in her hand she bore
A hollowe globe of glasse, that long before [9]
  She full of emptinesse had bladderèd,
  And all the world therein depicturèd :
Whose colours, like the rainbowe, euer vanishèd.

59.

Such watry orbicles [1] young boyes do blowe
Out of their sopy shells, and much admire
The swimming world, which tenderly they rowe
With easie breath, till it be wauèd higher :
But if they chaunce but roughly once aspire,
  The painted bubble instantly doth fall.
  Here when she came, she 'gan for musique call,
And sung this wooing song, to welcome Him withall :—

  Loue is the blossome whear thear blowes
  Euery thing that liues or growes :
  Loue doth make the heau'ns to moue,
  And the sun doth burne in loue :
  Loue the strong and weake doth yoke,
  And makes the yuie climbe the oke ;
  Vnder whose shadowes lions wilde,
  Soft'ned by loue, growe tame and mild ;
  Loue no med'cine can appease,
  He burnes the fishes in the seas ;

---

[1] Soap-bubbles.   Dr Richardson, as before, quotes Fletcher
above. G.

Not all the skill his wounds can stench,[1]
Not all the sea his fire can quench :
Loue did make the bloody spear
Once a leuie coat to wear,
While in his leaues thear shrouded lay
Sweete birds, for loue, that sing and play :
And of all loue's ioyfull flame,
I the bud and blossome am :
  Onely bend Thy knee to mee,
  Thy wooeing shall Thy winning bee.

See, see the flowers that belowe,
Now as fresh as morning blowe ;
And of all, the virgin rose,
That as bright Aurora showes ;
How they all vnleauèd die,
Loosing their virginitie ;
Like vnto a summer-shade,
But now borne, and now they fade.
Euery thing doth passe away,
Thear is danger in delay :
Come, come gather then the rose,
Gather it, or it you lose :
All the sand of Tagus' shore
Into my bosome casts his o re :
All the valleys' swimming corne
To my house is yeerely borne ;

[2] Staunch. G.

Euery grape of euery vine
Is gladly bruis'd to make me wine,
While ten thousand kings, as proud,
To carry vp my train haue bow'd,
And a world of ladies send me
In my chambers to attend me :
All the starres in heau'n that shine,
And ten thousand more, are mine.
　　Onely bend Thy knee to mee,
　　Thy wooing shall Thy winning bee.

60.

Thus sought the dire Enchauntress in His minde
Her guilefull bayt to haue embosomèd ;
But He her charmes dispersèd into winde,
And her of insolence admonishèd ;
And all her optique glasses shatterèd.
　So with her sire to Hell shee took her flight,
　(The starting ayre flew from the damnèd spright,)
Whear deeply both[1] aggriev'd, plungèd themselues in
　　night.

61.

But to their Lord, now musing in His thought,
A heauenly volie of light angels flew,
And from His Father Him a banquet brought,
Through the fine element ; for well they knew,
After His Lenten fast He hungrie grew ;

[1] = Presumption and Satan.   G.

And, as He fed, the holy quires combine
To sing a hymne of the celestiall Trine ;
All thought to passe, and each was past all thought
    divine.

62.

The birds' sweet notes, to sonnet out their ioyes,
Attemper'd to the layes angelicall ;
And to the birds, the winds attune their noyse,
And to the winds, the waters hoarcely call,
And Eccho back againe revoycèd all ;
    That the whole valley rung with victorie.
    But now our Lord to rest doth homeward flie :
See how the Night comes stealing from the mountains
    high !

CHRIST'S
TRIVMPH OVER DEATH.

THE ARGUMENT.

Christ's tryumph ouer death on the crosse, exprest. I. In generall by His ioy to vndergoe it, singing before He went to the garden : Matt. xxvi. 30, st. 1—3—by His griefe in the vndergoing it : st. 4—6—by the obscure fables of the Gentiles typing it : st. 7, 8—by the cause of it in Him, His loue : st. 9—by the effect it should haue in us : st. 10—12—by the instrument, the cursed tree : st. 13.—II. Exprest in particular : 1. By His fore-passion in the garden : st. 14—25—by His passion it selfe amplified. (1.) From the general causes : st. 26, 27 : parts, and effects of it : st. 28, 29. (2.) From the particular causes : st. 30, 31 parts, and effects of it—in heauen : st. 32—36—in the heauenly spirits : st. 37—in the creatures sub-celestiall : st. 38—in the wicked Jewes : st. 39—in Iudas : st. 40—51—in the blessed saints, Ioseph [of Arimathea,] &c., st. 52—67.

1.

SO downe the siluer streames of Eridan,[1]
  On either side bank't with a lilly wall,
Whiter then both, rides the triumphant swan,
And sings his dirge, and prophesies his fall,
Diuing into his watrie funerall :
  But Eridan to Cedron must submit
  His flowry shore ; nor can he enuie it,
If when Apollo sings, his swans doe silent sit.

2.

That heau'nly voice I more delight to heare,
Then gentle ayres to breath, or swelling waues
Against the sounding rocks their bosomes teare,
Or whistling reeds, that rutty[2] Iordan laues,
And with their verdure his white head embraues

---

[1] The Po : The Saviour as "He singing goes" (st. 3) over
Cedron to His death, is likened to the "triumphant swan" sailing
down the silver Po—whiter than the lilies on its banks, and singing
its dirge before it dies. G.

[2] Query, 'course'-forming Jordan? Dr Richardson, as before,
quotes under 'rut.' G.

To chide the windes, or hiuing bees, that flie
About the laughing bloosms of sallowie,[1]
Rocking asleepe the idle groomes that lazie lie.

3

And yet, how can I heare Thee singing goe,
When men incens'd with hate Thy death foreset?
Or els, why doe I heare Thee sighing so,
When Thou inflam'd with loue, their life doest get,
That loue, and hate, and sighs, and songs are met;
   But thus, and onely thus Thy loue did craue,
   To sende Thee singing for vs to Thy graue,
While we sought Thee to kill, and Thou sought'st vs to
    saue.

4.

When I remember Christ our burden beares,
I looke for glorie, but find miserie;
I looke for ioy, but finde a sea of teares;
I looke that we should liue, and finde Him die;
I looke for angels' songs, and heare Him crie:
   Thus what I looke I cannot finde so well;
   Or rather, what I finde, I cannot tell,
These bankes so narrowe are, those streames so highly
    swell.

5.

Christ suffers, and in this His teares begin;
Suffers for vs—and our ioy springs in this;

---

[1] Willows : Cf. Dr Richardson as before, s. v.   G.

Suffers to death—here is His manhood seen ;
Suffers to rise—and here His Godhead is.
For man, that could not by himselfe haue ris,
  Out of the graue doth by the Godhead rise,
  And God, that could not die, in manhood dies,
That we in both might liue by that sweete sacrifice.

6.

Goe, giddy braines, whose witts are thought so fresh,
Plucke all the flowrs that Nature forth doth throwe,
Goe sticke them on the cheekes of wanton flesh ;
Poor idol (forc't at once to fall and growe)
Of fading roses, and of melting snowe !
  Your songs exceede your matter; this of mine
  The matter which it sings, shall make diuine :
The starres dull puddles guild, in which their beauties
    shine.

7.

Who doth not see drown'd in Deucalion's[1] name
(When earth his men, and sea had lost his shore)
Old Noah? and in Nisus'[2] lock, the fame
Of Sampson yet aliue ; and long before
In Phaëthon's, mine owne fall I deplore :
  But he that conquer'd hell, to fetch againe
  His virgin widowe, by a serpent slaine,
Another Orpheus was then dreaming poets feigne :

---

[1] Ovid, *Met.* I. 260, &c. G.
[2] Apollod. III. 15. §§ 5, 6, 8. G.

8.

This taught the stones to melt for passion,
And dormant sea, to heare him, silent lie;
And at his voice, the watrie nation
To flocke, as if they deem'd it cheape, to buy
With their owne deaths his sacred harmonie:
    The while the waues stood still to heare his song,
    And steadie shore wau'd with the reeling throng
Of thirstie soules, that hung vpon his fluent tongue.

9.

What better friendship then to couer shame?
What greater loue then for a friend to die?
Yet this is better to asself the blame;[1]
And this is greater, for an enemie:
But more then this, to die, not suddenly,
    Nor with some common death, or easie paine,
    But slowely, and with torments to be slaine;
O depth, without a depth, farre better seene, then saine![2]

10.

And yet the Sonne is humblèd for the slaue,
And yet the slaue is proude before the Sonne;
Yet the Creator for His creature gaue
Himselfe and yet the creature hasts to runne
From his Creator, and self-good doth shunne;

---

[1] Self-blame. G.   [2] Said. G.

And yet the Prince, and God Himselfe doth crie
To man, His traitour, pardon not to flie :
Yet man his[1] God, and traytour doth his prince defie.

11.

Who is it sees not that he nothing is,
But he that nothing sees ?   What weaker brest,
Since Adam's armour fail'd, dares warrant his ?
That, made by God of all His creatures best,
Strait made himselfe the woorst of all the rest :
  " If any strength we haue, it is to ill ;
  " But all the good is God's, both pow'r and will : "
The dead man cannot rise, though he himself may kill.

12.

But let the thorny Schools their punctualls
Of wills, all good, or bad, or neuter diss :[2]
Such ioy we gainèd by our parentalls,
That good, or bad, whether I cannot wiss,
To call it a mishap or happy miss,
  That fell from Eden, and to Heau'n did rise :
  Albee the mitred card'nall more did prize
His part in Paris then his part in Paradise.[3]

---

[1] Cattermole misprints 'is.' G.   [2] = Discuss? G.
[3] A favourite monition of the Puritan Divinity, *e.g.* Thomas
Brooks of Cardinal BORBONIUS : Cf. my edn. of BROOKS, Vol. IV.
p. 55 : and under BOURBON in Index. G.

13.

A tree was first the instrument of strife,
Whear Eue to sinne her soul did prostitute ;
A tree is now the instrument of life,
Though ill that trunke and this faire body suit :
Ah, cursed tree ! and yet O blessed fruit ! [1]
  That death to Him, this life to vs doth giue :
  Strange is the cure, when things past cure reviue,
And the Physitian dies, to make his patient liue.

14.

Sweete Eden was the arbour of delight,
Yet in his hony flowrs our poyson blew ;
Sad Gethseman the bowre of balefull night,
Whear Christ a health of poyson for vs drewe,
Yet all our hony in that poyson grewe :
  So we from sweetest flowrs could sucke our bane,
  And Christ from bitter venome could againe
Extract life out of death, and pleasure out of paine.

---

[1] Very pretty is St. Austin's remark upon this passage : [St. Luke XXIII. 45] "Christ," saith he, " in rescuing the poor thief upon the cross was but quits with the devil, for the devil took man from God out of the midst of Paradise ; Christ takes this poor man from Satan, when he was no less than in the very jaws of hell. *Satan ruined man on the forbidden tree,* and Christ saves them on the cursed tree." MARCH *in loco,* quoted by FORD in the Gospel of St. Luke Illustrated. G.

15.

A man was first the author of our fall,
A man is now the author of our rise ;
A garden was the place we perisht all,
A garden is the place He payes our price ;
And the Old Serpent with a newe deuise,
   Hath found a way himselfe for to beguile :
   So he, that all men tangled in his wile,
Is now by one man caught, beguil'd with his own guile.

16.

The dewie night had with her frostie shade
Immant'led all the world, and the stiffe ground
Sparkled in yce ; onely the Lord, that made
All for Himselfe, Himselfe dissolvèd found :
Sweat without heat ; and bled without a wound :
   Of heau'n, and earth, and God, and man forlore,[1]
   Thrice begging helpe of those whose sinnes He bore,
And thrice denièd of those, not to denie had swore.[2]

---

[1] Forlorn, lost : Dr Richardson, as before, quotes Fletcher above.
G.

[2] Richardson and Cattermole change 'those' into 'one,' and,
literally taken, the correction is admissible : but they overlook—as
is commonly done—that all the disciples had made the same pro-
fession and promise with St. Peter, *e.g.* St. Mark xiv. 31. [St.
Peter] " He spake the more vehemently, If I should die with Thee,
I will not denie Thee in any wise. *Likewise also said they all.*"—
By 'forsaking' Him and 'fleeing' they all 'denied' their Lord

17.

Yet had He beene alone of God forsaken,
Or had His bodie beene imbroyl'd alone
In fierce assault; He might, perhaps haue taken
Some ioy in soule, when all ioy els was gone;
But that with God—and God to heau'n is flow'n :
   And Hell it selfe out from her graue doth rise,
   Black as the starles night : and with them flies,
Yet blacker then they both, the sonne of blasphemies.

18.

As when the planets with vnkind aspect,
Call from her caues the meager pestilence;
The sacred vapour, eager to infect,
Obeyes the voyce of the sad influence,
And vomits vp a thousand noysome sents :
   The well of life, flaming his golden flood
   With the sicke ayre, fevers the boyling blood,
And poysons all the bodie with contagious food.

19.

The bold physitian, too incautelous,
By those he cures himselfe is murdered;

though only St. Peter's articulate denial is told in detail. He
indeed excelled the others, for he 'followed' still, albeit 'afar off.'
Hence Fletcher, in the spirit, and looking deeper than Richardson'
Cattermole, and the rest, is accurate :=And thrice denied (*i.e.*
refused) the help He thrice begged (see previous line) in the Garden, by those who had sworn not to deny (in another sense).   G.

Kindnes infects, pitie is dangerous ;
And the poore infant, yet not fully bred,
Thear whear he should be borne, lies burièd.
  So the darke prince, from his infernall cell,
  Casts vp his griesly torturers of Hell,
And whets them to revenge, with this insulting spell :—

20.

' See how the world smiles in eternall peace ;
While we, the harmles brats and rustie throng
Of night, our snakes in curles doe pranke and dresse :
Why sleep our drouzie scorpions so long ?
Whear is our wonted vertue to doe wrong ?
  Are we our selues ? or are we Graces growen ?
  The sonnes of hell or heau'n ? was neuer knowne
Our whips so ouer-moss't and brands so deadly blowne !

21.

' O long desirèd, neuer-hop't for howre,
When our Tormentour shall our torments feele !
Arme, arme, your selues, sad Dires[1] of my pow'r,
And make our Iudge for pardon to vs kneele :
Slise, launch,[2] dig, teare Him with your whips of steele :
  My selfe in honour of so noble prize,
  Will powre you reaking blood, shed with the cries
Of hastie heyres,[3] who their owne fathers sacrifice.

---

[1] Diræ, the Furies. G.   [2] = Lance. G.   [3] Heirs. G.

22.

With that a flood of poyson, blacke as Hell,
Out from his filthy gorge, the beast did spue,
That all about His blessed bodie fell,
And thousand flaming serpents hissing flew
About His soule, from hellish sulphur threw,
     And euery one brandish't his firie tongue,
     And woorming all about His soule they clung;
But He their stings tore out, and to the ground them
     flung.

23.

So haue I seene a rock's heroique brest,
Against proud Neptune, that his ruin threats,
When all his waues he hath to battle prest,
And with a thousand swelling billows beats
The stubborne stone, and foams, and chafes, and frets
     To heaue him from his root, vnmooued stand;
     And more in heapes the barking surges [1] band,
The more in pieces beat, flie weeping to the strand.

24.

So may wee oft a vent'rous father see,
To please his wanton sonne, his onely ioy,
Coast all about, to catch the roving bee,

---

[1] Cf. Milton later in Comus (l. 258) "chid her barking waues."   G.

And stung himselfe, his busie hands employ
To saue the honie for the gamesome boy ;
   Or from the snake her rank'rous teeth erace,
   Making his child the toothles serpent chace,
Or, with his little hands, her tum'rous [1] gorge embrace.

25.

Thus Christ Himselfe to watch and sorrow giues,
While deaw'd in heavie sleepe, dead Peter lies :
Thus man in his owne graue securely liues,
While Christ aliue, with thousand horrours dies,
Yet more for theirs then His owne pardon cries :
   No sinnes He had, yet all our sinnes He bare ;
   So much doth God for others' euills care,
And yet so careles men for their owne euills are.

26.

See drouzie Peter, see whear Iudas wakes,
Whear Iudas kisses Him whom Peter flies :
O kisse more deadly then the sting of snakes !
False loue more hurtfull then true injuries !
Aye me ! how deerly God His seruant buies !
   For God His man at His owne blood doth hold,
   And man his God, for thirtie pence hath sold :
So tinne for siluer goes, and dunghill drosse for gold.

---

[1] Southey misprints 'tim'rous.' G.

27.

Yet was it not enough for Sinne to chuse
A seruant, to betray his Lord to them ;
But that a subiect must his king accuse ;
But that a pagan must his God condemne ;
But that a Father must His Sonne contemne,
  But that the Sonne must His owne death desire ;
  That prince and people, seruant and the Sire,
Gentil and Jewe, and He against Himselfe conspire ?

28.

Was this the oyle, to make thy saints adore Thee,
The froathy spittle of the rascall throng ?
Are these the virges,[1] that ar borne before Thee,
Base whipps of corde, and knotted all along ?
Is this thy golden scepter against wrong,
  A reedie cane ? is that the crowne adornes
  Thy shining locks, a crowne of spiny thornes ?
Ar theas the angels' himns, the priests' blasphemous
    scornes ?

29.

Who euer sawe Honour before asham'd ;
Afflicted Majestie ; debasèd Height ;
Innocence guiltie ; Honestie defam'd ;
Libertie bound ; Health sick ; the sunne in night ?
But since such wrong was offred vnto Right,

[1] Rods, as before.   G.

Our night is day, our sicknes health is growne
Our shame is veil'd : this now remaines alone
For vs : since He was ours that wee bee not our owne.

30.

Night was ordeyn'd for rest, and not for paine,
But they, to paine their Lord, their rest contemne ;
Good lawes to saue what bad men would haue slaine,
And not bad iudges, with one breath, by them
The innocent to pardon, and condemne :
 Death for reuenge of murderers, not decaie
 Of guiltles blood : but now, all headlong sway
Man's murderer to saue, man's Sauiour to slaie.

31.

Fraile multitude ! whose giddy lawe is list [1]
And best applause is windy flattering ;
Most like the breath of which it doth consist,
No sooner blowne but as soone vanishing,
As much desir'd as little profiting ;
 That makes the men that haue it oft as light
 As those that giue it ; which the proud inuite,
And feare ;—the bad man's friend, the good man's hypo-
  crite.

32.

It was but now their sounding clamours sung,
'Blessèd is He that comes from the Most High !'

   [1] Choice. G.

And all the mountaines with ' Hosanna !' rung ;
And nowe, 'Away with Him—away !' they crie,
And nothing can be heard but ' Crucifie !'
    It was but now, the crowne it selfe they saue
    And golden name of King vnto Him gaue ;
And nowe, no king, but onely Cæsar, they will haue.

33.

It was but now they gatherèd blooming May,
And of his armes disrob'd the branching tree,
To strowe with boughs and blossomes all Thy[1] way ;
And now the branchlesse truncke a crosse for Thee
And May dismai'd, Thy coronet must be :
    It was but now they wear so kind, to throwe
    Their owne best garments whear Thy feet should goe,
And now, Thy selfe they strip, and bleeding wounds
      they show.

34.

See whear the Author of all life is dying :
O fearefull day ! He dead, what hope of liuing ?
See whear the hopes of all our liues are buying :
O chearfull day ! they bought, what feare of grieuing ?
Loue, loue for hate, and death for life is giuing :
    Loe, how His armes are stretcht abroad to grace thee,
    And, as they open stand, call to embrace thee !
Why stai'st Thou then, my soule? O flie, flie, thither,
      hast thee !

[1] Cattermole misprints ' the.' G.

35.

His radious head, with shamefull thornes they teare,
His tender backe, with bloody whipps they rent,
His side and heart they furrowe with a spear,
His hands and feete, with riuing nayles they tent;[1]
And, as to disentrayle His soule they meant,
   They iolly at his griefe, and make their game,
   His naked body to expose to shame,
That all might come to see, and all might see, that
   came.

36.

Whereat the heau'n put out his guiltie eye,
That durst behold so execrable sight,
And sabled all in blacke the shadie skie;
And the pale starres, strucke with vnwonted fright,
Quenchèd their euerlasting lamps in night;
   And at His birth, as all the starres heau'n had
   Wear not enough, but a newe star was made,
So now, both newe and old and all, away did fade.

37.

The mazèd[2] angels shooke their fierie wings,
Readie to lighten vengeance from God's throne,
One downe his eyes vpon the manhood flings,
Another gazes on the Godhead : none
But surely thought his wits were not his owne;

---

[1] Stretch : Dr Richardson has overlooked this example. G.
[2] Southey misprints 'amazed.' G.

Some flew to looke if it wear very Hee
But when God's arm vnarmèd they did see,
Albee they sawe it was, they vow'd it could not bee.

38.

The sadded aire hung all in cheerlesse blacke,
Through which the gentle windes soft sighing flewe,
And Iordan into such huge sorrowe brake,
(As if his holy streame no measure knewe,)
That all his narrowe bankes he ouerthrewe;
 The trembling earth with horrour inly shooke,
 And stubborne stones, such griefe vnus'd to brooke,
Did burst, and ghosts awaking from their graues gan
  looke.

39.

The wise philosopher cried, all agast,
'The God of Nature surely languishèd!'
The sad Centurion cried out as fast,
The Sonne of God, the Sonne of God was dead;[1]
The headlong Iew hung downe his pensiue head,
 And homewards far'd; and euer, as he went,
 He smote his brest, half desperately bent:
The verie woods and beasts did seeme His death lament.

40.

The gracelesse traytour round about did looke
(He lok't not long, the deuill quickely met him)

[1] St. Luke XXIII. 47. G.

To finde a halter, which he found, and tooke;
Onely a gibbet nowe he needes must get him;
So on a wither'd tree he fairly set him.
    And helpt him fit the rope, and in his thought
    A thousand furies with their whippes, he brought;
So thear he stands, readie to Hell to make his vault.

41.

For him a waking bloodhound, yelling loude,
That in his bosome long had sleeping layde;
A guiltie conscience, barking after blood,
Pursuèd eagerly, ne euer stai'd
Till the betrayer's selfe it had betray'd.
    Oft chang'd he place, in hope away to winde;
    But change of place could neuer change his minde:
Himselfe he flies to loose, and followes for to finde.

42.

Thear is but two wayes for this soule to haue,
When parting from the body, forth it purges;
To fly to heau'n, or fall into the graue,
Where whippes of scorpions, with the stinging scourges,
Feed on the howling ghosts, and firie surges
    Of brimstone, rowle about the caue of night;
    Where flames doe burne, and yet no sparke of light,
And fire both fries and freezes the blaspheming spright.
                               O

43.

Thear lies the captiue soule, aye-sighing sore,
Reckoning a thousand yeares since her first bands;
Yet staies not thear, but addes a thousand more,
And at another thousand neuer stands,
But tells to them the starres, and heapes the sands :
    And now the starres are told, and sands are runne,
    And all those thousand thousand myriads done,
And yet but now, alas ! but now all is begunne.

44.

With that a flaming brand a Furie catch't
And shooke, and tos't it rounde in his wilde thought :
So from his heart all ioy, all comfort snatch't
With eu'ry starre of hope ; and as he sought
(With present feare, and future griefe distraught)
    To flie from his owne heart, and aide implore
    Of Him, the more He giues, that hath the more,
Whose storehouse is the heauens, too little for His store:

45.

'Stay wretch on earth,' cried Satan—'restles rest ;
Know'st thou not Iustice liues in heau'n ; or can
The worst of creatures liue among the best :
Among the blessèd angels cursèd man ?
Will Iudas now become a Christian ?

Whither will Hope's long wings transport thy minde?
Or canst thou not thy selfe a sinner finde?
Or cruell to thy selfe, wouldst thou haue Mercie kinde?

46.

'He gave thee life : why shouldst thou seeke to slay Him?
He lent thee wealth : to feed thy avarice?
He cal'd thee friend: what, that thou shouldst betray Him?
He kis't thee, though He knew His life the price ;
He wash't thy feet : shouldst thou His sacrifice?
 He gaue thee bread, and wine, His bodie, blood,
 And at thy heart, to enter in He stood ;
But then I entred in, and all my snakie brood.[1]

47.

As when wild Pentheus, growne madde with fear,
Whole troupes of hellish haggs about him spies ;
Two bloodie sunnes stalking the duskie sphear,
And twofold Thebes runs rowling in his eyes ;
Or through the scene staring Orestes flies,
 With eyes flung back vpon his mother's ghost,
 That, with infernall serpents all embost,
And torches quencht in blood, doth her stern sonne
  accost : [2]

48.

Such horrid Gorgons, and misformèd formes
Of damnèd fiends, flew dauncing in his heart,

---

[1] Euripides, Bacch. 816, 954, &c.: Theocritus XXVI. 10.   G.
[2] See Euripides, Sophocles, Aeschylus.   G.

That, now, vnable to endure their stormes,
'Flie, flie,' he cries, 'thyselfe, what ere thou art,
Hell, hell, alreadie burnes in eu'ry part.'
   So downe into his torturer's armes he fell,
   That readie stood his funeralls to yell,
And in a clowd of night to waft him quick [1] to Hell.

49.

Yet oft he snatch't, and started as he hung :
So when the senses halfe enslumb'red lie,
The headlong bodie, readie to be flung
By the deluding phansie, from some high
And craggie rock, recovers greedily,
   And clasps the yeelding pillow, halfe asleep
   And, as from heav'n it tombled to the deepe,
Feeles a cold sweat through euery trembling member
    creepe.

50.

Thear [2] let him hang, embowellèd in blood,
Thear neuer any gentle shepheard feed
His blessed flocks, nor euer heav'nly flood [3]
Fall on the cursed ground, nor holesome seed,
That may the least delight or pleasure breed :

---

[1] Living, alive, as before. G.
[2] Misprinted 'Whear.' G.
[3] Richardson and Cattermole misprint 'food.' G.

Let neuer Spring visit his habitation,
But nettles, kixe,[1] and all the weedie nation,
With emptie elders grow : sad signes of desolation !

51.

Thear let the Dragon keep his habitance,
And stinking karcasses be throwne avaunt ;
Faunes, Sylvans, and deformèd Satyrs daunce,
Wild-cats, wolues, toads, and skreech-owles direly chaunt;
Thear euer let some restles spirit haunt,
 With hollow sound, and clashing cheynes, to scarr
 The passenger, and eyes like to the starr
That sparkles in the crest of angrie Mars afarr.

52.

But let the blessed deawes for euer showr
Vpon that ground, in whose faire fields I spie
The bloodie ensigne of our Sauiour :
Strange conquest, whear the Conquerour must die,
And He is slaine, that winns the victorie !
 But He that liuing, had no house, to owe it,
 Now had no graue : but Ioseph must bestowe it :
O runne, ye saints apace, and with sweete flowrs
  bestrowe it !

---

[1] Hemlock. The late lamented Dr Tregelles informed me that in Welsh and the ancient Cornwall, the word is *cegyx ;* the *c* being hard *k*.   G.

53.

And ye glad spirits, that now sainted sit
On your cœlestiall thrones, in beawtie drest,
Though I your teares recoumpt, O let not it
With after-sorrowe wound your tender brest,
Or with new griefe vnquiet your soft rest :
    Inough is me your plaints to sound againe
    That neuer could inough my selfe complaine :
Sing, then, O sing aloude, thou Arimathean swaine !

54.

But long he stood, in his faint arms vphoulding
    The fairest spoile heau'n euer forfeited,
With such a silent passion griefe vnfoulding
That, had the sheete but on himselfe beene spread,
He for the corse might haue been buried :
    And with him stood the happie theefe that stole
    By night his owne saluation, and a shole
Of Maries, drownèd, round about him sat, in dole.

55.

At length (kissing His lipps before he spake,
As if from thence he fetcht againe His ghost)
To Mary thus, with teares, his silence brake :
' Ah, woefull soule ! what ioy in all our cost,
When Him we hould, we haue alreadie lost ?

Once did'st thou loose thy Sonne, but found'st againe,
Now find'st thy Sonne, but find'st Him lost and slaine.
Ay mee! though He could death, how canst thou life
    sustaine?

56.

' Whear ere, deere Lord, thy Shadowe houereth,
Blessing the place, wherein it deigns abide,
Looke how the Earth darke horrour couereth,
Cloathing in mournfull black her naked side,
Willing her shadowe vp to heau'n to glide,
    To see, and if it meet Thee wandring thear;
    That so, and if her selfe must misse Thee hear,
At least her shadow may her dutie to Thee bear.

57.

' See how the sunne in day-time cloudes his face,
And lagging Vesper, loosing his late teame,
Forgets in heau'n to runne his nightly race;
But, sleeping on bright Oeta's[1] top, doeth dreame
The world a chaos is; no ioyfull beame
    Looks from his starrie bowre, the heau'ns do mone,
    And trees drop teares, least we should greeue alone;
The windes haue learn't to sigh, and waters hoarcely
    grone.

58.

' And you sweete flow'rs, that in this garden growe,
Whose happie states a thousand soules enuie!

    [1] Mountain in south of Thessaly. G.

Did you your owne felicities but knowe,
Yourselues, vnpluckt [1] would to his funerals hie—
You neuer could in better season die :
   O that I might into your places slide !
   The gate of heau'n stands gaping in His side ; [2]
Thear in my soule should steale, and all her faults should
    hide. [3]

59.

'Are theas the eyes that made all others blind ?
Ah ! why ar they themselues now blemishèd ?
Is this the face, in which all beawtie shin'd ?
What blast hath thus His flowers debellishèd ?
Ar these the feete that on the watry head
   Of the vnfaithfull ocean passage found ?
   Why goe they now so lowely vnder ground,
Wash't with our woorthless tears, and their owne pre-
    cious wound ?

60.

'One hem but of the garments that He wore
Could medicine [4] whole countries of their paine ;
One touch of this pale hand could life restore ;
One word of these cold lips reuiue the slaine :
Well, the blinde man, Thy Godhead might maintaine :

---

[1] Southey misprints 'uppluck'd.'   G.
[2] Cf. Hebrews x. 20.   G.
   [3] "Rock of Ages ! cleft for me
     Let me hide myself in Thee."—TOPLADY.   G.
[4] A Shakesperian word.   See Cymbeline IV. 2, and Othello
   III. 3.   G.

What, though the sullen Pharises repin'd ?
He that should both compare, at length would finde
The blinde man onely sawe, the seers all wear blinde.

61.

' Why should they thinke Thee worthy to be slaine ?
Was it because Thou gau'st their blinde men eyes ?
Or that Thou mad'st their lame to walke againe ?
Or for Thou heal'dst their sick men's maladies ?
Or mad'st their dumbe to speake, and dead to rise ?
  O could all these but any grace haue woon,
  What would they not to saue Thy life haue done ?
The dumb man would haue spoke, and lame man would
    haue runne.

62.

' Let mee, O let me neere some fountaine lie,
That through the rocke heaues vp his sandie head ;
Or let me dwell vpon some mountaine high,
Whose hollowe root and baser parts ar spread
On fleeting waters, in his bowells bred,
  That I their streames, and they my teares may feed :
  Or, cloathèd in some hermit's ragged weed,
Spend all my daies, in weeping for this cursèd deed.

63.

' The life, the which I once did loue, I leaue ;
The loue, in which I once did liue, I loath ;

I hate the light, that did my light bereaue :
Both loue, and life, I doe despise you both.
O that one graue might both our ashes cloath !
　　A loue, a life, a light, I now obteine,
　　Able to make my age growe young againe—
Able to saue the sick, and to reuiue the slaine.

64.

'Thus spend we teares, that neuer can be spent,
On Him, that sorrow now no more shall see ;
Thus send we sighs, that neuer can be sent,
To Him that died to liue, and would not be,
To be thear whear He would.　Here burie we
　　This heau'nly earth ; here let it softly sleepe,
　　The fairest Sheapheard of the fairest sheepe : '
So all the bodie kist, and homeward went to weepe.

65.

So home their bodies went, to seeke repose,
But at the graue they left their soules behinde :
O who the force of loue cœlestiall knowes !
That can the cheynes of Nature's self vnbinde,
Sending the bodie home without the minde :
　　Ah, blessed Virgin ! what high angel's art
　　Can euer coumpt thy teares, or sing thy smart,
When euery naile that pierst His hand, did pierce
　　thy heart ?

66.

So Philomel, perch't on an aspin sprig,
Weeps all the night her lost virginitie,
And sings her sad tale to the merrie twig,
That daunces at such ioyfull miserie,
Ne euer lets sweet rest inuade her eye ;
 But leaning on a thorne her daintie chest,
 For feare soft sleepe should steale into her brest,
Expresses in her song greefe not to be exprest.

67.

So when the larke, poore birde, afarre espi'th
Her yet vnfeather'd children (whom to saue
She striues in vaine) slaine by the fatall sithe,
Which from the medowe her greene locks doeth shaue,
That their warme nest is now become their graue ;
 The wofull mother vp to heauen springs,
 And all about her plaintiue notes she flings,
And their vntimely fate most pittifully sings.

CHRIST'S
TRIVMPH AFTER DEATH.

THE ARGUMENT.

Christ's triumph after death, 1—In His Resurrection, manifested by the effects in the creatures: st. 1—7.—In Himselfe: st. 8—12.—In His Ascension into Heauen; whose ioyes are described: st. 13—16.—(1) By the access of all good, the blessed societie of saints, angels, &c.: st. 17—19.—The sweete quiet and peace inioyed under God: st. 20.—Shadowed by the peace we enioy vnder our soueraigne: st. 21—26.—The beauty of the place: st. 27.—The caritie[1] (as the Schoole calls it) of the saints bodies: st. 28—31.—The impletion of the appetite: st. 32, 33.—The ioy of the senses, &c.: st. 34.—(2) By the amotion of all euill: st. 35, 36.—By the access of all good againe: st. 37.—In the glorie of the holie citie: st. 38.—In the beatificall vision of God: st. 39—42.—And of Christ: st. 43. [seqq

---

[1] Query, clarity? G.

Christ's Trivmph after Death.

BVT now the second morning, from her bowre
    Began to glister in her beames ; and nowe
The roses of the Day began to flowre
In th' easterne garden ; for heau'ns smiling browe
Halfe insolent for ioy begunne to showe :
    The early sunne came liuely dauncing out,
    And the bragge lambes ranne wantoning about,
That heau'n and earth might seeme in tryumph both to
    shout.

2

Th' engladded Spring, forgetfull now to weepe,
Began t' eblazon from her leauie bed ;
The waking swallowe broke her halfe-yeare's sleepe,
And euerie bush lay deeply purpurèd
With violets ; the wood's late-wintry head
    Wide flaming primroses set all on fire,
    And his bald trees put on their greene attire,
Among whose infant leaues the ioycous birds conspire.

3.

And now the taller sonnes (whom Titan warmes)
Of vnshorne mountaines, blowne with easie windes,
Dandled the Morning's childhood in their armes,
And if they chaunc't to slip the prouder pines,
The vnder corylets [1] did catch the shines,
  To guild their leaues ; sawe neuer happier yeare
  Such ioyfull triumph and triumphant cheare,
As though the aged world anew created wear.

4.

Say, Earth, why hast thou got thee new attire,
And stick'st thy habit full of dazies red ?
Seems that thou doest to some high thought aspire,
And some newe-found-out bridegroome mean'st to wed :
Tell me, ye trees, so fresh apparrellèd,
  So neuer let the spitefull canker wast you,
  So neuer let the heau'ns with lightening blast you,
Why goe you now so trimly drest, or whither hast you?

5.

Answer me, Iordan, why thy crooked tide
So often wanders from his neerest way,
As though some other way thy streame would slide,
And fain salute the place where something lay ?
And you, sweete birds, that, shaded from the ray,

[1] Copses. G.

Sit carolling and piping griefe away,
The while the lambs to heare you daunce and play :
Tell me, sweete birds, what is it you so faine would say?

6.

And thou, fair spouse of Earth, that euerie yeare
Gett'st such a numerous issue of thy bride,
How chance thou hotter shin'st, and draw'st more neere?
Sure thou somewhear some worthie sight hast spide,
That in one place for ioy thou canst not bide: [1]
  And you, dead swallowes, that so liuely now
  Through the flit [2] aire your wingèd passage rowe,
How could new life into your frozen ashes flowe?

7.

Ye primroses and purple violets, [3]
Tell me, why blaze ye from your leauie bed,
And wooe men's hands to rent you from your sets,
As though you would somewhear be carrièd,
With fresh perfumes and velvets garnishèd?
  But ah, I neede not aske, tis surely so,
  You all would to your Sauiour's triumphs goe :
There would ye all awaite and humble homage doe.

---

[1] Southey misprints 'hide.' G.

[2] Flitting = moving. Cf. "Christ's Victorie in Heauen, st. 22.
l. 2. G.

[3] Giles and Phineas Fletcher reserve their daintiest praise for these
flowers. G.

P

8.

Thear should the Earth herselfe with garlands newe
And louely flowrs embellishèd, adore :
Such roses neuer in her garland grewe,
Such lillies neuer in her brest she wore,
Like beautie neuer yet did shine before :
  Thear should the sunne another sunne behold,
  From whence himselfe borrowes his locks of gold,
That kindle heau'n, and earth with beauties manifold.

9.

There might the violet, and primrose sweet,
Beames of more liuely, and more louely grace,
Arising from their beds of incense meet ;
Thear should the swallowe see new life embrace
Dead ashes, and the graue vnheale [1] his face,
  To let the liuing from his bowels creepe,
  Vnable longer his owne dead to keepe :
Thear heau'n and earth should see their Lord awake from
    sleepe.—

10.

Their Lord, before by others iudg'd to die,
Now Iudge of all Himselfe ; before forsaken
Of all the world, that from His aide did flie,
Now by the saints into their armies taken ;
Before for an vnworthie man mistaken,

[1] Unveil or uncover. G.

Nowe worthy to be God confest ; before
With blasphemies by all the basest tore,
Now worshippèd by angels, that Him lowe adore.

11.

Whose garment was before indipt in blood,
But now imbright'ned into heau'nly flame,
The sunne it selfe outglitters, though he should
Climbe to the toppe of the celestiall frame,
And force the starres go [1] hide themselues for shame :
   Before, that vnder earth was burièd
   But nowe aboue [2] the heau'ns is carrièd,
And thear for euer by the angels heried ! [3]

12.

So fairest Phosphor, the bright morning starre,
But neewely washt in the greene element,
Before the drouzie Night is halfe aware,
Shooting his flaming locks with deaw besprent,
Springs liuely vp into the Orient,
   And the bright droue, fleec't all in gold, he chaces
   To drinke, that on the Olympique mountaine grazes,
The while the minor planets forfeit all their faces.

[1] Richardson, Southey and Cattermole misprint 'to.' G.
[2] Misprinted originally 'about :' corrected to 'above' in 1632 edn. G.
[3] Honoured, praised. G.

13.

So long he wandred in our lower spheare,
That heau'n began his cloudy starres despise,
Halfe enuious, to see on Earth appeare
A greater light then flam'd in his own skies :
At length it burst for spight, and out thear flies
   A globe of wingèd angels, swift as thought
    That on their spotted feathers liuely caught
The sparkling Earth, and to their azure fields it brought.

14.

The rest, that yet amazèd stood belowe,
With eyes cast vp, as greedie to be fed,
And hands vpheld, themselues to ground did throwe :
So when the Troian boy was rauishèd,
As through th' Idalian woods they saie he fled.
   His aged gardians stood all dismai'd,
    Some least he should have fallen back afraid,
And some their hasty vowes and timely prayers said.

15.

'Tosse vp your heads, ye euerlasting gates,[1]
And let the Prince of glorie enter in !'

[1] Dr. J. M. Neale in his "Hymns, chiefly Mediæval, on the Joys and Glories of Paradise" (1866) gives a selection of stanzas—beginning with this—from this 'Part' of Fletcher's poem, and pronounces them "perhaps the most beautiful original verses, in a strictly religious poem, which the English language possesses," and adds further,

At whose braue voly of sideriall States,
The sunne to blush and starres grow pale wear seene ;
When, leaping first from Earth He did begin
   To climbe his angells wings : then open hang
   Your christall doores ! so all the chorus sang
Of heau'nly birds, as to the starres they nimbly sprang.

16.

Hearke ! how the floods clap their applauding hands,
The pleasant valleyes singing for delight ;
The wanton mountaines daunce about the lands,
The while the fieldes struck with the heau'nly light,
Set all their flowrs a smiling at the sight ;
   The trees laugh with their blossoms, and the sound
   Of the triumphant shout of praise, that crown'd
The flaming Lambe, breaking through Heau'n hath
    passage found.

17.

Out leap the antique patriarchs, all in hast,
To see the powrs of Hell in triumph lead,
And with small starres a garland interchast
Of oliue-leaues they bore, to crowne His Head,
That was before with thornes degloried :

" The reader to whom this poem is new will, I think, allow that
nothing more exquisite was ever written than the 5, 6, 7, 10, 12, and
13 stanzas as here numbered : corresponding with 20, 28, 30, 33, 35
and 36 of the complete Poem."   G.

After them flewe the prophets, brightly stold
In shining lawne, and wimpled manifold.
Striking their yuorie harpes, strung all in chords of gold.

18.

To which the saints victorious carolls sung,
Ten thousand saints at once; that with the sound
The hollow vaults of heau'n for triumph rung:
The cherubins their clamours did confound
With all the rest, and clapt their wings around:
    Downe from their thrones the dominations flowe
    And at His feet their crownes and scepters throwe,
And all the princely soules fell on their faces lowe.

19.

Nor can the martyrs' wounds them stay behind,
But out they rush among the heau'nly crowd,
Seeking their heau'n out of their heau'n to find,
Sounding their siluer trumpets out so loude,
That the shrill noise broke through the starrie cloude,
    And all the virgin soules, in pure arraie,
    Came dauncing forth, and making joyeous plaie:
So Him they lead along into the courts of day.

20.

So Him they lead into the courts of day,
Whear neuer warre nor wounds abide Him more;

But in that house eternall peace doth plaie,
Acquieting the soules that newe before,[1]
Their way to heav'n through their owne blood did skore,
   But now, estrangèd from all miserie,
   As farre as heau'n and earth discoasted lie,
Swelter[2] in quiet waues of immortalitie !

21.

And if great things by smaller may be ghuest,
So, in the mid'st of Neptune's angrie tide
Our Britan Island, like the weedie nest
Of true halcyon, on the waues doth ride,
And softly sayling, skornes the water's pride :
   While all the rest, drown'd on the Continent
   And tost in bloodie waues, their wounds lament,
And stand, to see our peace, as struck with woonderment.[3]

22.

The ship of France, religious waues doe tosse,
And Greec it selfe is now growne barbarous ;
Spain's children hardly dare the ocean crosse,
And Belge's field lies wast and ruinous ;
That vnto those, the heau'ns ar invious,

---

[1] Southey misprints 'besore.' G.

[2] = Grow warm : Dr Neale changes to
     ' They bathe in quiet waves of immortality.' G.

[3] Misnumbered in edition of 1610 and also in those of 1632 and 1640 as ' 20 ' (*bis*) : so that there appear to be only 50 stanzas while there actually are 51. G.

And vnto them, themselues ar strangers growne,
And vnto these, the seas ar faithles knowne,
And vnto her, alas! her owne is not her owne.

23.

Here only shut we Ianus yron gates,
And call the welcome Muses to our springs,
And ar but [1] pilgrims from our heav'nly states
The while the trusty Earth sure plentie brings,
And ships through Neptune safely spread their wings.
    Go blessed Island, wander whear thou please,
    Vnto thy God, or men, Heau'n, lands or seas:
Thou canst not loose thy way, thy king with all hath peace.

24.

Deere prince! thy subjects' ioy, hope of their heirs,
Picture of Peace, or breathing image rather;
The certaine argument of all our prayrs,
Thy Harrie's [2] and thy countrie's louely father;
Let peace in endles ioyes for euer bath her
    Within thy sacred brest, that at thy birth
    Brough'st her with thee from Heau'n, to dwell on Earth,
Making our Earth a Heav'n, and paradise of mirth.

25.

Let not my liege misdeem [3] these humble laies
As lickt with soft and supple blandishment,

---

[1] Southey misprints here 'put' for 'but.' G.
[2] = Henry's *i.e.* Prince Henry whose death was so lamented by the nation. G.   [3] Southey misprints 'disdain.' G.

Or spoken to disparagon His praise;
For though pale Cynthia, neere her brother's tent,
Soone disappeares in the white firmament,
   And giues him back the beames before wear his;
   Yet when he verges, or is hardly ris,
She the viue image of her absent brother is.

26.

Nor let the Prince of Peace, his beadsman blame,
That with His stewart dares his Lord compare,
And heau'nly peace with earthly quiet shame:
So pines to lowely plants comparèd ar,
And lightning Phœbus to a little starre:
   And well I wot, my rime, albee vnsmooth
   Ne saies but what it meanes, ne meanes but sooth,
Ne harmes the good, ne good to harmefull person doth.[1]

27.

Gaze but vpon the house whear man embowrs;
With flowrs and rushes pauèd is his way,
Whear all the creatures ar his seruitours;
The windes do sweepe his chambers euery day;
And cloudes doe wash his rooms; the seeling gay
   Starrèd aloft, the guilded knobs embraue:
   If such a house God to another gaue,
How shine those glittering courts, He for Himselfe will
    haue?

[1] Cattermole drops, without marking the omission, stanzas 21, 22, 23, 24, 25 and 26. G.

28.

And if a sullen cloud, as sad as night,
In which the sunne may seeme embodied,
Depur'd[1] of all his drosse, we see so[2] white
Burning in melted gold his wat'rie head,
Or round with yuorie edges siluerèd,
    What lustre super-excellent will He
    Lighten on those that shall His sunneshine see,
In that all-glorious court in which all glories be?

29.

If but one sunne with his diffusive fires,
Can paint the starres, and the whole world with light,
And ioy, and life into each heart inspires,
And eu'ry saint shall shine in heau'n, as bright
As doth the sunne in his transcendent might,
    (As Faith may well beleeue what Truth once sayes)
    What shall so many sunnes' united rayes,
But dazle all the eyes that nowe in heau'n we praise?

30.

Here let my Lord hang vp his conquering launce,
And bloody armour with late slaughter warme,
And looking downe on His weake militants,
Behold His saints, mid'st of their hot alarme
Hang all their golden hopes vpon His arme;

---

[1] Purified. G.   [2] Cattermole misprints 'no.' G.

And in this lower field dispacing wide,
  Through windie thoughts, that would their sayles mis-
    guide,
Anchor their fleshly ships fast in His wounded side.[1]

31.

Here may the band, that now in tryumph shines,
And that (before they wear inuested thus)
In earthly bodies carried heauenly mindes,
Pitch [2] round about in order glorious,
Their sunny tents, and houses luminous ;
  All their eternall day in songs employing,
  Ioying their ende, without ende of their ioying,
While their Almightie Prince destruction is destroying.

32.

Full, yet without satietie, of that
Which whetts, and quiets greedy appetite,
Whear neuer sunne did rise, nor euer sat ;
But one eternall day, and endles light
Giues time to those whose time is infinite—
  Speaking with thought, obtaining without fee,
  Beholding Him whom neuer eye could see,
And magnifying Him that cannot greater be.

33.

How can such ioy as this want words to speake ?
And yet what words can speake such ioy as this ?

---

[1] The very striking close of this stanza is inserted with little variation in Phineas Fletcher's *Purple Island*, c. 12. st. 52. G.

[2] Cattermole corrects 'pitcht' by 'pitch :' adopted. G.

Far from the world, that might their quiet breake.
Here the glad soules the face of beauty kisse ;
Powr'd out in pleasure, on their beds of blisse ;
   And drunke with nectar-torrents, euer hold
   Their eyes on Him, whose graces manifold
The more they doe behold, the more they would behold.

34.

Their sight drinkes louely fires in at their eyes,
Their braine sweete incense with fine breath accloyes,
That on God's sweating [1] altar burning lies ;
Their hungrie eares feede on the heau'nly noyse,
That angels sing, to tell their vntould ioyes ;
   Their vnderstanding, naked truth ; their wills
   The all, and selfe-sufficient Goodnesse, fills :
That nothing here is wanting, but the want of ills.

35.

No sorrowe now hangs clowding on their browe,
No bloodles maladie empales their face,
No age drops on their hayrs his siluer snowe,
No nakednesse their bodies doeth embase,
No pouertie themselues and theirs disgrace,
   No feare of death the ioy of life deuours,
   No vnchast sleepe their precious time deflowrs,
No losse, no griefe, no change, waite on their wingèd hours.

    [1] Neale changes to ' That on the heavenly '   G.

36.

But now their naked bodies skorne the cold,
And from their eyes ioy lookes, and laughs at paine ;
The infant wonders how he came so old,
The old man how he came so young againe ;
Still resting, though from sleep they still refraine [1]
    Whear all are rich, and yet no gold they owe,[2]
    And all are kings, and yet no subjects knowe,
All full, and yet no time on foode they doe bestow.

37.

For things that passe are past :[3] and in this field
The indeficient Spring no Winter feares ;
The trees together fruit and blossome yield ;
Th' unfading lilly leaues of siluer beares,
And crimson rose a skarlet garment weares ;
    And all of these on the saints' bodies growe,
    Not, as they woont, on baser earth belowe :
Three riuers heer, of milke, and wine, and honie, flowe.

38.

About the holy citie rowles a flood
Of moulten chrystall, like a sea of glasse ;

---

[1] Changed (probably by misprint) to 'restraine' in 1632 edition. G.   [2] Own. G.

[3] Dr Neale says here 'He is simply translating the 'Nam transire transiit' of S. Peter Damiani :' but this is too strong. Rich and glowing as his Hymn *de Gloria Paradisi* is in other thoughts, he is poor and faint in the antithetic-ideas so vividly

On which weake streame a strong foundation stood :
Of liuing diamounds the building was,
That all things else, besides itselfe, did passe :[1]
   Her streetes, instead of stones, the starres did paue,
   And little pearles, for dust, it seem'd to haue ;
On which soft-streaming manna, like pure snowe, did
    wave.

39.

In midst of this citie cælestiall,
Whear the Eternall Temple should haue rose,
Light'ned the Idea[2] Beatificall :
End, and beginning of each thing that growes ;
Whose selfe no end, nor yet beginning knowes ;
   That hath no eyes to see, nor ears to heare ;
   Yet sees, and heares, and is all-eye, all-eare ;
That nowhear is contain'd, and yet is euery whear :

40.

Changer of all things, yet immutable ;
Before and after all, the first and last ;
That, moouing all, is yet immoueable ;
Great without quantitie ; in Whose forecast
Things past are present, things to come are past ;

worded by Fletcher in this stanza and the context. The most
hasty comparison will prove this. G.
  [1] Sur-pass. G.
  [2] Neale substitutes 'Vision.' G.

Swift without motion; to Whose open eye
The hearts of wicked men vnbrested lie ;
At once absent and present to them, farre, and nigh.[1]

41.

It is no flaming lustre, made of light ;
No sweet concent, or well-tim'd harmonie ;
Ambrosia, for to feast the appetite,
Or flowrie odour, mixt with spicerie ;
No soft embrace, or pleasure bodily ;
   And yet it is a kinde of inward feast,
   A harmony, that sounds within the brest,
An odour, light, embrace, in which the soule doth rest.

42.

A heav'nly feast, no hunger can consume ;
A light vnseene, yet shines in euery place ;
A sound, no time can steale ; a sweet perfume
No winds can scatter; an intire embrace
That no satietie can ere vnlace :
   Ingrac't into so high a fauour, thear
   The saints, with their beaw-peers[2] whole worlds outwear;
And things vnseene doe see, and things vnheard doe hear.

---

[1] Dr Neale remarks, 'One of our Poet's most careless lines.'
Surely, something like this would have been better ?—
   "To whom the dark is light : to whom the far is nigh ;"
but Fletcher's thought looks deeper :=God's eye is at once absent
(to the thoughtless wicked) and present (in fact) to them, far off
(in their forgetfulness) but nigh to them in reality. G.
   [2] Beau-pere=companion : Cf. Spenser F. Q. III. l. 35. G.

43.

Ye blessed soules, growne richer by your spoile ;
Whose losse, though great, is cause of greater gains ;
Here may your weary spirits rest from toyle,
Spending your endlesse eav'ning that remaines,
Among those white flocks and celestiall traines,
 That feed vpon their Sheapheard's eyes, and frame
 That heau'nly musique of so woondrous fame,
Psalming aloude the holy honours of His name ![1]

44.

Had I a voice of steel to tune my song,
Wear euery verse as smoothly fil'd as glasse,[2]
And euery member turnèd to a tongue,
And euery tongue wear made of sounding brasse ;
Yet all that skill, and all this strength, alas !
 Should it presume to guild [3] wear misadvis'd,
 The place, whear Dauid hath new songs devis'd,
As in his burning throne he sits emparadis'd.

45.

Most happie prince, whose eyes those starres behold,
Treading ours vnder feet ! now maist thou powre

---

[1] Dr Neale adds here, " He is thinking no doubt of the Vesper Hymn :
   Largire clarum vesperem
   Quo vita nunquam decidat :
both Poets, of course drawing their inspiration from Zech. xiv. 7." G.   [2] Southey has ' smooth as smoothest glass.' G.
 [3] He substitutes ' t' adorn.' G.

That ouerflowing skill, whearwith of ould
Thou woont'st to combe [1] rough speech ; now maist
    thou showr
Fresh streames of praise vpon that holy bowre,
   Which well we Heaven call ; not that it rowles
   But that it is the hauen of our soules—
Most happie prince, whose sight so heau'nly sight
    behoulds !

46.

Ah, foolish sheapheards, that wear woont esteem
Your god all rough and shaggy-hair'd to bee ;
And yet farre wiser, sheapheards then ye deeme ;
For who so poore (though who so rich) as hee
When, with vs hermiting [2] in lowe degree,
   He wash't His flocks in Jordan's spotles tide ;
   And, that His deare remembrance aie might bide, [3]
Did to vs come, and with vs liu'd, and for vs di'd ?

47.

But now so liuely colours did embeame
His sparkling forehead, and so [4] shiny rayes

---

[1] Here also he has 'smooth.' G.

[2] Southey reads 'When sojourning with us in low degree.'
Richardson and Cattermole 'When with us sojourning in low
degree.' G.

[3] The same mis-read 'And that his dear remembrance might
abide.' G.

[4] Southey misprints 'such.' G.

Q

Kindled his flaming locks, that downe did stream
In curles along his necke, whear sweetly playes
(Singing His wounds of loue in sacred layes)
 His deerest Spouse,[1] Spouse of the deerest Lover,
 Knitting a thousand knots ouer and ouer,
And dying still for loue; but they her still recover :—

48.

Faire Egliset,[2] that at His eyes doth dresse
Her glorious face; those eyes from whence ar shed
Infinite belamours ;[3] whear, to expresse
His loue, High God all heav'n as captive leads,
And all the banners of His grace dispreads,
 And in those windowes doth His armes englaze
 And on those eyes the angels all doe gaze,
And from those eies the lights of Heau'n doe gleane [4]
  their blaze.

49.

But let the Kentish lad,[5] that lately taught
His oaten reed the trumpet's siluer sound—
Young Thyrsilis, and for his musique brought

---

 [1] The Church. G.
 [2] Richardson, Southey, and Cattermole, substitute 'Fairest of Fairs.' G.
 [3] Southey reads 'attractions infinite :' = attractions or love-spells. G.
 [4] Southey reads 'obtain,' and Richardson and Cattermole 'catch.' G.
 [5] Phineas Fletcher.—See our Memorial-Introduction. G.

The willing sphears from heau'n, to lead a round
Of dauncing nymphs and heards,[1] that sung, and crown'd
　Eclecta's Hymen with ten thousand flowrs
　　Of choycest prayse ; and hung her heau'nly bow'rs
With saffron garlands, drest for nuptiall paramours ;—

50.

Let his shrill trumpet with her siluer blast,
Of faire Eclecta and her spousall bed,
Be the sweet pipe, and smooth encomiast :
But my greene Muse, hiding her younger head
Vnder old Chamus' flaggy banks, that spread
　Their willough locks abroad, and all the day
　　With their owne watry shadowes wanton play—
Dares not those high amours, and loue-sick songs assay.

51.

Impotent words, weake lines,[2] that striue in vaine—
In vaine, alas, to tell so heau'nly sight !—
So [3] heav'nly sight, as none can greater feigne,
Feigne what he can, that seemes of greatest might :
　Might any yet compare with infinite ?
　　Infinite sure those ioyes, my words but light ;
Light is the pallace where she dwells—O blessèd wight ! [4]

[1] Richardson and Cattermole read 'swains.' G

[2] Misprinted 'sides ' in 1610 edn., and which Southey repeats. G.

[3] Southey here, by misprinting 'To' for 'so,' and in line 5th
' could' for ' might ' misses the echoing repetition—a device afterwards used by Milton.   See our Memorial-Introduction in Phineas
Fletcher. G.

[4] Richardson and Southey read ' O then how bright.' G.

Reverse of p. 84.

Ruina cœli pulchra : iam terris decus,
Deusque : proles matris innuptæ, et pater :
Sine matre natus, sine patre excrescens caro :
Quem nec mare, æther, terra, non cœlum capit,
Vtero puellæ totus angusto latens ;
Æquævus idem patri, matre antiquior :
Heu domite victor, et triumphator ; tui
Opus opifexque ; qui minor quam sis, eo
Maior resurgis : vita, quæ mori velis,
Atque ergo possis ; passa finem Æternitas.
Quid tibi rependam, quid tibi rependam miser?
Vt quando ocellos mollis inuadit quies,
Et nocte membra plurimus Morpheus premit,
Auide videmur velle de tergo sequens
Effugere monstrum, et plumbeos frustra pedes
Celerare ; media succidimus ægri fuga ;
Solitum pigrescit robur, os quærit viam,
Sed proditurus moritur in lingua sonus :
Sic stupeo totus, totus hæresco, intuens
Et sæpe repeto, forte si rependerem :
Solus rependit ille, qui repetit bene.

G. FLETCHER.

Τέλειον ἐστι, καὶ τελῶν Θεὸς τέλος.*

---

* In 1632 there follows here
’Εστι τελῶν τὸ τέλος· τέλος ἐστὶ Θεὸς τὸ τέλειον.   G.

Appendix.

ENGRAVINGS IN THE RE-ISSUE OF 2ND EDITION (1632) IN 1640.

1. The Birth of Christ—opposite page 1.   At bottom these lines :—

> A new way here that prophets text may pass
> for truth : the oxe his owner knew, the ass
> his master's crib : thus thus incradled lay
> your King, your Lord, your Christ : there fix, there stay
> thy stoopinge, low, deiiected thoughts ; shall I
> since he lay thus depressed, care where I lie.
> Esay I. 3.

2. The Circumcision of Christ—opposite page 23. At bottom these lines :—

> View well this sacred portraiture, and see
> what pangs thy Sauio[or] felt, and all for thee :
> Wilt thou returne a sacrifice may please
> him who had felt all this? be then all these :
> Be thou both preist and knife : re-act each part
> thy selfe againe, Go circumcise thy heart.

3. The Baptism of Christ—opposite page 26.   At bottom these lines :—

> How many riddlinge thoughts strangly appeare
> Unfolded in this shadow : for first here

I see the Fountaine in the Streams : I see
the water wa[s]hd by washing in't : And wee
through nature black to pitch and inck, are scour'd
to snow, while water's on an other pour'd
I see againe.   Ile not say all I can
least I turne Jordan to an ocean.

4. The Temptation of Christ—opposite page 30.   At
bottom these lines :—

'Tis written : Thus the tempter taught : (and thus
by Scriptures wrack'd he oft preuailes on vs
weake flesh and blood) But that he thus did dare
By Moses and the prophets to insnare
the sonne of God ; thinck it not strange that he
become confounded in his policie
for sure it could but slender hopes afford
he by the Scriptures should orecome ye Word.

5. The Crucifixion of Christ—opposite page 49.   At
bottom these lines :—

What you see here does but the picture show
of sorrowes picture : miracle of woe !
Greefe was miscall'd till now : what plaints before
e're mou'd the bowells of the earth or toare
the rocks ? nay more, the heaun's put out their light
And truc'd with darkness to auoide that sight.
Blind Israel ! this this your hardness shewes
ye then turn'd stones whilst thus those stones turn'd Jewes.

6. The Resurrection of Christ—opposite page 69.
At bottom these lines :—

Forget those horrid stiles of death : see here
who died, and by his presence there
inbalm'd the graue.   See here who rose : and so
left hell infeebled, and the powers below

and death suppress'd. So that a child (no doubt)
may safly play w^{tht} now the sting's pluck'd out.

7. The Ascension of Christ—opposite page 81. At
bottom these lines :—

> Tis finish'd : and hees now gon vp on high
> rich in the spoyles of hell : in maiesty,
> and glorie (and glorie glorious farre
> above all words) each glimpse treads out a starre,
> dazles the sun : And whether true this bee
> here written, follow him, and you shall see.

' Geo. Yate ' is the ' sculpt[or]' of these ' engravings' which are
grotesque in the extreme, though in the ' Baptism ' and ' Ascension '
there are evident reminiscences of the great sacred Painters. Everywhere perspective and proportion are violated.—The ' Temptation '
is ludicrous in its attempt to group the three temptations together.
Generally the faces are hideous. It is just possible that as these
Engravings did not appear until 1640 and so were posthumous, the
Verses may belong to Phineas not Giles : but their place seems
appropriate in Giles' volume. G.

MINOR POEMS.

NOTE.

The sources of these minor poems are given in the places. G.

A Canto vpon the Death of Eliza.[1]

THE early Howres were readie to unlocke
    The doore of Morne, to let abroad the Day;
When sad Ocyroe sitting on a rocke,
    Hemmed [2] in with teares, not glassing as they say
    Shee woont, her damaske beuties (when to play
Shee bent her looser fancie) in the streame,
That sudding [3] on the rocke, would closely seeme
To imitate her whitenesse with his frothy creame.

But hanging from the stone her careful head,
    That shewed (for griefe had made it so to shew)
A stone itselfe, that only differèd,
    That those without, these streames within, did flow,
    Both euer ranne; yet neuer lesse did grow;

---

[1] Originally published in 'Sorrowe's Joy, or a Lamentation for our Deceased Soveraigne Elizabeth, with a Triumph for the Prosperous succession of our Gratious King James. Printed by John Legat, printer to the University of Cambridge, 1603.' Our text is taken from Nichol's 'Progresses of James I.,' Vol. I. pp. 17—19. In the margin are variations from the reprint in Nichol's 'Progresses of Queen Elizabeth,' Vol. III. 257—259. G.

[2] Hemmd. G.

[3] Query—foaming as in frothy (soap) 'suds?' G.

And tearing from her head her amber haires,
Whose like or none, or onely Phœbus weares,
Shee strowd them on the flood to waite vpon her teares.

About her many Nymphs sate weeping by,
   That when shee sang were woont to daunce and
     leape;
And all the grasse that round about did lie,
   Hung full of teares, as if that meant to weepe;
   Whilst th' vndersliding streames did softly creepe,
And clung about the rocke with winding wreath,
To heare a Canto of Elizae's[1] death;
Which thus poore nymph shee sung, whilest Sorrowe lent
   her breath.

Tell me, ye blushing currols that bunch out,
   To cloath with beuteous red your ragged sire[2]
To let the sea-greene mosse curle round about,
   With soft embrace (as creeping vines do wyre
   Their loved elmes) your sides in rosie tyre;
So let the ruddie vermeyle of your checke
Make stain'd carnations fresher liueries seeke,
So let your braunched armes grow crooked, smooth, and
   sleeke.

So from your growth late be you rent away,
   And hung with silver bels and whistles shrill;

    [1] Elizaes. G.
    [2] Misprinted 'fire' in Prog. of King James. G.

Vnto those children be you giuen to play,
   Where blest Eliza raign'd ; so neuer ill
   Betide your caues, nor them with breaking spill ;
Tell me if some vncivill hand should teare
Your branches hence, and place them otherwhere ;
Could you still grow, and such fresh crimson ensignes
     beare ?

Tell me, sad Philomele, that yonder sit'st
   Piping thy songs vnto the dauncing twig,
And to the waters fall thy musicke fit'st ;
   So let the friendly prickle never digge
   Thy watchfull breast with wound, or small, or bigge,
Whereon thou lean'st ; so let the hissing snake,
Sliding with shrinking silence, neuer take
Th' vnwarie foote, whilst thou perhaps hangst half [1] awake.

So let the loathèd lapwing, when her nest
   Is stolne away, not as shee vses, flie,
Cousening the searcher of his promis'd feast,
   But, widdow'd of all hope, still *Itis* crie,
   And nought but *Itis*, *Itis* till shee die.
Say, sweetest querister of the airie quirè,
Doth not thy Tereu, Tereu, then expire,
When Winter robs thy house of all her greene attire ?

Tell me, ye veluet-headed violets
   That fringe the crooked banke, with gawdie blewe ;

     [1] Halfe. G.

So let with comely grace your pretie [1] frets
    Be spread ; so let a thousand [2] *Zephyrs* sue
    To kisse your willing heads, that seeme t' eschew
Their wanton touch with maiden modestie ;
So let the siluer dewe but lightly lie,
Like little watrie worlds within your azure skie.

So when your blazing leaues are broadly spread,
    Let wandring nymphes gather you in their lapps,
And send you where Eliza lieth dead,
    To strow the sheete that her pale bodie wraps ;
    Aie me, in this I enuie your good haps ;
Who would not die, there to be buried?
Say if the sunne denie his beames to shedde
Upon your liuing stalkes, grow you not witherèd ?

Tell me, thou wanton brooke, that slipst away
    T' avoid the straggling banks still flowing cling,
So let thy waters cleanely tribute pay,
    Vnmixt with mudde, vnto the sea your king ;
    So neuer let your streames leaue murmuring,
Vntil they steale by many a secret furt [3]
To kisse those walls that built Elizaes Court,
Drie you not when your mother springs are choakt with
    durt?

Yes, you all say, and I say, with you all,
    Naught without cause of ioy can ioyous bide,

---

[1] Prettie. G.   [2] Thousand. G.   [3] = forth? G.

Then me, vnhappie nymph, whom the dire fall
    Of my ioyes spring :—but there, aye mee, shee cried,
    And spake no more ; for sorrow speech denied,
And downe into her watrie lodge did goe ;
The very waters when shee sunke did showe
With many wrinkled [1] ohs, they sympathiz'd her woe :

The sunne in mourning clouds inveloped,
    Flew fast into the westearne world to tell
Newes of her death ; Heaven itselfe sorrowed
    With teares that to the earthes dank bosome fell ;
    But when the next Aurora 'gan to deale
Handfuls of roses 'fore the teame of day,
A shepheard [2] droue his flocke by chance that way,
And made the nymph to dance that mournèd yesterday.

                    G. FLETCHER, Trinit.

---

[1] Wrinckled. G.   [2] Sheappheard. G.

AFTER PETRONIUS.

(FROM TANNER MSS., VOL. 465, FOL. 42.[1])

Nisis amore pio pueri, &c.

IT was at euening, and in Aprill mild,
  Of twelue sounes of the yeare, the fairest child ;
When Night and Day their strife to peace doe bring,
To haue an equall interest in the Spring,
The sunne being arbiter : I walkt to see
How Nature drew a meddow, and a tree,
In orient colours ; and to smell what sent
Of true perfume the winds the aire had lent.
When with a happy carelesse glance I spy
One pace, a shade : Encolpus cry'd 'tis I ;
And soe vnmaskt his forehead, brancht more faire
Than locks of grasse—our motley Rhea's haire.
I had mine eyes soe full of such a freind,
That Flora's pride was dimm'd ; and in the end
I askt some time, before I could perswade
My senses it was Spring ; the silken blade
Of cowslips lost their grace ; the speckled pancie
Came short to flatter, though he smil'd, my fancie.

---

[1] On the margin Bancroft has written that he had obtained this poem from a Mr Blois, and he notes that (as *supra*) it was from the Encolpus of Petronius.

If later seasons had the roses bredd,
I doubt the modest damaske had turn'd redd,
Stain'd with a parallel ; but it was good
They swadled were, like infants, in the bud ;
Solsequium,[1] gladd of this excuse, begunne
To close his blushes with the setting sunne.
Thrice chanting philomel beganne a song,
Thrice had no audience for Encolpus' tongue.
This thorne did touch her breast to be rejected,
And tun'd a moane ; not heard, she was neglected.
I thought vncurteous Time would wait, but Night
Appear'd, Orion's whelpes had chas'd the light
Into the Westerne couerts ; judge from hence
How farre a beauty commands reuerence.
The neighbour starres in loue were waxen clearer,
The farthest shott methought, to view him nearer.
My Vranoscopy said, the moone did cast
Faint beames and sullen glimpses ; when at last
I spy'd in her a new and vncouth spott,—
Doubtles through envy all the rest she gott :
And then she held her palenes in a shrowd
Borrowing the pleighted curtaines of a clowd.[2]
Flowers, birds, and starres, all to Encolpus yields,
As to Adonis doe Adonis fields.
Oh had some other, thus describ'd, and seene !
I came a partiall judge, to praise the screene.

                                        G. FLETCHER.

[1] Sunflower.

[2] Cf. Milton later, "play in the *flighted clouds*" (Comus, l. 300).

                                                    R

From Reward of the Faithfull.[1]

(1.) THE HEAVENLY COUNTRY.

. . . . "Which diuine thought wee shall not find in the hearts alone of the children of light, that haue the starres of heauen shining thicke in them, (Hebr. 11, 16) but in

---

[1] THE
REWARD
of the Faithfull.
Math. 5. 6.
They shall be satisfied.
THE LABOVR OF
the Faithfull.
Genes. 26. 12.
Then Isaac sowed in that Land.
THE GROVNDS
of our Faith.
Acts 10. 43.
To him giue all the Prophets witnesse.
At London printed by B. A. for
Beniamin Fisher, and are to
be sold at the signe of the *Tal-
bot* in Pater-noster row
1623.
16°. [10 leaves [unpaged] and 1 leaf blank and pp. 419 : some of the pages are mis-numbered. See Introduction. G.

the minds of heathen men, that lay shadowed in their owne naturall wisedome, out of which the banisht Consul of Rome, Boetius, could sing

> Hæc, dices, memini patria est mihi,
> Hinc ortus, hic sistam gradum.

> O this my country is, thy soule shall say,
> Hence was my birth, and here shall be my stay."
>
> (pp. 29, 30.)

[Boethius, Cons. Phil. IV., metr. I, l. 25, 26.   G.]

(2.) THE ROSE and 'BLACK BUT COMELY.'

" Cleane opposite are these glories, and delights, and this ambition to those of our vnder-world.   Gather all the roses of pleasure that grow vpon the earth, sayes not the Greek Epigram truely of them :

> Τὸ ῥόδον ἀκμάζει βαιὸν χρόνον, ἢν δὲ παρέλθῃ,
> ζητῶν εὑρήσεις οὐ ῥόδον, ἀλλὰ βάτον.

> The Rose is faire and fading, short and sweet,
> Passe softly by her :
> And in a moment you shall see her fleet,
> And turne a bryer.

They looke fairely, but they are sodainely dispoiled : whereas, contrary, all the flowers of Paradise (like the Church, *Cant.* I. 5. 6.) sun-burnt and frosted with the heat and cold of this tempestuous world, looke black and homely, but flourish inwardly with diuine beauty, and are all glorious within. So that wee may well say of the Church as the Poet sings :—

> She's black : what then ? so are dead coales, but cherish,
>   And with soft breath them blow,
> And you shall see them glow as bright and flourish,
>   As spring-borne Roses grow.   (pp. 120, 121.)

[The author of the Epigram on the Rose seems unknown : but Jakobs gives a German translation as follows :—

" Wenige Tage nur währt die Rosenzeit ; sind sie verschwunden,
    Siehst du die Rose nicht mehr ; sondern die Dornen allein."

Dr Johnson quotes it in his 'Rambler,' No. 71, with the sole difference of παρέλθῃς for the last word of the first line : which elsewhere occurs as παρέλθῃ (as in Fletcher). Johnson gives no author's name but translates

> " Soon fades the rose; once past the fragrant hour,
>   The loiterer finds a bramble for a flower."

[See Notes and Queries, 4th. S. 11th April 1868 : p. 351, and Anthologia Græca, IV. 126, ed. Jacobs.]

A Correspondent of 'Notes and Queries,' with reference to the Epigram, communicates an amusing Greek pun from it, which he heads 'Cane and Birch.'—"The occasion of it was a complaint of a friend to an old-fashioned pedagogue that, objecting to the corporal punishment of little boys at school, he had sent his son to one where it was said *birch* was unknown, but found that a very cruel and severe use of *the cane* was substituted for it. Ah !" said the old-fashioned school-master exultingly, whose meditations, like Fielding's Thwackum's, were full of birch,

" Ζητῶν εὑρήσεις οὐ 'ΡΟΔΟΝ ἀλλὰ ΒΑΤΟΝ."

The reply was pedantic, but it was appropriate. [As before, May 16th, p. 467.]

Perhaps it may be well to remember on the whole, the fine words of Dr F. W. Faber :—" Roses grow on briars, say the wise men of the world, with that sententious morality which thinks to make virtue truthful by making it dismal. Yes ! but as the very different spirit of piety would say, it is a truer truth that briars bloom with roses. If roses have thorns, thorns also have roses. This is the rule of life. Yet everybody tells us one side of this truth, and nobody tells us the other."—(" The Precious Blood," p. 216.)

[The second Epigram *supra*, is too corruptly given in the Greek (by Fletcher) for restoration : and too unimportant to spend pains on. G.]

(3.) THE RICH POOR MAN.

"Let vs graunt Diues the happinesse to die a rich man, which he shall neuer doe (for as the heathen sings of death,

> Involuit humile pariter et celsum caput.
> Æquatque summis infima.

Death and the Graue, make euen all estates.
There, high, and low, and rich, and poor are mates." (p. 203.)[1]

[Boethius : De Cons. Phil. lib. II., metr. 7, l. 13, 14. G.]

---

[1] LIVESEY (as before) gives this more tersely :—

'There is no difference : Death hath made
Equal the sceptre and the spade.' (p. 66.) G.

(4.) UNGODLY RICH.

"To speake soothly, as the last of the best, and the best of the last, Poets saies of all morall helpes which Fabricius, and Cato, and Brutus, three of the most famous of the Romane Worthies thought to eternize themselues by,

> Cum sera vobis rapiet hoc etiam dies,
> Iam vos secunda mors manet :

So may the vngodly rich more truly say of himselfe, and all worldly meanes, whereby he hoped to perpetuate [1] his life and memorie.

> The poor man dies but once : but O that I
> Already dead, haue yet three deaths to die.

For, being dead in his bodie, he still remaines aliue in his soule, estate, and posteritie to suffer death, and therefore death is said *to gnaw, and feed vpon him.* Psal. 49. 14. (p. 205-207.)" [Boethius is the poet referred to, *supra:* De Cons : Phil : lib ii. metr. 7, l. 25, 26.   G.]

(5.) THE 'GODS' ACCUSED.

"Neither did simple women onely, but the wisest of the heathen Gouernors loade their Gods with their proper crimes :

> ——ἐγὼ δ' οὐκ αἴτιός εἰμι,
> Ἀλλὰ Ζεὺς καὶ μοῖρα καὶ ἠεροφοῖτις Ἐρινύς.

---

[1] Misprinted 'perpetrate.'   G.

Sayes great Agamemnon, alas !

> It was not he that did them injurie,
> But Ioue and Fate, and the night Furie.

But Iupiter's answer is recorded by the same Poet :

> Ἐξ ἡμῶν γάρ φασι κάκ' ἔμμεναι οἱ δὲ καὶ αὐτοὶ
> Σφῇσιν ἀτασθαλίῃσιν ὑπέρμορον ἄλγε' ἔχουσιν.

> Men say their faults are ours when their own wils
> Beyond their fate, are authours of their ills." (pp. 232, 235.)
>   [Homer Iliad XIX. 86, 87. and Od. I. 33, 34.   G.]

(6.) HUSBANDRY.

" The Art of husbandry . . . . wants both schollers
and teachers, meeting, very seldom with such religious
votaries towards them as the Prince of the Latin Poets
was, who in his Georgicks, or Poeticall Husbandrie,
breaks out into this godly wish :

> Me vero primum dulces, &c.
> No, first of all O let the Muses wings
> Whose sacred fountaine in my bosome springs,
> Receiue, and landing mee aboue the starres,
> Shew me the waies of heuen : but if the barres
> Of vnkinde Nature stoppe so high a flight,
> The Woods and Fields shall be my next delight."   (pp.
>   273, 274.)

>   [Virgil, Georg. II. 475-478, 483, 485.   G.]

(7.) OTHERS.

It is indeede the nature of al men to think other mens
liues more happy then their owne.

> Optat ephippia bos piger, optat arare caballus.
> Faine would the Oxe the horse's trappins weare ;
> And faine the Horse the oxes yoake would beare. (p. 283.)

[Horace Epist. 1. 14, 43.   G.]

FINIS.

PRINTED BY BALLANTYNE AND COMPANY
EDINBURGH AND LONDON

A List of Books

PUBLISHED BY

CHATTO & WINDUS

74 & 75, PICCADILLY, LONDON, W.

ADVERTISING, A HISTORY OF, from the Earliest Times. Illustrated by Anecdotes, Curious Specimens, and Biographical Notes of Successful Advertisers. By HENRY SAMPSON. Crown 8vo, with Coloured Frontispiece and Illustrations, cloth gilt, 7s. 6d.

ÆSOP'S FABLES TRANSLATED INTO HUMAN NATURE. By C. H. BENNETT. Crown 4to, 24 Plates beautifully printed in Colours, with descriptive Text, cloth extra, gilt, 6s.

"For fun and frolic the new version of Æsop's Fables must bear away the palm. There are twenty-two fables and twenty-two wonderful coloured illustrations : the moral is pointed, the tale adorned. This is not a juvenile book, but there are plenty of grown-up children who like to be amused at Christmas, and indeed at any time of the year : and if this new version of old stories does not amuse them they must be very dull indeed, and their situation one much to be commiserated."—*Morning Post.*

AINSWORTH'S LATIN DICTIONARY. The only Modern Edition which comprises the Complete Work. With numerous Additions, Emendations, and Improvements, by the Rev. B. W. BEATSON and W. ELLIS. Imperial 8vo, cloth extra, 15s.

AMUSING POETRY. A Selection from the Best Writers. Edited, with Preface, by SHIRLEY BROOKS. Fcap. 8vo, cloth, gilt edges, 3s. 6d.

ANACREON. Translated by THOMAS MOORE, and Illustrated by the exquisite Designs of GIRODET. Oblong 8vo, Etruscan gold and blue, 12s. 6d.

ARTEMUS WARD, COMPLETE.— The Works of CHARLES FARRER BROWNE, better known as ARTEMUS WARD. With fine Portrait, facsimile of Handwriting, &c. Crown 8vo, cloth extra, 7s. 6d.

AS PRETTY AS SEVEN, and other Popular German Stories. Collected by LUDWIG BECHSTEIN. With Additional Tales by the Brothers GRIMM, and 100 Illustrations by RICHTER. Small 4to, green and gold, 6s. 6d. ; gilt edges, 7s. 6d.

ASTLE ON WRITING.—THE ORIGIN AND PROGRESS

OF WRITING, as well Hieroglyphic as Elementary, Illustrated by Engravings taken from Marbles, Manuscripts, and Charters, Ancient and Modern; also Some Account of the Origin and Progress of Printing. By THOMAS ASTLE, F.R.S., F.A S., late Keeper of Records in the Tower of London. Royal 4to, half-Roxburghe, with 33 Plates (some Coloured), price £1 15s. A few Large Paper copies, royal folio, half-Roxburghe, the Plates altogether unfolded, price £3 3s.

BACON'S (Francis, Lord) WORKS, both English and Latin, with

an Introductory Essay, Biographical and Critical, and copious Indexes. Two Vols., imperial 8vo, with Portrait, cloth extra, £1 4s.

BANKERS, A HANDBOOK OF LONDON ; with some Account of

their Predecessors, the Early Goldsmiths, together with Lists of Bankers, from the Earliest London Directory printed in 1677, to the Official List of 1875. By F. G. HILTON PRICE. Crown 8vo, cloth extra, 7s. 6d.   [*In the press.*

BARDSLEY'S OUR ENGLISH SURNAMES : Their Sources

and Significations. By CHARLES WAREING BARDSLEY, M.A. SECOND EDITION, revised throughout, considerably Enlarged, and partially rewritten. Crown 8vo, cloth extra, 9s.

"Mr. Bardsley has faithfully consulted the original mediæval documents and works from which the origin and development of surnames can alone be satisfactorily traced. He has furnished a valuable contribution to the literature of surnames, and we hope to hear more of him in this field."—*Times.*

BAUER AND HOOKER'S GENERA OF FERNS; in which

the Characters of each Genus are displayed in a series of magnified dissections and figures, highly finished in colours, after the drawings of FRANCIS BAUER, with letterpress by Sir WILLIAM HOOKER. Imperial 8vo, with 120 beautifully Coloured Plates, half-morocco, gilt, £5 5s.

BEAUTIFUL PICTURES BY BRITISH ARTISTS: A Gather-

ing of Favourites from our Picture Galleries. In Two Series. The FIRST SERIES• including Examples by WILKIE, CONSTABLE, TURNER, MULREADY LANDSEER, MACLISE, E. M. WARD, FRITH, Sir JOHN GILBERT, LESLIE, ANSDELL, MARCUS STONE, Sir NOEL PATON, FAED, EYRE CROWE, GAVIN, O'NEIL, and MADOX BROWN. The SECOND containing Pictures by ARMYTAGE, FAED, GOODALL, HEMSLEV, HORSLEY, MARKS, NICHOLLS, Sir NOEL PATON, PICKERSGILL, G. SMITH, MARCUS STONE, SOLOMON, STRAIGHT, E. M. WARD, and WARREN. All engraved on Steel in the highest style of Art. Edited, with Notices of the Artists, by SYDNEY ARMYTAGE, M.A. Price of each Series, imperial 4to, cloth extra, gilt and gilt edges, 21s. *Each Volume is Complete in itself.*

BELL'S (Sir Charles) ANATOMY OF EXPRESSION, as

connected with the Fine Arts. Fifth Edition, with an Appendix on the Nervous System by ALEXANDER SHAW. Illustrated with 45 beautiful Engravings. Imp. 8vo, cloth extra, gilt, 16s.

BINGHAM'S ANTIQUITIES of the CHRISTIAN CHURCH.

A New Edition, revised, with copious Index. Two Vols., imperial 8vo, cloth extra, £1 4s.

"A writer who does equal honour to the English clergy and to the English nation, and whose learning is to be equalled only by his moderation and impartiality."— *Quarterly Review.'*   .

BIOGRAPHICAL AND CRITICAL DICTIONARY OF RE-

CENT AND LIVING PAINTERS AND ENGRAVERS, both English and Foreign. By HENRY OTTLEY. Being a Supplementary Volume to "Bryan's Dictionary." Imperial 8vo, cloth extra, 12s.

⁎⁎ *This is the only work giving an account of the principal living painters of all countries.*

BLAKE'S WORKS.—A Series of Reproductions in Facsimile of the Works of WILLIAM BLAKE, including the "Songs of Innocence and Experience," "The Book of Thel," "America," "The Vision of the Daughters of Albion," "The Marriage of Heaven and Hell," "Europe, a Prophecy," "Jerusalem," "Milton," "Urizen," "The Song of Los," &c. These Works will be issued both coloured and plain. [*In preparation.*

"Blake is a real name, I assure you, and a most extraordinary man he is, if he still be living. He is the Blake whose wild designs accompany a splendid edition of Blair's 'Grave.' He paints in water-colours marvellous strange pictures—visions of his brain—which he asserts he has seen. They have great merit. I must look upon him as one of the most extraordinary persons of the age."—CHARLES LAMB.

BLANCHARD'S (Laman) POEMS. Now first Collected. Edited, with a Life of the Author (including numerous hitherto unpublished Letters from Lord LYTTON, LAMB, DICKENS, ROBERT BROWNING, and others), by BLANCHARD JERROLD. Crown 8vo, cloth extra. [*In preparation.*

BOCCACCIO'S DECAMERON; or, Ten Days' Entertainment. Translated into English, with Introduction by THOMAS WRIGHT, Esq., M.A., F.S.A. With Portrait after RAPHAEL, and STOTHARD'S beautiful Copperplates. Crown 8vo, cloth extra, gilt, 7s. 6d.

BOLTON'S SONG BIRDS OF GREAT BRITAIN. Illustrated with Figures, the size of Life, of both Male and Female ; of their Nests and Eggs, Food, Favourite Plants, Shrubs, Trees, &c. &c. Two Vols. in One, royal 4to containing 80 beautifully Coloured Plates, half-Roxburghe, £3 13s. 6d.

BOOKSELLERS, A HISTORY OF. Including the Story of the Rise and Progress of the Great Publishing Houses, in London and the Provinces, and of their greatest Works. By HARRY CURWEN. Crown 8vo, with Frontispiece and numerous Portraits and Illustrations, cloth extra, 7s. 6d.

"In these days, ten ordinary Histories of Kings and Courtiers were well exchanged against the tenth part of one good History of Booksellers."—THOMAS CARLYLE.

"This stout little book is unquestionably amusing. Ill-starred, indeed, must be the reader who, opening it anywhere, lights upon six consecutive pages within the entire compass of which some good anecdote or smart repartee is not to be found."—*Saturday Review.*

BOUDOIR BALLADS : Vers de Société. By J. ASHBY STERRY. Crown 8vo, cloth extra. [*In preparation.*

BRAND'S OBSERVATIONS ON POPULAR ANTIQUITIES, chiefly Illustrating the Origin of our Vulgar Customs, Ceremonies, and Superstitions. Arranged and revised, with Additions, by Sir HENRY ELLIS. A New Edition, with fine full-page Illustrations. Crown 8vo, cloth extra, gilt, 7s. 6d. [*In the press.*

BRET HARTE'S CHOICE WORKS in Prose and Poetry. With Introductory Essay by J. M. BELLEW, Portrait of the Author, and 50 Illustrations. Crown 8vo, cloth extra, 7s. 6d.

BREWSTER'S (Sir David) MARTYRS OF SCIENCE. A New Edition, in small crown 8vo, cloth extra, gilt, with full-page Portraits,4s. 6d.

BREWSTER'S (Sir David) MORE WORLDS THAN ONE, the Creed of the Philosopher and the Hope of the Christian. A New Edition, in small crown 8vo, cloth extra, gilt, with full-page Astronomical Plates, 4s. 6d.

BRIC-À-BRAC HUNTER (The) ; or, Chapters on Chinamania. By Major H. BYNG HALL. With Photographic Frontispiece. Crown 8vo, cloth, full gilt (from a special and novel design), 10s. 6d.

BRITISH ESSAYISTS (The) : viz., "Spectator," "Tatler," "Guardian," "Rambler," "Adventurer," "Idler," and "Connoisseur." Complete in Three thick Vols., 8vo with Portrait, cloth extra, £1 7s.

BROADSTONE HALL, and other Poems. By W. E. WINDUS.
With 40 Illustrations by ALFRED CONCANEN. Crown 8vo, cloth extra, gilt, 5s.

"This little volume of poems is illustrated with such vigour, and shows such a thoroughly practical knowledge of and love for sea-life, that it is quite tonic and refreshing. Maudlin sentimentality is carefully eschewed, and a robust, manly tone of thought gives muscle to the verse and elasticity of mind to the reader."—*Morning Post.*

BROCKEDON'S PASSES OF THE ALPS. Containing 109 fine Engravings by FINDEN, WILLMORE, and others ; with Maps of each Pass, and a General Map of the Alps by ARROWSMITH. Two Vols., 4to, half-bound morocco, gilt edges, £3 13s. 6d.

BULWER'S (Lytton) PILGRIMS OF THE RHINE. With Portrait and 27 exquisite Line Engravings on Steel, by GOODALL, WILLMORE, and others ; after Drawings by DAVID ROBERTS and MACLISE. Crown 8vo, cloth extra, top edges gilt, 10s. 6d.

BUNYAN'S PILGRIM'S PROGRESS. Edited by Rev. T. SCOTT. With 17 beautiful Steel Plates by STOTHARD, engraved by GOODALL ; and numerous Woodcuts. Crown 8vo, cloth extra, gilt, 7s. 6d.

BURNET'S HISTORY OF HIS OWN TIME, from the Restoration of Charles II. to the Treaty of Peace at Utrecht. With Historical and Biographical Notes and copious Index. Imp. 8vo, with Portrait, cloth extra, 13s. 6d.

BURNET'S HISTORY OF THE REFORMATION OF THE CHURCH OF ENGLAND. A New Edition, with numerous illustrative Notes and copious Index. Two Vols., imperial 8vo, cloth extra, £1 1s.

BYRON'S (Lord) LETTERS AND JOURNALS. With Notices of his Life. By THOMAS MOORE. A Reprint of the Original Edition, newly revised, complete in a thick Volume of 1060 pp., with Twelve full-page Plates. Crown 8vo, cloth extra, gilt, 7s. 6d.

"We have read this book with the greatest pleasure. Considered merely as a composition, it deserves to be classed among the best specimens of English prose which our age has produced. . . . The style is agreeable, clear, and manly, and, when it rises into eloquence, rises without effort or ostentation. Nor is the matter inferior to the manner. It would be difficult to name a book which exhibits more kindness, fairness, and modesty."—MACAULAY, in the *Edinburgh Review.*

CALMET'S BIBLE DICTIONARY. Edited by CHARLES TAYLOR. With the Fragments incorporated and arranged in Alphabetical Order. New Edition. Imperial 8vo, with Maps and Wood Engravings, cloth extra, 10s. 6d.

CANOVA'S WORKS IN SCULPTURE AND MODELLING. 150 Plates, exquisitely engraved in Outline by MOSES, and printed on an India tint. With Descriptions by the Countess ALBRIZZI, a Biographical Memoir by CICOGNARA, and Portrait by WORTHINGTON. A New Edition. Demy 4to, cloth extra, gilt, gilt edges, 31s. 6d.   [*In the press.*

CARLYLE (Thomas) ON THE CHOICE OF BOOKS. With New Life and Anecdotes. Small post 8vo, brown cloth, 1s. 6d.

CAROLS OF COCKAYNE ; Vers de Société descriptive of London Life. By HENRY S. LEIGH. Third Edition. With numerous Illustrations by ALFRED CONCANEN. Crown 8vo, cloth extra, gilt, 5s.

CARTER'S ANCIENT ARCHITECTURE OF ENGLAND. Including the Orders during the British, Roman, Saxon, and Norman Eras ; and also under the Reigns of Henry III. and Edward III. Illustrated by 103 large Copperplate Engravings, comprising upwards of Two Thousand Specimens. Edited by JOHN BRITTON. Royal folio, half-morocco extra, £2 8s.

*** *This national work on ancient architecture occupied its author, in drawing tching, arranging, and publishing, more than twenty years, and he himsel declared it to be the result of his studies through life.*

CARTER'S ANCIENT SCULPTURE NOW REMAINING
IN ENGLAND, from the Earliest Period to the Reign of Henry VIII.; consisting of Statues, Basso-relievos, Sculptures, &c., Brasses, Monumental Effigies,
Paintings on Glass and on Walls ; Missal Ornaments : Carvings on Cups, Croziers,
Chests, Seals ; Ancient Furniture, &c. &c. With Historical and Critical Illustrations by DOUCE, MEYRICK, DAWSON TURNER, and JOHN BRITTON. Royal
folio, with 120 large Engravings, many Illuminated, half-bound morocco extra,
£8 8s.

CATLIN'S ILLUSTRATIONS OF THE MANNERS, CUS-
TOMS, AND CONDITION OF THE NORTH AMERICAN INDIANS,
written during Eight Years of Travel and Adventure among the Wildest and most
Remarkable Tribes now existing. Containing 360 Coloured Engravings from the
Author's original Paintings. Two Vols., imperial 8vo, Cloth extra, gilt, the Plates
beautifully printed in Colours, £1 10s.

"One of the most admirable observers of manners who ever lived among the
aborigines of America."—HUMBOLDT'S *Cosmos.*

CATLIN'S NORTH AMERICAN INDIAN PORTFOLIO. Con-
taining Hunting Scenes, Amusements, Scenery, and Costume of the Indians of
the Rocky Mountains and Prairies of America, from Drawings and Notes made
by the Author during Eight Years' Travel. A series of 31 magnificent Plates,
beautifully coloured in facsimile of the Original Drawings exhibited at the Egyptian Hall. With Letterpress Descriptions, imperial folio, half-morocco, gilt,
£7 10s.

⁎ *Five of the above Drawings are now for the first time published.*

CHAMBERLAINE'S IMITATIONS OF DRAWINGS FROM
THE GREAT MASTERS in the Royal Collection. Engraved by BARTOLOZZI
and others. 74 fine Plates, mostly tinted ; including, in addition, "Ecce Homo,"
after GUIDO, and the scarce Series of 7 Anatomical Drawings. Imperial folio,
half-morocco, gilt edges, £5 5s.

CHATTO'S (W. Andrew) HISTORY OF WOOD ENGRAVING,
Historical and Practical. A New Edition, with an Additional Chapter. Illustrated
by 445 fine Wood Engravings. Imperial 8vo, half-Roxburghe, £2 2s.

"This volume is one of the most interesting and valuable of modern times."—*Art
Union.*

CHRISTMAS CAROLS AND BALLADS. Selected and
Edited by JOSHUA SYLVESTER. Cloth extra, gilt, gilt edges, 3s. 6d.

CICERO'S FAMILIAR LETTERS, AND LETTERS TO
ATTICUS. Translated by MELMOTH and HEBERDEN. With Life of Cicero by
MIDDLETON. Royal 8vo, with Portrait, cloth extra, 12s.

"Cicero is the type of a perfect letter-writer, never boring you with moral essays
out of season, always evincing his mastery over his art by the most careful consideration for your patience and amusement. We should rifle the volumes of antiquity in vain to find a letter-writer who converses on paper so naturally, so
engagingly, so much from the heart as Cicero."—*Quarterly Review.*

CLAUDE'S LIBER VERITATIS. A Collection of 303 Prints
after the Original Designs of CLAUDE. Engraved by RICHARD EARLOM. With
a descriptive Catalogue of each Print, Lists of the Persons for whom, and the Places
for which, the original Pictures were first painted, and of the present Possessors
of most of them. London : published by Messrs. Boydell and Co., Cheapside.
Printed by W. Bulmer and Co., Cleveland Row, 1777. Three Vols. folio, half-
morocco extra, gilt edges, £10 10s.

CLAUDE, BEAUTIES OF, containing 24 of his choicest Land-
scapes, beautifully Engraved on Steel, by BROMLEY, LUPTON, and others. With
Biographical Sketch and Portrait. Royal folio, in a portfolio, £1 5s.

COLLINS' (Wilkie) NOVELS. New Illustrated Library Editions, price 6s. each, with Frontispiece and several full-page Illustrations in each Volume:—

The Woman in White. Illustrated by Sir JOHN GILBERT and F. A. FRASER.

Antonina; or, The Fall of Rome. Illustrated by Sir JOHN GILBERT and ALFRED CONCANEN.

Basil. Illustrated by Sir JOHN GILBERT and M. F. MAHONEY.

The Dead Secret. Illustrated by Sir JOHN GILBERT and H. FURNISS.

The Queen of Hearts. Illustrated by Sir JOHN GILBERT and ALFRED CONCANEN.

The Moonstone. Illustrated by G. DU MAURIER and F. A. FRASER.

Man and Wife. Illustrated by WILLIAM SMALL.

Hide and Seek; or, The Mystery of Mary Grice. Illustrated by Sir JOHN GILBERT and M. F. MAHONEY.

Poor Miss Finch. Illustrated by GEORGE DU MAURIER and EDWARD HUGHES.

Miss or Mrs.? Illustrated by S. L. FILDES and HENRY WOODS.

The New Magdalen. With Illustrations by GEO. DU MAURIER and C. S. R.

The Frozen Deep. Illustrated by G. DU MAURIER and M. F. MAHONEY.

My Miscellanies. With Steel-plate Portrait of the Author, and Illustrations by ALFRED CONCANEN.

COLLINS' (Wilkie) THE LAW AND THE LADY. Three Vols., crown 8vo, 31s. 6d.
"*Edwin.* Read any novels lately?—*Angelina.* Just read an awfully nice book, 'The Law and the Lady.' One of the heroes is a monstrosity without legs, 'Miserrimus Dexter,' don't you know. Awfully clever.—*Edwin.* O yes. Read the book myself. Clever notion, the idiotic man-woman, eh, wasn't it?—*Angelina.* O yes, awfully good."—*Punch.*
"An exceedingly clever novel, full of admirable writing, abounding in a subtle ingenuity which is a distinct order of genius. . . . . 'The Law and the Lady' will be read with avidity by all who delight in the romances of the greatest master the sensational novel has ever known."—*World.*

COLMAN'S HUMOROUS WORKS.—Broad Grins, My Nightgown and Slippers, and other Humorous Works, Prose and Poetical, of GEORGE COLMAN. With Life and Anecdotes by G. B. BUCKSTONE, and Frontispiece by HOGARTH. Crown 8vo, cloth extra, gilt, 7s. 6d.

CONEY'S ENGRAVINGS OF ANCIENT CATHEDRALS, Hôtels de Ville, Town Halls, &c., including some of the finest Examples of Gothic Architecture in France, Holland, Germany, and Italy. 32 large Plates, imperial folio, half-morocco extra, £3 13s. 6d.

CONQUEST OF THE SEA (The). A History of Diving from the Earliest Times. By HENRY SIEBE. Profusely Illustrated. Crown 8vo, cloth extra, gilt, 4s. 6d.
"We have perused this volume, full of quaint information, with delight. Mr. Siebe has bestowed much pains on his work; he writes with enthusiasm and fulness of knowledge."—*Echo.*
"Really interesting alike to youths and to grown-up people."—*Scotsman.*

CONSTABLE'S GRAPHIC WORKS. Comprising 40 highly finished Mezzotinto Engravings on Steel, by DAVID LUCAS; with descriptive Letterpress by C. R. LESLIE, R.A. Folio, half-morocco, gilt edges, £2 2s.

COTMAN'S ENGRAVINGS OF THE SEPULCHRAL BRASSES IN NORFOLK AND SUFFOLK. With Letterpress Descriptions, an Essay on Sepulchral Memorials by DAWSON TURNER, Notes by Sir SAMUEL MEYRICK, ALBERT WAY, and Sir HARRIS NICOLAS, and copious Index. New Edition, containing 173 Plates, two of them splendidly Illuminated. Two Volumes, small folio, half-morocco extra, £6 6s.

COTMAN'S ETCHINGS OF ARCHITECTURAL REMAINS, chiefly Norman and Gothic, in various Counties in England, but principally in Norfolk, with Descriptive Notices by DAWSON TURNER, and Architectural Observations by THOMAS RICKMAN. Two Vols., imperial folio, containing 240 spirited Etchings, half-morocco, top edges gilt, £8 8s.

COTMAN'S LIBER STUDIORUM. A Series of Landscape Studies and Original Compositions, for the Use of Art Students, consisting of 48 Etchings, the greater part executed in "soft ground." Imperial folio, half-morocco, £1 11s. 6d.

COWPER'S POETICAL WORKS. Including his Translation of HOMER. Edited by the Rev. H. F. CARY. With Portrait and 18 Steel Engravings after HARVEY. Royal 8vo, cloth extra, gilt edges, 10s. 6d.

"I long to know your opinion of Cowper's Translation. The *Odyssey* especially is surely very Homeric. What nobler than the appearance of Phœbus at the beginning of the *Iliad*—lines ending with ' Dread sounding-bounding in the silver bow'?"—CHARLES LAMB, *in a Letter to Coleridge.*

CREASY'S MEMOIRS OF EMINENT ETONIANS; with Notices of the Early History of Eton College. By Sir EDWARD CREASY, Author of "The Fifteen Decisive Battles of the World." A New Edition, brought down to the Present Time, with Illustrations. Crown 8vo, cloth extra. [*In the press.*

CRUIKSHANK AT HOME. Tales and Sketches by the most Popular Authors. With numerous Illustrations by ROBERT CRUIKSHANK and ROBERT SEYMOUR. Also, CRUIKSHANK'S ODD VOLUME, or Book of Variety, Illustrated by Two Odd Fellows—SEYMOUR and CRUIKSHANK. Four Vols. bound in Two, fcap. 8vo, cloth extra, gilt, 10s. 6d.

CRUIKSHANK'S COMIC ALMANACK. Complete in TWO SERIES: The FIRST from 1835 to 1843 ; the SECOND from 1844 to 1853. A Gathering of the BEST HUMOUR of THACKERAY, HOOD, MAYHEW, ALBERT SMITH, A'BECKETT, ROBERT BROUGH, &c. With 2000 Woodcuts and Steel Engravings by CRUIKSHANK, HINE, LANDELLS, &c. Crown 8vo, cloth gilt, two very thick volumes, 15s.; or, separately, 7s. 6d. per volume.

CRUIKSHANK'S UNIVERSAL SONGSTER. The largest Collection extant of the best Old English Songs (upwards of 5000). With 8 Engravings on Steel and Wood by GEORGE and R. CRUIKSHANK, and 8 Portraits. Three Vols., 8vo, cloth extra, gilt, 21s.

CUSSANS' HANDBOOK OF HERALDRY. With Instructions for Tracing Pedigrees and Deciphering Ancient MSS.; Rules for the Appointment of Liveries, Chapters on Continental and American Heraldry, &c. &c. By JOHN E. CUSSANS. Illustrated with 360 Plates and Woodcuts. Crown 8vo, cloth extra, gilt and emblazoned, 7s. 6d.

CUSSANS' HISTORY OF HERTFORDSHIRE. A County History, got up in a very superior manner, and ranging with the finest works of its class. By JOHN E. CUSSANS. Illustrated with full-page Plates on Copper and Stone, and a profusion of small Woodcuts. Parts I. to VIII. now ready, 21s. each.

⁎ *An entirely new History of this important County, great attention being given to all matters pertaining to Family History.*

CUVIER'S ANIMAL KINGDOM, arranged after its Organization : forming a Natural History of Animals, and an Introduction to Comparative Anatomy. New Edition, with considerable Additions by W. B. CARPENTER and J. O. WESTWOOD. Illustrated by many Hundred Wood Engravings, and numerous Steel Engravings by THOS. LANDSEER, mostly Coloured. Imperial 8vo, cloth extra, 18s.

8 BOOKS PUBLISHED BY

CYCLOPÆDIA OF COSTUME ; or, A Dictionary of Dress—Regal, Ecclesiastical, Civil, and Military—from the Earliest Period in England to the reign of George the Third. Including Notices of Contemporaneous Fashions on the Continent, and preceded by a General History of the Costumes of the Principal Countries of Europe. By J. R. PLANCHÉ, Somerset Herald. To be Completed in Twenty-four Parts, quarto, at Five Shillings each, profusely illustrated by Coloured and Plain Plates and Wood Engravings.—A Prospectus will be sent upon application. [*In course of publication.*]

"There is no subject connected with dress with which 'Somerset Herald' is not as familiar as ordinary men are with the ordinary themes of everyday life. The gathered knowledge of many years is placed before the world in this his latest work, and when finished, there will exist no work on the subject half so valuable. The numerous illustrations are all effective—for their accuracy the author is responsible ; they are well drawn and well engraved, and, while indispensable to a proper comprehension of the text, are satisfactory as works of art."—*Art Journal.*

"These, the first numbers of a Cyclopædia of Ancient and Modern Costume, give promise that the work, when complete, will be one of the most perfect works ever published upon the subject. The illustrations are numerous and excellent, and would, even without the letterpress, render the work an invaluable book of reference for information as to costumes for fancy balls and character quadrilles."—*Standard.*

"Destined, we anticipate, to be the standard English work on dress."—*Builder.*

"Promises to be a very complete work on a subject of the greatest importance to the historian and the archæologist."—*Tablet.*

"Beautifully printed and superbly illustrated."—*Standard*, second notice.

D'ARBLAY'S (Madame) DIARY AND LETTERS. Edited by her Niece, CHARLOTTE BARRETT. A New Edition, in Four Vols., 8vo. Illustrated by numerous fine Portraits engraved on Steel. [*In the press.*]

DIBDIN'S (T. F.) BIBLIOMANIA ; or, Book-Madness : A Bibliographical Romance. With numerous Illustrations. A New Edition, with a Supplement, including a Key to the Assumed Characters in the Drama. Demy 8vo, half-Roxburghe. 21s. ; a few Large Paper copies, half-Roxburghe, the edges altogether uncut, at 42s. [*In the press.*]

DICKENS' LIFE AND SPEECHES. Royal 16mo, cloth extra, 2s. 6d.

DISCOUNT TABLES, on a new and simple plan ; to facilitate the Discounting of Bills, and the Calculation of Interest on Banking and Current Accounts, &c. ; showing, without calculation, the number of days from every day in the year to any other day. By THOMAS READER. Post 8vo, cloth extra, 7s.

DIXON'S (Hepworth) NEW WORK.—WHITE CONQUEST : AMERICA IN 1875. 2 vols. demy 8vo, cloth extra, 30s. [*In the press.*]

DON QUIXOTE : A Revised Translation, based upon those of MOTTEUX, JARVIS, and SMOLLETT. With 50 Illustrations by ARMSTRONG and TONY JOHANNOT. Royal 8vo, cloth extra, gilt, 10s. 6d.

DON QUIXOTE IN SPANISH.—EL INGENIOSO HIDALGO DON QUIJOTE DE LA MANCHA. Nueva Edicion, corregida y revisada. Por MIGUEL DE CERVANTES SAAVEDRA. Complete in One Volume, post 8vo, nearly 700 pages, cloth extra, price 4s. 6d.

DRURY'S ILLUSTRATIONS of FOREIGN ENTOMOLOGY. Containing, in 150 beautifully Coloured Plates, upwards of 600 Exotic Insects of the East and West Indies, China, New Holland, North and South America, Germany, &c. With important Additions and Scientific Indexes, by J. O. WESTWOOD, F.L.S. Three Vols., 4to, half-morocco extra, £5 5s.

DULWICH GALLERY (The): A Series of 50 beautifully Coloured Plates, from the most celebrated Pictures in this Collection, executed by the Custodian, R. COCKBURN, and mounted upon Cardboard, in the manner of Drawings. Imperial folio, in portfolio, £16 16s.

DUNLOP'S HISTORY OF FICTION: Being a Critical and
Analytical Account of the most celebrated Prose Works of Fiction, from the
Earliest Greek Romances to the Novels of the Present Day, with General Index.
Third Edition, royal 8vo, cloth extra, 9s.

DUNRAVEN'S (The Earl of) THE GREAT DIVIDE: A
Narrative of Travels in the Upper Yellowstone in the Summer of 1874. With
numerous striking full-page Illustrations by VALENTINE W. BROMLEY. Demy 8vo,
cloth extra, with Maps and Illustrations. [*In the press.*

EARLY ENGLISH POETS. A New Series is in preparation,
Edited, with Introductions and copious Notes, by the Rev. A. B. GROSART.
The following are in the press :—THE COMPLETE WORKS OF GILES FLETCHER,
B.D.—THE WORKS OF SIR JOHN DAVIES.—THE WORKS OF SIR PHILIP SIDNEY.

ELLIS'S (Mrs.) MOTHERS OF GREAT MEN. A New Edi-
tion, with Illustrations by VALENTINE BROMLEY. Crown 8vo, cloth gilt, 6s.

EMANUEL ON DIAMONDS AND PRECIOUS STONES ;
Their History, Value, and Properties; with Simple Tests for ascertaining their
Reality. By HARRY EMANUEL, F.R.G.S. With numerous Illustrations, Tinted
and Plain. A New Edition, crown 8vo, cloth extra, gilt, 6s.

ENGLISHMAN'S HOUSE (The): A Practical Guide to all in-
terested in Selecting or Building a House, with full Estimates of Cost, Quantities,
&c. By C. J. RICHARDSON. Third Edition. With nearly 600 Illustrations.
Crown 8vo, cloth extra, 7s. 6d.

*** This book is intended to supply a long-felt want, viz., a plain, non-technical
account of every style of house, with the cost and manner of building; it gives
every variety, from a workman's cottage to a nobleman's palace.*

FAIRHOLT.—TOBACCO : Its History and Associations; in-
cluding an Account of the Plant and its Manufacture ; with its Modes of Use
in all Ages and Countries. By F. W. FAIRHOLT, F.S.A. With Coloured Frontispiece and upwards of 100 Illustrations by the Author. Crown 8vo, cloth extra,
6s. [*In the press.*

FARADAY'S CHEMICAL HISTORY OF A CANDLE.
Lectures delivered to a Juvenile Audience. A New Edition, Edited by W.
CROOKES, Esq., F.C.S., &c. Crown 8vo, cloth extra, with numerous Illustra-
tions, 4s. 6d.

FARADAY'S VARIOUS FORCES OF NATURE. A New
Edition, Edited by W. CROOKES, Esq., F.C.S., &c. Crown 8vo, cloth extra, with
numerous Illustrations, 4s. 6d.

FIGUIER'S PRIMITIVE MAN : A Popular Manual of the pre-
vailing Theories of the Descent of Man as promulgated by DARWIN, LYELL, Sir
JOHN LUBBOCK, HUXLEY, E. B. TYLOR, and other eminent Ethnologists. Translated from the last French edition, and revised by E. B. T. With 263 Illustrations. Demy 8vo, cloth extra, gilt, 9s.

"An interesting and essentially popular resumé of all that has been written on
the subject. M. Figuier has collected together the evidences which modern researches have accumulated, and has done this with a considerable amount of care.
He endeavours to separate the inquiry respecting Primitive Man from the Mosaic
account of Man's creation, and does not admit that the authority of Holy Writ is in
any way questioned by those labours which aim at seeking the real epoch of Man's
first appearance upon earth. . . . An interesting book, with 263 illustrations, of
which thirty are full-page engravings, confessedly somewhat fanciful in their com-
binations, but which will be found on examination to be justified by that soundest evidence, the actual discovery of the objects of which they represent the use."—*Athenæum.*

FINGER-RING LORE: Historical and Anecdotal. By WILLIAM
JONES, F.S.A. With Hundreds of Illustrations of Curious Rings of all Ages and
Countries. Crown 8vo, cloth extra, gilt, 7s. 6d. [*In the press.*

FINISH TO LIFE IN AND OUT OF LONDON ; or, The Final Adventures of Tom, Jerry, and Logic. By PIERCE EGAN. Royal 8vo, cloth extra, with spirited Coloured Illustrations by CRUIKSHANK, 21*s.*

FLAGELLATION AND THE FLAGELLANTS.—A History of the Rod in all Countries, from the Earliest Period to the Present Time. By the Rev. W. COOPER, B.A. Third Edition, revised and corrected, with numerous Illustrations. Thick crown 8vo, cloth extra, gilt, 12*s.* 6*d.*

FOX'S BOOK OF MARTYRS: The Acts and Monuments of the Church. Edited by JOHN CUMMING, D.D. With upwards of 1000 Illustrations. Three Vols., imperial 8vo, cloth extra, £2 12*s.* 6*d.*

GELL'S TOPOGRAPHY OF ROME AND ITS VICINITY. A New Edition, revised and enlarged by E. H. BUNBURY. With a large mounted Map of Rome and its Environs (from a careful Trigonometrical Survey). Two Vols., 8vo, cloth extra, 15*s.*

GELL AND GANDY'S POMPEIANA; or, The Topography, Edifices, and Ornaments of Pompeii. With upwards of 100 Line Engravings by GOODALL, COOKE, HEATH, PYE, &c. Demy 8vo, cloth extra, gilt, 18*s.*

GEMMER'S (Mrs.) PLEASANT RHYMES FOR LITTLE READERS. By CAROLINE M. GEMMER (GERDA FAY). With numerous Illustrations. Crown 8vo, cloth extra.   [*In the press.*

GEMS OF ART : A Collection of 36 Engravings, after Paintings by REMBRANDT, CUYP, REYNOLDS, POUSSIN, MURILLO, TENIERS, CORREGGIO, GAINSBOROUGH, NORTHCOTE, &c., executed in Mezzotint by TURNER, BROMLEY, &c. Folio, in Portfolio, £1 11*s.* 6*d.*

GENIAL SHOWMAN; or, Show Life in the New World. Adventures with Artemus Ward, and the Story of his Life. By E. P. HINGSTON. Third Edition. Crown 8vo, Illustrated by W. BRUNTON, cloth extra, 7*s.* 6*d.*

GIBBON'S ROMAN EMPIRE (The Decline and Fall of the). With Memoir of the Author, and full General Index. Imperial 8vo, with Portrait, cloth extra, 15*s.*

GILBERT'S (W. S.) DRAMATIC WORKS (" A Wicked World," "Charity," "Palace of Truth," "Pygmalion," "Trial by Jury," &c.). One Vol., crown 8vo, cloth extra.   [*In the press.*

GIL BLAS.—HISTORIA DE GIL BLAS DE SANTILLANA. Por LE SAGE. Traducida al Castellano por el PADRE ISLA. Nueva Edicion, corregida y revisada. Complete in One Vol., post 8vo, cl. extra, nearly 600 pp., 4*s.* 6*d.*

GILLRAY'S CARICATURES. Printed from the Original Plates, all engraved by Himself between 1779 and 1810; comprising the best Political and Humorous Satires of the Reign of GEORGE THE THIRD, in upwards of 600 highly spirited Engravings. Atlas folio, half-morocco extra, gilt edges, £7 10*s.*—There is also a Volume of the SUPPRESSED PLATES, atlas folio, half-morocco, 31*s.* 6*d.*— Also, a VOLUME OF LETTERPRESS DESCRIPTIONS, comprising a very amusing Political History of the Reign of GEORGE THE THIRD, by THOS. WRIGHT and R. H. EVANS. Demy 8vo, cloth extra, 15*s.* ; or half-morocco, £1 1*s.*

GILLRAY, THE CARICATURIST : The Story of his Life and Times, and Anecdotal Descriptions of his Engravings. Edited by THOMAS WRIGHT, Esq., M.A., F.S.A. With 83 full-page Plates, and numerous Wood Engravings. Demy 4to, 600 pages, cloth extra, 31*s.* 6*d.*

"High as the expectations excited by this description [in the Introduction] may be, they will not be disappointed. The most inquisitive or exacting reader will find ready gathered to his hand, without the trouble of reference, almost every scrap of narrative, anecdote, gossip, scandal, or epigram, in poetry or prose, that he can possibly require for the elucidation of the caricatures."—*Quarterly Review.*

GLEIG'S CHELSEA PENSIONERS : Saratoga, the Rivals, and other Stories. By the Rev. G. R. GLEIG, late Chaplain to Her Majesty's Forces. Post 8vo, illustrated boards, 2s.

GOLDEN LIBRARY.
Square 16mo (Tauchnitz size), cloth, extra gilt, price 2s. per Vol.

BYRON'S DON JUAN.

CLERICAL ANECDOTES : Humours of "the Cloth."

HOLMES'S AUTOCRAT OF THE BREAKFAST TABLE. With an Introduction by GEORGE AUGUSTUS SALA.

HOLMES'S PROFESSOR AT THE BREAKFAST TABLE.

HOOD'S WHIMS AND ODDITIES. Both Series Complete in One Volume, with all the original Illustrations.

IRVING'S (Washington) TALES OF A TRAVELLER.

IRVING'S (Washington) TALES OF THE ALHAMBRA.

JESSE'S (Edward) SCENES AND OCCUPATIONS OF COUNTRY LIFE; with Recollections of Natural History.

LAMB'S ESSAYS OF ELIA. Both Series Complete in One Vol.

LEIGH HUNT'S ESSAYS : A Tale for a Chimney Corner, and other Pieces. With Portrait, and Introduction by EDMUND OLLIER.

MALLORY'S (Sir Thomas) MORT D'ARTHUR : The Stories of King Arthur and of the Knights of the Round Table. Edited by B. M. RANKING.

PASCAL'S PROVINCIAL LETTERS. A New Translation, with Historical Introduction and Notes, by T. M'CRIE, D.D., LL.D.

POPE'S COMPLETE POETICAL WORKS. Reprinted from the Original Editions.

ROCHEFOUCAULD'S MAXIMS AND MORAL REFLEC- TIONS. With Notes, and an Introductory Essay by SAINTE-BEUVE.

ST. PIERRE'S PAUL AND VIRGINIA AND THE INDIAN COTTAGE. Edited, with Life, by the Rev. E. CLARKE.

SHELLEY'S EARLY POEMS, AND QUEEN MAB, with Essay by LEIGH HUNT.

SHELLEY'S LATER POEMS : Laon and Cythna, &c.

SHELLEY'S POSTHUMOUS POEMS, the SHELLEY PAPERS, &c.

SHELLEY'S PROSE WORKS, including A Refutation of Deism, Zastrozzi, St. Irvyne, &c.

WHITE'S NATURAL HISTORY OF SELBORNE. Edited, with additions, by THOMAS BROWN, F.L.S.

GOLDEN TREASURY OF THOUGHT. An Encyclopædia of Quotations from Writers of all Times and all Countries. Selected and Edited by THEODORE TAYLOR. Crown 8vo, cloth gilt, and gilt edges, 7s. 6d.

GOSPELS (The Holy). Illustrated with upwards of 200 Wood Engravings, after the best Masters, and every page surrounded by ornamental Borders. Handsomely printed, imperial 4to, cloth, full gilt (Grolier style), 10s. 6d.

GRAMMONT (Count), MEMOIRS OF. By ANTHONY HAMIL-TON. A New Edition, with a Biographical Sketch of Count Hamilton, numerous Historical and Illustrative Notes by Sir WALTER SCOTT, and 64 Copperplate Portraits by EDWARD SCRIVEN. 8vo, cloth extra, 12s. 6d.   [*In the press.*

GREENWOOD'S (James) LOW-LIFE DEEPS : An Account of Strange Fish to be found there ; including "The Man and Dog Fight," with much additional and confirmatory evidence ; "With a Tally-Man," "A Fallen Star," "The Betting Barber," "A Coal Marriage," &c. With Illustrations in tint by ALFRED CONCANEN. Crown 8vo, cloth extra, gilt, 7s. 6d. [*In the press.*]

GREENWOOD'S WILDS OF LONDON ; Descriptive Sketches from Personal Observations and Experience of Remarkable Scenes, People, and Places in London. By JAMES GREENWOOD, the "Lambeth Casual." With 12 Tinted Illustrations by ALFRED CONCANEN. Crown 8vo, cloth extra, gilt, 7s. 6d.
"Mr. James Greenwood presents himself once more in the character of 'one whose delight it is to do his humble endeavour towards exposing and extirpating social abuses and those hole-and-corner evils which afflict society.'"—*Saturday Review.*

GREVILLE'S CRYPTOGAMIC FLORA. Comprising the Principal Species found in Great Britain, inclusive of all the New Species recently discovered in Scotland. Six Vols., royal 8vo, with 360 beautifully Coloured Plates, half-morocco, gilt, £7 7s. ; the Plates uncoloured, £4 14s. 6d.
"A truly admirable work, which may be honestly designated as so excellent, that nothing can be found to compete with it in the whole range of Indigenous Botany ; whether we consider the importance of its critical discussions, the accuracy of the drawings, the minuteness of the analyses, or the unusual care which is evident in the publishing department."—LOUDON.

GRIMM.—GERMAN POPULAR STORIES. Collected by the Brothers GRIMM, and Translated by EDGAR TAYLOR. Edited, with an Introduction, by JOHN RUSKIN. With 22 Illustrations after the inimitable designs of GEORGE CRUIKSHANK. Both Series Complete. Square crown 8vo, 6s. 6d. ; gilt leaves, 7s. 6d.
"The illustrations of this volume . . . . are of quite sterling and admirable art, of a class precisely parallel in elevation to the character of the tales which they illustrate ; and the original etchings, as I have before said in the Appendix to my 'Elements of Drawing,' were unrivalled in masterfulness of touch since Rembrandt (in some qualities of delineation, unrivalled even by him). . . . . To make somewhat enlarged copies of them, looking at them through a magnifying glass, and never putting two lines where Cruikshank has put only one, would be an exercise in decision and severe drawing which would leave afterwards little to be learnt in schools."—*Extract from Introduction by* JOHN RUSKIN.

GUYOT'S EARTH AND MAN ; or, Physical Geography in its Relation to the History of Mankind. With Additions by Professors AGASSIZ, PIERCE, and GRAY. With 12 Maps and Engravings on Steel, some Coloured, and a copious Index. A New Edition. Crown 8vo, cloth extra, gilt, 4s. 6d.

HAKE'S (T. GORDON) NEW SYMBOLS : Poems. By the Author of "Parables and Tales." Crown 8vo, cloth extra. [*In the press.*]

HALL'S (Mrs. S. C.) SKETCHES OF IRISH CHARACTER. With numerous Illustrations on Steel and Wood, by DANIEL MACLISE, Sir JOHN GILBERT, W. HARVEY, and G. CRUIKSHANK. 8vo, cloth extra, gilt, 7s. 6d.
"The Irish sketches of this lady resemble Miss Mitford's beautiful English Sketches in 'Our Village,' but they are far more vigorous and picturesque and bright."—*Blackwood's Magazine.*

HALL-MARKS (BOOK OF) ; or, Manual of Reference for the Goldsmith and Silversmith. By ALFRED LUTSCHAUNIG. Crown 8vo, with 46 Plates of the Hall-marks of the different Assay Towns of the Kingdom. 7s. 6d.

HARRIS'S AURELIAN ; A Natural History of English Moths and Butterflies, and the Plants on which they feed. A New Edition. Edited, with Additions, by J. O. WESTWOOD. With about 400 exquisitely Coloured Figures of Moths, Butterflies, Caterpillars, &c., and the Plants on which they feed. Small folio, half-morocco extra, gilt edges, £3 13s. 6d

HAYDON'S (B. R.) MEMOIR, CORRESPONDENCE, AND TABLE-TALK. By his Son, F. W. HAYDON. Comprising a large number of hitherto unpublished Letters from KEATS, WILKIE, SOUTHEY, WORDSWORTH, KIRKUP, LAMB, LEIGH HUNT, LANDSEER, and others. Two Volumes, demy 8vo, cloth extra, illustrated with a Portrait and facsimiles of many interesting Sketches; including a Portrait of HAYDON drawn by KEATS, and HAYDON'S Portraits of WILKIE, KEATS, LEIGH HUNT, and MARIA FOOTE, Sketched by him in his Journals. *[In the press.*

HEEREN'S HISTORICAL WORKS. Translated from the German by GEORGE BANCROFT, and various Oxford Scholars. Six Vols., 8vo, cloth extra, £1 16s.; or, separately, 6s. per volume.

₊ *The Contents of the Volumes are as follows:*—Vols. 1 and 2. Historical Researches into the Politics, Intercourse, and Trade of the Ancient Nations of Asia; 3. Researches into the Politics, Intercourse, and Trade of the Ancient Nations of Africa, including the Carthaginians, Ethiopians, and Egyptians; 4. History of the Political System of Europe and its Colonies; 5. History of Ancient Greece, with Historical Treatises; 6. A Manual of Ancient History, with special reference to the Constitutions, Commerce, and Colonies of the States of Antiquity.

" Prof. Heeren's Historical Researches stand in the very highest rank among those with which modern Germany has enriched European literature."—*Quarterly Review.*

" We look upon Heeren as having breathed a new life into the dry bones of Ancient History. In countries, the history of which has been too imperfectly known to afford lessons of political wisdom, he has taught us still more interesting lessons—on the social relations of men, and the intercourse of nations in the earlier ages of the world. His work is as learned as a professed commentary on the ancient historians and geographers, and as entertaining as a modern book of travels."—*Edinburgh Review.*

HISTORICAL PORTRAITS; Upwards of 430 Engravings of Rare Prints. Comprising the Collections of RODD and GRAINGER, RICHARDSON, CAULFIELD, &c. With Descriptive Text to every Plate, giving a brief outline of the most important Historical and Biographical Facts and Dates connected with each Portrait, and references to original Authorities. In Three Vols., royal 4to, Roxburghe binding, price £6 6s. *[In the press.*

THE ORIGINAL HOGARTH.

HOGARTH'S WORKS. ENGRAVED BY HIMSELF. 153 fine Plates, with elaborate Letterpress Descriptions by JOHN NICHOLS. Atlas folio, half-morocco extra, gilt edges, £7 10s.

" I was pleased with the reply of a gentleman who, being asked which book he esteemed most in his library, answered 'Shakespeare'; being asked which he esteemed next best, answered 'Hogarth.'"—CHARLES LAMB.

HOGARTH'S WORKS. With Life and Anecdotal Descriptions of the Pictures, by JOHN IRELAND and JOHN NICHOLS. 160 Engravings, reduced in exact facsimile of the Originals. The whole in Three Series, 8vo, cloth, gilt, 22s. 6d.; or, separately, 7s. 6d. per volume.

HOGARTH'S WORKS. Engraved by T. COOK. 84 Plates, atlas folio, half-morocco, £5.

HOGARTH MORALIZED: A Complete Edition of all the most capital and admired Works of WILLIAM HOGARTH, accompanied by concise and comprehensive Explanations of their Moral Tendency, by the late Rev. Dr. TRUSLER; to which are added, an Introductory Essay, and many Original and Selected Notes, by JOHN MAJOR. With 57 Plates and numerous Woodcuts. New Edition, revised, corrected, and enlarged. Demy 8vo, hf.-Roxburghe, 12s. 6d.

HOGARTH'S FIVE DAYS' FROLIC; or, Peregrinations by Land and Water. Illustrated by Tinted Drawings, made by HOGARTH and SCOTT during the Journey. Demy 4to, cloth extra, gilt, 10s. 6d.

HOLBEIN'S PORTRAITS OF THE COURT OF HENRY THE EIGHTH. A Series of 84 exquisitely beautiful Tinted Plates, engraved by BARTOLOZZI, COOPER, and others, and printed on Tinted Paper, in imitation of the Original Drawings in the Royal Collection at Windsor. With Historical Letterpress by EDMUND LODGE, Norroy King of Arms. Imperial 4to, half-morocco extra, gilt edges, £5 15s. 6d.

HOLBEIN'S PORTRAITS OF THE COURT OF HENRY VIII. CHAMBERLAINE's Imitations of the Original Drawings, mostly engraved by BARTOLOZEI. London: printed by W. BULMER & Co., Shakespeare Printing Office, 1792. 92 splendid Portraits (including 8 additional Plates), elaborately tinted in Colours, with Descriptive and Biographical Notes, by EDMUND LODGE, Norroy King of Arms. Atlas fol., half-morocco, gilt edges, £20.—The same, PROOF IMPRESSIONS, uncoloured, half-Roxburghe, £18.

HONE'S SCRAP-BOOKS: The Miscellaneous Collections of WILLIAM HONE, Author of "The Table-Book," "Every-Day Book," and "Year-Book": being a Supplementary Volume to those works. Now first published. With Notes, Portraits, and numerous Illustrations of curious and eccentric objects. Crown 8vo. [*In preparation.*

HOOD'S (Thomas) CHOICE WORKS, in Prose and Verse. Including the Cream of the Comic Annuals. With Life of the Author, Portrait, and over Two Hundred original Illustrations. Crown 8vo, cloth extra, gilt, 7s. 6d. [*In the press.*

HOOD'S (Tom) FROM NOWHERE TO THE NORTH POLE: A Noah's Arkæological Narrative. By TOM HOOD. With 25 Illustrations by W. BRUNTON and E. C. BARNES. Square crown 8vo, in a handsome and specially-designed binding, gilt edges, 6s.

"Poor Tom Hood! It is very sad to turn over the droll pages of 'From Nowhere to the North Pole,' and to think that he will never make the young people, for whom, like his famous father, he ever had such a kind, sympathetic heart, laugh or cry any more. This is a birthday story, and no part of it is better than the first chapter, concerning birthdays in general, and Frank's birthday in particular. The amusing letterpress is profusely interspersed with the jingling rhymes which children love and learn so easily. Messrs. Brunton and Barnes do full justice to the writer's meaning, and a pleasanter result of the harmonious co-operation of author and artist could not be desired."—*Times.*

HOOD'S (Tom) HUMOROUS WORKS. Edited, with an Introduction, by his Sister, FRANCES FREELING BRODERIP. Crown 8vo, cloth extra, and numerous Illustrations, 6s. [*In the press.*

HOOKER'S (Sir William) EXOTIC FLORA. Containing Figures and Descriptions of Rare or otherwise interesting Exotic Plants. With Remarks upon their Generic and Specific Characters, Natural Orders, Culture, &c. Containing 232 large and beautifully Coloured Plates. Three Vols., imperial 8vo, cloth extra, gilt, £6 6s.

HOOKER AND GREVILLE'S ICONES FILICUM; or, Figures and Descriptions of Ferns, many of which have been altogether unnoticed by Botanists, or have been incorrectly figured. With 240 beautifully Coloured Plates. Two Vols., folio, half-morocco, gilt, £12 12s.

HOPE'S COSTUME OF THE ANCIENTS. Illustrated in upwards of 320 Outline Engravings, containing Representations of Egyptian, Greek, and Roman Habits and Dresses. A New Edition. Two Vols., royal 8vo, with Coloured Frontispieces, cloth extra, £2 5s.

HORNE.—ORION. An Epic Poem, in Three Books. By RICHARD HENGIST HORNE. With Photographic Portrait. TENTH EDITION. Crown 8vo, cloth extra, 7s.

"Orion will be admitted, by every man of genius, to be one of the noblest, if not the very noblest poetical work of the age. Its defects are trivial and conventional, its beauties intrinsic and supreme."—EDGAR ALLAN POE.

HUME AND SMOLLETT'S HISTORY OF ENGLAND. With a Memoir of HUME by himself, Chronological Table of Contents, and General Index. Imperial 8vo, with Portraits of the Authors, cloth extra, 15s.

HUNT'S (Robert) DROLL STORIES OF OLD CORNWALL; or, POPULAR ROMANCES OF THE WEST OF ENGLAND. With Illustrations by GEORGE CRUIKSHANK. Crown 8vo, cloth extra, gilt, 7s. 6d.

ITALIAN MASTERS (DRAWINGS BY THE): Autotype Facsimiles of Original Drawings. With Critical and Descriptive Notes by J. COMYNS CARR. Atlas folio, half-morocco, gilt. [In preparation.

ITALIAN SCHOOL OF DESIGN (The): 91 beautiful Plates, chiefly Engraved by BARTOLOZZI, after Paintings in the Royal Collection by MICHAEL ANGELO, DOMENICHINO, ANNIBALE CARACCI, and others. Imperial 4to, half-morocco, gilt edges, £2 12s. 6d.

JARDINE'S (Sir Wm.) NATURALIST'S LIBRARY. 42 vols. Fcap. 8vo, illustrated by over 1200 Coloured Plates, with numerous Portrait and Memoirs of eminent Naturalists, half (imitation) calf, full gilt, top edges gilt, £9 9s.; or, separately, cloth extra, 4s. 6d. per Vol., as follows:—
Vols. 1 to 4. British Birds; 5. Sun Birds; 6 and 7. Humming Birds; 8. Game Birds; 9. Pigeons; 10. Parrots; 11 and 12. Birds of West Africa; 13. Fly Catchers; 14. Pheasants, Peacocks, &c.; 15. Animals—Introduction; 16. Lions and Tigers; 17. British Quadrupeds; 18 and 19. Dogs; 20. Horses; 21 and 22. Ruminating Animals; 23. Elephants, &c.; 24. Marsupialia; 25. Seals, &c.; 26. Whales, &c.; 27. Monkeys; 28. Insects—Introduction; 29. British Butterflies; 30. British Moths, &c.; 31. Foreign Butterflies; 32. Foreign Moths; 33. Beetles; 34. Bees; 35. Fishes—Introduction, and Foreign Fishes; 36 and 37. British Fishes; 38. Perch, &c.; 39 and 40. Fishes of Guiana; 41. Smith's Natural History of Man; 42. Gould's Humming Birds.

JENNINGS' (Hargrave) ONE OF THE THIRTY. With numerous curious Illustrations. Crown 8vo, cloth extra, 10s. 6d.

JENNINGS' (Hargrave) THE ROSICRUCIANS: Their Rites and Mysteries. With Chapters on the Ancient Fire and Serpent Worshippers, and Explanations of Mystic Symbols in Monuments and Talismans of Primeval Philosophers. Crown 8vo, with 300 Illustrations, 10s. 6d.

JERROLD'S (Douglas) THE BARBER'S CHAIR, AND THE HEDGEHOG LETTERS. Edited, with an Introduction, by his Son, BLANCHARD JERROLD. Crown 8vo, with Steel-plate Portrait, cloth extra, 7s. 6d.
"Better fitted than any other of his productions to give an idea of Douglas Jerrold's amazing wit; the 'Barber's Chair' may be presumed to give as near an approach as is possible in print to the wit of Jerrold's conversation."—*Examiner.*

JOHNSON'S ENGLISH DICTIONARY. Printed verbatim from the Author's Last and most Complete Edition, with all the Examples in full; to which are prefixed a History of the Language and a Grammar of the English Tongue. Imperial 8vo, cloth extra, 15s.

JOHNSON'S LIVES OF ENGLISH HIGHWAYMEN, PIRATES, AND ROBBERS. With Additions by WHITEHEAD. Fcap. 8vo, 16 Plates, cloth extra, gilt, 5s.

JOSEPHUS (The Works of). Translated by WHISTON. Containing both the "Antiquities of the Jews," and the "Wars of the Jews." Two Vols., 8vo, with 52 Illustrations and Maps, cloth extra, gilt, 14s.

KINGSLEY'S (Henry) NUMBER SEVENTEEN: A Novel. In Two Vols., crown 8vo, cloth extra, price 21s., at all Libraries.

KNIGHT'S (H. Gally) ECCLESIASTICAL ARCHITECTURE
OF ITALY, from the time of Constantine to the Fifteenth Century, with Introduction and descriptive Text. Complete in Two Series; the FIRST, to the end of
the Eleventh Century; the SECOND, from the Twelfth to the Fifteenth Century;
containing 81 beautiful Views of Ecclesiastical Buildings in Italy, several of them
Illuminated in gold and colours. Imperial folio, half-morocco extra, price £3 13s. 6d.
each Series.

LAMB'S (Charles) COMPLETE WORKS, in Prose and Verse,
reprinted from the Original Editions, with many pieces now first included in
any Edition, and Notes and Introduction by R. H. SHEPHERD. With Two Portraits and facsimile of a page of the "Essay on Roast Pig." Crown 8vo, cloth
extra, gilt, 7s. 6d.
"A complete edition of Lamb's writings, in prose and verse, has long been
wanted, and is now supplied. The editor appears to have taken great pains to bring
together Lamb's scattered contributions, and his collection contains a number of
pieces which are now reproduced for the first time since their original appearance in
various old periodicals."—*Saturday Review.*

LAMB (Mary and Charles) : THEIR POEMS, LETTERS, and
REMAINS. With Reminiscences and Notes by W. CAREW HAZLITT. With
HANCOCK's Portrait of the Essayist, Facsimiles of the Title-pages of the rare First
Editions of Lamb's and Coleridge's Works, and numerous Illustrations. Crown
8vo, cloth extra, 10s. 6d.; Large Paper copies, 21s.
"Must be consulted by all future biographers of the Lambs."—*Daily News.*
"Very many passages will delight those fond of literary trifles ; hardly any
portion will fail in interest for lovers of Charles Lamb and his sister."—*Standard.*

LAMONT'S YACHTING IN THE ARCTIC SEAS : An Examination of Routes to the North Pole, during Five Voyages of Sport and
Discovery in the Neighbourhood of the Great Ice Pack. By JAMES LAMONT,
F.G.S., F.R.G.S., Author of "Seasons with the Sea-Horses." Edited, with
numerous full-page Illustrations, by WILLIAM LIVESAY, M.D. Demy 8vo, cloth
extra, with Maps and Illustrations.   [*In the press.*

LANDSEER'S (Sir Edwin) ETCHINGS OF CARNIVOROUS
ANIMALS. Comprising 38 subjects, chiefly Early Works, etched by his Brother
THOMAS or his Father, with Letterpress Descriptions. Roy. 4to, cloth extra 15s.

LEE (General Robert): HIS LIFE AND CAMPAIGNS. By
his Nephew, EDWARD LEE CHILDE. With Steel-plate Portrait by JEENS, and
a Map. Post 8vo, 9s.

LIFE IN LONDON; or, The Day and Night Scenes of Jerry
Hawthorn and Corinthian Tom. WITH THE WHOLE OF CRUIKSHANK'S VERY
DROLL ILLUSTRATIONS, in Colours, after the Originals. Cr. 8vo, cloth extra, 7s. 6d.

LINTON'S (Mrs. E. Lynn) PATRICIA KEMBALL : A Novel.
New and Popular Edition, with a Frontispiece by GEORGE DU MAURIER. Crown
8vo, cloth extra, gilt, 6s.
"A very clever and well-constructed story, original and striking, and interesting
all through. . . . A novel abounding in thought and power and interest."—*Times.*
"Perhaps the ablest novel published in London this year (1874) . . . We know of
nothing in the novels we have lately read equal to the scene in which Mr. Hamley
proposes to Dora . . . We advise our readers to send to the library for the story."
—*Athenæum.*
"This novel is distinguished by qualities which entitle it to a place apart from the
ordinary fiction of the day ; . . . displays genuine humour, as well as keen
social observation. . . . Enough graphic portraiture and witty observation to
furnish materials for half a dozen novels of the ordinary kind."—*Saturday Review.*

LINTON'S (Mrs. E. Lynn) JOSHUA DAVIDSON, CHRIS-
TIAN AND COMMUNIST. SIXTH EDITION, with a New Preface. Small
crown 8vo, cloth extra, 4s. 6d.

LONDON.—WILKINSON'S LONDINA ILLUSTRATA; or, Graphic and Historical Illustrations of the most Interesting and Curious Architectural Monuments of the City and Suburbs of London and Westminster (now mostly destroyed). Two Vols., imperial 4to, containing 207 Copperplate Engravings, with historical and descriptive Letterpress, half-bound morocco, top edges gilt, £5 5s.

⁎⁎ An enumeration of a few of the Plates will give some idea of the scope of the Work:—St. Bartholomew's Church, Cloisters, and Priory, in 1393; St. Michael's, Cornhill, in 1421; St. Paul's Cathedral and Cross, in 1616 and 1656; St. John's of Jerusalem, Clerkenwell, 1660; Bunyan's Meeting House, in 1687; Guildhall, in 1517; Cheapside and its Cross, in 1547, 1585, and 1641; Cornhill, in 1599; Merchant Taylors' Hall, in 1599; Shakespeare's Globe Theatre, in 1612 and 1647; Alleyne's Bear Garden, in 1614 and 1647; Drury Lane, in 1792 and 1814; Covent Garden, in 1732, 1794, and 1809; Whitehall, in 1638 and 1697; York House, with Inigo Jones's Water Gate, circa 1626; Somerset House, previous to its alteration by Inigo Jones, circa 1600; St James's Palace, 1660; Montagu House (now the British Museum) before 1685, and in 1804.

LONGFELLOW'S PROSE WORKS, Complete. With Portrait and Illustrations by VALENTINE BROMLEY. 800 pages, crown 8vo, cloth gilt, 7s. 6d.

⁎⁎ This is by far the most complete edition ever issued in this country. "Outre-Mer" contains two additional chapters, restored from the first edition; while "The Poets and Poetry of Europe," and the little collection of Sketches entitled "Driftwood," are now first introduced to the English public.

LONGFELLOW'S POETICAL WORKS. With numerous fine Illustrations. Crown 8vo, cloth extra, gilt, 7s. 6d. [*In the press.*

LOST BEAUTIES OF THE ENGLISH LANGUAGE. An Appeal to Authors, Poets, Clergymen, and Public Speakers. By CHARLES MACKAY, LL.D. Crown 8vo, cloth extra, 6s. 6d.

LOTOS LEAVES: Original Stories, Essays, and Poems, by WILKIE COLLINS, MARK TWAIN, WHITELAW REID, JOHN HAY, NOAH BROOKS, JOHN BROUGHAM, P. V. NASBY, ISAAC BROMLEY, and others. Profusely Illustrated by ALFRED FREDERICKS, ARTHUR LUMLEY, JOHN LA FARGE, GILBERT BURLING, GEORGE WHITE, and others. Crown 4to, handsomely bound, cloth extra, gilt and gil edges, 21s.

"A very comely and pleasant volume, produced by general contribution of a literary club in New York, which has some kindly relations with a similar coterie in London. A *livre de luxe,* splendidly illustrated."—*Daily Telegraph.*

MACLISE'S GALLERY OF ILLUSTRIOUS LITERARY CHARACTERS. (THE FAMOUS FRASER PORTRAITS.) With Notes by the late WILLIAM MAGINN, LL.D. Edited, with copious Additional Notes, by WILLIAM BATES, B.A. The volume contains 83 CHARACTERISTIC PORTRAITS, now first issued in a complete form. Demy 4to, cloth gilt and gilt edges, 31s. 6d.

"One of the most interesting volumes of this year's literature."—*Times.*
"Deserves a place on every drawing-room table, and may not unfitly be removed from the drawing-room to the library."—*Spectator.*

MACQUOID'S (Katharine S., Author of "Patty," &c.) THE EVIL EYE, and other Stories. With 8 Illustrations by THOMAS R. MACQUOID and PERCY MACQUOID. Crown 8vo, cloth extra, price 6s. [*In the press.*

MADRE NATURA versus THE MOLOCH OF FASHION. By LUKE LIMNER. With 32 Illustrations by the Author. FOURTH EDITION, revised and enlarged. Crown 8vo, cloth, extra gilt, 2s. 6d.

"Agreeably written and amusingly illustrated. Common sense and erudition are brought to bear on the subjects discussed in it."—*Lancet.*

MAGNA CHARTA. An exact Facsimile of the Original Document in the British Museum, printed on fine plate paper, nearly 3 feet long by 2 feet wide, with the Arms and Seals of the Barons emblazoned in Gold and Colours. Price 5s.

A full Translation, with Notes, printed on a large sheet, price 6d.

MANTELL'S PICTORIAL ATLAS OF FOSSIL REMAINS. With Additions and Descriptions. 4to, 74 Coloured Plates, cloth extra, 31s. 6d.

AUTHOR'S CORRECTED EDITION.

MARK TWAIN'S CHOICE WORKS. Revised and Corrected throughout by the Author. With Life, Portrait, and numerous Illustrations. 700 pages, cloth extra, gil 7s. 6d.

MARK TWAIN'S PLEASURE TRIP on the CONTINENT of EUROPE. Post 8vo, illustrated boards, 2s:

MARRYAT'S (Florence) OPEN! SESAME! Three Vols., crown 8vo, 31s. 6d.

"A story which arouses and sustains the reader's interest to a higher degree than, perhaps, any of its author's former works. . . . A very excellent story."—*Graphic.*

MARSTON'S (Dr. Westland) DRAMATIC and POETICAL WORKS. Collected Library Edition, in Two Vols., crown 8vo. [*In the press.*

MARSTON'S (Philip Bourke) SONG TIDE, and other Poems. Second Edition. Crown 8vo, cloth extra, 8s.

"This is a first work of extraordinary performance and of still more extraordinary promise. The youngest school of English poetry has received an important accession to its ranks in Philip Bourke Marston."—*Examiner.*

MARSTON'S (P. B.) ALL IN ALL : Poems and Sonnets. Crown 8vo, cloth extra, 8s.

"Many of these poems are leavened with the leaven of genuine poetical sentiment, and expressed with grace and beauty of language. A tender melancholy, as well as a penetrating pathos, gives character to much of their sentiment, and lends it an irresistible interest to all who can feel."—*Standard.*

MAXWELL'S LIFE OF THE DUKE OF WELLINGTON. Three Vols., 8vo, with numerous highly finished Line and Wood Engravings by Eminent Artists. Cloth extra, gilt, £1 7s.

MAYHEW'S LONDON CHARACTERS: Illustrations of the Humour, Pathos, and Peculiarities of London Life. By HENRY MAYHEW, Author of "London Labour and the London Poor," and other Writers. With nearly 100 graphic Illustrations by W. S. GILBERT and others. Crown 8vo, cloth extra, 6s.

"Well fulfils the promise of its title. . . The book is an eminently interesting one, and will probably attract many readers."—*Court Circular.*

MILLINGEN'S ANCIENT UNEDITED MONUMENTS; comprising Painted Greek Vases, Statues, Busts, Bas-Reliefs, and other Remains of Grecian Art. 62 beautiful Engravings, mostly Coloured, with Letterpress Descriptions. Imperial 4to, half-morocco, £4 14s. 6d.

MEYRICK'S ENGRAVED ILLUSTRATIONS OF ANCIENT ARMS AND ARMOUR. 154 highly finished Etchings of the Collection at Goodrich Court, Herefordshire, engraved by JOSEPH SKELTON, with Historical and Critical Disquisitions by Sir S. R. MEYRICK. Two Vols., imperial 4to, with Portrait, half-morocco extra, gilt edges, £4 14s. 6d.

MEYRICK'S PAINTED ILLUSTRATIONS OF ANCIENT
ARMS AND ARMOUR : A Critical Inquiry into Ancient Armour as it existed
in Europe, but particularly in England, from the Norman Conquest to the Reign of
Charles II. ; with a Glossary, by Sir S. R. MEYRICK. New and greatly improved
Edition, corrected throughout by the Author, with the assistance of ALBERT WAY
and others. Illustrated by more than 100 Plates, splendidly Illuminated in gold
and silver ; also an additional Plate of the Tournament of Locks and Keys. Three
Vols., imperial 4to, half-morocco extra, gilt edges, £10 10s.

"While the splendour of the decorations of this work is well calculated to excite
curiosity, the novel character of its contents, the very curious extracts from the rare
MSS. in which it abounds, and the pleasing manner in which the author's anti-
quarian researches are prosecuted, will tempt many who take up the book in idleness,
to peruse it with care. No previous work can be compared, in point of extent,
arrangement, science, or utility, with the one now in question. 1st. It for the first
time supplies to our schools of art, correct and ascertained data for costume, in its
noblest and most important branch—historical painting. 2nd. It affords a simple,
clear, and most conclusive elucidation of a great number of passages in our great
dramatic poets—ay, and in the works of those of Greece and Rome--against which
commentators and scholiasts have been trying their wits for centuries. 3rd. It
throws a flood of light upon the manners, usages, and sports of our ancestors, from
the time of the Anglo-Saxons down to the reign of Charles the Second. And lastly,
it at once removes a vast number of idle traditions and ingenious fables, which one
compiler of history, copying from another, has succeeded in transmitting through
the lapse of four or five hundred years.

"It is not often the fortune of a painful student of antiquity to conduct his readers
through so splendid a succession of scenes and events as those to which Dr. Meyrick
here successively introduces us. But he does it with all the ease and gracefulness
of an accomplished *cicerone*. We see the haughty nobles and the impetuous knights
—we are present at their arming—assist them to their shields—enter the well-
appointed lists with them—and partake the hopes and fears, the perils, honours, and
successes of the manly tournaments. Then we are presented to the glorious damsels,
all superb and lovely, in ' velours and clothe of golde and dayntie devyces, bothe in
pearls and emerawds, sawphires and dymondes,'— and the banquet, with the serving
men and bucklers, servitors and trenchers—kings and queens—pageants, &c. &c.
We feel as if the age of chivalry had returned in all its glory."—*Edinburgh Review.*

MILTON'S COMPLETE WORKS, Prose and Poetical. With an
Introductory Essay by ROBERT FLETCHER. Imp. 8vo, with Portraits, cl. extra, 15s.

" It is to be regretted that the prose writings of Milton should, in our time, be so
little read. As compositions, they deserve the attention of every man who wishes to
become acquainted with the full power of the English language. They abound
with passages compared with which the finest declamations of Burke sink into
insignificance. They are a perfect field of cloth of gold. The style is stiff with
gorgeous embroidery. Not even in the earlier books of the ' Paradise Lost' has the
great poet ever risen higher than in those parts of his controversial works in which
his feelings, excited by conflict, find a vent in bursts of devotional and lyric rapture.
It is, to borrow his own majestic language, 'a sevenfold chorus of hallelujahs and
harping symphonies.' "—MACAULAY.

MITFORD'S (Mary Russell) COUNTRY STORIES. With
5 Steel-plate Illustrations. Fcap. 8vo, cloth extra, gilt edges, 3s. 6d.

MONTAGU'S (Lady Mary Wortley) LETTERS AND WORKS.
Edited by Lord WHARNCLIFFE. With important Additions and Corrections,
derived from the Original Manuscripts, and a New Memoir. Two Vols., 8vo,
with fine Steel Portraits, cloth extra, 18s.

" I have heard Dr. Johnson say that he never read but one book through from
choice in his whole life, and that book was Lady Mary Wortley Montagu's
Letters."—BOSWELL.

MOSES' ANTIQUE VASES, Candelabra, Lamps, Tripods, Paterae,
Tazzas, Tombs, Mausoleums, Sepulchral Chambers, Cinerary Urns, Sarcophagi,
Cippi, and other Ornaments. 170 Plates, several of which are coloured ; with
historical and descriptive Letterpress by THOS. HOPE, F.A.S. Small 4to, cloth
extra, 18s.

MONUMENTAL INSCRIPTIONS OF THE WEST INDIES,
from the Earliest Date, with Genealogical and Historical Annotations, &c., from
Original, Local, and other Sources. Illustrative of the Histories and Genealo-
gies of the Seventeenth Century, the Calendars of State Papers, Peerages, and
Baronetages. With Engravings of the Arms of the Principal Families. Chiefly
collected on the spot by Capt. J. H. LAWRENCE-ARCHER. Demy 4to, half-
Roxburghe, gilt top, 42s.

MUSES OF MAYFAIR: Vers de Société of the Nineteenth Cen-
tury. Including Selections from TENNYSON, BROWNING, SWINBURNE, ROSSETTI,
JEAN INGELOW, LOCKER, INGOLDSBY, HOOD, LYTTON, C.S.C., LANDOR, AUSTIN
DOBSON, HENRY LEIGH, &c. &c. Edited by H. CHOLMONDELEY-PENNELL.
Crown 8vo, cloth extra, gilt, gilt edges, 7s. 6d.

NAPOLEON III., THE MAN OF HIS TIME. From Carica-
tures. Part I. THE STORY OF THE LIFE OF NAPOLEON III., as told by J. M.
HASWELL. Part II. THE SAME STORY, as told by the POPULAR CARICATURES
of the past Thirty-five Years. Crown 8vo, with Coloured Frontispiece and over
100 Caricatures, 7s. 6d.

NATIONAL GALLERY (The). A Selection from its Pictures.
By CLAUDE, REMBRANDT, CUYP, Sir DAVID WILKIE, CORREGGIO, GAINSBOROUGH,
CANALETTI, VANDYCK, PAUL VERONESE, CARACCI, RUBENS, N. and G. POUS-
SIN, and other great Masters. Engraved by GEORGE DOO, JOHN BURNETT,
WM. FINDEN, JOHN and HENRY LE KEUX, JOHN PYE, WALTER BROMLEY, and
others. With descriptive Text. Columbier 4to, cl. extra, full gilt and gilt edges, 42s.

NICHOLSON'S FIVE ORDERS of ARCHITECTURE (The
Student's Instructor for Drawing and Working the). Demy 8vo, with 41 Plates,
cloth extra, 5s.

NIEBUHR'S LECTURES ON ROMAN HISTORY, delivered
at the University of Bonn. Translated into English from the Edition of Dr. M.
ISLER, by H. le M. CHEPMELL, M.A., and FRANZ DEMMLER, Ph.D. Three.
vols., fcap. 8vo, half (imitation) calf, full gilt back, and top edge gilt, price 13s. 6d.

OLD BOOKS—FACSIMILE REPRINTS.

ARMY LISTS OF THE ROUNDHEADS AND CAVALIERS
IN THE CIVIL WAR, 1642. SECOND EDITION, Corrected and considerably
Enlarged. Edited, with Notes and full Index, by EDWARD PEACOCK, F.S.A.
4to, half-Roxburghe, 7s. 6d.

D'URFEY'S (" Tom") WIT AND MIRTH; or, PILLS TO PURGE
MELANCHOLY. Being a Collection of the best Merry Ballads and Songs, Old
and New. Fitted to all Humours, having each their proper Tune for either
Voice or Instrument; most of the Songs being new set. London: Printed by
W. Pearson, for J. Tonson, at Shakespeare's Head, over against Catherine
Street in the Strand, 1719. An exact reprint. In Six Vols., large fcap. 8vo,
printed on antique laid paper, antique boards, £3 3s.

EARLY NEWS SHEET.—The Russian Invasion of Poland in
1563. (Memorabilis et perinde stupenda de crudeli Moscovitarum Expedi-
tione Narratio, e Germanico in Latinum conversa.) An exact Facsimile of a
Contemporary Account, with Introduction, Historical Notes, and full Translation.
Large fcap. 8vo, antique paper, half-Roxburghe, 7s. 6d.

ENGLISH ROGUE (The), described in the Life of MERITON
LATROON, and other Extravagants, comprehending the most Eminent Cheats
of both Sexes. By RICHARD HEAD and FRANCIS KIRKMAN. A Facsimile
Reprint of the rare Original Edition (1665-1672), with Frontispiece, Facsimiles
of the 12 Copperplates, and Portraits of the Authors. In Four Vols., large fcap.
8vo, printed on antique laid paper, and bound in antique boards, 36s.

HOGG'S JACOBITE RELICS OF SCOTLAND: The Songs,
Airs, and Legends of the Adherents to the House of Stuart. Collected and Illustrated by JAMES HOGG. Two Vols, demy 8vo. ORIGINAL EDITION. Cloth extra, 28s.

IRELAND FORGERIES.—Confessions of WILLIAM HENRY
IRELAND. Containing the Particulars of his Fabrication of the Shakespeare
Manuscripts : together with Anecdotes and Opinions (hitherto unpublished) of
many Distinguished Persons in the Literary, Political, and Theatrical World.
A Facsimile Reprint from the Original Edition, with several additional Facsimiles. Fcap. 8vo, antique paper and boards, 10s. 6d.; a few Large Paper
copies, at 21s.

JOE MILLER'S JESTS : The politest Repartees, most elegant
Bons-mots, and most pleasing short Stories in the English Language. London :
printed by T. Read. 1739. A Facsimile of Orig. Edit. 8vo, half-morocco, 9s. 6d.

LITTLE LONDON DIRECTORY OF 1677. The Oldest Printed
List of the Merchants and Bankers of London. Reprinted from the Rare Original,
with Introduction by J. C. HOTTEN. 16mo, binding after the original, 6s. 6d.

MERRY DROLLERY, Complete ; or, a Collection of Jovial Poems,
Merry Songs, Witty Drolleries, intermingled with Pleasant Catches. Collected
by W.N.C.B.R.S.J.C., Lovers of Wit. The two Parts in 1 Vol. A page-for-page
and literal reprint. Edited, with Indexes and Notes, by J. WOODFALL EBSWORTH,
M.A. Cantab. Large fcap. 8vo, antique paper and cloth boards, 12s. 6d : Large
paper copies, 25s.

MUSARUM DELICIÆ ; or, The Muses' Recreation, 1656 ; Wit
Restored, 1658 ; and Wit's Recreations, 1640. The whole compared with the
Originals. With all the Wood Engravings, Plates, Memoirs, and Notes. A New
Edition, in Two Vols., large fcap. 8vo, antique paper and boards, 21s.

MYSTERY OF THE GOOD OLD CAUSE. Sarcastic Notices
of those Members of the Long Parliament that held Places, both Civil and
Military, contrary to the Self-denying Ordinance of April 3, 1645 ; with the Sums
of Money and Lands they divided among themselves. Sm. 4to, half-morocco, 7s. 6d.

RUMP (The) ; or, An Exact Collection of the Choicest POEMS and
SONGS relating to the late Times, and continued by the most eminent Wits ; from
Anno 1639 to 1661. A Facsimile Reprint of the rare Original Edition (London,
1662), with Frontispiece and Engraved Title-page. In Two Vols.. large fcap.
8vo, printed on antique laid paper, and bound in antique boards, 17s. 6d.

WESTMINSTER DROLLERIES : Being a Choice Collection of
Songs and Poems sung at Court and Theatres. With Additions made by a
Person of Quality. Now first reprinted in exact Facsimile from the Original
Editions of 1671 and 1672. Edited, with an Introduction on the Literature of the
Drolleries, a copious Appendix of Notes, Illustrations, and Emendations of Text,
Table of Contents, and Index of First Lines, by J. WOODFALL EBSWORTH, M.A.,
Cantab. Large fcap. 8vo, antique paper and boards, 12s. 6d.; Large Paper
copies, 25s.

OLD DRAMATISTS.

BEN JONSON'S WORKS. With Notes, Critical and Explanatory,
and a Biographical Memoir by WM. GIFFORD. Edited by Col. CUNNINGHAM.
Complete in Three Vols., crown 8vo, cloth extra, gilt, with Portrait, 6s. each.

CHAPMAN'S (George) COMPLETE WORKS. Now first
Collected. In Three Volumes, crown 8vo, cloth extra, with two Frontispieces, price
18s.; or, separately, 6s. per vol. Vol. I. contains the Plays complete, including
the doubtful ones ; Vol. II. the Poems and Minor Translations, with an Introductory Essay by ALGERNON CHARLES SWINBURNE ; Vol. III. the Translations of
the Iliad and Odyssey.

MARLOWE'S WORKS. Including his Translations. Edited,
with Notes and Introduction, by Col. CUNNINGHAM. Crown 8vo, cloth extra,
gilt, with Portrait, price 6s.

MASSINGER'S PLAYS. From the Text of WM. GIFFORD.
With the addition of the Tragedy of "Believe as You List." Edited by Col.
CUNNINGHAM. Crown 8vo, cloth extra, gilt, with Portrait, price 6s.

OLD SHEKARRY'S FOREST AND FIELD: Life and Adventure in Wild Africa. With 8 Illustrations. Crown 8vo, cloth extra, gilt, 6s.

OLD SHEKARRY'S WRINKLES; or, Hints to Sportsmen and Travellers upon Dress, Equipment, Armament, and Camp Life. A New Edition, with Illustrations. Small crown 8vo, cloth extra, gilt, 6s.

"The book is most comprehensive in its character, nothing necessary to the paraphernalia of the travelling sportsman being omitted, while the hints are given in that plain, unvarnished language which can be easily understood. There are numerous illustrations, and the book has been excellently brought out by the publishers."—*Sportsman.*

ORIGINAL LISTS OF PERSONS OF QUALITY; Emigrants; Religious Exiles; Political Rebels; Serving Men Sold for a Term of Years; Apprentices; Children Stolen; Maidens Pressed; and others who went from Great Britain to the American Plantations, 1600–1700. From MSS. in Her Majesty's Public Record Office. Edited by JOHN CAMDEN HOTTEN. Crown 4to, cloth gilt, 700 pages, 38s. Large Paper copies, half-morocco, 60s.

"This volume is an English Family Record, and as such may be commended to English families, and the descendants of English families, wherever they exist."—*Academy.*

O'SHAUGHNESSY'S (Arthur) AN EPIC OF WOMEN, and other Poems. Second Edition. Fcap. 8vo, cloth extra, 6s.

O'SHAUGHNESSY'S LAYS OF FRANCE. (Founded on the "Lays of Marie.") Second Edition. Crown 8vo, cloth extra, 10s. 6d.

O'SHAUGHNESSY'S MUSIC AND MOONLIGHT: Poems and Songs. Fcap. 8vo, cloth extra, 7s. 6d.

"It is difficult to say which is more exquisite, the technical perfection of structure and melody, or the delicate pathos of thought. Mr. O'Shaughnessy will enrich our literature with some of the very best songs written in our generation."—*Academy.*

OTTLEY'S FACSIMILES OF SCARCE AND CURIOUS PRINTS, by the Early Masters of the Italian, German, and Flemish Schools. 129 Copperplate Engravings, illustrative of the History of Engraving, from the Invention of the Art (the Niellos printed in Silver). Imperial 4to, half-bound morocco, top edges gilt, £6 6s.

OUIDA'S NOVELS.—Uniform Edition, crown 8vo, cloth extra, gilt, price 5s. each.

Folle Farine.	**Held in Bondage**; or, Granville de Vigne.
Idalia. A Romance.	
Chandos. A Novel.	**Puck.** His Vicissitudes, Adventures, &c.
Under Two Flags.	**A Dog of Flanders**, and other Stories.
Cecil Castlemaine's Gage.	
Tricotrin. The Story of a Waif and Stray.	**Strathmore**; or, Wrought by his Own Hand.
Pascarèl. Only a Story.	**Two Little Wooden Shoes.**

"Keen poetic insight, an intense love of nature, a deep admiration of the beautiful in form and colour, are the gifts of Ouida."—*Morning Post.*

PALEY'S COMPLETE WORKS. Containing the Natural Theology, Moral and Political Philosophy, Evidences of Christianity, Horæ Paulinæ, Clergyman's Companion, &c. Demy 8vo, with Portrait, cloth extra, 5s.

PERCY'S RELIQUES OF ANCIENT ENGLISH POETRY. Consisting of Old Heroic Ballads, Songs, and other Pieces of our Earlier Poets, together with some few of later date, and a copious Glossary. Medium 8vo, with Engraved Title and Frontispiece, cloth extra, gilt, 5s.

PARKS OF LONDON: Their History, from the Earliest Period to the Present Time. By JACOB LARWOOD. With numerous Illustrations, Coloured and Plain. Crown 8vo, cloth extra, gilt, 7s. 6d.

PLATTNER'S MANUAL OF QUALITATIVE AND QUANTI-TATIVE ANALYSIS WITH THE BLOWPIPE. From the last German Edition. Revised and enlarged by Prof. TH. RICHTER, Royal Saxon Mining Academy. Translated by Prof. H. B. CORNWALL, School of Mines, New York. Edited by T. HUGO COOKESLEY. With numerous Illustrations. Demy 8vo, cloth extra, 21s.
"'Plattner's Manual' deservedly stands first among all other works on this sub-ject, and its appearance in English will be hailed by all those who are occupied in the analysis of mineral ores, but who, from ignorance of the German language, have been hitherto unable to study it. It is a work of great practical as well as scientific value."—*Standard.*
"By far the most complete work extant on a subject of growing practical import-ance and of extreme interest."—*Mining Journal.*

PLUTARCH'S LIVES, Complete. Translated by the LANGHORNES. New Edition, with Medallion Portraits. In Two Vols., 8vo, cloth extra, 10s. 6d.

POE'S (Edgar Allan) CHOICE PROSE AND POETICAL WORKS. With BAUDELAIRE'S "Essay." 750 pages, crown 8vo, Portrait and Illustrations, cloth extra, 7s. 6d.

PRACTICAL ASSAYER: A Guide to Miners and Explorers. Giving directions, in the simplest form, for assaying bullion and the baser metals by the cheapest, quickest, and best methods. By OLIVER NORTH. With Tables and Illustrative Woodcuts. Crown 8vo, 7s. 6d.

PRIVATE BOOK OF USEFUL ALLOYS AND MEMO-RANDA FOR GOLDSMITHS AND JEWELLERS. By JAMES E. COLLINS, C.E. Royal 16mo, 3s. 6d.

PROUT, FATHER.—THE FINAL RELIQUES OF FATHER PROUT. Collected and edited, from MSS. supplied by the family of the Rev. FRANCIS MAHONY, by BLANCHARD JERROLD. With Portrait and Fac-similes. [*In the press.*

PUCK ON PEGASUS. By H. CHOLMONDELEY-PENNELL. Pro-fusely illustrated by JOHN LEECH, H. K. BROWNE, Sir NOEL PATON, J. E. MILLAIS, JOHN TENNIEL, RICHARD DOYLE, ELLEN EDWARDS, and other Artists. Seventh Edition, crown 8vo, cloth extra, gilt, price 5s.
"The book is clever and amusing, vigorous and healthy."—*Saturday Review.*

PUGIN'S ARCHITECTURAL WORKS.

APOLOGY FOR THE REVIVAL OF CHRISTIAN ARCHI-TECTURE. With 10 large Etchings. Small 4to, cloth extra, 5s.

EXAMPLES OF GOTHIC ARCHITECTURE, selected from Ancient Edifices in England. 225 Engravings by LE KEUX, with descriptive Letterpress by E. J. WILLSON. Three Vols., 4to, half-morocco, £3 13s. 6d.

FLORIATED ORNAMENTS. 31 Plates in Gold and Colours, royal 4to, half-morocco, £1 16s.

GOTHIC ORNAMENTS. 90 Plates, by J. D. HARDING and others. Royal 4to, half-bound, £1 16s.

ORNAMENTAL TIMBER GABLES. 30 Plates. Royal 4to, cloth extra, 18s.

SPECIMENS OF GOTHIC ARCHITECTURE, from Ancient Edifices in England. 114 Outline Plates by LE KEUX and others. With descrip-tive Letterpress and Glossary by E. J. WILLSON. Two Vols., 4to, half-morocco, £1 16s.

TRUE PRINCIPLES OF POINTED OR CHRISTIAN ARCHITECTURE. With 87 Illustrations. Small 4to, cloth extra, 10s. 6d.

PUNIANA; or, Thoughts Wise and Other-Why's. A New Collection of Riddles, Conundrums, Jokes, Sells, &c. In Two Series, each containing 3000 of the best Riddles, 10,000 most outrageous Puns, and upwards of fifty beautifully-executed Drawings by the Editor, the Hon. HUGH ROWLEY. Price of each Volume, in small 4to, blue and gold, gilt edges, 6s. *Each Series Complete in itself.*

"A witty, droll, and most amusing work, profusely and elegantly illustrated."—*Standard.*

PURSUIVANT OF ARMS (The); or, Heraldry founded upon Facts. A Popular Guide to the Science of Heraldry. By J. R. PLANCHÉ, Esq., Somerset Herald. To which are added, Essays on the BADGES OF THE HOUSES OF LANCASTER AND YORK. With Coloured Frontispiece, five full-page Plates, and about 200 Illustrations. Crown 8vo, cloth extra, gilt, 7s. 6d.

QUEENS AND KINGS, AND OTHER THINGS: A Rare and Choice Collection of Pictures, Poetry, and strange but veritable Histories, designed and written by the Princess HESSE-SCHWARZBOURG. Imprinted in gold and many colours by the Brothers DALZIEL, at their Camden Press. Imperial 4to, cloth gilt and gilt edges, £1 1s.

RABELAIS' WORKS. Faithfully translated from the French, with variorum Notes, and numerous Characteristic Illustrations by GUSTAVE DORÉ. Crown 8vo, cloth extra, 700 pages, 7s. 6d.

READE'S (Winwood) THE OUTCAST. Cr. 8vo, cloth extra, 5s.

"He relaxed his mind in his leisure hours by the creation of a new religion."—*Standard.*

"A work of very considerable power, written with great pathos and evident earnestness."—*Athenæum.*

REMARKABLE TRIALS AND NOTORIOUS CHARACTERS. From "Half-Hanged Smith," 1700, to Oxford, who shot at the Queen, 1840. By Captain L. BENSON. With nearly Fifty spirited full-page Engravings by PHIZ. Crown 8vo, cloth extra, gilt, 7s. 6d.

ROLL OF BATTLE ABBEY; or, A List of the Principal Warriors who came over from Normandy with William the Conqueror, and Settled in this Country, A.D. 1066-7. Printed on fine plate paper, nearly three feet by two, with the principal Arms emblazoned in Gold and Colours. Price 5s.

ROLL OF CAERLAVEROCK, the Oldest Heraldic Roll; including the Original Anglo-Norman Poem, and an English Translation of the MS. in the British Museum, By THOMAS WRIGHT, M.A. The Arms emblazoned in Gold and Colours. In 4to, very handsomely printed, extra gold cloth, 12s.

ROMAN CATHOLICS IN THE COUNTY OF YORK IN 1604 (A List of). Transcribed from the MS. in the Bodleian Library, and Edited, with Notes, by EDWARD PEACOCK, F.S.A. Small 4to, cloth extra, 15s.

ROSCOE'S LIFE AND PONTIFICATE OF LEO THE TENTH. Edited by his Son, THOMAS ROSCOE. Two Vols., 8vo, with Portraits and numerous Plates, cloth extra, 18s.

** Also, an Edition in One Vol. 16mo, cloth extra, price 3s.

ROSCOE'S LIFE OF LORENZO DE' MEDICI, called "THE MAGNIFICENT." A New and much improved Edition. Edited by his Son, THOMAS ROSCOE. Demy 8vo, with Portraits and numerous Plates, cloth extra, 9s.

ROSS'S (C. H.) STORY OF A HONEYMOON. With numerous Illustrations by the Author. Fcap. 8vo, illustrated boards, 2s.

ROWLANDSON (Thomas): HIS LIFE AND TIMES. With
the History of his Caricatures, and the Key to their Meaning. With very numerous full-page Plates and Wood Engravings. Demy 4to, cloth extra, gilt and
gilt edges, 31s. 6d. *[In preparation.*

SAINT-SIMON (MEMOIRS OF THE DUKE OF), during the
Reign of Louis the Fourteenth and the Regency. Translated from the French
and Edited by BAYLE ST. JOHN. A New Edition, in Three Vols., 8vo, with
numerous Steel-plate Illustrations. *[In preparation.*

**SALA (George Augustus) ON COOKERY IN ITS HISTO-
RICAL ASPECT.** With very numerous Illustrations by the AUTHOR. Crown
4to, cloth extra, gilt. *[In preparation.*

SEVEN GENERATIONS OF EXECUTIONERS.

SANSON FAMILY, Memoirs of the, compiled from Private Documents in the possession of the Family (1688-1847), by HENRI SANSON. Translated
from the French, with an Introduction by CAMILLE BARRÈRE. Two Vols., 8vo,
cloth extra. *[In the press.*

*** Sanson was the hereditary French executioner, who officiated at the decapita-
tion of Louis XVI.*

SCHOLA ITALICA; or, Engravings of the finest Pictures in the
Galleries at Rome. Imperial folio, with 40 beautiful Engravings after MICHAEL
ANGELO, RAPHAEL, TITIAN, CARACCI, GUIDO, PARMIGIANO, &c., by VOLPATO
and others, half-bound morocco extra, £2 12s. 6d.

**SCHOPENHAUER'S THE WORLD AS WILL AND IMA-
GINATION.** Translated by Dr. FRANZ HÜFFER, Author of "Richard Wagner
and the Music of the Future." *[In preparation.*

SCOTT'S COMMENTARY ON THE HOLY BIBLE. With
the Author's Last Corrections, and beautiful Illustrations and Maps. Three Vols.,
imperial 8vo, cloth extra, £1 16s.

"SECRET OUT" SERIES.
Crown 8vo, cloth extra, profusely Illustrated, price 4s. 6d. each.

ART OF AMUSING: A Collection of Graceful Arts, Games,
Tricks, Puzzles, and Charades. By FRANK BELLEW. 300 Illustrations.

HANKY-PANKY: Very Easy Tricks, Very Difficult Tricks, White
Magic, Sleight of Hand. Edited by W. H. CREMER. 200 Illustrations.

MAGICIAN'S OWN BOOK: Performances with Cups and Balls,
Eggs, Hats, Handkerchiefs, &c. All from Actual Experience. Edited by W. H.
CREMER. 200 Illustrations.

MAGIC NO MYSTERY: Tricks with Cards, Dice, Balls, &c.,
with fully descriptive Directions. Numerous Illustrations. *[In the press.*

MERRY CIRCLE (The): A Book of New Intellectual Games and
Amusements. By CLARA BELLEW. Numerous Illustrations.

SECRET OUT: One Thousand Tricks with Cards, and other Recreations: with entertaining Experiments in Drawing-room or "White Magic."
By W. H. CREMER. 300 Engravings.

SEYMOUR'S (Robert) HUMOROUS SKETCHES. 86 Clever
and Amusing Caricature Etchings on Steel, with Letterpress Commentary by
ALFRED CROWQUILL. A New Edition, with Biographical Notice, and Descriptive List of Plates. Royal 8vo, cloth extra, gilt edges, 15s.

SHAKESPEARE.—THE FIRST FOLIO. Mr. WILLIAM SHAKE-
SPEARE's Comedies, Histories, and Tragedies. Published according to the true
Origina Copies. London, Printed by ISAAC IAGGARD and ED. BLOUNT.
1623.—An exact Reproduction of the extremely rare Original, in reduced facsimile
by a photographic process—thus ensuring the strictest accuracy in every detail.
Small 8vo, half Roxburghe, 10s. 6d. *[In the press.*

SHAKESPEARE.—THE LANSDOWNE EDITION. Beautifully printed in red and black, in small but very clear type. Post 8vo, with engraved facsimile of DROESHOUT'S Portrait, cloth extra, gilt, gilt edges, 14*s*.; or, illustrated by 37 beautiful Steel Plates, after STOTHARD, cloth extra, gilt, gilt edges, 18*s*.

SHAKESPEARE, THE SCHOOL OF. Including "The Life and Death of Captain Thomas Stukeley," with a New Life of Stucley, from Unpublished Sources; "A Warning for Fair Women," with a Reprint of the Account of the Murder; "Nobody and Somebody;" "The Cobbler's Prophecy;" Histriomastix;" "The Prodigal Son," &c. Edited, with Introductions and Notes, by R. SIMPSON, Author of "An Introduction to the Philosophy of Shakespeare's Sonnets." Two Vols., crown 8vo, cloth extra. [*In the press.*

SHAW'S ILLUMINATED WORKS.

ALPHABETS, NUMERALS, AND DEVICES OF THE MIDDLE AGES. Selected from the finest existing Specimens. 4to, 48 Plates (26 Coloured), £2 2*s*.; Large Paper, imperial 4to, the Coloured Plates very highly finished and heightened with Gold, £4 4*s*. [*New Edition preparing.*

ANCIENT FURNITURE, drawn from existing Authorities. With Descriptions by Sir S. R. MEYRICK. 4to, 74 Plates, half-morocco, £1 11*s*. 6*d*.; or, with some Plates Coloured, 4to, half-morocco, £2 2*s*.; Large Paper copies, imperial 4to, all the Plates extra finished in opaque Colours, half-morocco extra, £4 14*s*. 6*d*.

DECORATIVE ARTS OF THE MIDDLE AGES. Exhibiting, in 41 Plates and numerous beautiful Woodcuts, choice Specimens of the various kinds of Ancient Enamel, Metal Work, Wood Carvings, Paintings on Stained Glass, Venetian Glass, Initial Illuminations, Embroidery, Fictile Ware, Bookbinding, &c.; with elegant Initial Letters to the various Descriptions. Imperial 8vo, half-morocco extra, £1 8*s*.

DRESSES AND DECORATIONS OF THE MIDDLE AGES, from the Seventh to the Seventeenth Centuries. 94 Plates, beautifully Coloured, a profusion of Initial Letters, and Examples of Curious Ornament, with Historical Introduction and Descriptive Text. Two Vols., imperial 8vo, half-Roxburghe, £5 5*s*.

ELIZABETHAN ARCHITECTURE (DETAILS OF). With Descriptive Letterpress by T. MOULE. 4to, 60 Plates, half-morocco, £1 5*s*.; Large Paper, imperial 4to, several of the Plates Coloured, half-morocco, £2 12*s*. 6*d*.

ENCYCLOPÆDIA OF ORNAMENT. Select Examples from the purest and best Specimens of all kinds and all Ages. 4to, 59 Plates, half-morocco, £1 1*s*.; Large Paper copies, imperial 4to, with all the Plates Coloured, half-morocco, £2 12*s*. 6*d*.

ILLUMINATED ORNAMENTS OF THE MIDDLE AGES, from the Sixth to the Seventeenth Century. Selected from Missals, MSS., and early printed Books. 66 Plates, carefully coloured from the Originals, with Descriptions by Sir F. MADDEN, Keeper of MSS., Brit. Mus. 4to, half-Roxburghe, £3 13*s*. 6*d*.; Large Paper copies, the Plates finished with opaque Colours and illuminated with Gold, imperial 4to, half-Roxburghe, £7 7*s*.

LUTON CHAPEL: A Series of 20 highly-finished Line Engravings of Gothic Architecture and Ornaments. Imperial folio, India Proofs, half-morocco, £2 8*s*.

ORNAMENTAL METAL WORK: A Series of 50 Copperplates, several Coloured. 4to, half-morocco, 18*s*.

SHAW AND BRIDGENS' DESIGNS FOR FURNITURE, with Candelabra and Interior Decoration. 60 Plates, royal 4to, half-morocco, £1 1*s*. Large Paper, imperial 4to, the Plates Coloured, half-morocco, £2 8*s*.

SHELLEY'S EARLY LIFE. From Original Sources. With Curious Incidents, Letters, and Writings, now First Collected. By D. F. MACCARTHY Crown 8vo, with Illustrations, cloth extra, 7*s*. 6*d*.

SHERIDAN'S COMPLETE WORKS, with Life and Anecdotes.

Including his Dramatic Writings, printed from the Original Editions, his Works in Prose and Poetry, Translations, Speeches, Jokes, Puns, &c.; with a Collection of Sheridaniana. Crown 8vo, cloth extra, gilt, with 10 full-page Tinted Illustrations, 7s. 6d.

"Whatever Sheridan has done, has been, *par excellence*, always the *best* of its kind. He has written the best comedy (School for Scandal', the *best* drama (the Duenna), the *best* farce (the Critic), and the *best* address (Monologue on Garrick); and, to crown all, delivered the very best oration (the famous Begum Speech) ever conceived or heard in this country."—BYRON.

"The editor has brought together within a manageable compass not only the seven plays by which Sheridan is best known, but a collection also of his poetical pieces which are less familiar to the public, sketches of unfinished dramas, selections from his reported witticisms, and extracts from his principal speeches. To these is prefixed a short but well-written memoir, giving the chief facts in Sheridan's literary and political career; so that with this volume in his hand, the student may consider himself tolerably well furnished with all that is necessary for a general comprehension of the subject of it."—*Pall Mall Gazette.*

SIGNBOARDS: Their History. With Anecdotes of Famous Ta-

verns and Remarkable Characters. By JACOB LARWOOD and JOHN CAMDEN HOTTEN. With nearly 100 Illustrations. SEVENTH EDITION. Crown 8vo, cloth extra, 7s. 6d.

"Even if we were ever so maliciously inclined, we could not pick out all Messrs. Larwood and Hotten's plums, because the good things are so numerous as to defy the most wholesale depredation."—*The Times.*

SILVESTRE'S UNIVERSAL PALÆOGRAPHY; or, A Collec-

tion of Facsimiles of the Writings of every Age. Containing upwards of 300 large and beautifully executed Facsimiles, taken from Missals and other MSS., richly Illuminated in the finest style of art. A New Edition, arranged under the direction of Sir F. MADDEN, Keeper of MSS., Brit. Mus. Two Vols., atlas folio, half-morocco, gilt, £31 10s.

Also, a Volume of HISTORICAL AND DESCRIPTIVE LETTERPRESS, by CHAMPOLLION FIGEAC and CHAMPOLLION, Jun. Translated, with Additions, by Sir F. MADDEN. Two Vols., royal 8vo, half-morocco, gilt, £2 8s.

"This great work contains upwards of three hundred large and beautifully executed facsimiles of the finest and most interesting MSS. of various ages and nations, illuminated in the highest style of art. The cost of getting up this splendid publication was not far from £20,000."—*Alibone's Dict.*

"The great work on Palæography generally—one of the most sumptuous works of its class ever published."—*Chambers's Encyclopædia.*

SLANG DICTIONARY (The): Etymological, Historical, and

Anecdotal. An ENTIRELY NEW EDITION, revised throughout, and considerably Enlarged. Crown 8vo, cloth extra, gilt, 6s. 6d.

"We are glad to see the Slang Dictionary reprinted and enlarged. From a high scientific point of view this book is not to be despised. Of course it cannot fail to be amusing also. It contains the very vocabulary of unrestrained humour, and oddity, and grotesqueness. In a word, it provides valuable material both for the student of language and the student of human nature."—*Academy.*

"In every way a great improvement on the edition of 1864. Its uses as a dictionary of the very vulgar tongue do not require to be explained."—*Notes and Queries.*

"Compiled with most exacting care, and based on the best authorities."—*Standard.*

SMITH'S HISTORICAL AND LITERARY CURIOSITIES:

Containing Facsimiles of autographs, Scenes of Remarkable Events, Interesting Localities, Old Houses, Portraits, Illuminated and Missal Ornaments, Antiquities, &c. 4to, with 100 Plates (some Illuminated), half-morocco extra, £2 5s.

SMITH (Thomas Assheton), REMINISCENCES of the LATE;

or, The Pursuits of an English Country Gentleman. By Sir J. E. EARDLEY WILMOT, Bart. New Edition, with Portrait, and plain and coloured Illustrations. Crown 8vo, cloth extra, 7s. 6d.

SMOKER'S TEXT-BOOK. By J. HAMER, F.R.S.L. Exquisitely printed from "silver-faced" type, cloth, very neat, gilt edges, 2s. 6d.

SOUTH'S (Dr. Robert) SERMONS. With Biographical Memoir, Analytical Tables, General Index, &c. Two Vols., royal 8vo, cloth extra, 15s.

SOUTHEY'S COMMON-PLACE BOOK. Edited by his Son-in-Law, J. W. WARTER. Second Edition. Four Vols., medium 8vo, with Portrait, cloth extra, £1 10s.

SOWERBY'S MANUAL OF CONCHOLOGY: A Complete Introduction to the Science. Illustrated by upwards of 650 etched Figures of Shells and numerous Woodcuts. With copious Explanations, Tables, Glossary, &c. 8vo, cloth extra, gilt, 15s. ; or, the Plates beautifully Coloured, £1 8s.

SPECTATOR (The), with the Original Dedications, Notes, and a General Index. Demy 8vo, with Portrait of ADDISON, cloth extra, 9s.

STEDMAN'S (Edmund Clarence) VICTORIAN POETS : Critical Essays. Crown 8vo, cloth extra, 9s. *[In the press.* Abstract of Contents :—The Period—Walter Savage Landor—Thomas Hood—Matthew Arnold — Bryan Waller Procter — Elizabeth Barrett Browning—Alfred Tennyson—Tennyson and Theocritus—Miscellaneous Poets—Robert Browning. Latter-Day Poets: Robert Buchanan—Dante Gabriel Rossetti—William Morris—Algernon Charles Swinburne.

STOTHARD'S MONUMENTAL EFFIGIES OF GREAT BRITAIN, selected from our Cathedrals and Churches. With Historical Description and Introduction, by JOHN KEMPE, F.S.A. A NEW EDITION, with a large body of Additional Notes by JOHN HEWITT. Imperial 4to, containing 147 beautifully finished Etchings, all Tinted, and some Illuminated in Gold and Colours, half-morocco, £9 9s. ; Large Paper, the whole Illuminated in body-colours, half-morocco, £15 15s. *[In the press*

STOW'S SURVEY OF LONDON, written in the Year 1598. Edited by W. J THOMS, F.S.A. A New Edition, with Copperplate Illustrations, large 8vo, half-Roxburghe, price 9s.

STRUTT'S DRESSES AND HABITS OF THE ENGLISH, from the Establishment of the Saxons in Britain to the Present Time. With an Historical Inquiry into every branch of Costume, Ancient and Modern. New Edition, with Explanatory Notes by J. R. PLANCHÉ, Somerset Herald. Two Vols., royal 4to, with 153 Engravings from the most Authentic Sources, beautifully Coloured, half-Roxburgh, £6 6s. ; or the Plates splendidly Illuminated in Silver and Opaque Colours, in the Missal style, half-Roxburghe, £15 15s.

STRUTT'S REGAL AND ECCLESIASTICAL ANTIQUITIES OF ENGLAND : Authentic Representations of all the English Monarchs, from Edward the Confessor to Henry the Eighth ; with many Great Personages eminent under their several Reigns. New Edition, with critical Notes by J. R. PLANCHÉ, Somerset Herald. Royal 4to, with 72 Engravings from Manuscripts, Monuments, &c., beautifully Coloured, half-Roxburghe, £3 3s. ; or the Plates splendidly Illuminated in Gold and Colours, half-morocco, £10 10s.

STRUTT'S SPORTS AND PASTIMES OF THE PEOPLE OF ENGLAND ; including the Rural and Domestic Recreations, May Games, Mummeries, Shows, Processions, Pageants, and Pompous Spectacles, from the Earliest Period to the Present Time. Illustrated by One Hundred and Forty Engravings, in which are represented most of the popular Diversions, selected from Ancient Manuscripts. Edited by WILLIAM HONE, Author of the "Everyday Book." Crown 8vo, cloth extra, gilt, price 7s. 6d. A few LARGE PAPER COPIES have been prepared, uniform with the "Dresses," with an extra set of Copperplate Illustrations, carefully Coloured by hand, from the Originals, price 63s. *[In the press.*

STUBBS' ANATOMY OF THE HORSE. 24 fine Copperplate Engravings on a very large scale. Imperial folio, cloth extra, £1 1s.

SUMMER CRUISING IN THE SOUTH SEAS. By CHARLES WARREN STODDARD. With Twenty-five Illustrations by WALLIS MACKAY. Crown 8vo, cloth, extra gilt, 7s. 6d.

SWIFT'S CHOICE WORKS, in Prose and Verse. With Memoir, Portrait, and numerous Illustrations. Cr. 8vo, cl. extra, gilt, 7s. 6d. [*In the press.*

SYNTAX'S (Dr.) THREE TOURS, in Search of the Picturesque, in Search of Consolation, and in Search of a Wife. With the whole of ROWLANDSON's droll full-page Illustrations, in Colours, and Life of the Author by J. C. HOTTEN. Medium 8vo, cloth extra, gilt, 7s. 6d.

SWINBURNE'S WORKS.

QUEEN MOTHER AND ROSAMOND. Fcap. 8vo, 5s.

ATALANTA IN CALYDON. A New Edition. Crown 8vo, 6s.

CHASTELARD: A Tragedy. Fcap. 8vo, 7s.

POEMS AND BALLADS. Fcap. 8vo, 9s.

WILLIAM BLAKE: A Critical Essay. With Facsimile Paintings, Coloured by Hand, after Drawings by BLAKE and his Wife. Demy 8vo, 16s.

SONGS BEFORE SUNRISE. Crown 8vo, 10s. 6d.

BOTHWELL: A Tragedy. Two Vols., crown 8vo, 12s. 6d.

GEORGE CHAPMAN: An Essay. Crown 8vo, 7s.

SONGS OF TWO NATIONS: DIRÆ, A SONG OF ITALY, ODE ON THE FRENCH REPUBLIC. Crown 8vo, 6s.

ESSAYS AND STUDIES. Crown 8vo, 12s.

Also, fcap. 8vo, cloth extra, price 3s. 6d.

ROSSETTI'S (W. M.) CRITICISM UPON SWINBURNE'S POEMS AND BALLADS.

TAYLOR'S HISTORY OF PLAYING CARDS: Ancient and Modern Games, Conjuring, Fortune-Telling, and Card Sharping, Gambling and Calculation, Cartomancy, Old Gaming-Houses, Card Revels and Blind Hookey, Picquet and Vingt-et-un, Whist and Cribbage, Tricks, &c. With Sixty curious Illustrations. Crown 8vo, cloth extra, gilt, price 7s. 6d.

THACKERAYANA: Notes and Anecdotes. Illustrated by a profusion of Sketches by WILLIAM MAKEPEACE THACKERAY, depicting Humorous Incidents in his School-life, and Favourite Characters in the books of his every-day reading. Large post 8vo, with Hundreds of Wood Engravings and Five Coloured Plates, from Mr. Thackeray's Original Drawings, cloth, full gilt, gilt top, 12s. 6d.

THEODORE HOOK'S CHOICE HUMOROUS WORKS, with his Ludicrous Adventures, Bons-mots, Puns, and Hoaxes. With a new Life of the Author, Portraits, Facsimiles, and Illustrations. Cr. 8vo, cloth extra, gilt, 7s. 6d.

THESEUS: A GREEK FAIRY LEGEND. Illustrated, in a series of Designs in Gold and Sepia, by JOHN MOYR SMITH. With Descriptive Text. Oblong folio, price 7s. 6d.

THIERS' HISTORY OF THE FRENCH REVOLUTION. Roy. 8vo, cloth extra, 15s.

"The History of the French Revolution by Thiers is a celebrated and popular book in France—and I believe in Europe. It combines the compactness and unity of the book, the order and arrangement of the journal, the simplicity of the biography, the valuable and minute details of the autobiography, and the enthusiasm, the passion, and the indignation of the pamphlet. There are in many parts of this great book, whole chapters which read as if they had been written with the sword." —JULES JANIN, *in the Athenæum.*

THIERS' HISTORY OF THE CONSULATE AND EMPIRE
OF FRANCE UNDER NAPOLEON. Royal 8vo, cloth extra, 15s.

THOMSON'S SEASONS, and CASTLE OF INDOLENCE.
With a Biographical and Critical Introduction by ALLAN CUNNINGHAM, and over
50 fine Illustrations on Steel and Wood. Crown 8vo, cloth extra, gilt, 7s. 6d.
[*In the press.*

THORNBURY'S (Walter) HISTORICAL AND LEGENDARY
BALLADS AND SONGS. Illustrated by J. WHISTLER, JOHN TENNIEL, A. F.
SANDYS, W. SMALL, M. J. LAWLESS, J. D. WATSON, G. J. PINWELL, F. WALKER,
T. R. MACQUOID, and others. Handsomely printed, crown 4to, cloth extra,
gilt and gilt edges, 21s. [*In preparation.*

TIMBS' ENGLISH ECCENTRICS and ECCENTRICITIES:
Stories of Wealth and Fashion, Delusions, Impostures and Fanatic Missions,
Strange Sights and Sporting Scenes, Eccentric Artists, Theatrical Folks, Men of
Letters, &c. By JOHN TIMBS, F.S.A. With nearly 50 Illustrations. Crown 8vo,
cloth extra, 7s. 6d.

" The reader who would fain enjoy a harmless laugh in some very odd company
might do much worse than take an occasional dip into 'English Eccentrics.'
Beaux, preachers, authors, actors, monstrosities of the public shows, and leaders of
religious impostures, will meet him here in infinite, almost perplexing, variety. The
queer illustrations, from portraits and caricatures of the time, are admirably suited
to the letterpress."—*Graphic.*

TIMBS' CLUBS AND CLUB LIFE IN LONDON. With
ANECDOTES of its FAMOUS COFFEE HOUSES, HOSTELRIES, and TAVERNS. By
JOHN TIMBS, F.S.A. With numerous Illustrations. Cr. 8vo, cloth extra, 7s. 6d.

TOURNEUR'S (Cyril) COLLECTED WORKS, including a
unique Poem, entitled " The Transformed Metamorphosis ; " and " Laugh and Lie
Down ; or, The World's Folly." Edited, with a Critical Preface, Introductions,
and Notes, by J. CHURTON COLLINS. Post 8vo, cloth extra, 10s. 6d.
[*In preparation.*

TURNER'S (J. M. W.) LIBER FLUVIORUM; or, River
Scenery of France. 62 highly-finished Line Engravings by WILLMORE, GOODALL,
MILLER, COUSENS, and other distinguished Artists. With descriptive Letterpress
by LEITCH RITCHIE, and Memoir by ALARIC A. WATTS. Imperial 8vo, cloth
extra, gilt edges, £1 11s. 6d.

TURNER (J. M. W.) and GIRTIN'S RIVER SCENERY.
20 beautiful Mezzotinto Plates, engraved on Steel by REYNOLDS, BROMLEY,
LUPTON, and CHARLES TURNER, principally after the Drawings of J. M. W.
TURNER. Small folio, in Portfolio, £1 11s. 6d.

TURNER'S (J. M. W.) LIFE AND CORRESPONDENCE.
Founded upon Letters and Papers furnished by his Friends and Fellow-Academi-
cians. By WALTER THORNBURY. New Edition, entirely rewritten and added
to. With numerous Illustrations. Two Vols., 8vo, cloth extra.[*In preparation.*

TURNER GALLERY (The) : A Series of Sixty Engravings from
the Principal Works of JOSEPH MALLORD WILLIAM TURNER. With a Memoir
and Illustrative Text by RALPH NICHOLSON WORNUM, Keeper and Secretary,
National Gallery. Handsomely half-bound, India Proofs, royal folio, £10 ;
Large Paper copies, Artists' India Proofs, elephant folio, £20.—A Descriptive
Pamphlet will be sent upon application.

VAGABONDIANA ; or, Anecdotes of Mendicant Wanderers
through the Streets of London ; with Portraits of the most Remarkable, drawn
from the Life by JOHN THOMAS SMITH, late Keeper of the Prints in the British
Museum. With Introduction by FRANCIS DOUCE, and Descriptive Text. With
the Woodcuts and the 32 Plates, from the original Coppers. Crown 4to, half-
Roxburghe, 12s. 6d.

VYNER'S NOTITIA VENATICA: A Treatise on Fox-Hunting, the General Management of Hounds, and the Diseases of Dogs : Distemper and Rabies ; Kennel Lameness, &c. By ROBERT C. VYNER. Sixth Edition, Enlarged. With spirited Coloured Illustrations by ALKEN. Royal 8vo, cloth extra, 21s.

WALPOLE'S (Horace) ANECDOTES OF PAINTING IN ENGLAND. With some Account of the principal English Artists, and incidental Notices of Sculptors, Carvers, Enamellers, Architects, Medallists, Engravers, &c. With Additions by the Rev. JAMES DALLAWAY. New Edition, Revised and Edited, with Additional Notes, by RALPH N. WORNUM, Keeper and Secretary, National Gallery. Three Vols., 8vo, with upwards of 150 Portraits and Plates, cloth extra, £1 7s.

WALPOLE'S (Horace) ENTIRE CORRESPONDENCE. Chronologically arranged, with the Prefaces and Notes of CROKER, Lord DOVER, and others ; the Notes of all previous Editors, and Additional Notes by PETER CUNNINGHAM. Nine Vols., 8vo, with numerous fine Portraits engraved on Steel, cloth extra, £4 1s.
"The charm which lurks in Horace Walpole's Letters is one for which we have no term ; and our Gallic neighbours seem to have engrossed both the word and the quality—'elles sont piquantes,' to the highest degree. If you read but a sentence, you feel yourself spell-bound till you have read the volume."—*Quarterly Review.*

WALPOLE'S (Horace) ROYAL AND NOBLE AUTHORS OF ENGLAND, SCOTLAND, AND IRELAND; with Lists of their Works. A New Edition, Annotated, considerably Enlarged, and brought down to the Present Time. Illustrated by nearly 200 Copperplate Portraits. Six Vols., 8vo, cloth extra. [*In preparation.*

WALTON AND COTTON, ILLUSTRATED.—THE COM- PLETE ANGLER ; or, The Contemplative Man's Recreation : Being a Discourse of Rivers, Fish-ponds, Fish and Fishing, written by IZAAK WALTON ; and Instructions how to Angle for a Trout or Grayling in a clear Stream, by CHARLES COTTON. With Original Memoirs and Notes by Sir HARRIS NICOLAS, K.C.M.G. With the 61 Plate Illustrations, precisely as in Pickering's two-volume Edition. Complete in One Volume, large crown 8vo, cloth antique, 7s. 6d.

WARRANT TO EXECUTE CHARLES I. An exact Facsimile of this important Document, with the Fifty-nine Signatures of the Regicides, and corresponding Seals, on paper to imitate the Original, 22 in. by 14 in. Price 2s.

WARRANT TO EXECUTE MARY QUEEN OF SCOTS. An exact Facsimile of this important Document, including the Signature of Queen Elizabeth and Facsimile of the Great Seal, on tinted paper, to imitate the Original MS. Price 2s.

WATERFORD ROLL (The).—Illuminated Charter-Roll of Waterford, Temp. Richard II. The Illuminations accurately Traced and Coloured for the Work from a Copy carefully made by the late GEORGE V. DU NOYER, Esq., M.R.I.A. Those Charters which have not already appeared in print will be edited by the Rev. JAMES GRAVES, A.B., M.R.I.A. Imperial 4to, cloth extra, gilt, 36s. [*Nearly ready.*

WELLS' JOSEPH AND HIS BRETHREN: A Dramatic Poem. By CHARLES O. WELLS. With an Introductory Essay by ALGERNON CHARLES SWINBURNE. Crown 8vo, cloth extra, 8s. [*In the press.*

WESTWOOD'S PALÆOGRAPHIA SACRA PICTORIA: being a Series of Illustrations of the Ancient Versions of the Bible, copied from Illuminated Manuscripts, executed between the Fourth and Sixteenth Centuries. Royal 4to, with 50 beautifully Illuminated Plates, half-bound morocco, £3 10s.

WILD'S ENGLISH CATHEDRALS. Twelve select examples of the Ecclesiastical Architecture of the Middle Ages ; beautifully coloured, after the Original Drawings by CHARLES WILD. Imperial folio, in portfolio, £4 4s.

WILD'S FOREIGN CATHEDRALS. Twelve fine Plates, im-
perial folio, coloured, after the Original Drawings, by CHARLES WILD. In portfolio, £4 4s.

"These splendid plates are unequalled, whether bound as a volume, treasured in
a portfolio, or framed for universal admiration."—*Athenæum.*

WILSON'S AMERICAN ORNITHOLOGY; or, Natural History
of the Birds of the United States; with the Continuation by Prince CHARLES
LUCIAN BONAPARTE. NEW AND ENLARGED EDITION, completed by the
insertion of above One Hundred Birds omitted in the original Work, and Illustrated by valuable Notes, and Life of the Author, by Sir WILLIAM JARDINE.
Three Vols., 8vo, with a fine Portrait of WILSON, and 103 Plates, exhibiting
nearly four hundred figures of Birds accurately engraved and beautifully printed in
Colours, half-bound morocco. A few Large Paper copies will also be issued, with
the Plates all carefully Coloured by hand.   [*In the press.*

"The History of American Birds by Alexander Wilson is equal in elegance to the
most distinguished of our own splendid works on Ornithology."—CUVIER.

WILSON'S FRENCH-ENGLISH AND ENGLISH-FRENCH
DICTIONARY; containing full Explanations, Definitions, Synonyms, Idioms,
Proverbs, Terms of Art and Science, and Rules for the Pronunciation of each
Language. Compiled from the Dictionaries of the French Academy, BOYER,
CHAMBAUD, GARNIER, LAVEAUX, DES CARRIÈRES and FAIN, JOHNSON, and
WALKER. Imperial 8vo, 1,323 closely-printed pages, cloth extra, 15s.

WONDERFUL CHARACTERS: Memoirs and Anecdotes of
Remarkable and Eccentric Persons of every Age and Nation. By HENRY
WILSON and JAMES CAULFIELD. Crown 8vo, cloth extra, with 61 full-page
Engravings, 7s. 6d.

WRIGHT'S (Andrew) COURT-HAND RESTORED; or, Stu-
dent's Assistant in Reading Old Deeds, Charters, Records, &c. Folio, half-
morocco, 10s. 6d.

WRIGHT'S CARICATURE HISTORY of the GEORGES
(House of Hanover). With 400 Pictures, Caricatures, Squibs, Broadsides,
Window Pictures, &c. By THOMAS WRIGHT, Esq., M.A., F.S.A. Crown 8vo,
cloth extra, 7s. 6d.

"Emphatically one of the liveliest of books, as also one of the most interesting.
Has the twofold merit of being at once amusing and edifying."—*Morning Post.*

WRIGHT'S HISTORY OF CARICATURE AND OF THE
GROTESQUE IN ART, LITERATURE, SCULPTURE, AND PAINT-
ING, from the Earliest Times to the Present Day. By THOMAS WRIGHT,
M.A., F.S.A. Profusely Illustrated by F. W. FAIRHOLT, F.S.A. Large post
8vo, cloth extra, gilt, 7s. 6d.

"Almost overwhelms us with its infinite research. Mr. Wright dexterously guides
the reader to a full survey of our English caricature, from its earliest efforts to the
full-blown blossoms of a Rowlandson or a Gillray. The excellent illustrations of
Mr. Fairholt add greatly to the value of the volume."—*Graphic.*
" A very amusing and instructive volume."—*Saturday Review.*

XENOPHON'S COMPLETE WORKS. Translated into English.
Demy 8vo, with Steel-plate Portrait, a thick volume of 770 pages, 12s.

YANKEE DROLLERIES. Edited, with Introduction, by GEORGE
AUGUSTUS SALA. In Three Parts, each Complete in itself. Crown 8vo, cloth
extra, 3s. 6d. per Vol.

J. OGDEN AND CO., PRINTERS, 172, ST. JOHN STREET, E.C.

www.ingramcontent.com/pod-product-compliance
Lightning Source LLC
Chambersburg PA
CBHW060554030726
47498CB00005B/1384